MW01194597

PRAISE FOR THE ROXY REINHARDT MYSTERY SERIES

"These are amazing books!"

"A great and well told story, it has well-defined characters,
a good bit of humor, and a bit of a suspense."

"Great new series, my personal favorite."

"Oh my goodness, oh my goodness! I've loved your books
since I turned the first page, but this one stole my heart!"

"*Louisiana Lies* was awesome!"

"The story was brilliantly plotted out and wonderfully
written, you could barely wait to turn the pages to see
where the tale would take you next."

"Excellent story, very clever."

"I read your book until the wee hours last night.... couldn't
put it down!!"

"All the food made me very hungry and really wanting to
visit New Orleans!"

"Absolutely loved it!!!"

"You've done a great job. Truly. This one shines."

"I just want you to know how much I like Roxy. She
makes me smile."

THE ROXY REINHARDT MYSTERIES

THE ROXY REINHARDT MYSTERIES

BOOKS 1-3

ALISON GOLDEN

HONEY BROUSSARD

Published by Mesa Verde Publishing
P.O. Box 1002
San Carlos, CA 94070

ISBN-13: 978-0-9887955-7-0

Edited by
Marjorie Kramer

"To read a book for the first time is to make an acquaintance with a new friend. To read it for a second time is to meet an old one."
(Chinese proverb)

For a limited time, you can get the first books in each of my series - *Chaos in Cambridge, The Case of the Screaming Beauty, Hunted, and Mardi Gras Madness* - plus updates about new releases, promotions, and other Insider exclusives, by signing up for my mailing list at:

https://www.alisongolden.com/roxy

A ROXY REINHARDT MYSTERY

MARDI GRAS MADNESS

USA *TODAY* BESTSELLING AUTHOR
ALISON GOLDEN WITH
HONEY BROUSSARD

MARDI GRAS MADNESS

BOOK ONE

Published by Mesa Verde Publishing
P.O. Box 1002
San Carlos, CA 94070

Edited by
Marjorie Kramer

CHAPTER ONE

"**W**HAT IS *WRONG* with you?" the man said.

Roxy Reinhardt blinked over and over trying to get her view of the world to clear. As it was, everything looked blurry with unshed tears. The call center desks looked warped as the fluid in her eyes distorted everything, stretching out desks and squeezing people until it all looked as wrong as it felt. *Please don't let me cry...please don't let me cry.*

"Sir," Roxy said, praying her voice wouldn't shake, "I have to remind you to remain non-abusive in your interactions with customer service." She adjusted her headset and swallowed hard. "It would be easier for us to troubleshoot your washing machine problems if you were a little calmer."

"I am calm!" the man at the other end of the line shouted, adding a strong curse word for good measure.

"Okay," said Roxy, just about holding it together enough that her voice didn't tremble. "Just a second, please." She hit the "Hold" button and exhaled deeply trying to calm herself. What she didn't expect was a little sob to come out, too.

Jade had heard and turned around with a nasty gleeful look on her face. "Are you *crying*, Roxy?" she asked, her eyes shining. Straightening up in her seat, Roxy tucked her blonde flyaways behind her ears.

"No," Roxy said quickly. Some days this job felt so much like high school. It was as though bullies picked on her, sneered at her, and followed her around. She always seemed to have to "protect" herself from Jade, as well as Chloe, the girl in front who was mercifully taking what seemed to be a long, drawn-out technical call.

Roxy tried to take no notice. All she wanted to do was go to the office each morning, work hard, save her money, go home and spend the evening snuggling on the couch with her boyfriend Ryan and fluffy white princess cat Nefertiti. Was that too much to ask?

Apparently it was, as Jade and Chloe always seemed to have something smart and cutting to say. In Chloe's case, it was often clothed as a "compliment."

"Oh, Roxy, your hair looks nice today. At least, it looks *so* much better than it did yesterday," or "Oh, Roxy, I wish I had a figure like yours. All the men chase after me because of my curves, and it's just *so* annoying."

Roxy was short, only five-feet-two. She had a slim, small-boned figure with which she was mostly at peace. But she was frequently carded and even mistaken for her boyfriend's much younger sister, despite being 24.

Roxy was generally secure enough in herself to recognize these young women, her co-workers, as insecure and rude and their "compliments" as silliness. However, today she wasn't able to just let their comments roll off her back quite so easily. She took a deep breath. In truth it felt like everything in her life was falling apart, and she had no clue how to patch it back together again.

Always one to try and look on the bright side, at times like these she would tell herself, "At least I still have my savings." Having grown up in a semi-rural, impoverished home in Ohio, this money that she had put aside was very important to her. The cushion of money made her feel so *safe*.

Roxy didn't make all that much as a call center customer service rep, but she religiously transferred a couple hundred dollars into her savings account each month. It meant bringing in sandwiches and coffee in a flask instead of buying them from the store next door like everyone else, but it was worth it for the glorious feeling of security. Heck, it meant coming to her miserable call center job day in and day out, but if that's what it took, that's what it took. She would pay the price of 50 percent boredom, 50 percent stress for the peace of mind she felt when she checked her bank balance—something she did at *least* once a day. Seeing that dollar amount next to her name was thrilling to Roxy.

But not even her nest egg could save her from her other Big Problem.

Ryan, her tall, dark, six-foot-five boyfriend, was slipping away. No, he was *wrenching* himself away. No matter what Roxy did, he kept getting ruder and more distant—saying more and more hurtful things as the days went by. It wasn't his raised voice that hurt her so much; it was the look in his eyes. All the warmth had gone. He looked through her like she was a complete stranger.

Her eyes welled up again.

She suddenly remembered her abusive customer at

the end of the phone. She pressed the "Hold" button to go back to the call but got nothing but a *beeeeeep* on the other end. He'd already hung up. Roxy flopped her head forward into her hands and swallowed. She'd give anything not to cry here. *Anything.* The customer would call back and report her for leaving him on hold for so long, and her supervisor would dock her pay instantly, she just knew it.

Angela, her boss, was a cold, hard woman who prided herself on being "no-nonsense" with her employees, which in this case meant she was a real witch. Any little mistake, she docked pay. Didn't meet your call target for the day? Docked pay. Got to your desk one minute late? Docked pay. If anyone got sick or pregnant, she treated them like they'd made a terrible, unworthy choice and were exaggerating their symptoms.

Roxy felt her phone vibrate in her bag. She knew it would be Ryan—he was the only one who called her. Preferring a quiet, almost silent life, she had very few friends, and her mom never called. She'd never met her father, so it couldn't possibly be him. Roxy felt a huge urge to reach down and check her phone surreptitiously. Cell phones, however, were strictly forbidden in the office. Getting caught using it one time was a fineable offense. Twice? Termination of employment would be instantaneous.

Roxy valued her job too much to check her phone, but her mind ran wild trying to work out about what Ryan might have texted her. Was it a "Sorry for being a jerk, honey bun, let's move on," kind of text? Or, much more likely, a variation on "You're so unambitious, and you're holding my life back." The latter seemed to be his latest complaint.

Roxy couldn't ruminate for too long, however, because the phone on her desk rang again—a new customer service call to take. "Good afternoon, you're through to Modal Appliances, Inc. My name's Roxy. How may I help you today?"

CHAPTER TWO

"**O**H, HELLO," THE voice of an elderly lady said. "I've just bought a new washing machine, and I can't work out all these complicated buttons. Do you think you could help me with that?"

"Of course, ma'am," Roxy said with a forced smile. "Do you know what model of machine you bought by any chance?"

"No, dear, I'm afraid I don't."

"No problem," Roxy said. "Let me walk you through how to find that out. There's a special sticker on the back of the machine."

"Oh, thank you," the old lady said. "That would be very kind of you, Roxy."

"You're so welcome."

Roxy's favorite calls were those where she could help people who were polite and respectful, even grateful, and she dared to believe that perhaps her day was looking up just the tiniest bit.

But then she caught sight of Angela, her supervisor,

marching over. From where Roxy sat, it didn't look like Angela was using her "We're-Hitting-Targets-And-I'm-Giving-You-A-Huge-Bonus" walk. It was more like "I'm-On-The-Warpath-And-About-To-Give-You-Hell."

Angela's eyes locked onto Roxy and didn't leave her face.

Jade, even though she was on a call, noticed her storm by and turned to flash her eyes wide at Roxy, evidently delighted by the promise of impending drama. Roxy's fingers began to shake ever so slightly as Angela came to a stop next to Roxy's desk and towered over her, folding her arms. Roxy looked up, but Angela flapped at her dismissively, signaling that she should get back to the call.

Roxy pulled up the relevant manual on her screen and prepared to talk the elderly woman through the buttons on her machine. Roxy couldn't concentrate what with Angela looming over her, however, and she made a couple of mistakes as she explained. She sputtered and wondered if Angela had noticed. What was she thinking? Of course, Angela had noticed.

"Thank you, dear," the elderly woman said at the end of the call. "I *think* I understand now."

"I'm glad to hear it," Roxy said. She tried to put good-natured friendliness into the call like she always did, but she was so anxious that it came out all rushed and a tad insincere. "If you have any more questions please feel free to call us again. Thank you for calling Modal Appliances, Inc. Have a nice day." Roxy spun her chair around to face Angela.

Her supervisor launched into a lecture before Roxy even had the time to blink. "You do know I've just had some idiot yelling at me, telling me that you had *hung up on him* and that he was going to complain about Modal

Appliances' customer service to anyone who would listen because we don't value our customers."

"Oh...," Roxy took a deep breath and looked up at Angela. She tried to meet her eyes, but it was hard. Angela's gaze felt like a pair of lasers boring into her. "Well, I didn't hang up on him. I just put him on hold for a moment, to..."

"To what?" Angela exploded!

"To collect myself," Roxy bravely continued. She *hated* confrontation. "Because he was being abusive."

"To *collect* yourself," Angela said with a mocking smile. "Oh, well that's just swell. Are you sure you're cut out for this job, Roxy?"

Roxy felt a lump in her throat. It was such an unfair question. She had consistently met her targets and often had customers tell her how kind and helpful she was. An elderly gentleman had even once said that she had made his week. "Yes" was all Roxy could come out with.

Angela snorted. "Not convincing. Pack your stuff."

"W...what?"

"Take your bag and your lunchboxes and go," Angela said, pointing toward the door at the end of the corridor between the cubicles.

"Go...you mean, like, forever?"

Angela was already walking away. "I haven't decided yet. I'll call you if I want you to come back."

"But..." Roxy began. Angela was already too far away to hear her.

Now the world *did* begin to distort and warp with her tears. She packed her lunch things into her handbag and took her favorite pen—a purple fluffy thing with a cat on it that wrote as smooth as anything—from the desktop. There was nothing else of hers there.

She didn't look at Jade or Chloe, but that didn't stop her from hearing them gossip about her.

"About time, if you ask me," Chloe said, in a whisper that was much too loud to be tactful. "Maybe we can finally get someone hired who actually fits in."

"Right?" Jade said, "And, hopefully someone with more fashion sense."

Roxy knew they were being snarky and mean, but that didn't stop their comments from stinging. She swung her bag over her shoulder and strode down the aisle of the office determined not to look at anyone. She kept her head high as if she were full of confidence, and, thankfully, she made it to the door without stumbling in her kitten heels as she had sometimes done in the past. However, a tear did slide down her cheek, and she had to quickly wipe it away.

Once in her car—the smallest, most reliable car Roxy had been able to find without putting herself into debt— she had a good cry. Tears streamed down her cheeks as she bent forward to turn on the ignition. She even had a little wail as she drove back to the apartment she shared with Ryan. She hadn't cried in so incredibly long that it felt weirdly good to do so. All her sadness, disappointment, humiliation—and yes, anger—gushed from beneath her long, dark eyelashes in watery rivulets that she couldn't have stopped if she'd tried.

As Roxy climbed the stairs to her apartment, she paused in the dingy stairwell. How should she be? Should she wipe all her tears away and put on a brave face? Maybe then Ryan wouldn't think of her as such a drag. Or should she allow herself to cry in front of him so he could see how upset all this was making her? Then, perhaps, he'd find an iota of emotion—preferably a supportive one—and wrap her up in his strong arms like he used to.

But Roxy didn't know what he would do anymore. She felt like she didn't know *him* anymore. She still really wanted to. She had this desperate urge to reconnect with him, to rekindle their spark. But how? She'd tried pretty much everything. And this on top of her dismissal made her so unsure that she couldn't be certain of the ground beneath her feet.

Roxy looked at herself in her makeup mirror and scrubbed at her blotchy face with a tissue. Her lashes clumped but the light hitting the surface of her moist eyes made them shine. One of her gold stud earrings was missing.

Roxy was an attractive young woman. A few times throughout her life she had been told that she was beautiful, a compliment she vigorously denied. Her insecurity made her shake in the face of such approval. She would blush furiously.

But, in truth, her pale skin was like alabaster while her bone structure was delicate. She had deep blue, heavy-lidded, almond-shaped eyes that sat atop a neat, upturned nose. She had a full, small mouth. As she looked in the mirror she could see that her nose was red and her lips were swollen, both a result of her tears.

Roxy's oval face and fine features were accentuated by her short, blond hair. The length of it was one of the few things upon which Roxy stood firm. While her boyfriend objected to her hair being so short, Roxy detested spending time styling it. The result was a "wash and go" cut that was perfect for her, even though the "swish" that Ryan craved was lacking.

Roxy patted down her plain white t-shirt, and beige

skirt, flattening out the wrinkles and turned the key in the lock of the apartment door. She felt numb. Nefertiti, a cat with a cute squashed-up face and an abundance of pristine white fur, was waiting for her in the hallway as usual.

"Hello, my sweet girl," Roxy said, giving the cat a rub under her chin. She straightened up. "Ryan?"

Ryan worked as a graphic designer from the comfort of their couch and was mostly home, but Roxy's voice echoed around the apartment. There was no reply. She headed into the bedroom to see if he was asleep. He wasn't there. Her heart dropped. She saw the closet. His side was empty, the hangers askew.

Roxy dove into her purse for her phone remembering that she hadn't yet read his text message. Her heart hammered.

Bye, Roxy. I'm moving in with my new girlfriend. Thanks for the fun times.

CHAPTER THREE

ROXY DIDN'T GET dinner. She didn't even change out of her work clothes. Usually, the first thing she'd do when she got in was shower, slip into some clean pajamas and fluffy cat slippers that looked quite like Nefertiti, and pad around the apartment for the rest of the evening.

But today, Roxy simply crashed onto the bed and fell asleep fully clothed, with Nefertiti curled up beside her.

Ten hours later—as if it were the next moment—Roxy woke up in the same position that she had collapsed into the previous night. For a glorious moment or two, she enjoyed the golden morning sunlight streaming through the blinds and the feeling of wellbeing that her good, long sleep had given her, but then reality came crashing down. Ryan wasn't there. Ryan wasn't in her *life*. And she didn't even know if she had a job to go to.

Her mind started running. Would she have to dip into her savings? She could barely afford this apartment on her own *with* her job, let alone without it. Back when they had first rented it, she'd preferred a far more modest place so she could save even more of her paycheck. But Ryan had picked out this sleek one-bedroom, wooden-floored, white-walled apartment, and she'd have gone along with pretty much anything to make him happy. Now she'd gotten used to it.

Roxy's mind continued to race. What if she *had* lost her job? Where would she live? How would she eat? In her mind's eye, she could see it all too clearly—her savings spent, her car sold, the money from that spent too. Next she'd be destitute, on the street, cold and dirty with no one to care for or about her. Roxy's heart began to beat more quickly.

But then again, what if Angela did ask her back? What should she do? Sink deeper and deeper into this black hole of misery where her life crumbled to nothingness as Jade and Chloe looked on and laughed? As Angela tormented her day after day? As customers called up to curse at her for their washing machine woes? After all that, she'd come home to an empty apartment where Nefertiti would be the only ray of light in her otherwise dismal existence. None of the available options sounded good.

Nefertiti must have padded out of the room during the night, leaving the bed empty. Roxy rolled over onto her side, feeling thoroughly miserable and having talked herself into a depression as deep as the Grand Canyon. It was at times like these that she wished she had a friend, a true friend, someone who really understood her. Sure, there were a couple of people from school that she messaged on Facebook now and then, and one or two women from her old job that she sometimes went out with on the weekend. But she had no one who she could ugly-cry to on the phone and with whom she could share her woes.

Eventually, Roxy swallowed back her tears, and with no phone call from Angela forthcoming, she moped around the house. Days like this called for a huge tub of ice cream, but she didn't have any in the freezer, and the thought of going to the store to buy some seemed to demand the amount of energy required to climb Mount Everest. The idea of *seeing* anyone felt horrifying.

Roxy sprawled out on the couch, arranging herself around Nefertiti's curled-up, white, fluffy softness and flipped through TV stations. There were Lifetime movies and some others she hadn't heard of, but a Tuesday morning didn't exactly get top programming. She tried to settle down to watch a *Dr. Phil*—anything—but neither her mind nor her body would settle, and she felt like launching the remote at the TV set. This was so unlike her that she startled herself.

Roxy sighed deeply and went to the kitchen. She shoved a six-pack of yogurts from the refrigerator into the freezer hoping that would be an adequate substitute for ice cream. She purposefully walked back out of the kitchen before she leaned against the doorframe. "Oh, what's the point, Nefertiti?" Roxy said. But she could see from her place at the doorway that even the cat was ignoring her. Nefertiti was sitting bolt upright, staring at the TV.

"Hey," Roxy said with her first little smile of the day. Nefertiti looked so human as she sat on the sofa watching television, it made Roxy laugh. "What's so interesting, Nef?"

Roxy stepped forward into the living room and turned to look at the screen.

"Oh...," she said. She watched the bright colors of a carnival flash up. The weirdest feeling overcame her—a feeling she'd never had before. She sat down beside Nefertiti; her eyes now glued to the screen. "Oh...," she said again. It was like she was watching something she'd seen or been a part of before, almost like nostalgia for something she'd never really known but knew about instinctively.

Roxy watched as carnival dancers spun and flashed their bright costumes, revelers packing the streets. She watched women in skimpy bright outfits, their bodies painted, twirling and dancing and laughing and looking *so* carefree. That was one thing Roxy wished she could be, carefree.

"Taste real life," a woman's voiceover on the commercial said. "Taste real culture. Taste Mardi Gras in New Orleans. We're waiting for you." The pounding sound of drums in the background matched the pounding of Roxy's heart.

Once the commercial had ended and an ad for some kind of drug had started, Roxy let out a little breath like *she'd* been dancing among the bright colors and booming drums. "Well," she breathed, looking at Nefertiti. She trailed off not quite knowing what to say. How could you explain *that* feeling? And why had Nefertiti been so interested? The fluffy cat sat back down again and curled up on the couch. Sinking back into her sleepy zone, she purred just a little.

Roxy felt baffled and, all of a sudden, not depressed at all.

She began tickling Nefertiti under her chin, and before she could stop it, a new, slightly scandalous idea was forming in her head.

"No, you couldn't *possibly*," Roxy said to herself out loud. But a huge smile was spreading over her face. "Not sensible Roxy. She'd *never* do that." But talking the idea down only served to make a new rebellious streak in her gain strength. She got up feeling like a new person, full of energy, and sauntered over to the bedroom to get her laptop.

"All right," Roxy said, mentally preparing herself for what lay ahead. She threaded her fingers together and pushed her palms out in a stretch. She bobbed her head from side to side like a boxer preparing to enter the ring. "Okay." Butterflies danced in her stomach, but it felt thrilling rather than nerve-wracking. "I'm going to *do this*."

She placed her fingertips on the keyboard, typed a few words, and pressed "Return."

CHAPTER FOUR

"HAVE I COMPLETELY and utterly lost my mind?" Roxy said to Nefertiti. She almost couldn't believe what she was doing. She had nearly had a panic attack when she realized that she was eating into her savings for the first time *ever*. The bus she was traveling in had been at a service station at the time. Now, Roxy poked her finger into Nefertiti's travel box, trying unsuccessfully to stroke her. "Have I gone totally crazy?"

The middle-aged lady across the aisle from Roxy clearly thought so by the look she shot her, though in fairness that was probably because Roxy had prattled on to Nefertiti constantly about all kinds of nonsense for the past three hours.

For her part, Roxy couldn't believe that she was now over 800 miles away from her home state of Ohio. She hadn't *ever* been that far before. The furthest she'd ventured was to visit some of Ryan's family in the Chicago suburbs.

That had been an uncomfortable visit. It was the first

time she'd met Ryan's mom, who kept calling him, "My little Ry-Ry," waiting on him hand and foot, and undermining Roxy at every opportunity. She had made snide little "jokes" about her son's girlfriend, and Ryan had laughed along.

Roxy drifted into silence as she stared out the window as Alabama raced by. Her heart hurt a little. Life had changed so quickly. She thought she had been so *happy*—with Ryan, with her job, with her cozy little life, with her cute apartment that she'd now given notice on, and with her little rusty car that she'd sold just before she left. All of the money went into her savings account, of course. But had she really been satisfied and content with her life? The overwhelming feeling Roxy got as she whizzed down the country to the South was *No, she had not!*

She felt free now in a way she never had before. Her tension was easing. Her disappointing memories were disappearing in the rearview mirror of the bus. She was breaking into smiles more easily, and she alternately tapped her feet as she managed her pent-up energy. Roxy had been gone for fewer than 18 hours.

Perhaps leaving it all behind for a while wasn't going to be as hard as she thought. In a month she'd have to find somewhere to live and somewhere to work. Her new life wouldn't be one long Mardi Gras, but that was okay. When Roxy's pessimistic thoughts threatened to break through her excitement, she calmed herself with a lot of soothing self-talk, letting herself know it was fine to dip into her savings. That's what they were for—to give her just the right amount of freedom she needed to explore. She settled back in her seat and let out a long breath. Things were going to be fine. They were, *weren't they?*

Roxy drifted off to sleep at some point. She was awakened when the bus driver spotted a stop sign at the last minute and screeched to a halt. She blinked blurrily and looked out the window. They were in New Orleans already? She was about to turn to the woman across the aisle and ask, but then she spotted a sign that said *"Craving Cajun?"* She couldn't *wait* to try the food. While her frame was petite, Roxy had a deceptively large appetite and enjoyed cuisine from around the world in rather large amounts.

That was one thing she could thank Ryan for—introducing her to international food. Along with Mexican, Chinese, Italian, and Indian fare, they'd also adventured into less-explored culinary territory. They'd tried Indonesian, Jamaican, and Polish food, and they *loved* a good Ethiopian meal from time to time.

"Stop thinking about him," Roxy whispered to herself. "This is *your* new life—not his! Not yours to share, but yours *alone.*" She was both extremely nervous and extremely exhilarated. She felt a buzzing sensation travel through her body. She couldn't wait to hop off the bus and locate the hotel where she was staying for the next month. *That* would be the beginning of her new life.

Roxy strolled down the New Orleans streets, pulling her case with one hand and holding Nefertiti's travel box in the other. She *sort of* knew where she was going, but she was enjoying the scenery and didn't mind too much that she was meandering a little. The sun was shining down, and Roxy felt sunny and optimistic.

She figured that she couldn't miss the guesthouse she was looking for. The pictures she'd seen made it look idyllic and so bright that she expected to squint. The flamingo pink frontage of the small hotel was what had attracted her, and when she found that they *did* accept pets, Roxy knew that it was the perfect place for her stay. The price was very reasonable, too, and they offered a hefty discount for month-long visits. Perfect.

Eventually though, Roxy stopped a sympathetic-looking woman in the street and asked her, "Do you know where *Evangeline's* guesthouse is?"

The woman's eyes flashed wide for a moment before she fixed her face into a smile. "Sure thing, sugar. You just go into the alleyway off this street, and it's a little way down there. You see it?" She pointed.

"Oh, sure, great," Roxy said.

The woman looked her over, her eyes curious. Roxy paused for a moment, wondering if she was violating any kind of local custom or unspoken rule. Perhaps her northern manners weren't up to snuff for those in the South. "Thank you, ma'am," she added, feeling a little uncomfortable but hoping she was saying the right thing.

"You're most welcome. Take care now."

Roxy followed the woman's directions and turned into a little alleyway. It was a very narrow cobblestone street, so narrow that only a small vehicle could have turned around in it. At the other end, there was an ivy-covered brick wall. Set within that was a tall, wrought iron gate beyond which she saw gravestones. Halfway down the alleyway, placed outside a café from which the most beautiful, sweet, pastry-baking smell was pouring, were set some tables and chairs. However, her attention was quickly snatched away by the building that faced them.

The sky above it was a deep, deep blue just as the

website had promised, and *Evangeline's* was indeed where it was supposed to be, nestled among a huddle of old wooden buildings. The narrow three-story structure was pink as the photographs had shown, but that was where reality collided with Roxy's expectations. It was like a truck hitting a brick wall.

The pictures Roxy had seen must have been taken years and years ago. Now the paint was patchy—baby pink in some places, salmon in others, and almost white at the very top where it caught the most sun. Some of the wooden trim boards had black streaks running through them and were half rotted away. There was a little balcony on the third floor that looked like it would collapse at any minute, and while the windows were clean, one of them had a massive crack across it. Even the courtyard out front was a scrub of weeds. Roxy would have assumed it was abandoned if many of the windows hadn't been open.

Roxy gulped. What *on earth* had she done?

"Okay, Nefertiti. Here's home for the next month." She tried to sound cheerful, but she had a horrible sinking feeling like her stomach was collapsing in on itself. Still, she thrust her head up and threw her shoulders back. There was no way she'd cry or break down or even doubt herself. She'd prove she wasn't boring. She'd prove she wasn't a pushover. She'd prove she wasn't afraid of anything. She'd prove she was adventurous, exciting Roxy, fully in control of her fabulous, fun, new life.

Roxy lugged her case over to the narrow weed-surrounded doorway and looked around for a doorbell. There wasn't one, so she knocked, plastering a smile on her face for whoever would greet her and waited for something to happen. No one came, so she knocked again, more forcibly this time. The door opened with a long creak. Roxy peered inside.

In the hallway, she could see some rather grand-looking pieces of furniture, a large armchair, an armoire, and a huge mirror. They appeared to be antiques. An ornate wooden staircase with a worn carpet led upward and around a corner. On the wall, there was even a gilt-framed portrait of a young woman with blonde flowing hair wearing a hat and an old-fashioned, floral, frilly dress. There, though, the potential grandeur of the hallway ended.

The antique furniture was rendered incongruous next to a cheap-looking laminate front desk, and under a strip light that was far too bright to be comfortable, their shabbiness was laid bare. Grey cobwebby masses darkened the high white wooden ceiling, and Roxy spied a long-legged spider making its slow descent down the wall behind the unmanned desk. It was all very strange.

Just then, a woman walked across the hallway and toward the staircase. She didn't notice Roxy, who watched her closely. Her dark hair was piled up into a messy bun at the back of her head, and she wore a lime green jogging suit and bright white sneakers. Roxy estimated the woman to be in her mid-forties and might have guessed that she was an avid runner but for the little extra weight she carried around her middle and the full face of makeup she had on. Still slightly stunned by the situation, Roxy didn't gather herself to speak, even as the woman began to jog up the stairs.

"Meeeooowwww," said Nefertiti.

At the sound, the woman swung around and put one hand to her chest in shock, gasping and leaning forward before unfurling herself and laughing when she saw

Roxy. "My goodness, you gave me a scare," she said. She came jogging back down the stairs.

"Sorry," Roxy said with a smile, glad for an opening to start a conversation. "This is Nefertiti. My cat. She can be quite vocal at times."

"I love cats," the woman said. "I used to have two. Not anymore, I'm afraid."

She didn't elaborate.

"Oh, right," Roxy said. "So...are you...I'm...I'm meant to be staying here...I mean to say, I'm arriving."

The woman laughed at her but not unkindly. "They give a good welcome at this place, don't they?"

"Umm...," Roxy didn't quite know what to say. "So...you don't work here?"

"Oh, no," said the woman. "I'm a guest, too."

"Oh, right. Are you staying for Mardi Gras?"

The woman laughed again, but this time with a little bitterness. "For Mardi Gras and then some. I'm not quite sure what I'm doing next."

"Me either," said Roxy, her shoulders relaxing. "I have a month booked, with nowhere to go at the end of it."

The woman's eyes brightened perceptibly. "Well, then, we're in the same boat, aren't we?" She gave Roxy a conspiratorial grin. "Man trouble. Am I right?"

CHAPTER FIVE

"**Y**OU ARE," ROXY said with a humorless chuckle before she could stop herself. She didn't normally share intimacies this quickly, if at all, but being alone in a new city seemed to have changed her.

The woman sighed dramatically. "Me too. I thought I had my life all figured out in New Jersey, but then my husband, well...let's say he found being faithful too taxing, and I found out about it. Stormed out that night with a suitcase, I did, and well, here I am!"

She looked genuinely happy about it.

"Yeah, my boyfriend wasn't exactly Prince Charming either," Roxy said.

"Oh well, what man is really?" the woman said. "I'm Louise, by the way."

"I'm Roxy. Have you been here long?"

"About, um...," Louise looked up at the cobwebs on the ceiling, "three weeks now."

"How do you like it?"

Louise's blue eyes twinkled. "Well, it's not exactly a 5-star experience, and the cemetery at the end of the alleyway is a little off-putting after dark, but once you taste Evangeline's meals and the pastries from across the way, you'll *never* want to leave."

Now, *that* sounded good. Roxy had never been a big cook or baker while her boyfriend, wrapped in cotton wool by his mother as he had been, hadn't known how to do anything domestic nor had he been inclined to try. He'd have ordered takeout every day, but Roxy was too budget-conscious for that. They had eaten a lot of chicken stir-fry and baked potatoes. Good, wholesome food prepared by someone else sounded heavenly.

"And it has great bones."

Roxy frowned. "What does?"

"This place...good bones. I'm an interior designer," Louise explained. "And I'm just *desperate* to redecorate this place. My mind runs wild with how I could make it truly splendid. It's got great potential. It's a shame they want to tear it down."

"They do?" Roxy said. She wondered who "they" were.

"Yes," Louise said. "Why anyone would want to knock a building of such *heritage* down is beyond me. I'd tell them to..."

Nefertiti interrupted her with a very loud, very annoyed *meeeoooowwww*.

"Oh!" Louise said. "That cat of yours is getting fed up with hearing us warble on. She wants to get settled in, I think."

Roxy was feeling apprehensive. *Evangeline's* looked like a dump. People wanted to tear it down, possibly before her month's stay was done, and who knew what horrors lurked in her room. She was torn between wanting to see more of the guesthouse and running back out the door. Was it going to be a cobweb-infested hovel? Or might it be quite charming in a rustic sort of way?

"Where *is* everyone?" Louise said, peering around. "Evangeline and Nat should be somewhere. Each one of them is crazier than the other, you know. And not exactly customer service whizzes either."

From the side door, in strode an androgynous young woman who looked to be in her early twenties. She was dressed head to toe in black: black t-shirt, black skinny jeans, black work boots. Her dark brown hair was cropped short, and her ears were adorned with multiple piercings. There was a tiny diamond stud in her nose. Her short-sleeved t-shirt revealed one entire arm covered in tattoos. Roxy, her eyes widening just a little, leaned in closer but quickly withdrew. She didn't want to be caught staring, especially not by this sharp-eyed, intimidating young woman.

"Well, what were you expecting at these prices?" the tattooed woman said with an English accent that was more Eliza Doolittle than Mary Poppins. "The Ritz?" A smirk pulled at her lips.

Louise chuckled, completely unembarrassed that her criticism of the guesthouse service had been overheard. "Oh, Nat. Not the Ritz. But maybe just a little common courtesy would be nice. I treat my house guests better, and they're not even paying."

"Of course you do," Nat said. "You don't get guests day-in and day-out though, do you?"

"Neither do you," Louise shot back, and there was a moment of stunned silence during which Roxy nervously looked back and forth between both women, as she gauged the atmosphere. After a second, Nat burst out laughing, followed by Louise. Roxy joined in although not quite so uproariously. "This is Roxy and her cat, who seems to be getting restless," Louise said when she'd calmed down.

Nat nodded at Roxy. "Hi. I'm Nat. You're here for a month, aren't you?"

Roxy swallowed, wondering what she had gotten herself into. "That I am."

"Come on then, don't be shy. I'll haul your luggage up for you," Nat said. She grabbed the handle from Roxy and rolled the case to the stairs. "You've got the room at the top, the one with the balcony. You can't actually go *out* on the balcony, because it'll fall down if you do, but you can open the top of the doors. Sam, he's our handyman, sort of chopped them in half or something. Don't ask me how."

Roxy followed behind obediently, while Louise gave her a wide-eyed look and smile of sympathy. As they walked up the stairs, Roxy found there was no need for polite conversation, because Nat just kept talking and talking.

"Now, we don't have any AC up here, so you might roast like a chicken." When she saw Roxy chewing her lip, Nat laughed. "Nah, I'm just joking. Well, you might in July or August, but you're not with us that long. You just open the windows in the front and the back, and you'll get a breeze going through. No problem. I've stayed up here heaps of times. Breakfast is *en famille* and starts at 8, dinner is at 6."

"Okay," Roxy said. She followed Nat up the creaking staircase and took the opportunity to check out her tattoos. There were some roses and crosses and skulls, and a mishmash of bare-breasted ladies, unicorns, band names, and what looked like gargoyles or demons. There was a pirate ship in amongst the madness, too.

Nat caught her looking as they reached the third floor, and flashed her a grin. "I'm working out what to get next. I'm addicted." Then she opened the white wooden door to Roxy's room. There was a key in the lock. "Here you are," she said.

Roxy stepped into the attic room. Though it smelled a little of old wood, it also smelled of freshly laundered cotton and delicious baked goods from across the narrow cobblestone alley. The half-door window contraptions didn't look as strange as they sounded and the windows were open wide, the white linen curtains flapping gently in the breeze.

The bed was large. A soft-looking white duvet lay over it. Across the room, next to an old armoire, there was a vintage dressing table with a white Louis-style stool. A rocking chair stood in the corner. The dark wooden floor was covered with a pale blue tasseled rug, and the whole place looked clean, welcoming, and comfortable.

Roxy sighed happily. She was pleasantly surprised.

"See? Not too shabby, huh? Like I said, dinner's at six, cocktails at five-thirty. See you then," Nat said. She unceremoniously plonked Roxy's case on the floor and spun around on her boot heel to leave Roxy alone.

When Nat had left, Roxy sat down on the bed and looked around. She felt a thrill pulse through her. Nefertiti gave a tiny mewl from her carrier, and Roxy leaned down to let her out, cuddling the fluffy cat to her chest.

"This isn't too bad, is it, Nef? There's adventure ahead, possibilities. Anything could happen." She buried her nose in Nefertiti's soft, white fur, feeling the hairs tickle her nose. "And it's all going to be okay."

CHAPTER SIX

E VANGELINE SURPRISED ROXY in numerous ways, not least by the fact that she appeared to be at least eighty years old. The guesthouse owner was short, stocky, and with a tanned face creased a thousand times with wrinkles. In her ears were big gold hoop earrings and around her waist an apron lay over her blue dress patterned with tiny flowers.

She passed through the dining room from time to time, giving Roxy and Louise cheerful waves as they waited for their dinner. She had a spring in her step and twinkling green eyes that lit up her face.

Every time she went through the white swinging door to the kitchen, a huge blast of fabulous-smelling air drifted outward—sausage and peppers and all kinds of savory flavors that Roxy couldn't quite put her finger on. Plus, something delicious was baking. Roxy sniffed the air and frowned, trying to identify the smell. *Oh, it was cornbread!*

"Smell awright, cher?" Evangeline said as she walked by, throwing Roxy a wink.

"Smells like *heaven*," Roxy said cheerfully. She'd had a big tuna sandwich and a packet of chips on the bus on the way down but nothing since, despite the bakery across the road calling her name. Now she was ravenous. "I can't wait."

Evangeline looked her up and down as she pushed the swing door with her behind and grinned. "I think we need to get some good ole Creole spice into you, cher. Get you smiling and bright and a little round, like Louise here."

Louise laughed, pretending to be outraged. "Evangeline!"

Evangeline laughed. "Many men like a little more meat on the bones, Louise, don't 'cha know? If you've still got your eye on Sam..."

"I have not!" Louise protested, this time quite serious.

Evangeline snickered and disappeared into the kitchen, throwing another wink in Roxy's direction. She returned with two glasses. The drink inside was thick and creamy and white, with chocolate dust on top. "Your brandy milk punch. Usually for brunch, but since both of y'all missed that..."

"Thank you," Roxy said. "It looks scrumptious."

"It *is*," said Louise leaning in and whispering. "That's *why* I've been missing brunch. I've been putting on weight thanks to all this fabulous Creole cooking. I'm trying to get it off by running in the mornings and *not* sipping at sugary drinks any time of day, but especially at breakfast. I can't keep my nose out of the sugar bowl if I start early. I'll be the size of a house before Evangeline's through with me if I'm not careful."

"Oh, life's too short to eat dull food, child," said Evangeline, overhearing as she once more made her way back into the kitchen. They heard her start to berate someone about something or other. Her words were laced with French and made Roxy pause as she sipped on her brandy milk punch, which was indeed scrumptious.

Roxy turned to Louise, "So how...?"

She trailed off. It was clear Louise wasn't listening. She was flicking her hair behind her shoulder, sitting up straight, and pushing her lips into a pout. She was looking over Roxy's shoulder toward the doorway that led out from the lobby.

Roxy followed her gaze and despite Louise's bad manners, immediately appreciated what was causing her to behave in this odd fashion. The guy who had just come through the doorway was gorgeous.

He was tall for one thing and broad-shouldered for another, the kind of man who looked like he could lift small, slight Roxy with his little finger. The huge saxophone case he carried was dwarfed in his strong arms. He had tousled sandy hair and dark eyes that betrayed a little shyness but which were in direct contradiction to his confident walk.

"Hi Sam," Louise said. Her voice got a little high and childlike. Roxy suppressed a cringe.

Sam looked awkward. "Hi, Louise." He looked at Roxy, then back at Louise, obviously expecting an introduction, but Louise was far too busy batting her eyelashes at him to cotton on.

"I'm...," Roxy began, but unexpectedly, her voice caught in her throat. She cleared it and ended up in a coughing fit. She tried to sip a little punch to soothe her throat, but it didn't help. She grabbed a napkin, and Sam leaned his saxophone case against the wall to give her a firm pat on the back.

"Sorry," Roxy said through yet another cough, her voice tight and constricted. "I'm Roxy Reinhardt." Her eyes were watering, and she laughed at herself through the coughs—what else was there to do?

Sam opened his mouth, but before he could speak, a booming voice came from the doorway, "And I'm Elijah Walder, if you don't mind!" An extremely slender man with sparkling eyes stepped in, holding aloft a white paper box like it was a tray. He came over to the table. He was wearing a black bow tie atop a white short-sleeved shirt printed with coffee cups. "Roxy, did I hear?" he said, sticking his free hand out.

"You did," Roxy said with a smile, taking his hand and shaking it quickly.

"Good to have another lovely, bright, and pretty flower around to liven up the place. Besides me, of course," he said. He strode away toward the kitchen door with his hips swaying from side to side as he did so; the box he held aloft moving in concert with them. "Better get these in to Evangeline," he said cheerfully, "before I get yelled at." He turned and cupped his hand to his mouth. "You know what she's like," he whispered.

Elijah was like a whirlwind, passing through the room so quickly no one had a chance to react. Roxy wasn't sure how she felt about being called a "lovely, bright, and pretty flower," but he seemed to mean it kindly.

Sam thrust his hands into his pockets and laughed, watching the skinny man flounce into the kitchen. "Elijah owns the bakery across the street."

"He does?" Roxy asked. "It smelled *spectacularly* good earlier. I'll be in there every single day, I'll bet."

Sam pulled up a chair from the next table. "I wouldn't blame you."

Louise leaned her elbows on the table and focused on him. From the way she was blinking owlishly in his direction, her mascara-thickened lashes batting furiously, Roxy doubted Louise had noticed Elijah at all. "Sam knows how to do *everything*," Louise said, in a husky, low-toned voice.

"Is that so?" Roxy said.

"Of course not," Sam retorted.

"It *is*," said Louise, leaning over and pushing Sam playfully on his bicep with her fingertips.

Sam blushed. Roxy reckoned it was with embarrassment but suspected that Louise would interpret it as a sign of attraction.

"He's got his own *very* successful laundry business," Louise continued. "He plays the sax like an absolute god. He fixes just about everything around here. *And* he manages to maintain an incredible physique." Her eyelashes flickered. "Did you bring that monster of a car with you today?"

Sam stared at the floor, then at the ceiling. He laughed. "Yes, yes, I did."

Louise turned to Roxy. "He has this *incredible* deep red car. What is it, Sam?"

"A Rolls Royce Phantom," he said. "But it's just...it's nothing. It's the one luxury I allow myself."

"It costs more than my *house!*" Louise said excitedly.

Sam turned quickly as they heard the front door open and close. A woman came into the room, and he sounded far too relieved when he said, "Sage! So good to see you!"

CHAPTER SEVEN

S AGE WAS A tall, willowy African-American woman. She looked to be in her late thirties. Long, mermaid-like hair in a mixture of pastel colors fell in ribbons to her waist. She wore billowing, purple linen robes. Around her neck were draped multiple chains, each one weighed down by a stone that lay on her breastbone. A laptop satchel sat at her right hip, the strap crossing her body. She raised her palms as she laughed good-naturedly at Sam's words. "It is a pleasure to lay eyes upon you, too, Samuel." The mellow tone of her voice was like honey and had that lovely New Orleans lilt. "Along with all the souls present here today," she looked at Louise and Roxy, then around the room, "both seen and unseen."

"This is Sage Washington," Sam told Roxy. "She keeps the guesthouse website up to date and about a thousand other things." He flashed his eyes wide, and by the way he did so, Roxy could tell he meant a thousand other *unusual* things. But there wasn't a trace of mocking in his look; he treated Sage and the rest of them with great respect.

"The website?" Roxy said. Sage seemed such an ethereal soul, Roxy couldn't imagine her knowing what a computer was, let alone working one.

"Yes, sugar," Sage said. "But that's just my day job. I do tarot readings and all sorts of other spiritual work. I connect with the spirit world daily."

"*And* the not-so-spirit world," Sam said. They all laughed.

"It's true," Sage said. "I'd say connecting with the spirit world is my true calling, but I love my computer work, too."

Sage beamed a huge smile at Roxy, "So who are you, sugar?" she asked her.

"I'm Roxy. I'm from Ohio. I arrived here today."

"Greetings," Sage said. "You have a beautiful aura."

"Oh," said Roxy, a little taken aback. "Um, thank you."

"Evangeline not done yet?" Sage said, reaching into her bag. "I could whip out my laptop and finish the last bit of programming for this client, before..."

"You won't be bringing any screens to *my* table!" Evangeline said, bursting through the kitchen door, carrying a steaming plate in each hand. "The only thing on this table is going to be my jambalaya. I made a special one for you, honey."

"I'm a vegetarian," Sage explained to Roxy.

Elijah and Nat followed Evangeline out, all carrying plates.

"Put the tables together, why don't ya, Sam." Evangeline said.

"Sure," he replied, "but I've come for the washing. I heard you had a problem with the machine today."

"Yes, yes," Evangeline said impatiently. "You can pick it up later. Now, sit down and eat."

"Are you *sure* you don't want me to buy you a new washing machine? I could donate one of..."

"Charity," she hissed at him. "Now be quiet, we have a new guest."

"Sorry," Sam said. He looked a little shamefaced as he realized he'd been indiscreet. "Roxy, you'll love Evangeline's feast. Her food is the best."

Soon he'd dragged all the lace-covered tables into a neat row. Louise watched his bulging biceps the whole while, but the others arranged the chairs around the table as they anticipated tucking in to their hot plates of food.

Roxy noticed that Sam studiously avoided sitting next to Louise and ended up between Evangeline and Nat. The younger woman had bustled out of the kitchen and, with a grin, had plonked herself down gracelessly beside Roxy. Roxy couldn't tell what to make of the English woman. There was a definite edge to her, what with the piercings and the tattoos and the big biker boots, but she seemed nice enough. Elijah sat between Louise and Sage on the other side of the table.

"Now, Roxy," Evangeline said, "everyone else is used to this already, but let me tell you specially, cher. This is real Creole jambalaya, with salt pork, smoky sausage, shrimp, and a secret spice mix that's been in my family since before your grandmomma was born. It's got a little kick to it." She nodded at the jugs on the table—one of ice water, the other lemonade—and then at the bottles of red wine. "So go ahead and fill your glass with whatever beverage you'd prefer."

"That sounds like an invitation to me," Elijah said. He'd also joined them at the table. "Let's be getting ourselves going."

"But don't let Louise guzzle down all the wine over there," Evangeline said, "or she'll be flirtin' with the floor mop by the time the evenin's through."

"I will not!" Louise exclaimed.

Evangeline chuckled to herself. "If you say so, cher." Then she lifted her glass and said, *"Laissez les bons temps rouler!"*

Louise flashed Roxy a grin. "That's something about having a good time."

And they certainly *did* have a good time. The jambalaya was delicious, deep and rich with flavor and spice. The red wine was robust and warm, and it made Roxy feel all cozy. Best of all, Sam and Elijah got up after dinner and treated them to a live jazz show. Elijah demonstrated some deft finger work on the grand piano that sat in the corner, while Sam filled the whole room with beautiful, rich saxophone melodies. Soothed nearly to sleep, Roxy nibbled her dessert—a delicious pastry from Elijah's bakery—and felt the happiest and satisfied she had been in a long, long time.

Just as they were about to wrap up, Evangeline nodded at Sage, who reached into her bag and pulled out a well-worn deck of cards. Roxy wondered if she was about to start doing magic tricks, or if they were going to play poker. Neither was her sort of thing.

"Tarot cards," Louise explained to her. "It's their little after-dinner ritual." She rolled her eyes.

But no one was paying Louise much attention. Sipping on her wine, Evangeline watched keenly as Sage laid out the cards, face down.

"Let's go for a quick one today," Sage said. "I've got some programming to do before bed."

"I want a reading," Evangeline rushed to say. "About..." She widened her eyes significantly, "you know, this place." She looked over at Roxy and then back at Sage. "A fast one is fine."

"All right," Sage said. "Choose two cards."

Evangeline, her gnarled hand hovering over the cards, quickly pulled two back toward her. She flipped them over.

Sage gasped. "The Ten of Swords and The Tower. Oh gosh."

"What does it mean? What does it mean?" Evangeline asked.

Sage bit her lip. "Umm... well, it doesn't look good. But if we're looking for the positive..."

"I don't want the positive," Evangeline snapped. "I want the cold, hard truth."

Roxy peered over and saw that the Ten of Swords card depicted a man lying dead with ten swords sticking out of his back.

"Okay," Sage said. She gulped. "Well, the Ten of Swords means you're about to experience an unwelcome surprise. And..." She sounded reluctant to go on.

"And...?" Evangeline said impatiently.

"Well, The Tower means everything's about to change—and not the rainbows and unicorns kind of change," said Sage.

"Hmm," Evangeline said. She was silent as she dipped her head and stared at the floor in deep thought, sipping her wine.

"Well, that's cheerful. Lucky they're just cards picked at random, eh?" Elijah said with a grin. He bit into his third pastry. Roxy wondered how on earth he stayed so slim, him being such a talented baker and surrounded by deliciousness all day. He was as thin and lanky as a beanpole.

Judging by the worn state of her card deck, Sage, who clearly believed heart and soul in tarot readings, didn't say anything. She simply bit her lip and looked up at Evangeline. Her eyes were full of anxiety.

CHAPTER EIGHT

T HE NEXT MORNING, it took a while for Roxy to register where she was. Nefertiti was curled up in front of her face as usual, but she had to blink and lie back for a couple of seconds to remember that she was at *Evangeline's* guesthouse in New Orleans and that her regular life was indeed over.

It hadn't helped that she'd dreamed of Ryan giving her the most beautiful bouquet of flowers and telling her that she was his soul mate. Tears stung in her eyes as she realized her dream hadn't been real. She'd have never called their love a grand passion, but when the relationship was working, it had been cozy and comforting and familiar, which was just how Roxy wanted life to be.

They'd had their problems, and Ryan was a real jerk at times, but she'd swept all that under the carpet to keep the relationship going. A fat lot of good that had done her. Now he was off, pursuing *his* Grand Passion, it seemed, and Roxy was alone with no job, using up her precious savings without a plan. She stared at the ceiling. Was she really here because of a *commercial?!* At the time, her decision had felt so *right*, like the universe had ordered the stars in the perfect configuration just for her. Now it seemed ridiculous.

"Oh, Neffi, what have I done?" she said. Nefertiti pushed her nose under Roxy's chin and purred loudly as her owner tickled her. Roxy sighed. "Well, at least *you* sound happy."

She hauled herself up, wondering what she was going to do for the day, and the day after, and the day after that. She knew there was a Mardi Gras party in the area that night—Louise had told her—but she was *not* in a party mood.

Even after a shower in the tiny bathroom and slipping into one of her favorite outfits, a denim sundress with a large ruffle neckline and lace hem, Roxy looked into the mirror and sighed heavily again. She tried a smile. It was little and pathetic, only just turning up the corners of her mouth, but it was a smile nonetheless. She inched her feet into silver sandals that sparkled with rhinestones and bent over to feed Nefertiti, using the little carry bowl and one of the cat food sachets she'd brought along with her. Her cat tucked in with delight. Unlike her owner, she was unperturbed by her surroundings. "Maybe *I'll* feel better after breakfast," Roxy said.

But her image of beignets—a type of square donut that New Orleans is famous for—and coffee while reading pamphlets that would tell her about local tourist spots she should visit was shattered by the sound of raised voices in the hallway. She could hear them as she came down the stairs. She tried to make them out. One was easy. It was the quivering but fierce tones of Evangeline. The other was a man's voice, one she didn't recognize.

"I've told you 'no' a thousand times, haven't I? No, no,

no, and no. When will you people get that message into your head, huh? Are you stupid or just senile?" Evangeline raged.

The man's voice was tense. "You and I know that you're pathetic and desperate, clinging onto this dump of a place. Do what any right-thinking person would do and take the money."

"Like hell, I will!" Evangeline shot back.

They were so embroiled in hurling insults, they barely seemed to notice Roxy walking past. Evangeline was like a crackling, spitting fire. The man was losing his temper, too. His face was red, and he had a bead of sweat in his mustache. He was very tall and snappily dressed, but Evangeline didn't seem the least bit intimidated, even though he positively towered over her.

Roxy slunk into the dining room, her nerves on edge. She looked around the room to see pastel-haired Sage tapping away at her laptop, absentmindedly eating a beignet, her eyes glued to the screen. She seemed to be completely oblivious to the drama unfolding in the hallway.

Louise was there too, sitting at a table in her running gear, her hair scraped back into a ponytail. She smiled at Roxy sheepishly and beckoned for her to come over and sit opposite. Roxy had planned to sit alone, but she wasn't sure how she could now, not without looking very rude.

"Morning," Louise said.

"Good morning," said Roxy, making an effort to sound cheerful.

"I'm..." Louise's eyes darted about awkwardly as she sipped her coffee. She looked down at her bowl of fruit. "I'm so embarrassed about yesterday." She lowered her voice. "I think I came on a little strong with Sam, don't you? You know, with the flirting?"

Roxy shifted in her seat, not knowing what to say. Louise stared at her with eager eyes. "Oh, I don't know," Roxy said eventually. "I'm most definitely *not* a relationship expert."

Louise puffed out a weary breath and leaned back in her chair. "Me either. I mean, he's good looking, and tall and talented, but I've just gotten out of a marriage, for goodness' sake. I think I just like him being around." She laughed self-consciously. "He's quite a comforting figure. Any time anything goes wrong around here, it's like, 'Oh, Sam'll fix it.'" She wiggled her head from side to side as she spoke.

Roxy nodded. "Talking of things going wrong..." She was about to ask what on earth was going on with Evangeline and the suited stranger outside in the hallway, but before she could, Evangeline herself stormed in and over to Sage's table. She dropped into the chair opposite and buried her head in her hands. Roxy was pretty sure she was crying.

Sage came out of her laptop daze. "The cards don't tell lies," she said. She rubbed Evangeline's arm.

"Maybe I should sell. That guy, Richard Lomas, certainly thinks so," Evangeline said. She pulled one hand away from her face and thumbed in the direction of the lobby where Roxy had passed her arguing with the man. The elderly woman roughly wiped her eyes with a napkin and sat up straight, jerking her arm away from Sage. "He works for TML Property Developers. He says it would be better for me to retire and put this place up for sale—specifically so he can buy it. Thing is, he's right. There are more repairs than I can keep up with and not enough guests. And the ones we have barely bring in enough money to take care of 'em. But he wants to tear the old girl down. Seems no one values New Orleans heritage no more. Y'all want to demolish these beautiful old places and build shiny, soulless apartment complexes in their place."

"Not everyone," Sage said. "Not you."

"Perhaps swimming against the tide is a waste of darn time, after all," Evangeline said bitterly. "Maybe I *am* standing in the way of *development* and *progress*. If I sold to Richard Lomas or some other developer, I could walk away and buy a nice little cottage. No more gettin' up at 6 AM to cook and clean for other people. I could sleep in and grow a pretty yard to sit in. I could get a little dog." She brightened up at the thought.

Nat came out of the kitchen, a white frilly apron over the top of her dark, edgy clothes. Her gaze flitted over Evangeline's face, and then to Sage. "Oh, what is it now?" she said, exasperated. "Can't be that you're bottling it, surely?" Nat said.

"I'm not sure I want to run a guesthouse no more, cher," Evangeline replied, wearily. "Much as I love the people. And the cooking, now and again."

"So what are you going to do?" Nat said, deadly serious now. Her wide, amused eyes were filled with concern, and a small frown creased her forehead. "Chuck me out onto the street?" Her voice rose high with tension on the last word.

Louise called over. "*I'll* hire you when I buy one," she said to Nat. "I'd *love* to have a little guesthouse just like this."

"You try runnin' one 'fore you say that," Evangeline said. "Especially *this* one. What with the upkeep and the dry rot and everythin' wearin' out because it's all 100 years old, it's not easy. You have to have a real love of old architecture."

Roxy felt like she was in an alternate universe. She'd never been in a place where staff and guests spoke so freely to each other. It was almost like they were a bickering, but affectionate, family. Growing up, it had just been Roxy and her mom. There had been no extended family, and things had always been tense and difficult.

These easy exchanges, these expressions of feeling, the acceptance that the people around her showed for one another was unfamiliar to her, but she liked it. It felt refreshing. She felt a little like an outsider right now, but maybe, in the month she would be there, she'd learn to fit in, and this level of honesty and sense of freedom would rub off on her.

Louise ate her last piece of fruit. "Well, I'm going to have to think of *something* to do long term. I can't be a lady of leisure for the rest of my life. I'm too young for that even if I could afford it." She stood. "Anyhow, I'm off for my jog. Gotta run off last night's dinner." She stretched her arms above her head and gave them all a wave as she headed out.

"Now, what I *actually* came out here for was to ask you, Roxy," Nat said, "what you would like for breakfast? We have eggs, sausages, bacon, grits, biscuits, muffins, pancakes, omelets, toast..."

"Wow!" Roxy said. Talk about options! She would certainly be having fun with her breakfasts over the next month, but she was still set on her original vision. "Do you have beignets, too?"

"As long as I haven't eaten them all," Nat said,

throwing her a wink. She leaned her head toward the kitchen. "Yep, yep, we do. Anything to drink?"

"Coffee, please. With cream and sugar."

"Coming right up."

"Now, Evangeline," said Sage as sternly as she could with that smooth-as-cream voice of hers. "I got up early to finish my programming job, so I have the day free. What can we do to cheer you up?"

"Me?" Evangeline said, incredulous. "I don't need cheering up, cher." Her eyes belied her words but then sparkled with appreciation at the kindness Sage had shown her. She slapped her thighs. "I've got plenty of jobs to be gettin' on with." She pushed the three-quarter length sleeves of her green, floral print dress up over her elbows and headed to the kitchen. "You know, that Richard Lomas might not agree," she said, pointing to the place outside the room where she and the red-faced man had been arguing. "But I believe that this place is wonderful." She smiled at Roxy. "You have a good day, now, cher."

Sage watched Evangeline's retreating figure as it disappeared into the kitchen before turning to Roxy. "What are you doing today, sweetheart?" she asked. "I'm heading to our local botanica. That's a spiritual supplies store. It may not be your thing, but it's a great walk over there, and the sun is blessing us with its rays this morning. Nat's coming. What do you say?"

Roxy smiled. She felt quite comfortable with Sage despite her strange ideas. "Sure," she said. "I'd love to see more of the city. When do we leave?"

CHAPTER NINE

AS IT TURNED out, Roxy loved the botanica. She'd never been in such a place before. She breathed in its musky, sweet smell as she peered at all the unfamiliar objects on the shelves. There were little statues of Mother Mary, the saints, and other figures she didn't recognize. There were candles in every color, oils in tiny bottles, and so many scents, Roxy became intoxicated. There were crystals, engraved boxes, a basket of pewter "charms." There were even snowglobes labeled "love," "money," and "revenge."

Nat stood in the doorway, her arms folded over her chest. She looked distinctly unimpressed. "Come *on*," she kept saying. "How hard is it to choose between a bunch of candles or a handful of crystals?" Roxy looked up and saw pulses of anxiety play across Nat's face. She looked disturbed by the energy of the store though she did clutch a packet of incense sticks.

Sage smiled, her eyes appearing only half-focused. "I've ventured outside the realm of time so that I may deeply pleasure my soul."

"Yeah, I'm sure Evangeline will buy *that* when I tell her why I'm late," Nat grumbled.

Roxy had no idea what to buy. She turned another corner and came upon a whole new assortment of seemingly random objects—a huge collection of silk flowers, bottle after bottle of Florida Water, silver goblets filled with shiny black stones, and a line of human skulls which looked much too real for Roxy's liking. She took the time to remind herself that, of course, they *weren't* real. They couldn't possibly be. But still...

She could have stayed to explore the store all day until she came upon the skulls. They sent a jolting shiver up her spine, and she went to join Nat at the entrance. By now, Nat was mumbling "weirdos" and "absolute rubbish" under her breath. Feeling a little intimidated by this rather brittle, young English woman, Roxy pretended to study a rack of herbs while they waited for Sage to finish up.

On the way back to the guesthouse, Sage and Nat had a good-natured—but still heated—argument. Nat started it.

"So Sage, what miracle in a bag did you buy this time?"

"Candles for my archangel altar," Sage said, ignoring Nat's sarcasm.

"And what's *that* when it's at home?" Nat asked with a snort.

Roxy, too, was a little curious and equally skeptical, but she would never have been so outwardly scornful.

"An archangel altar is a portal to facilitate contact with certain benevolent spirits from the unseen world," Sage said serenely.

"Oh brother," Nat said, rolling her eyes.

"No one's asking *you* to believe in it, honey," Sage said smoothly. "It's not your fault. Society has conditioned us to not believe anything beyond the bounds of modern science. And that's okay."

Nat shrugged. "Meh. I didn't like science at school either. I like things I can see and touch, and you can't see atoms, can you? Well, they can with their super-super-super-microscope thingies, but not with 'the naked eye.' No, I like to think about what I can see right in front of me. Like now, we have to get back to *Evangeline's* because I have to make lunch, and if I don't, she's going to go crazy on me. That's what *I* believe in."

Sage sighed. "Well, everyone's different."

Nat looked her up and down, "And thank goddess for that!"

Roxy hated the mounting tension, but then Nat and Sage burst out laughing, and Nat threw her arm around Sage's shoulders. "I do love you, you crazy witch lady."

Sage chuckled. "And I love you, too, you...you...thug!"

They all laughed at that.

"Oh, look, is that Sam?" Roxy said, pointing a little way down a side street on the other side of the road. His flashy car was parked on the sidewalk. Sam was wearing reflective sunglasses and looked pretty flashy himself. He was speaking with a couple of guys who looked a little shady. They saw Sam count out a wad of bills and hand them to one of the men. Roxy frowned. "What is he doing?"

Nat shrugged her shoulders. "Who knows? He's very private about what he does outside of the guesthouse and laundry."

Roxy continued to look over as they passed and wondered what he could be doing. The transaction didn't look very savory.

When they reached the narrow cobbled street that housed Evangeline's guesthouse and Elijah's wonderful bakery, they spotted a woman wearing a navy pencil skirt and jacket up ahead of them. It was hard *not* to spot her because just then she caught the heel of her bright red stiletto in the cobblestones and went flying forward. She collapsed onto one of Elijah's tables and stayed there prostrate over it for a few seconds until she peered around to see who might have seen her ungainly fall. Carefully, she straightened up, tugged on her pencil skirt, and wriggled it back into place. She smoothed down her thick, shoulder-length blonde hair, flicking what might have been crumbs off her jacket.

As Roxy, Sage, and Nat got closer, they could see the woman was furious. A deep frown creased her forehead, and she blew air from her nose like an angry bull. Tears shone in her eyes, too, and when she noticed them, she flushed a deep shade of pink. "Oh...," she said. Roxy felt a little sorry for her.

"Hi there," Nat said, uncharacteristically smiley. "Have you come to stay at *Evangeline's*?"

"Evange—? *That!*" the woman replied. She spun around, looking up at Roxy's rickety balcony in disgust. Roxy began to feel distinctly *less* sorry for her. "Of course not. I'm looking for Richard Lomas. Have you seen him?" Her eyes like lasers drilled into the three of them, and her lips, bearing remnants of red lipstick that matched her shoes, curled into a snarl.

Nat crumpled her brow.

"The name sounds familiar," Sage said. "Um..."

"Tall guy," the woman said, flicking up her chin. "Snappy suit. Property developer. Attitude to match."

"Oh!" everyone said, even Roxy.

"Yes, we know him." Nat crossed her arms over her chest. "Are you one of them? The demon developers?"

"No," the woman practically spat. "My name is Mara Lomas. He's my husband. How do you know him?"

"He's been trying to persuade Evangeline to sell her building to him. So he can tear it down," Nat said, "but it's not for sale."

Roxy wasn't at all sure Nat should be sharing this kind of information with a stranger on the street, but before she could say anything, Mara started snarling again.

"Well, if you see the slippery snake, tell him I'm in town, I know exactly what he's done, I know all about his *cozy* little double life *and* his mistress." She laughed bitterly. "And tell him, he'd better say goodbye to his beloved Aston Martin, too, because that's the *first* thing I'm going to make my lawyers take from him." She looked the three of them up and down. No one knew quite what to say. She nodded her head fractionally upward. "Just tell him I'm looking for him, okay?"

Nat shrugged. "Okay."

"Good." Mara began to stride away purposefully, but her exit wasn't quite as dramatic and impressive as it could have been. She had to quickly change her stride to a totter as she picked her way carefully over the cobblestones in her three-inch heels.

"I hope for blessings on your soul," Sage called out after her. She looked genuinely concerned.

Mara waved dismissively. "Pray for *his* soul," she called back. "He's going to need all the protection he can get!" Her voice reverberated around the small side street; then she turned the corner and was gone.

CHAPTER TEN

"WHOA," WHISPERED ROXY admiringly. She wished *she* had been a little more Mara-esque toward *her* ex. Some threats and stiletto strutting might have been quite empowering, but at least she hadn't sobbed down the phone or had some other humiliating reaction. She had retained her self-respect.

Roxy's shoulders slumped when she thought of her ex-boyfriend. Without any idea of who his new girlfriend was or what she looked like, Roxy tortured herself with images of a tall, picture-perfect bronzed beauty with a gorgeous curvy body and thick, flowing, long hair. She'd be a brunette, of course, Roxy was sure. Ryan had loved to remind Roxy that he preferred dark-haired women. Dark-haired, *long-haired* women. As she considered this, she wondered whether she had been with someone who was deliberately cruel, who determinedly sought to undermine her, who *wanted* her to feel bad about herself? A frown creased the bridge of her nose.

"Are you all right?" Sage said. The African-American woman peered at her with concern.

"Oh, yes, yes, I'm fine." Roxy woke up from her daydream and shook her head. "Yes, fine. Um, I must go. I'd better feed Nefertiti."

"You can let her roam around, you know," Nat said. "We just have to make sure the front door is closed for a bit so she doesn't go outside and get lost. To make sure, Evangeline will put butter on her paws for a couple of days. Then she'll *never* stray far."

Roxy smiled. "Sounds like a plan."

"Aha!" a voice from behind them called out.

They turned to see Elijah coming from his bakery, holding his signature white boxes. "You've got a beignet monster staying with you, huh?" he said. "*Evangeline's* alone would keep my bakery going at the moment. Is it you, Roxy?" He narrowed his eyes as he pointed a finger and wagged it accusingly.

"Look at how skinny she is," Nat said, laughing. "She's not scarfing down thousands of those things now, is she?"

Elijah gestured down at his own impossibly wiry body.

"Not everyone has the metabolism of a stick insect," Nat said.

He gave her a fake frown and wiggled his finger again. "You'll never get a job anywhere else, Miss, talking to people like that. I hope you're kissing Evangeline's shoes."

Nat laughed again, but a little less heartily this time. She punched him in the arm.

"Anyhow," he said, "who's coming to see the Krewe du Vieux with me tonight? Their parade is in the French

Quarter. I was thinking of heading there then maybe taking a cruise down the river."

"Wow!" Roxy said, her eyes lighting up. "I'll come!" She paused. "What's the Krewe du Vieux?" she added.

"It's a Mardi Gras parade known for its wild, adult themes. They usually include political comedy, and they have some of the best brass and traditional jazz bands in New Orleans," Elijah said.

"Sounds great!" Roxy replied.

"If we're feeling brave enough we'll hit their after-party, too. It's called the Krewe du Vieux Doo. Try saying *that* fast," he added.

"Krewe du Vieux Doo, Krewe du Vieux Doo, Krewe du Vieux Doo, Krewe du Vieux Doo, Krewe du Vieux Doo, Krewe du Vieux Doo," Nat said.

"Okay, okay," Elijah retorted, flapping his free hand to calm her down. "I didn't mean for you to take me literally."

"Krewe du Vieux Doo," Sage said, elongating the vowels in the words, and shaking her head. "They should respect the vast spiritual heritage of Voodoo more carefully if you ask me. They're making a mockery of it. You know, it's a tradition thousands of years old from Central and West Africa."

"Yeah, yeah," Nat said. "But they just want to have *fun!* Relax a bit, Sage. You can't take *everything* seriously. Elijah, I'll be there. With Roxy *and* Sage."

"Sounds more and more like a party every moment," Elijah said with a grin. "I like it. Sam's coming, too."

"That means Louise will be there with her eyelashes," said Nat. "Oh, bless her little heart."

That evening, they all met in the lobby and walked down to the French Quarter together. Sage was in her trademark flowing robes, a pale lilac this time. The color matched the tones in her hair. Nat also wore what was proving to be her uniform—black jeans and a scary-looking band t-shirt. A big pink tongue splayed out from a skull and crossbones that was emblazoned across the front of her top. In contrast, Louise wore a figure-hugging baby blue dress and stood too close to Sam, who kept edging away. He was more conventional in jeans and a button-down shirt. To Roxy's eye, and probably Louise's, he looked more handsome than ever. Roxy had kept things simple with a long patterned rust-colored skirt and a cream peasant top, but Elijah wore a bright purple suit with a pair of shiny black crocodile shoes.

Evangeline stood at the doorway, Nefertiti in her arms. The guesthouse owner had indeed given the cat butter that afternoon, and Nefertiti had appreciated the treat enormously. The elderly woman watched the younger people with tears welling up in her eyes. "This is the last time you'll do this, leave from here to go to the parade. It's the end of an era," she said. She snuggled her head against Nefertiti's.

"You've decided to sell?" Sage asked.

Evangeline nodded. "I've called that developer. It's all over. This place will be just rubble by the end of the summer." Her voice caught in her throat. "So y'all go on. Jump up in the carnival for me, and send old *Evangeline's* out with the best of memories, won't you?"

"Of course we will," Louise said. She wrapped Evangeline in a hug.

They walked to the French Quarter a little subdued,

but Elijah kept telling everyone jokes and striding forward cheerfully. He made everyone feel a little better. Everyone, that is, except Nat. She kept looking up and around at all the buildings and didn't join in with any of the conversations.

Roxy watched Nat for a while, wondering what was causing her to be so nervous and if she knew Nat well enough to ask her if she was all right. After a few minutes' observation, Roxy decided against it. She didn't want to get her head bitten off for reaching out, and experience had taught her that might well happen. Instead, she fell into step beside Nat and they walked side by side in silence.

New Orleans looked truly beautiful as they walked through it. There were string lights dotted around the tops of buildings and hanging over roadways. They were like little fairies who had decided to bless the city with their magic. It was warm for the time of year, too.

"Lovely, isn't it, this place?" Roxy said to Nat.

"Not really," Nat replied. "I've seen better." She sounded nonchalant and dismissive, but her voice cracked.

Silence fell once more. They walked on for a while, falling behind the others. "So how did you end up here?" Roxy tried again.

"No particular reason."

"But you must have come here for something. You don't end up in New Orleans by accident." Roxy was surprising herself. She wasn't usually so forward.

"It's a long story," Nat said, staring resolutely ahead. She quickened her pace and walked away as Roxy wondered what that long story might be.

CHAPTER ELEVEN

PART FROM WHAT Elijah had told her, Roxy had no idea what to expect from the Krewe du Vieux parade, but she was very excited and curious to see it. They had gotten there early, and yet the streets were already lined with people waiting for the parade to start. The atmosphere on the street was buzzing as the group settled down at a table outside a fancy-looking restaurant where the tables were covered in linens and a replica oil lamp sat on every one. The air was getting a little colder. The sun had set and the cool wind rushed over the darkened Mississippi River.

"Café Brûlots all round to warm us up?" Elijah asked.

"Oh, yes!" everyone except Roxy said. She had no idea what a Café Brûlot was.

Sam sat down beside her. "You're in for a real treat," he said. "Café Brûlots are spiced liqueur coffees that they flame up right in front of you, watch."

Roxy looked at him warily. He seemed like such a good, generous person, but she wondered whether he was completely honest. There was that business with giving money to men on the side street and the flashy car. How did he afford such a thing? Was she just being paranoid? Oh, why was life so confusing?

A waiter in a jacket and bow tie came up to the table rolling a cart with a bowl set on top. He straightened and poured some liquor into a ladle.

"That's cognac and Curaçao. The spices are already in the bowl," Sam said in his lovely low voice. Roxy could feel the heat of his body next to her, and she struggled to keep her heart from racing. After all, he was very, very handsome. And Louise was right. He emanated stability and capability. He seemed like a guy who would step in and save the day if necessary, whatever it took. Safe. Solid. A protector. Still, she couldn't put her worries to rest.

The waiter set the alcohol on fire, and blue flames leaped up in a chaotic fiery dance. He ladled the flaming liquid over an orange that had been mostly peeled, its skin trailing downward in a spiral into the bowl. More blue flames jumped up, but the waiter doused them with a brown liquid.

"And there's the coffee going in!" Louise said. She giggled girlishly and brushed her hand against Sam's.

He jerked his away with a laugh. "Indeed, and now for the sugar." He got up and went to stand next to Elijah.

The waiter poured sugar into the bowl and ladled the spiced coffee, cognac and Curaçao mixture into small coffee glasses. He finished by adding a dollop of whipped cream. "Voilà!"

The table burst into applause.

"Bravo, bravo!" Elijah said, and he gathered up the

coffee cups as best he could, carrying three between his fingers.

Sam scooped up the other three coffees, and soon they were all sipping and sighing with delight. Roxy savored hers, drinking it ever so slowly. The brandy and coffee and cream together were warming, but the hints of orange and spice and cinnamon took the drink to a whole new level of "ahhhh."

"Like drinking a hug," Nat said.

Roxy smiled. "It *is* kind of like that!" She winced a little at the strength of the brandy, though. "They don't scrimp on the alcohol, do they?"

Sam laughed. "They certainly don't."

Just then, police sirens started to blare, and blue lights flashed among the crowd.

"Hey, what's going on?" Roxy said, getting up and looking around. She was a little jumpy at the best of times —the result of growing up with a mother who could be unpredictable. Sirens made her edgy.

"They're clearing the road for the parade!" Sage said, clapping her hands. "Let's go stand a little nearer and get a good look!"

The crowd wasn't too dense, and they managed to get a great spot almost immediately. Roxy's head swirled a little when she got up, though. The brandy had been strong, and she was beginning to regret not having eaten anything since breakfast.

Brightly dressed people, some adorned with strings of fairy lights, began to walk down the middle of the street while music pumped away in the background. Roxy smiled at the colorful spectacle, the cold air hitting her face, joyous people all around her. She saw a woman with blue hair, a pink cone hat, a purple basque, and fishnets wave extravagantly to the crowd. Her friend, wearing a pirate hat, skull mask, and a ruffled gown, swayed silently to the music.

"Look at the horse!" Sage said, nudging Roxy.

Roxy peered down the end of the street and saw a large, stocky, dark brown horse making its slow way toward them. It was pulling a parade float dressed in lights and swathes of bright fabric. A huge jester's head was displayed on the front of the float while a couple of people stood on top of it wildly waving colored rags around a sculpture of the Statue of Liberty.

Next came a large group of people dressed in old-time clothes—men with tailcoats and tricorn hats, ladies with powdered faces, towering curly wigs, and corseted dresses in all kinds of vivid colors: fuchsia, turquoise, crimson, and canary yellow. They all laughed and joked and danced and drank as they proceeded down the center of the street.

Roxy couldn't help but bounce along to the rhythm of the music, too. Most everyone did, and Elijah was near leaping about. Only Nat stood still, looking uncharacteristically shy and withdrawn. Roxy thought she might try to talk to her again later, but for now, she was entranced by the throbbing beat, happy screams, whoops, and cheers that reverberated all around her.

Soon a brass band was marching by, a whole assortment of men and women playing French horns and trumpets and saxophones and other instruments that Roxy didn't know the names of. A percussion section followed behind with a man banging a big bass drum. The music was happy and cheerful and somewhat disorderly. It made Roxy want to dance.

As soon as the parade had passed and people were simply milling around, Elijah jumped out into the road with them. "Who's hitting the after-party with me?"

"I'd much prefer the boat ride," Sage said.

"I think I need to eat something," said Roxy. "That Café Brûlot has gone straight to my head!"

"Me too," Louise said, giggling. She stumbled into Sam and put her hand on his chest. "Oops! Silly me!"

Sam carefully moved her hand away and steadied her on her feet. "Whoa there, lady," he said.

"What about you, Nat?" Elijah said, looking over. She had her arms crossed protectively over her chest, and her face was solemn. "Cat got your tongue this evening?"

All of a sudden, Nat burst into tears, shocking everyone. She quickly swallowed and wiped her eyes hurriedly, saying, "Sorry, I'm sorry." She turned to leave. The group followed her.

"What's wrong, cher?" Elijah said, putting his arm around her like a big brother.

"What *am* I going to do? *Evangeline's* closing!" Nat said, her voice strangled by another suppressed sob. "I won't be able to stay!"

"What do you mean?" Sage said. "You can get another job."

"But that's just it!" said Nat. "I can't." She lowered her voice. "I don't have a work visa. I came to the US to work as a nanny. Of course, that all went to pot, as does *everything* in my life, but Evangeline took me on and paid me under the table. It was lovely of her, and I will be eternally grateful...but...but, basically, I'm...well, I'm an illegal immigrant!"

"Oh," Elijah said, taken aback. Sage leaned over and,

encircling Nat's shoulders with her arm, kissed her on the head. "There, there."

Louise smiled brightly. "Well, you don't have to worry, sweetie. I've made up my mind. I'm not going to let Evangeline sell the place to a developer just so he can tear it down. I'm going to buy it myself. I intend to do it up and make it into an upscale boutique hotel. You can keep working there." Louise looked Nat over. "Maybe more... behind the scenes, but you'll get paid. We'll be one big happy family. Perhaps Evangeline will stay on and continue with the cooking. I sure hope so. I'm going to make her an offer she can't refuse as soon as I get back."

Sam said, "Louise, I was thinking of buying it, too." He looked uncomfortable. "I have some...uh...spare change lying around. It makes sense for Evangeline to sell especially to someone who will protect the building, but the thing is, I don't think she will hear of it. I've already floated the idea, and she says that I'm just interested in buying it as a favor for her—and her pride won't allow it! I think she's made up her mind to sell to this developer now. She'll get a decent price without sacrificing her dignity. Don't be surprised if she turns you down."

"That woman can be so stubborn!" Nat said.

"Indeed, she can," said Sage smoothly. "But everything will turn out all right in the end. The spirits will make sure of it."

"But what if it doesn't?" said Nat. "What if I end up being carted back to England? The whole point of leaving there was to start a new life. I have nothing to go back to."

Nat's words got Roxy thinking about her own situation. Where would she go once this month was up? What would she do? If this developer shut *Evangeline's* down right away, would she even be able to stay for the full month she'd booked? Would she get her money back? Roxy bit her lip, beginning to feel as bad as Nat did. Her own future looked just as uncertain.

CHAPTER TWELVE

"LET'S TALK ABOUT this tomorrow," Elijah said. "Come on, let's eat and drink all our troubles away tonight. Problems can wait until the morning."

He led them to a run-down restaurant with pool tables in the back. From the outside it was shabby. It had peeling paint and a wooden door that badly needed staining. Inside it was gloomy, but Roxy could see if she peered hard enough that the interior was...exactly the same as the exterior. The wooden tables and chairs had seen better days, and the tiled floor was cracked and uneven.

"Hello, André!" Elijah said loudly as he crossed the threshold. Everyone in the restaurant turned to look at him. "He owns this place," Elijah explained to the others.

André, the heavyset owner with a huge handlebar mustache said, "Elijah!" just as animatedly. He came over and embraced Elijah with a hug, slapping him on the back.

"Table for a million, please," Elijah said, gesturing at

the group. He scanned his eyes over them all. "I mean, six."

Despite the surroundings that hadn't promised much, they had the most gorgeous meal. Roxy chose a chicken and andouille gumbo to start, a lovely thick, buttery, tomatoey, highly seasoned stew. Next, she had a shrimp étouffée, a dish chock full of shrimp on a bed of rice. It had a deep, spicy, but slightly sweet flavor that she just couldn't get enough of.

While they ate, they all chattered away, even Nat, who seemed better for having gotten her worries out. Fueling their conversation was a crisp chardonnay that Elijah described as having 'undertones of oak and smoke.' Glass after glass had gone down easily. Despite having filled herself up with savory courses, and sharing a plate of pralines with Nat, Roxy felt quite light-headed when she stood up. Everyone else seemed pretty merry, too. All except for Sage, who was a teetotaler.

"Boat ride next?" Elijah said to everyone, his voice slurring a little.

"I think...I think I might just fall in the Mississippi River," Louise said. "Which one of you strong men will jump in and save me, huh?" She looked straight at Sam.

"Oh, will you stop making a spectacle of yourself?" Nat said, a little too loudly. Nat's inhibitions were quite low *without* any alcohol in her system, so after a few drinks, Roxy was pretty sure she would say anything she darn well pleased. Nat was about to prove her theory correct.

"Look at you. He's young enough to be your *son*. We all know you're going through some kind of midlife crisis, but please, find someone your own age."

Ouch. There was a horrible pregnant pause, and

Roxy hoped this wasn't going to turn into an awful argument. Everyone watched Louise, waiting to see how she'd react.

She burst out laughing. "Oh, let me have my little fun. Ever heard of living it up?" She held out her empty glass. "Elijah, pour me some more!"

"I think you've had quite enough!" he said. "And I've had far too much to be some lifeguard if you fall out of the boat. Let's get you home."

Louise giggled. "Okay! Home time!"

While Elijah escorted a very wobbly Louise back to *Evangeline's*, Nat, Sage, Roxy, and Sam headed off to catch the boat. Roxy was relieved to get out of the hot restaurant. The thick, fragrant air had steamed up all the windows, and the chatter and laughter of the patrons, along with all the glass clinking and plate clattering, made the atmosphere loud and overwhelming. As she walked outside, Roxy enjoyed the cold air hitting her face once more, and the four of them meandered down to the riverfront.

Roxy couldn't help but notice Sam in the warm glow of the streetlights. She looked up at him. From her viewpoint, the backdrop was a dark sky, with a sprinkling of stars shining here and there. He caught her looking and smiled down at her.

Snap out of it, Rox! She shook her head and turned around. She saw some stragglers from the last of the parade.

"I can't see any boats," Nat said. She was a few steps ahead of them and a little unsteady on her feet. "I'll go check at the kiosk."

"I'm coming with you," said Sage. She linked her arm

firmly in Nat's before she could wriggle away, and they made off into the night. Sam continued after them.

Roxy was watching the last of the parade performers. "Shoot, I should have gotten a photo!" she said. She pulled her phone out of her bag and lined up a shot before the performers disappeared from view. "Oh, it doesn't look that good," she muttered to herself and fiddled with her phone. "It's a little dark. Maybe if I turn on the flash?"

She got a couple of shots in but they weren't great either. She tried the zoom; it made everything blur. She decided to get a little closer.

Roxy was so intent on what she was doing that she didn't notice she was alone at the riverside. As she walked forward, she sensed a tall, broad figure move up behind her. Momentarily, she thought it was Sam, until...

"Listen," a voice said behind her. "Give me that phone, or you'll regret it."

She spun around. "What?" before recoiling in horror.

There, in front of her was a man in a black and silver carnival mask, ribbons trailing from it. She gave a little scream. She looked over her shoulder, but the carnival stragglers had gone. So had her friends.

"You heard me," the man with the mask said. "Pay attention, I've got a gun." He patted his waist and moved closer. "You're a pretty little thing, aren't you?"

"Here, take it! Have the phone!" Roxy said, holding it out to him, her heart beating so fast she felt it would jump out of her chest. She began to back away. She fumbled her phone, and it fell to the ground.

The man walked up to her slowly, seeming to savor her fear.

"Sam!" she hollered. "Sam, help!"

"Sam, help!" the man mocked her. He pushed his face close to hers.

"Hey!" a voice bellowed through the still night air.

Sam had heard her. He came running. "Get out of here right now!" he yelled as he quickly covered the ground between them.

"Or what?" the man spat. He turned to face Sam.

"He's got a weapon!" Roxy shouted.

But Sam stepped right up to the man, his eyes filled with rage, his hands ready for a fight as he cleared the assailant by several inches. "I said get out of here," he said, in a quiet, intimidating voice. "Trust me, you're gonna want to do as I say."

The man jerked toward him, his face inches from Sam's. Sam didn't even flinch. Then, like an animal who knows that retreat is the better course of action in the face of a stronger foe, the man sloped away. Sam and Roxy stood frozen until he'd turned a corner and was out of sight.

"Oh my," Roxy said, dropping her hands to her sides and allowing herself to finally breathe.

"Are you all right?" Sam asked. He came closer, and put his arm around her shoulder, looking her over with concern in his eyes. "Did he hurt you?"

"No, no, not at all," Roxy said. "He just gave me a scare, is all."

"I'm so sorry that happened to you. On your first night out in New Orleans, too. That's bad luck. You must think we're all criminals now."

"No," said Roxy. "No, I don't. Not at all."

"Do you want to go back to *Evangeline's*?" he asked. "I'll walk you there if you want." Seeing her phone still on the ground, Sam picked it up and handed it to her.

Roxy took the phone from him. She thought about Sam's question. "No, I'd like to go on the boat ride, please."

Sam smiled. "You're a brave one, aren't you?"

"Not usually," Roxy replied.

"I don't believe you," he said.

Little did he know. They walked down the riverside together.

"So are you sure you like it here?" he asked after a while.

"It's only been a day, but so far I love it," Roxy said quietly. "I love the food, the atmosphere, the carnival, *Evangeline's*—everything! There's danger everywhere, I know that much."

Roxy had grown up in a tough neighborhood. This wasn't the first time she'd been mugged. It was almost a daily occurrence where she came from. People who knew her were often surprised by how little these sorts of things rattled her. It was emotional situations that made her nervous.

"Good," Sam said. He paused before resuming, "What about...what about...the people?"

Roxy looked up. He looked away, and then looked back again.

She smiled and said softly, "The people are wonderful."

Just at that moment, they heard Nat's voice shouting back at them, cutting through the darkness, "There's one more boat tonight! It gets here in fifteen minutes!"

"Well, fifteen minutes isn't too long to wait," Roxy said.

"No," Sam agreed, with a half-smile Roxy found very attractive. "Not when there's good company to be had."

CHAPTER THIRTEEN

N EXT MORNING, THE atmosphere at breakfast was dire. Roxy was silent. Louise was sullen. Nat's service was fitful and slow. No one spoke. The fun of the carnival had passed. Only dejection and sore heads were left in its wake. Nefertiti had come downstairs with Roxy, but after a couple of minutes, she left. Plainly not even her cat could tolerate the mood and Roxy felt depressed. It felt as though she were living beneath a large dark cloud, one that could burst at any moment.

"Sam was right," Louise said to Roxy, eventually. "Evangeline rejected my offer. Said she was already committed to Lomas. She's expecting him here any minute to sign papers." A crash from the kitchen made both of them wince. It was followed by raised voices and finally a heavy silence.

Roxy pondered this news. If Evangeline sold the guesthouse, where would she go? She couldn't imagine staying in any other establishment. Roxy then berated herself for getting attached so quickly. She barely knew these people. So why then, did she want to go magic shopping with Sage again, and learn more about those mysterious tarot cards? Why then, did she want to cut through Nat's tough exterior and become friends? Why then, did she want to keep eating Evangeline's exquisite meals and learn about New Orleans culture? And why then, did she want to stick around and get to know Sam?

Roxy munched through her beignets. She couldn't even touch her coffee—it reminded her too much of the Café Brûlot from the previous night, which now lived on as a lingering headache.

Once she was done eating, Roxy sat alone at the table, flicking through the local newspaper aimlessly. There was coverage of the carnival procession alongside the usual articles about properties for sale and local events. They made Roxy feel a little lost and lonely. Much as she liked it, New Orleans wasn't home, but Ohio wasn't either. Nor was with her mother. She didn't *have* a home. The only constant she had in her life was Nefertiti. Everything felt bleak, despite the beautiful morning sunlight streaming through the windows.

"We were supposed to sign the papers this morning, and now he doesn't even have the decency to show up!" Evangeline shouted in the kitchen.

Roxy heard the clatter of a saucepan. "I've had enough!" Nat shouted back. "If you're so desperate to sell this place and ruin everything, I'll get him for you myself! What hotel is he staying at?"

"I don't have a choice, Nat!"

"What hotel is he staying at?" Nat repeated fiercely.

"The gosh-darned Fontainebleau!" Evangeline shot back at her.

"Right, then!" Nat came out of the kitchen and threw her apron down on the table next to Roxy.

Despite Nat's fury and complete unwillingness to hide it, Roxy wasn't so intimidated by her anymore. If anything, she felt quite comfortable. After all, they were in the same boat. If *Evangeline's* closed down, both of them would have a serious problem.

"I'm coming with you," Roxy said, surprising herself with her boldness.

"Fine," said Nat. She was already striding out of the room, her chin stuck up high. Roxy had to scurry behind her to catch up, even when they were out on the street. Nat had long legs and kept up quite a pace in her heavy combat boots. They marched to the hotel in complete silence.

The hotel lobby was a shiny, marble affair, and Nat couldn't have looked more out of place. She didn't seem to care, though, or even notice. She marched right up to the front desk.

"I want to speak to a guest, Richard Lomas, please. Can you ring his room?"

"Of course...er, Miss," the young man at the desk said, looking taken aback. He looked Lomas up on his computer and dialed a number on the phone. "I'm afraid there's no answer."

"Try again, please," Nat said firmly.

"We have a policy—"

"Fine," said Nat. "Can you go up and see if he's there?" She paused, her eyebrows arched. "Please."

The man clenched his jaw as he stood up. "Yes, Miss," he said insincerely. "And who should I say wants to see him?" He looked her up and down. Nat's tattoos stood out even more than normal in the staid, chrome and neutral-shaded lobby.

Nat straightened up and held her head high. "The management of *Evangeline's*. He'll know."

"Please wait over there," the man said. He gestured toward a couple of luxury couches in the seating area where suited businesspeople tapped away on laptops and swilled coffee.

"Thank you," said Roxy. Nat was already walking away. When Roxy sat down, she found herself fidgeting. She drummed her fingers against the leather arms of her chair.

"I don't know where I'm going to go either," Roxy said quietly. "My boyfriend left me. I have no job to go back to."

Nat looked out over the room to avoid making eye contact with her. "Hmph. You can go stay with your family."

"I don't have any family," Roxy said. "I don't know my dad. And...well, my mom and I don't get on."

Nat looked at her then, surprised, as if she were considering Roxy from a whole new perspective. "Oh...I thought...well, I don't know. You just seem like the kind of person who'd have a wonderful family who loves you, who you could go home to on the holidays, eat massive amounts of food, and have a laugh with."

Roxy chuckled. "I wish!"

Nat frowned and pursed her lips. "Are you sure? You look so...normal."

"I do my best," Roxy admitted. "Looks like I'm doing a better job than I thought."

"My parents would love to have a daughter like you," Nat said ruefully. "Unfortunately, they can't stand the sight of me. I'd hate to go back to England with my tail between my legs, deported."

"I know what you mean," Roxy said, feeling a rush of recognition. "Every time something goes wrong, my mom loves to tell me how bad I am at being a grown-up. I haven't told her anything about my job or my boyfriend —*ex*-boyfriend. It would give her too much ammunition. I find it better to say nothing."

"Sounds just like my dad." Nat sighed. "Perhaps we're not quite as different as we look."

"Maybe not," Roxy said. Nat gave her a little smile and leaned over. She held out her fist. Roxy met it with her own—a fist bump! She didn't think she'd ever done one before. It wasn't conventional, but it worked. Their shared experience bonded them together.

Shortly afterward, the receptionist came out of the shining silver elevator in the hotel lobby. "There's no answer from his room," he told Nat. "I'm afraid you'll have to try again later."

At that moment, Nat's phone rung. It was Elijah. Nat put the call on speakerphone. Roxy could hear a voice, it sounded like Louise's, wailing and sobbing in the background.

"This was supposed to be...the beginning...of my new...life!" She sounded utterly hysterical.

And no wonder.

For it was Louise, it turned out, who had found the missing property developer. He was in the cemetery at the end of the alleyway, behind one of the graves. He was dead, a bullet through his chest.

Louise had come across Richard Lomas' body on her morning jog. At first, she thought he was passed out drunk and shook him, but..."Deathly cold!" she'd reported through sobs. "Deathly cold! And with a gunshot wound!"

Now, Roxy sat in the corner of the dining room at *Evangeline's*, feeling numb as the drama played out before her. They had raced back to the guesthouse from the hotel, and Nat had gone straight into panic mode. She couldn't stop making tea and coffee and plying everyone with beignets. "A cup of tea will make everything better," she kept saying over and over.

"It's her crazy English way," Evangeline explained. She sat slumped in a chair, periodically shaking her head, biting her lip, and wringing her hands. Elijah had rushed over when he heard Louise's screams, and his complexion was now a shade of green that matched his shirt. He hovered in the doorway, looking unsure of himself. In the corner, Sage took Louise in her arms and rocked her gently, stroking her hair to calm her. Slowly, Louise's wails subsided to sobs, then to a whimper as the shock of her discovery abated.

9-1-1 had been called, and as the small group waited for the police, the friends sat mostly in silence, all quietly contemplating Louise's discovery, what it could mean, and wondering what on earth would happen next.

CHAPTER FOURTEEN

DETECTIVE WILLIAM JOHNSON was a robust man in his early sixties with thick glasses and a bald head. He wasn't particularly tall or large, but he was sturdy and sure on his feet. He somehow dwarfed the dining room. He wore a sharp black suit and had the look of a bull that was about to charge.

As soon as he stepped into the room, Sage shivered. "Bad vibes," Roxy heard her whisper. "Very bad vibes."

Roxy couldn't have agreed more. Johnson seemed to make the very air turn cold and hostile. He was deeply unsettling, and the cruel glimmer in his eyes made Roxy feel like running upstairs and pulling the comforter over her head. As he looked over at Evangeline, Roxy could have sworn she heard him growl.

"Right, listen up! It seems that this was the last place the victim was seen alive." His eyes swiveled to Evangeline. They were beady, threatening. "He was talking to you." Johnson looked back at the others and said, "So you'll all stay here until you've spoken with me one by one."

Sam came running into the dining room, his eyes wild with anxiety. "Elijah called me. Is everyone okay?"

Detective Johnson sneered. "We're all fine, thank you, Superman. But now that you're here, you can sit yourself down, too."

"Right," Sam said, a little defensively. Roxy couldn't help but notice he looked pretty nervous, just as Nat did. Did he have something to hide, too? He avoided Johnson's eyes and rounded his broad shoulders like he was trying to make himself smaller, inconspicuous. "Well, I'm glad everything's being taken care of." Sam sat down on a chair by the door.

"Shall I fix everyone some coffee?" Nat said. When she got no response, "Maybe tea would be better?" She bit her lip and rushed into the kitchen.

"You first," Johnson said, pointing at Roxy.

"M... me?" said Roxy.

The detective sneered again. "Yes. You."

"Oh, but I wasn't even here when the body was found. I just came back."

Johnson stared at her. "Roxy Reinhardt, right? I've heard that you were at the victim's *hotel* when the body was found! I want to know why."

He took her to a side room off the lobby, which Evangeline and Nat used as a place to dump stuff in order to keep everywhere else clean. There was a mess of files, some with papers poking out as they tried to make their escape onto the floor. An old washing machine stood in the corner, and an assortment of random items, including napkins, plates, bed linen, and bizarrely, a bicycle wheel, were crammed into the rest of the space.

There was just about enough room for two chairs. Johnson set his recording device on top of a stack of files and sniffed. "Well, this will have to do." He then stated the date and time for the benefit of the recording. "Now please give me your full name."

"Roxanne Melissa Reinhardt," Roxy said.

"Date of birth?"

"2, 27, 1995."

"Address?"

"Well...I'm kind of *between* addresses," she said. She really didn't want to elaborate about her breakup to this stern-faced, hard-hearted detective, but he looked at her with one eyebrow cocked. It clearly meant, "Explain." She tried to put a positive spin on things. "I'm starting a new life," she said, holding her head high. "I wanted a change of scenery."

"Tell me about what you were doing before and where," Johnson said flatly.

She had to go into detail, it seemed.

"And how did you end up in New Orleans?" he said when she had finished.

"By bus," she said.

He sighed, exasperated. "No, *why* New Orleans in particular?"

Roxy gulped. What could she say? Because her *cat* had alerted her to a commercial, which had stirred a feeling deep inside her that she didn't understand? And she'd simply abandoned her former life and left? How ridiculous did *that* sound? In fact, it *was* ridiculous. What on earth was she doing with her life?

"Ms. Reinhardt?" Johnson said. He was watching her suspiciously.

She realized she had better come up with an answer

fast. "Well, what with my ex-boyfriend leaving and me having a stressful time at work, I was attracted here by the, um, cuisine. It intrigued me. I thought it would be good to go somewhere...interesting." Roxy's palms were sweating, but she didn't want to wipe them against her jeans in case it made her look guilty.

"So, you left your job and your home town indefinitely because of...Creole and Cajun *food*?" Detective Johnson did not sound impressed. Roxy didn't know if that was because he suspected her of lying, or that he considered her life choices to be ludicrous.

"Something like that, sir."

"Ooookay, then," Johnson said. He continued on. "Richard Lomas died from a gunshot wound in the early hours of this morning. Also this morning, you accompanied...someone...to the Fontainebleau Hotel where he was staying, in order to track him down. Why was that?"

Roxy could feel her hands trembling. Authority figures always made her feel afraid. "Well..." she began, and her voice wobbled. "Evangeline had decided she was going to sell the guesthouse to Mr. Lomas and had arranged for him to come over and sign the papers. He didn't turn up. The atmosphere here was tense, and I decided a walk would do me good. So when Nat said she was going to find him, Mr. Lomas, that is, I decided on the spur of the moment to go with her. Evangeline was angry that he hadn't shown up."

"Right," the detective said. "Evangeline is a well-known figure in these parts. She's been part of the establishment for decades. What is not clear is why she would decide to sell to this developer. She's well-known in town as a conservationist, wanting to keep old buildings alive. She's also known as someone who never gives up, even in the face of a sensible, logical proposition." The veins in Johnson's temples stood out, and his jaw muscle twitched as a dark cloud of annoyance swept over his face as he spoke. Roxy got the feeling there was some history between the two that she didn't know about. His animosity seemed extreme and out of place for so early in an investigation. "I find it hard to believe she would sell her property knowing that he would tear it down and develop the area beyond all recognition."

"I think she's at the end of her rope," Roxy said. "Exhausted by the responsibility and drudgery of running such a place. I'm sure she didn't do it if that's what you mean. Kill Mr. Lomas," Roxy blurted out. "I mean, why would she? She wanted to sell her property to him."

Johnson smirked. "Is that so? Well, thank you for that important insight. Tell me again, which police department did you transfer from to come here?"

CHAPTER FIFTEEN

"I...UH...." ROXY stumbled.

"So who do *you* think did it?" Johnson said, leaning forward, his eyes bright, his voice full of fake enthusiasm. He was mocking her.

Roxy felt heat flush her cheeks. A sense of shame burned in her chest, but since she'd been asked the question, she decided to answer it. "Probably Mara Lomas. That's his wife. She came over yesterday, telling us to inform her husband that she knew what he was doing. Something about an affair."

"Right," Johnson said, raising his eyebrows and looking a little more interested in what she had to say. "She came over here?"

"Yes, she was in the street outside."

"That's mighty convenient for Evangeline," he muttered under his breath. He coughed and looked down at his notebook. When he looked back up at Roxy, his eyes were shining.

His expression sent a shiver through Roxy. What *was* his beef with Evangeline? Did he hold a grudge against her? He wasn't being logical, that was for sure. Or without bias, it would seem.

"Not convenient at all," Roxy said firmly. "How would killing Lomas help her? His wife has a far stronger motive." Roxy wasn't quite sure where she was finding the courage to speak out like this, but her sense of fair play was acute. And justice wasn't being done here.

"I'm not interested in your speculation," Johnson snapped, despite the fact he had been asking for just that a minute or so ago.

A silence stretched out between them. Roxy played with her fingers in her lap while Johnson sat back and let out a sigh. Roxy doubted he ever felt uncomfortable. He had far too much confidence and self-assurance. It was very off-putting.

"Is this place going to be shut down?" she asked.

"Not yet," Johnson said with a snort. "There's no reason for it. However, if a certain someone happens to be guilty and is carted off to jail, it won't be able to continue. It will have to be sold, probably to another developer who will tear it down. No one will buy it and retain it in its current state." He looked around with disgust as if he had found himself in a stinking pigpen.

"Actually, two people said they would buy it, aside from the developer."

"And you tell me that *now*?" Detective Johnson said, leaning forward. "Who? We may have to protect them from..." Roxy knew he *desperately* wanted to say Evangeline, but he couldn't, because the tape was running. "Harm," he said eventually. "Give me their names."

"Louise, the other guest," Roxy said, "the one who found the body. She's an interior designer. And Sam, the handyman and laundryman. He plays the saxophone," she added and regretted it immediately. The instrument Sam played was completely irrelevant to the inquiry.

"Okay," Johnson said. "We need to make sure they stay safe. They might be in danger. Are either of them putting pressure on Evangeline to sell?"

"I don't think so," Roxy said. "They seemed to be offering a way to preserve the building and for Evangeline to stay on in some capacity. They didn't want to tear it down. They wanted to keep the guesthouse as is, improve it, update it. Their offers seemed to be acts of genuine kindness."

Detective Johnson opened his eyes wide and shook his head slowly. Roxy stopped herself from speaking. He was still being illogical. There was no sane reason to suspect Evangeline. "Right," he said. "So you would say they're on Evangeline's side?"

Roxy was getting a little sick of his line of questioning. He seemed so closed-minded, so dogged in his dislike of Evangeline. Every time he said her name his lip literally curled. "I don't know," she said, a little more sharply than she'd usually have managed toward an authority figure. "I'm new around here. I don't know anything about sides."

"Whatever," he said. His voice thickened into a monotonous drawl and his eyes glazed over as he said, "Can you account for your whereabouts last night?"

Roxy explained about the parade, then the meal, and the boat ride. She told him of her near mugging, and how afraid she had been, and how Sam had come to her rescue.

"Why are you going red?" Detective Johnson said.

That only made her blush deeper, and stammer for the right words to say. "It's... it's hot in here."

Johnson rolled his eyes. "Can you tell me what Evangeline was doing last night? Was she with you at the parade? At the meal? On the boat ride?"

"No," Roxy said. "She stayed here. She said she'd been to enough carnival parades to last a lifetime, and she didn't feel like it. I think she was very sad. She seemed to have resigned herself to selling this guesthouse, but she doesn't really want to."

"Conjecture," Detective Johnson snapped. "You have no idea what she was thinking. And she was here, alone, not far from where the victim was found. Very suspicious."

"Well, I do know that she was holding Nefertiti when we left. Nefertiti's a very good companion when you're not feeling your best. And she's a very good judge of character."

"Who on earth is Nefertiti?" Johnson said irritably.

"My cat."

Johnson smirked. "And we can trust your cat to be a reliable character witness, can we?" He rolled his eyes again. "Anything more to say?"

"I don't think so," Roxy said. She couldn't stand being around this guy. She wanted to get away from him as quickly as possible. Roxy burned to say something to him about how he was assuming all kinds of bad things about Evangeline, but a shadowy fear swirled within her and sucked her voice down her throat. She lost her nerve. She wasn't brave or bold enough.

"No," Roxy said eventually, more firmly this time.

"Right. Interview over." Johnson snapped off the machine. "Now, I want to see the girl you went to the hotel with, whatever her name is; the strange looking one who works here, the one with all the tattoos, wears only black."

"That's Nat." Roxy felt for Nat. She was going to sweat. Roxy hoped Nat was a good actress because before she had even blinked, Johnson would have decided that her close relationship with Evangeline meant Nat was probably an accomplice to some crime that existed only in his mind. And that was before he knew of her illegal status.

"Nat," Johnson said disapprovingly. "Go and get her. And tell her to bring me some coffee and beignets. And don't scrimp on the beignets, you hear?"

CHAPTER SIXTEEN

"THAT GUY," NAT said furiously. "Who the heck does he think he is?"

"Right?" Roxy agreed.

"He is deeply entrapped by his ego," Sage said. "His true self is lost somewhere so deep within him that he doesn't know who he is."

"Well, I know exactly *what* he is," said Nat. "A complete and utter..."

"He thinks Evangeline's the murderer," Roxy said, cutting Nat off before she said something she might regret. "And seemingly without any evidence."

After Johnson had finished speaking with her, Roxy had watched the others, Nat, Evangeline, Louise, Elijah, Sage, and briefly, Sam, go into the small junk room one by one. They had all traipsed out again a while later, their faces blank. Judging by the look on the detective's face when he finally emerged, no one, it seemed, had had any information that was remotely useful.

In need of a break, Roxy, Sage, and Nat had decided to take a walk down by the Mississippi River. Sage had said she was feeling "energetically tied up" and Roxy knew exactly what she meant. The African-American woman looked particularly serene that morning, in long, flowing robes the color of golden sunlight. She had pulled back her now-braided mermaid hair into a topknot and adorned it with yellow-gold flowers. They were real, Roxy could tell, the petals had begun to droop a little.

"Of course it wasn't Evangeline," Nat snapped. "It's *got* to be the guy's wife."

"That's what I told him as well," said Roxy. "She's got to be the main suspect, surely?" Then an idea struck her. "Sage?" she said, then paused because she realized the idea sounded silly.

Sage looked at her. "What is it, good soul?"

"I don't know...this sounds kind of dumb." Roxy wasn't afraid to say it in front of Sage, but she *was* scared of Nat's reaction. Sniggering was the most likely one.

"Go ahead," Sage said smoothly. She gave Nat a warning look. Roxy wondered if Sage's skills included mind reading.

She blew out a little breath and looked over the river. She tried to find a way to phrase what she was about to say so that it didn't sound preposterous. "You know that you know magic and everything...?"

"Yes," Sage said, her face lighting up.

"Like the cards and stuff. I was wondering if there was any way to...well, to find out who did it. Using magic."

"Oh, come on, Rox," said Nat. Sage shot her another look, but it didn't stop her. "If that were the case, we wouldn't need detectives or police or anything. Sage isn't Harry Potter, you know, and this is New Orleans, not Hogwarts."

"I know, but..." Roxy struggled to reply. She knew it was a crazy idea.

"Well, good friends, there *are* ways to do so," said Sage, mellow despite Nat's derision. "But it requires very advanced magic. I have been practicing for thirty-three years, and even I wouldn't trust my own ability at that level. Magic of that form is...complex."

"Then who would be able to do it?" Roxy asked. "Can we find someone like that?"

"It would need to be one who has trained with a long line of indigenous priests, perhaps an advanced magician from Haiti or the Congo, or somewhere deep in the heart of South America. Certainly not me, unfortunately."

"Oh, what rubbish!" Nat said. "You don't really *believe* in all this magic stuff, do you, Sage? Sure, you mess around with the cards and buy your lotions and potions and incense. But it doesn't really *mean* anything, does it? It's just a source of comfort, a hobby. It's not *real*."

"That is grossly disrespectful, Nat," Sage said calmly.

"Yeah, but, come on! Magic? Even little kids grow out of that by the time they're 7 or 8. Yet here you are, a grown person, actually professing to believe in this stuff?"

"Everyone believes in different things," Roxy said, trying to smooth the atmosphere over.

"People around the world have used magic for thousands and thousands of years," Sage said. "Since the beginning of time. Whole societies have depended upon it. Look at the Ancient Egyptians, for example."

"Why would I do that?" Nat said dismissively.

Roxy looked up to the sky.

To her surprise, Sage actually laughed gently. "You haven't done any in-depth research into magic throughout the ages, have you?" she asked Nat.

"No, I have not," Nat retorted.

"Have you read a single book on magic?"

"Well, no, but..."

"Exactly," Sage said smoothly. "You're simply projecting your uneducated prejudice onto me, without even knowing what you're talking about. And we are supposed to be friends, Nat. You're devaluing the foundation of my entire existence. That is *not* what friends do."

Roxy found her heart beating faster. "I don't think she meant to..."

"Nat knows exactly what she's doing," said Sage, her voice getting harder. The light caught her eyes and Roxy could see tears reflected in them. "Magic is my life. Magic saved me from...well, let's say I haven't had the easiest life. Magic is why I'm here today."

Nat dropped her head and stared at her combat boots.

"And because Nat is stressed about this situation and her own *precarious* status, she starts picking a fight with me to let off some steam." Sage drew herself up to her full height. She was nearly six-feet tall. "Hear this, Nat. You need to be more aware of your feelings and be honest about them. The more you hide and suppress them, the more they come out in toxic leaks like this. You have hurt me with your words, very deeply. But I will choose the higher road." Her voice wobbled. "I'll see you all later." Sage glided away, her golden robes swishing.

CHAPTER SEVENTEEN

ROXY COULD HEAR her heart beating against her chest. She and Nat walked on in silence, neither of them wanting to talk about what had just happened. Soon they found a bench, and Nat flopped down on it. Roxy joined her. They both stared across the rippling river for a while.

"She's right, you know," Nat said eventually. "I am worried about being found out and deported *and* this whole murder thing. I knew what I was saying was hurtful, but there was something in me that just kept pushing on and on, wanting to keep going until she got mad at me. But Sage never gets mad. Not really. "

Roxy couldn't understand what Nat was talking about. The idea of riling someone up until they got upset seemed both pointless and abhorrent to her.

"Now she's gone off, I feel kind of relieved," Nat said. "But also horrible. Because she's really upset now."

"Maybe you could go after her and apologize?" Roxy suggested. "She's probably at the magic store."

"How ironic," Nat said, shaking her head.

Roxy watched a cloud being carried by the wind through the cold, blue sky. "Do you really believe what you said about magic?"

Nat sighed. "I don't know. Like Sage said, I don't know anything about it, really. I guess I'm a skeptic, but I haven't looked into it. Not properly. It just seems so, oh I don't know, pie in the sky, airy-fairy."

"I've never really come across it before," said Roxy. "I don't know if I believe in it, but it is interesting. Since I've been here, I realize there are a *lot* of things I don't know about. My life has been...sheltered."

Nat laughed, but not unkindly. "That's why I left England. I was born in London's East End and my parents have worked hard all their lives. They wanted the best for me but our ideas of what that looked like were different. I was expected to go to university, get a clean, respectable office job, get married, have 2.3 kids or what-ever, and a mortgage, preferably on a house in the suburbs. To them that was success, but just saying that bores me, let alone *doing* it for the rest of my life."

It sounded lovely to Roxy, but she could appreciate it wasn't for everyone. "You wanted more adventure."

"Yep," said Nat. "I got a nanny job here. My plan was to travel afterward. Go to India. Australia. Thailand." She laughed again, but it was hollow.

"You could still, couldn't you?"

"Yeah, I think so. But since I've overstayed my visa, I'm guessing they'll never let me back into the US once I leave."

"Oh."

"When I do leave or get deported, I'm going to be leaving for good. So, as much as I want to explore the world, I'm not sure I can bring myself..." Nat looked around. "New Orleans has become like home to me now. And Evangeline's like...not my mum exactly, but oh, I don't know, my crazy great aunt, or something. I don't want *Evangeline's* to get shut down."

"Me, neither," said Roxy. "I'm already feeling attached to the place, and I've only been here a couple of days."

Nat gave a smile tinged with a little sadness.

"Sage is very wise," Nat said. "The magic stuff aside, she just *is* magic. She knows a lot of stuff. Before I met her, I'd *never* be here talking to you about emotions and stuff. I'd be somewhere down there..." She pointed to a bridge. "Probably *under* there, drinking away my sorrows, sure that no one would understand, and that I was the only person in the world with problems." She laughed at herself. "Sage is very wise."

Roxy smiled. "She does seem like a very special person."

"Yep," Nat said. She got up from the bench. "Let's go find her, and I can tell her what a total idiot I am."

Roxy stood and gave Nat a side hug. "You're not a total idiot."

"Oh, really I am," Nat said raising her eyebrows.

"We need to make a plan," Roxy said firmly. "A plan of how we're going to find out who *really* killed that developer. I feel sure Johnson will try to pin the murder on Evangeline, and that'll ruin everything as well as be a terrible miscarriage of justice." Roxy felt a great sense of loyalty toward these people already. "If he isn't going to investigate fairly, then *we* will."

Nat looked at Roxy in surprise. "You're feistier than I thought," she said.

Roxy smiled back, remembering something her old

English teacher had said. He'd been the only teacher who hadn't treated her as if she were invisible. *Roxy, you're soft on the outside, but steely underneath, where it counts.* Roxy had never believed him but now, she felt it. It was a rush. "Thanks," she said to Nat.

CHAPTER EIGHTEEN

SAGE TOOK NAT'S bumbling apology outside the magical supply store very graciously. In fact, she threw her arms around Nat's shoulders and squeezed her tight. "You know I love you, don't you, honey?"

Nat sniffed and swallowed hard. She bent her head into Sage's robed shoulder. She was the type to hold back tears at all costs, stiff upper lip and all that. "Yep," was all she could manage.

As they walked their way back to *Evangeline's*, the silence between them was companionable and restful after the emotional drama of earlier. The air was cold, but Roxy found it exhilarating. It chilled her cheeks as clouds cast a dark canopy over them, threatening rain. Sage had bought some strongly fragranced incense and even unlit, its mysterious musky smell wafted up from the paper bag she held and made the air around them sweet and unusual.

As they walked through the streets of the city, past a mixture of old, traditional buildings and flashing neon signs, Roxy felt something that she never had before. A sense of purpose, perhaps? *A mission?* A quest? But not only that...she felt a kinship. A *shared* goal. It struck her as she fell into step beside Nat and Sage.

For the first time, Roxy felt like she belonged. She felt like she mattered, that she was part of something bigger than herself. She stopped thinking in any sort of longing, tugging way about her ex-boyfriend. Instead, she wondered, "What on *earth* was I thinking?" And, quite miraculously, she stopped worrying and desperately craving security and stability. It was ironic that here, in a city she didn't know, with people she had just met, in an accommodation that could fall through at any moment, with the most uncertain future she had ever faced, she felt the safest she ever had.

Finally, Nat spoke up as they walked past a diner, and the air around them became thick and warm with the forceful smell of burgers and fries. It was so strong; it even drove away the scent of the incense that permanently swirled around Sage. "Oh heck, I'm starving," Nat said. "Let's grab some lunch here." She slipped her phone out of her pants pocket. "It's two o'clock already. I doubt Evangeline will be up to cooking today. I'm certainly not."

Sage, a vegetarian, ordered herself a portion of fries. Nat got a cheeseburger, fries and a milkshake. Roxy, meanwhile, realized that she'd barely nibbled at her beignets that morning, and there was a dull ache in her stomach. The events of the day had distracted her, but as whiffs of fast food assailed her, her hunger made itself known, and she felt slightly nauseous. She ordered a chicken burger and fries combo that came with a soda. The food arrived in minutes, and they carried their trays to one of the laminated tables. It was safe to say this was not one of New Orleans' finest eating establishments, but Roxy didn't care. Right then, something cheap, familiar, and fattening seemed the best option.

None of them said much until their food was mostly eaten. Roxy's mind wandered back to the case. "How are we going to prove to Johnson that the murderer is not Evangeline? I'm *sure* it's Mara Lomas. I mean, come on, she thought her husband was having an affair, and she *threatened* him—out loud and in public. She said he needed all the protection he could get. How on earth can Johnson think it was Evangeline with that evidence in front of him? It's a total open and shut case."

"One would think so," Sage said with a grimace. "But knowing the story between that man and Evangeline, I wouldn't be so sure."

"Aha! I *knew* there had to be a history between them!" Roxy exclaimed. "When he questioned me, he was acting like he loathed her. Why is that?"

Sage blew a stream of air out of her mouth and adjusted her golden robes. "Evangeline's always been quite an activist. That lady is *tough*, I tell you. When she believes in something and knows she's right, she'll hang on to the very end. It's actually most unlike her to have given in to this developer. It's sad, really. I think it's because her eyesight is deteriorating, but anyway, she's been a thorn in Johnson's side for years."

"In what sense?" Roxy asked.

"Hey!" Nat interrupted. "Look!"

Roxy turned to see Nat pointing at the TV on the wall. It was showing local news.

MURDER, it read at the bottom of the screen. There was a female reporter standing in front of the cordoned-off cemetery. Blue lights flashed. Police swarmed every-where behind her.

"Hey, would you turn it up, please?" Nat said to the young woman behind the counter.

The woman pressed her lips together and flicked her mousey brown ponytail with annoyance, but she complied with Nat's request. It was an old-fashioned boxy television, and the woman, who was quite short, had to reach up on tiptoes to press the volume button.

"The wife of the deceased is currently assisting police with their investigations," the reporter said, her hair blowing about her in the breeze.

"Aha!" Nat took a delighted sip on her milkshake, her eyes lighting up. "Well, there we go. Johnson has seen sense after all. 'Assisting with investigations' *always* means guilty as heck. It's just that they're not quite ready to charge her."

Roxy had been imagining Evangeline rattling around in jail, the other prisoners taking advantage of her as her eyesight got worse. She frowned as she sipped on her straw, even though her soda was long drained. "I certainly hope you're right," she said.

CHAPTER NINETEEN

T HEY CONTINUED TO stare at the TV even though the news report had moved on to more upbeat topics. The channel was now showing footage of the carnival celebrations.

"You know, I don't think Mara did it," Sage said.

"Of course she did," Nat scoffed.

But Roxy wasn't so quick to dismiss Sage. "What makes you say that?"

Sage looked straight at Roxy, her dark eyes flashing. "My intuition."

"Oh, for goodness..." Nat began, then seemed to remember their earlier argument and rushed to say, "Well, I mean, well, you know, I..." She couldn't find anything with which to elegantly finish off her sentence so she sighed and her shoulders slumped. "Sorry."

"Not to worry, sugar," Sage said. She threw Nat a wink and patted her hand.

Roxy's mind began to whir again. She had never *ever* trusted her intuition. In the past, she'd always felt too anxious to *have* any. Her decision to come to New

Orleans had been unique in that respect. Until that point, when faced with choices, Roxy had always gone for the safest option, the one with the least potential to go wrong. Now, however, feeling much more relaxed in New Orleans among her new friends, the strange gut feeling she had, the fluttering that told her, *No, something isn't quite right here,* stood out. She wondered what it could mean. If Mara hadn't killed the developer, then who had?

"Let's go," Nat said. "Now that they've caught that dead man's crazy wife, maybe Evangeline will think about keeping the guesthouse open. I want to persuade her."

"You know she can't afford to keep it going," said Sage, as they tipped their tray contents into the trash. "It's been running at a loss for ages."

"Yeah, but Sam said he'd buy it off her," Nat said breezily as if the deal had already been sealed. "And Louise is our backup. As annoying as she is, if she keeps the guesthouse open, I'll be her best friend for life."

Roxy laughed. "And maybe there'll finally be a steamy romance between her and Sam as they run the guesthouse together. It'd be like something out of a book."

Nat snorted. "In her dreams."

"She's alright," Roxy said as they walked back out onto the street.

"No, too old, too cougar," said Nat. "And she keeps totally embarrassing herself."

"She is suffering," Sage said. "I would say both her first and second chakras are severely out of balance."

Nat opened her mouth, then closed it again. She let out a huge happy sigh, swinging her arms as they walked. "Well, looks like that dumb Johnson won't be sniffing around for much longer. Let's go home and persuade

Evangeline and Sam and Louise or any combination of the above to keep *Evangeline's* open."

When they got back, they found that Evangeline was not in the mood to be persuaded to do anything, however. They found her sweeping the dining room and humming a furious tune, her lips pursed tightly together. Roxy saw her roughly wipe away a tear from her cheek.

Sam was in the corner bagging up tablecloths for laundering. He gave Nat a cautionary look as they walked in, but Nat ignored him.

"Did you see Mara Lomas has been arrested, Evangeline? We're all off the hook. You can relax. So promise me you're going to keep this place, and I won't get deported."

"She's not been arrested, just taken in for questionin'," Evangeline said, not looking up from her sweeping. "And your immigration status has nothin' to do with me. I helped you out when I didn't have to, so I don't appreciate you tryin' to put a guilt trip on me, Miss Natalie."

"*Don't* call me that," said Nat. All the confidence had seeped out of her voice.

"Now, there's things to do," said Evangeline, "and you've been out for far too long. You can begin by tacklin' that stack of teacups in the kitch'n."

Nat pressed her lips together and walked away to make a start on the cups, accompanied by a lot of banging and slamming.

Evangeline sighed. "I'm being horrible, aren't I?" she said to Sage.

Sage placed a hand on her arm and said in a quiet,

kind voice. "Perhaps you're not quite embodying your best self."

Evangeline burst into tears. "I'm sorry, Nat, cher," she said, going to the kitchen door and speaking through it. "I'm just so very upset about the guesthouse and if everythin's goin' to work out. Don't take old Evangeline so seriously. Don't take my words to heart, cher."

Evangeline pushed the door open and went into the kitchen, wrapping a surprised Nat up in a big, warmly reciprocated hug. Roxy and Sage exchanged glances. Despite their bickering back and forth, Nat and Evangeline were clearly quite fond of one another. But, oh the tension. Roxy was fit to wilt.

CHAPTER TWENTY

AFTER THE SECOND emotional reconciliation in as many hours, Roxy needed a break. She headed to her room. Nefertiti was on the stairs, attending to her complex self-grooming regimen. As soon as she saw Roxy, she sprang to her feet and wound her fuzzy, fluffy self round and round Roxy's ankles.

"Hello, beautiful girl," Roxy said, leaning down to tickle her under the chin.

Nefertiti purred loudly, then padded up the stairs alongside her owner.

"You like it here, don't you?" said Roxy before sighing emphatically. "Me too. I'm going to find a way to get us to stay here, Nef." She turned to look at Nefertiti's cute squashed up face. "We might have to do a little investigating, though. Oh, oh!" Roxy suddenly found herself knocked off her feet as she turned the corner of the stairs and fell sprawling across the staircase.

"Oh no!" Louise said. "Sorry!" Her voice was thick as if she had been crying. She was sitting on the stairs looking out of one of the old stained glass windows, her knees pulled up under her chin.

"It's okay," Roxy said, grabbing onto the stair rail to pull herself up. "I wasn't looking where I was going."

Louise wiped mascara from under her eyes, where it had begun to run in black streaks carried by her tears. "Are you hurt?"

"No," Roxy said, although her elbow ached a little where she'd banged it against a step. "Are you?"

"I'm fine," said Louise. She even tried a smile, but it looked so strained, hiding so much pain, that it tugged at Roxy's heart.

Roxy felt a little nervous at what she was about to do and tapped one hand into the palm of the other. In the past, she had always diverted herself from any drama or problem or worry as soon as she could. Anything that wasn't completely smooth sailing made her bite her lip and her pulse race. But this time, things felt different. She needed to do something.

Roxy sat down next to Louise and put an arm around her. "Something's up. What's wrong?"

Nefertiti clearly thought Louise had a lot of wrong going on, because she curled up at the feet of the two women and tucked her head under her paw, falling quickly into a snooze.

Louise looked down at the cat and gave a sad little smile. "She looks so cozy and happy and safe."

Roxy smiled. "She sure does."

Louise let out a long, sad sigh. "I wish I felt like that."

"It would be awesome to be a cat, wouldn't it?" Roxy agreed.

That made Louise laugh a little, her voice still tinged

with sadness. "Life would be a whole lot less complicated, that's for sure."

They sank into silence. Roxy looked at Louise out of the corner of her eye, trying to read her expression. "Is it... just that...well, you've been through so much already, what with your husband having an affair, you feeling like you had a new life ahead, and then this awful..." She couldn't bring herself to say the word. "This awful *thing* happened. You must be feeling like you don't know what to do and that things are hopeless anyway."

Louise widened her eyes. "Are you psychic? You read me like a book, Roxy. That's incredible."

"Oh, gosh," Roxy said quickly, flushing with embarrassment at the compliment. "No special skills here at all. I...I think it's quite easy to see."

Louise burst into tears. "So it's obvious to everyone that I'm a total mess?" she said thickly.

"Oh, no, no!" said Roxy. "That isn't what I meant at all!"

Louise gulped down tears, her face flushing. "Sorry, I apologize," she said. "I really do. A fully grown woman blubbing all over the place like this, it isn't dignified." She pulled herself up straight and attempted to regain her composure, but her face crumpled. "But you're right, it's just like you said. I had thought that this was to be my new start. But..."

"Didn't you say you wanted to buy the guesthouse?" Roxy said. "You still could. It would be a new start. A new life."

"I'm not sure I want to anymore. I can't..." Louise's eyes took on a glazed-over, faraway look as she trailed off.

"You can't what?"

"I can't stop...thinking about it. That moment."

Roxy paused for a second to fathom what Louise was talking about. From the traumatized look on her face, she gathered she must have meant the moment she stumbled across Richard Lomas' body.

"It's going to haunt me forever," Louise said. "His eyes...his eyes...they were open."

Roxy shuddered involuntarily.

"I want to get away," said Louise, firmly.

"You can do that," Roxy said. "You came here out of nowhere, didn't you say? Just like me. So you could go somewhere else. Anywhere."

Louise shook her head. "It's not the same anymore." Roxy could see she'd lost her confidence, her sense of adventure, her *joie de vivre*. "But I don't want to stay here, either," Louise added. "Anyway, I can't get away from myself, can I? I can't get away from what's in my own mind."

Roxy sighed. There was no answer to that. "I guess not." She was starting to feel a little depressed herself. She tried to come up with a positive thought. "Still, at least they've taken Mara Lomas, the developer's wife, in for questioning. That's progress, isn't it?"

"I guess," Louise said, looking unsure. "If she really is the killer. But it could have been..." She opened her mouth, and then closed it suddenly again. "Well, it could have been anyone."

Roxy's heart started thumping a little louder than usual. She looked at Louise. "Do you have an idea who the murderer might be?"

L OUISE PAUSED. HER eyes flickered. She was weighing something up in her mind. Eventually, she said, "No. We can all make our guesses, I'm sure. But I'd prefer the police find out who did it from the evidence."

"Yes," Roxy agreed. "You're absolutely right."

"But considering Lomas wanted to take over *Evangeline's*, as well as *other buildings*, and he didn't do business in a very honorable fashion from what I hear, they've probably got a massive suspect pool to work through."

"He wanted to buy up other buildings in the city?"

"Uh-huh," Louise said. "Before you arrived, I found him outside *Evangeline's* making a phone call. I heard him say something like 'I'm taking a look at two in the French Quarter, then I'll head over to Touro.'"

"Oh," said Roxy. She sat with that information for a moment and let it run through her mind. "Okay." Things seemed to be getting quite a lot more complicated all of a sudden. She slumped back against the stair feeling crushed.

Why on earth had she thought that *she* could find out who the killer was? After all, she was only an ex-call center operator? What did she know about investigations? What did she know about *anything*?

"Well…" she said, her mind a blank. "Right."

"Are you going to be staying on here?" Louise asked. "Or do you think you'll move on?"

"I…I'm not sure."

"Go out and see the world while you can, would be my advice," said Louise. "Whatever you do, don't settle down with a no-good man and waste half your life, like me." She gave a half-smile. "Hopefully, by the time you're my age, you'll have life a lot more figured out than I do."

Roxy tried to think of a way to respond to her politely, but there wasn't one. She just nodded a little awkwardly instead.

As if sensing the mood, Nefertiti got up and arched her back in a stretch. She began to pad up the stairs without so much as a backward look.

"It's been such a long day," Roxy said. "I'm going to see if I can nap the rest of the afternoon away."

"That sounds like a good plan," said Louise, offering her another small smile. She remained seated and watched, her eyes soulful and sad, as Roxy stood and followed her cat up the stairs.

Once they entered the loft, Roxy fed Nefertiti a packet of cat food and stood over her as she scarfed it down. When her cat had eaten her fill and raised her head to indicate she was done, Roxy dropped backward onto the bed.

She hadn't realized how tired she was until she sprawled out, her arms and legs spread like a starfish. She looked up at the white ceiling.

The next thing she knew, she awoke with a jerk. It was nighttime—the curtains were drawn, and there was a warm, cozy glow flooding the room. Someone had turned the lamp on. There was the most delicious smell—hearty and spicy and savory and warm.

Against the wall, Roxy saw Evangeline illuminated by the lamp. "Sorry to wake you, cher," she said. "I brought you your dinner. Thought you might like to have it up here. Sage had a tarot reading to do for a client. Nat's gone to listen to her music, and Louise is in her room with a bottle of brandy. So there's no dinner downstairs tonight."

"Sure," Roxy said, feeling quite disoriented as she sat up. "I'd love to have it up here. It smells delicious."

"Awright, cher." Evangeline brought the tray over from the side table and placed it on Roxy's lap. "It's real Creole comfort food. Red beans and rice with sausage and a glass of red wine." Roxy looked down and inhaled its spicy fragrance. "And then some Bananas Foster for dessert. To you, that's bananas browned in a whole heap of butter, sugar, and liquor, and served with vanilla ice cream. My momma used to make that for us as a real treat when I was growin' up. I always like to have it when things aren't so good. Reminds me of her, and how kind she was."

Roxy smiled. "That story will make me enjoy it all the more."

"Well, cher, I've leave you to your meal. I'll come up later for your tray. Just you leave it outside your door."

Roxy's mind, still dazed from her nap, spun as she tried to formulate a question. "Um, Evangeline?" There was so much to ask. Was she still going to sell the guesthouse? Did Roxy need to find somewhere else to go?

Would Nat get deported? Roxy looked up at the ceiling as she deliberated which question to lead with. As she did so, more questions popped into her mind. Why did Johnson dislike Evangeline so much? Why was Richard Lomas looking at other properties? Who did Evangeline believe the murderer to be? Was it her? Roxy's thoughts tied themselves in knots. She didn't really think Evangeline was the killer, but there was a part of her that knew no one could be trusted, not for sure. She had learned that growing up.

Evangeline laughed, as the silence stretched out. "Cat got your tongue?"

"What are you thinking about doing now?" Roxy blurted out.

"I can't say I'm sure yet," Evangeline said. "I *was* set on giving all this up." She cast her eyes around the room. "After all, my eyesight isn't what it used to be, and I don't have the energy I once had. I was all ready to sell to that developer fella, but it would be a real shame to let this place go, especially to have it torn down. Not many appreciate its beauty. She's an old girl, like me, but with a good structure, also like me." Evangeline laughed. "Yet, money is always...well, we don't have a money tree out front, do we?"

Roxy said, "I'm not sure Louise is still interested in taking it over, but what about Sam? Maybe he could put some money in the place and help renovate it. Then you would get more customers."

Evangeline's eye's hardened. "Charity, that would be." Her voice had hardened, too. "And Evangeline don't do charity." She bent down and gave Nefertiti a little tickle under the chin. "Ain't she so sweet? Yes, you are, cher! Yes, you are!" she said, cooing now. Roxy couldn't help but smile.

"Goodnight, Roxy. Enjoy your food, cher," the elderly woman said.

"Thanks, Evangeline. For everything."

The guesthouse owner paused by the door and looked back at Roxy with kindness in her eyes. "You're most welcome, cher."

CHAPTER TWENTY-TWO

BREAKFAST THE NEXT morning was another somber affair. Rain pounded at the windows. Outside, the light was a murky gray so dark they had to turn the lamps on. Roxy felt in limbo, and it seemed everyone else felt the same. Nobody spoke, except for Roxy when she gave Nat her order. Nat hadn't even asked her for it. She'd just turned up at the table and raised her eyebrows.

The silence remained unbroken until Elijah burst in with his cases of beignets. "Good morning!" he said jovially, walking across the room at a clip. Then he took in the atmosphere and stopped. "Well, we're a bunch of happy campers today, aren't we?" He laughed. "Don't you know? Today's the Endymion parade!"

He emphasized his words with an excited flourish that was remarkable given how many boxes of pastries he was balancing with one hand. No one replied except Roxy, who felt obliged to say something. She could only come up with a quiet, "Oh, okay."

"The weather's due to clear up by the afternoon. And

the place'll be full of kids and laughter and lots of bright colors and fun," he said. "Come on, we all deserve some relaxation time. It will be a distraction."

"There is a time for everything indeed," Sage said. She had popped in for breakfast as she often did, but today she looked run down, in comparison to her usual unruffled self. Her long mermaid hair looked unkempt. Even her robe didn't look right—the linen was all creased, and she'd spilled a drop of orange juice down the front. "Sometimes mourning and solemnity claim time for their own. We cannot always rush to distract ourselves from..."

"Oh, come now," Elijah said with a charming smile. "Let's take our minds off all the unpleasantness."

Sage opened her mouth, but quickly closed it and sighed deeply. She resumed munching on her beignet, poring over her laptop.

As he walked past her, Louise shot Elijah a nasty look. It was so nasty that Roxy was startled by it. After a moment Louise looked down at her oatmeal and stirred her spoon slowly around the bowl. She clearly lacked an appetite. Roxy didn't have one either, but that look perturbed her. Sure, Elijah could be a little insensitive to a mood, a little over the top, but Louise's expression wasn't one of annoyance, it was of pure hatred.

"What d'ya say, Nat? Evangeline?" Elijah said as he went into the kitchen.

Roxy turned back to Louise and scanned her face. The dark cloud had not left her features.

"We're not quite in the right mood for a parade, are we?" Roxy tried.

"Mmmm," Louise said. She was lost in her thoughts.

Roxy pressed on. "And you certainly don't look in the mood for fun."

"Oh, me?" said Louise. "I'm just thinking about liars, and how much I despise them."

They heard Elijah in the kitchen. Louise shot more daggers in his direction.

"Liars?" Roxy said.

"Yes, liars."

Elijah came out of the kitchen and said, "It's settled! We're leaving here at one o'clock after a quick lunch. See you then!"

"Bye," Louise said, in a sickly-sweet voice. She had an equally false smile to match. Her eyes remained cold. As soon as Elijah had turned his back, she grimaced, her face full of disgust. "I hate liars, Roxy."

Roxy leaned in. "What has Elijah lied about?" she asked quietly.

"Oh, not him in particular," Louise said. She leaned back in her chair and her voice lost its intensity, but she couldn't quite meet Roxy's eyes. Roxy would have put money on the fact that Louise was lying. "Just men in general."

"Is Elijah a cheat?" Roxy asked. "Does he even have a partner?"

"What does it matter?" Louise said. "Men are all cheaters and liars as far as I can tell. My husband, your boyfriend, Richard Lomas...and all the rest of them."

"I really don't think that's true," said Roxy. "Not all men."

Louise gave her a patronizing smile. "You're still a baby. You probably believe in Prince Charming. That a man will rush in on his charger to rescue you, and you'll both live happily ever after. But don't worry, it'll take a couple more betrayals to knock that belief out of you, but knock it out of you they will."

Roxy felt quite uncomfortable and a little angry at Louise's condescension. She shifted in her chair and looked at her without flinching. "You were staring at Elijah like you hated him. Why's that?"

Louise raised her eyebrows. "You're imagining things," she said. Her expression softened. "I'm sorry, we're all just tired and cranky and not thinking straight. Let's go to the parade later. I'm going to relax this morning. I suggest you do the same." Without another word, she got up from the table and left.

Roxy sat alone, looking out of the window when, all of a sudden, the lights went out. From the kitchen, the whirring sound of a mixer faded to nothing.

"Oh, for goodness' sake!" Roxy heard Evangeline shout. The old lady came barreling through from the kitchen. "The electricity's gone again," she called over furiously. "The wiring in this darn place," she said. She shook her head. "No wonder everyone wants to tear it down."

With Evangeline on the warpath, Roxy decided to take Louise's advice. It was a bit early for a nap, but she could escape up to her room for some quiet time. She took a beignet from the table and wrapped it in a napkin, hoping that some of her appetite might return later. Then she headed to the darkened hallway where Evangeline was flicking switches in an electrical box mounted in a closet, still muttering furiously. "Can't even see the darn thing."

"Looks like I arrived at just the right time," a cheery voice called out. They turned to see Sam running into the hallway from the wet cobbled street, ruffling his hair to shake the rain from it. "Hi there, Roxy."

"Hi," said Roxy, a little shyly.

"Electric gone again, Evangeline?"

"No, I just fancied turning the lights on and off and rummaging around in the dark for fun," Evangeline said humorlessly.

"Let me take a look," Sam said with a chuckle.

"I'm going back to the kitchen," Evangeline said. She spun on her heel and took off. "Come see me when you've fixed it. I told you this place was falling to pieces."

"Why don't you let me buy..."

Evangeline's crotchetiness turned to desperation. She spun around once more to face Roxy and Sam. She looked drained and exhausted. "Please, *stop*," she said. "Please." Then she disappeared into the kitchen.

CHAPTER TWENTY-THREE

SAM GRIMACED BUT moved on quickly. He flashed his phone light on the electrical box, pulled back a panel, and said, "Aha. It's just a couple of wires that need refitting. Evangeline should really do over the whole electrical system, but it's very expensive for a rewire when you have all these period features."

"Ah," Roxy said, wishing she could come out with something insightful, preferably witty. Or at the very least, *interesting*. "I just love the architecture here," was the best she could manage. She hated how simple and uninformed and unsophisticated that sounded. *She* sounded.

"Me too," he said. "Are you busy, Roxy? This is quite a fiddly job. I could pretend I'm some kind of superhero who could do this all by himself, but I just might end up electrocuting myself. Can I ask you to hold a box for me, with my fuses and tools? Then I can easily take what I need without bending down and letting go of a wire? I don't want to start an electrical fire or anything."

"Sure," Roxy said. She noticed that he had blushed a little, plus he was rambling. Perhaps *he* was a little shy, too.

"Thanks," he said. He dashed out into the rain to get tools from his van and quickly returned. "Great. If you could...just here would be amazing."

Roxy stood and held her hands out. Sam placed a tray from the inside of his toolbox over her hands and laid various tools and fuses and electrical parts on it like he was performing surgery.

"Right. Perfect," he said. He ducked his head into the electrical box and began to work.

Roxy waited for a moment, before saying, "You've offered to buy this place so many times. Why won't Evangeline take you up on it? Is it really just because she thinks it's charity?"

Sam sighed. "I don't know. I think she thinks I'm, um, humoring her."

"Well, are you?"

"No," he said. Sam looked into her eyes as he leaned over to take a fuse. "I just like things the way they are. Why not keep them the same? I can afford it. And I'd like to help. I've offered to pay for a full rewire in the past. Offered to fix the roof. Take care of the dry rot. But nada. Evangeline won't take any money to keep the place open. She won't take any money to move on. That woman is like a mule. Stubborn as anything. Won't go forward, won't go back." He peered deeply into the fuse box.

"Not to pry, but all these offers you're making sound real expensive. I didn't know the laundry business was quite so lucrative," Roxy said.

Sam's laugh was hollow. "Well, you know...life is full of surprises."

Just then, a horrible idea struck Roxy like a lightning bolt. She didn't even know where it came from. It wasn't a result of reasoning or deduction. It was something that flashed through her mind. Was it intuition?

Maybe Sam was getting bankrolled from somewhere. Maybe he used his laundry business as a front to get into all sorts of other "businesses." Perhaps he was a money launderer, buying up failing enterprises to funnel money on from who knows where. Perhaps that's why he was so keen to "help" Evangeline. Maybe *that* was how he got to own a fancy car. Perhaps he'd done this before. Perhaps that's what he'd been hiding all this time!

Roxy didn't know if her imagination was running away with her, or if she was really onto something. But she didn't want the warmth between them to skew her judgment, so she squinted and tried to look at Sam with a cold, objective eye.

He turned to pick another tool from the tray and gave her a lovely smile that drew up one corner of his mouth and showed off a dimple. "That's a real serious face," he said, his eyes dancing with mischief.

Roxy tried to view this, not as charming, but as suspicious and inappropriately irreverent, considering there had just been a murder.

"It appears to me that Detective Johnson will chase Evangeline down as the main suspect," said Roxy. "People say there's a history between them. Do you know what kind of history?"

"Sure, everyone knows," Sam said breezily. "There was a police corruption incident down here about 20 years ago. I was still a little kid back then, but I remember it. It was all over the news. Evangeline organized some major activism around it. You know, sit-ins, protests, that kind of stuff. Johnson was the accused guy's partner. They'd been best friends since childhood. Evangeline's efforts got the guy locked up for a good many years. Well, I should say his crimes are what got him locked up, but he might have gotten away with them if it weren't for her. Johnson has hated her ever since, by all accounts."

"Wow," Roxy said.

"Plus, she's made a lot of fuss over historic buildings getting torn down in the past. She turns up at city hall a lot, speaks at the meetings. She's well-known down there. She makes herself a thorn in certain people's sides, and that doesn't always go down so well. She won't back down and doesn't hesitate to demand what she thinks is right. So Johnson thinks she's somewhere between a menace and a pain in the ass, depending on what mood he's in. They don't see eye to eye at all."

"Do you think he'll try to pin the murder on her?"

Sam paused and looked at her. "I don't know. If he's as corrupt as his former partner, maybe." He laughed. "Though the way Evangeline's going on right now, I wouldn't be so sorry to see the back of her myself."

"Ouch!" Roxy said.

"Bit close to the bone? Yeah, you're probably right, I shouldn't have said it. We all love Evangeline. The place wouldn't be the same without her." Sam fiddled with the electrical box one more time, and the hall lit up.

"Yay!" Roxy said. "Well done."

Sam put on a silly voice and took a bow. "Thank you. I could not have done it without my assistant, the curious, resourceful, and beautiful Roxanne." He resumed his regular voice. "It is Roxanne, right?"

Roxy wrinkled her nose. "Only to my mom."

"Sorry, Roxy it is then."

They shared a smile.

There was a rustle behind them. Evangeline came rushing in. She squeezed Sam in a hug and kissed him on the cheek. "You're a genius, cher. Don't mind old Evangeline being grouchy. I'm feeling as lost as a polar bear in the Sahara, but that's no excuse. I'm sorry. To you too, Roxy."

"You're not lost," Sam said, smiling at her and squeezing her shoulder. "You're here with us, and you're in exactly the right place."

Roxy watched Sam looking down from his tall height at the diminutive figure of Evangeline and dreaded the idea that he could be faking for his own nefarious reasons. It felt unsettling, viewing someone she liked with suspicion. But years of feeling unsafe had prepared her—she was *well-versed* in not trusting people!

CHAPTER TWENTY-FOUR

I T FELT STRANGE to step out onto the bustling streets that afternoon. People were going about their business as though nothing untoward had happened. Roxy felt she was living in a parallel universe, one that was dark and confusing.

Thankfully, the weather had cleared up. The streets still glistened with the rain of the morning. The sidewalks were covered in watery patches where the blue sky was reflected. But the dark clouds had been chased away by the wind, leaving a cold, clear sky.

In the end, everyone decided to come along to the Endymion parade. Evangeline had taken some persuading; she'd seen a thousand carnivals she said, but Elijah hadn't taken no for an answer. Quite uncharacteristically, she had let herself be swayed. Roxy sidled up to Evangeline as they walked. She was desperate to talk about what Sam had disclosed to her about Evangeline's relationship with Detective Johnson.

"Can I ask you something?" Roxy said, trying to work out how she could phrase it diplomatically.

"Sure."

"Are you worried about Johnson holding a grudge, and trying to pin the murder on you? You know, after what happened." Diplomacy wasn't a skill Roxy possessed it would appear.

But Evangeline wasn't offended. She shook her head. "No. He can try if he likes, the truth will out. I'm innocent, cher. I don't have a motive, and that's that...No court would find me guilty." Evangeline peered at her. "How do you know what happened? You're quite the little detective, aren't 'cha?"

"Sam told me," Roxy said. "I think you're brave. I could never do the things he says that you've done."

Evangeline smiled at her. "Of course you could, cher. You may not see it in yourself yet, but there's a whole lot of moxie in there." She tapped the top of Roxy's chest and then laughed. "Moxie Roxy."

Roxy laughed, too.

"He won't try to pin it on me," Evangeline said. "What happened was a long time ago. It's in the past. And Johnson's not corrupt, not like his partner. He might *want* me to be the murderer, but at the end of the day, he's a good cop. We've come to...an understandin'. He leaves me alone to run my guesthouse. I leave him alone to do his job. That's all there is to it."

Roxy smiled. "Well, that sounds positive."

"I'm sure it'll be fine, cher. No need to worry yourself about me."

They settled into a comfortable silence.

Slightly ahead of them, Nat clutched a large bottle of iced tea that she swigged from every so often. She looked determined to enjoy herself. Next to her, Sage, in sky-blue robes, sashayed along. Every time a child passed, she gave them a big, kind smile. The children would smile back as they gravitated toward her and away from Louise who was a few steps behind. Louise walked with her head down, her hands thrust into the pockets of her pants, her lips in a flat line. She looked very unhappy. Bringing up the rear, Sam was light on his feet. He listened intently to Elijah. His friend was engrossed in telling a story, jabbing his finger to make his points.

Elijah clutched a huge basket of beignets and had brought another with him that Sam was carrying. "There'll be loads of families out enjoying themselves on St. Charles Avenue," he had explained. "We can sweeten up the occasion!"

Roxy noticed the vibrant shades of purple, green, and gold everywhere—on clothes and flags and decorations and strings of beads hanging around people's necks. One little girl was dressed head to toe in gold. Her dress was gold, her puffy coat was gold, her shoes were gold, her hair bows were gold, and even the beads on her frilly white socks were gold! She wore strings of plastic golden beads around her neck, too. Roxy saw her give Sam a gap-toothed smile as she passed, and he handed her a beignet with a wink.

As they walked along, the dazzling colors of the carnival passing by, Roxy's thoughts took a familiar turn—first they went to her uncertain future, and then they stuck like glue to the unsolved murder. Though she tried to focus on all the fun, sights, and sounds of the carnival, she couldn't help watching each of her party in turn. Were any of them the murderer? And if they were, what might their motivation be?

First, she looked at Evangeline. *Evangeline was desperate for a sale and killed Richard Lomas in a rage over the terms of a deal.* Roxy wondered if it could possibly be true. It probably wasn't, in all likelihood. She couldn't see how Evangeline would benefit from Lomas' death.

They turned onto St. Charles Avenue and into a huge crowd. Kids were raised high, sitting on their fathers' shoulders, waving to people on the parade floats, and squealing with excitement. Music pounded, colors flashed, everyone shouted with excitement. The smells of Creole spices and hot dogs and deep-fried donuts carried on the cold air.

"Woohoo!" Nat said. She took a huge swig from her iced tea bottle.

Nat. *Nat killed Richard Lomas because...she knew if Evangeline's closed down, she'd have nowhere to work or live and could be thrown out of the country.* It was a plausible motive. The only thing was that to have killed him, Nat would need to be extremely dark and devious. Roxy hadn't seen any sign of that in her. Hmm. Roxy sure hoped this theory wasn't true, but she knew she had to keep an open mind.

Next, she turned to Louise. Louise was very subdued and serious as she hung back. She was watching the parade without a smile, her expression flat. Roxy could deduce nothing from it.

*Louise killed Richard Lomas to...*Roxy let her imagination click into gear...*to get her paws on the guesthouse...?* It seemed quite a flimsy reason. Would a middle-aged divorcee have such fire in her belly over a "new life" project that she'd be willing to *murder?* Unlikely, but maybe. People had killed for less.

Roxy looked back at the parade. Folk on the carnival floats were dressed up as all kinds of crazy characters.

They tossed sweets and beads and tiny toys into the audience. Little kids scrambled and clutched at them. Many had bags to stuff their trinkets into. One small boy was so adorned with beads that Roxy was surprised he didn't keel over. She watched him as he stuffed his bag full of goodies, grabbing as many as his tiny hands could hold. Older kids hollered, "Throw me something, Mister!" Many adults joined in too, even those as old as Evangeline!

Elijah had given away nearly all his beignets, passing them to any kid nearby who hollered. His grin stretched all over his face. He seemed to be in his element when he was feeding people. Roxy studied him.

Elijah killed Richard Lomas because...he wanted to protect his own business? Perhaps...perhaps Elijah's bakery wasn't doing so well and it was Evangeline's daily pastry order that was keeping him afloat. If *Evangeline's* closed down perhaps Elijah's business would, too. By murdering the property developer, Elijah could scupper Evangeline's deal and his bakery business might survive.

Roxy immediately knew this theory was flawed. Elijah made deliveries all over town to various restaurants, hotels, private homes. His business wasn't struggling and in truth, she couldn't see Elijah as a likely suspect. His loud, bright breeziness seemed genuine. But then she thought back to that hateful look Louise had given him earlier. Maybe Louise knew something that Roxy didn't. Her mind began to spin.

"Hey Roxy," Sage said, bobbing up beside her with a grin. "Open your hand."

Roxy put out her palm with a smile, wondering what she was letting herself in for. Sage opened her fist over

Roxy's palm, and Roxy looked down to see a pile of glitter in her hand. It was a gorgeous mix of gold and deep purple.

"Fairy dust," Sage explained, opening her eyes wide and looking very serious. "It's collected from special fairy folk in Ireland and contains magical powers."

Roxy looked up into Sage's earnest eyes. "Oh, well, um, thank you."

Sage burst out laughing. "Oh, sugar, I'm having you on! It's just some glittery carnival fun. Though I guess there's no harm in making a wish with it if you want." She winked. "Never any harm in making wishes."

Roxy grinned. "Why not?" Roxy didn't know what to wish for. She'd never been one for wishing and dreaming. Worrying and procrastinating was more her style. Roxy closed her hand around the glitter and looked at Sage's amused but kind face.

Sage. *Sage killed Richard Lomas because...*

CHAPTER TWENTY-FIVE

R OXY TRIED TO work out what Sage would
have to lose if *Evangeline's* was sold off. Not
much, it seemed. She did some website work
for the elderly guesthouse owner, but that hardly sounded
lucrative compared with the corporate clients who were
constantly hiring her. In fact, Roxy had a hunch that the
work Sage did for the guesthouse was free of charge.
Maybe she had another reason, but Roxy doubted it.
Besides, Sage was a vegetarian. She didn't even believe in
killing *animals*. Roxy was hard-pressed to believe Sage
would ever kill a human being. This whole spiritual thing
couldn't be an act...could it? She looked over to the last of
their group.

Sam. *Sam killed Richard Lomas so that he could scoop
up the guesthouse from Evangeline and turn it into a
thriving business that laundered, not washing, but money,
maybe both!*

Of all the motives she'd come up with, Roxy had to
admit that this one seemed the most likely, except for the
fact that Sam seemed as straight as an arrow. She forced

herself to consider him though. She wondered how long Sam had been around. Was he really as much a part of the furniture as he looked? Or was he a relative stranger who had ingratiated himself for nefarious reasons?

Roxy watched the parade go by, feeling a little spaced-out and confused. Despite thinking in-depth about everyone, the situation didn't feel any clearer.

Her head pounded with all the twists and turns. Her brain couldn't hold all her thoughts, much like her clenched hand couldn't hold all the glitter. She could see the beautiful mix of purple and gold spilling through her fingers. What would she wish for?

She knew, of course, that glitter wouldn't *really* make anything happen. But it posed an interesting question... What *could* she wish for? What *did* she really want? If only she knew!

With a little jump, she shot her arm into the air and let go of the glitter. *I wish I knew what I wanted for my life! I wish I knew where I was going next!*

It seemed something of a non-wish, but it was the best she could come up with. At the very least, it was sincere. Drifting away above the heads of the crowd, the glitter caught the breeze and the gold and purple flecks dipped and swirled before fading to nothingness. Roxy watched it as it floated away.

As the group of friends ambled back to *Evangeline's* a couple of hours later, Roxy wondered about the idea of staying in New Orleans long term. She loved the music that seemed to seep from every corner of the city. She loved the bright shotgun houses that were painted just about every color under the sun—one hot pink, the next canary yellow, the next a deep forest green. She loved the food and wondered hopefully if it might bulk out her slight, childlike figure a little.

She loved...Well, it was hard to explain...But, she guessed, if she were being like Sage, she would have called it "the vibe." The place had a warm, wraparound feeling to it, like stepping into your favorite grandmother's kitchen, or at least what she imagined it would feel like if she had a favorite grandmother. Perhaps she did know what she wanted to do next after all...

As soon as they got back to the guesthouse, Evangeline was all smiles. Roxy realized it was the first time she'd seen her smile like that. She seemed lighter, happier.

"Everyone!" she said, clapping her hands at them in the hallway. "As y'all are here, I want to make an announcement. I've come to a big decision. First of all, I want to thank you for your offer to buy this old crumblin' place, Sam. I've known you since you were a child, cher, and your generosity has always shined. This ole lady is duly grateful."

On hearing this, Roxy immediately dismissed her earlier theory that Sam was a recent arrival and a fraud. If he was a cheat, he was deceiving people he had known for years. It seemed improbable.

Evangeline held her hand out for Louise to take. "But Louise and I have been talkin', and I've decided she is gonna be the new owner here."

Louise smiled a brave kind of smile and nodded like she was still trying to convince herself. "I know it's a bold move, but you only get one chance at life," she told the group. "I came here to start over, and that's what I'm going to do. I'm not going to be put off by what happened to Richard Lomas. It's a terrible tragedy, but I won't fall apart. You can rely on me, and I'll work like crazy to get *Evangeline's* back on its feet."

Evangeline nodded. "That's what I like to hear, cher."

"What will you do, Evangeline?" Sam asked. He looked tired but resigned.

"You'll have to find out, cher," Evangeline said with a wink and a sly smile.

Sam laughed. "Who knows what the next crazy chapter will be in Evangeline's book of life, huh?"

"You got that right, my boy."

"Congratulations, Louise! It is wonderful news. Don't forget, my bakery is at your service, night and day," Elijah said, taking Louise's hand. With a deep bow he planted a kiss on the back of it.

"Yes, congratulations," Sage said. "Let me know if you need the website updated."

Nat stared at Louise, mulishly. She looked threatening, but Roxy knew Nat well enough by now to know she was feeling very nervous. "Um, congratulations Louise," Nat mumbled. There was a pause. "Don't suppose you'll be keeping me on, will you?" she finally piped up, her voice tight and high.

"Of course, I will!" Louise said. "You might have to change up your clothing to match the new décor, but that's all."

"Right," said Nat, crossing her arms, but keeping her cool. "Thank you," she said, nodding.

"*Hello!*" A woman's voice carried through the lobby, her voice dripping with insincere gaiety. "How nice to find you all here. Have I interrupted something?"

They turned to the doorway.

"Mara Lomas!" Nat exclaimed. Mara smiled from ear

to ear. "What are you doing here? We thought you were in police custody!"

Mara looked distinctly disheveled compared with the last time they had seen her. Her stilettos had been replaced by old running shoes. Her hair was straggly and pulled back in a messy bun. Her face was still a picture of fury, though. "The police have finally seen sense and accepted that I didn't murder my husband. Now I want to find out who did. I know that Richard was trying to cut a deal here before he was shot so it was probably one of you guys."

Roxy's eyes flickered down to Mara's hand—she was wearing her wedding ring. Roxy was sure she hadn't been wearing it the last time she saw her.

"What do you care?" Nat said. "You hated the guy. He was cheating on you. You didn't exactly sound like his greatest fan when you came over here before."

Mara strode up to Nat and grabbed her by the face, her hand under Nat's chin, her fingers pushing into her cheeks. "Don't you *dare* talk about me and my dead husband like that!"

"Get off me!" Nat said, gripping Mara's wrist and tearing the woman's hand from her face.

"You keep quiet if you can't tell me something helpful, do you hear?" Mara shouted. A tear fell down her cheek, and she wiped it away, furious. "Tell me, who killed my husband? Who?"

No one said anything.

"Tell me!" Mara screamed, her eyes popping.

"I'm sorry, cher," Evangeline said. "We don't have no idea what happened to..."

"It was one of you," said Mara, narrowing her eyes. She picked up a letter knife from the hallway table and pointed it at each of the folks assembled in front of her. "I'm sure of it. Now you're all covering for each other. I know it. I do. I'm 100% certain."

Roxy's heart was beating faster than usual. It always did when someone yelled or got mad (or was waving a knife at her).

"No one knows who killed Richard," Sam said softly. "We want to know, too, but none of us are investigators."

"Maybe not. I bet one of you is a murderer though," said Mara, bitterness lacing her voice.

"Detective Johnson is still investigating," Elijah said. "I'm sure he'll find out who is responsible in the end."

"Him!" Mara said. She snorted. "He likes to play the big shot. He has traumatized me all over again. *Helping them with their inquiries.* That's no way to treat a grieving widow, is it?"

"No, it isn't," Sam agreed. His deep voice could be wonderfully soothing. "He's not the gentlest guy in town, but he's a good detective. He simply wants to find out what happened to your husband, that's all."

It seemed that Sam's compassion took all the wind out of Mara's sails. "Well," she said, dropping the letter knife. "I'll be back, but don't think any of you are off the hook. I *will* find out who did this. And they *will* be sorry."

She left, a little wobbly on her feet as she strode away, but thanks to her running shoes, she negotiated the cobblestones a little easier than she had last time.

As she watched Mara leave, Roxy was almost sure that what she'd just witnessed couldn't have been a performance. Mara had *not* killed Richard Lomas. Roxy was certain. She would have put money on it. So, if it wasn't her, *who was it?*

CHAPTER TWENTY-SIX

T HAT NIGHT, ROXY couldn't sleep. Now, the idea was really dawning on her that she may well be sleeping under the same roof as a murderer. Or at the very least, associating with one. She hated the thought and her brain buzzed with theories until she got a headache.

She opened her eyes and stared at the ceiling, trying to shut her mind down so she could drift off to sleep. It wasn't working. Nefertiti was curled up next to her. She was purring so loudly she sounded like some sort of engine. Roxy absentmindedly pushed her fingertips through Nefertiti's fur as her mind did all sorts of gymnastics she couldn't control.

It was then that she heard a bloodcurdling scream. It came from the room below her. Roxy sat bolt upright, her heart racing. "Oh, my gosh!"

Roxy scrambled out of bed and rushed from the room. Then she realized she could be in danger and didn't have a weapon. She looked around. What could she use? Her eyes fell upon a large candlestick, and she rushed to snatch it up. She doubted she'd have the strength to swing it around or cause some real damage if it came to it, but it was better than nothing.

She rushed down the stairs in bare feet and came across Louise, who was outside her room, clutching her chest, hyperventilating.

"Oh, my goodness, what happened?!" Roxy asked. "Are you okay?"

Louise gulped and tried to catch a breath. "I don't...I don't know! Someone was in my bedroom!" Her voice was slurred, and Roxy caught the scent of whiskey heavy on her breath.

"What? Who?"

"I don't know!" Louise squeaked. "It was dark. I couldn't see. I think he thought I was asleep, but then I gave him such a fright when I got up that he jumped out of the window. I tried to look down the street but I couldn't make him out—he was wearing all black and a ski mask." She leaned against the doorframe, still breathing heavily.

Roxy puffed out a breath. "This is getting serious now, Louise."

"Right?" Louise let out another big breath. "Oh, Roxy," she said. "I have to tell you."

"What? What do you have to tell me?"

Louise looked around, as though someone might be lurking in the stairway. "Come into my room. I want to show you something," she hissed.

Louise snapped on the light, and Roxy saw that her eyes were bloodshot. The path she made toward the bed was winding and wobbly.

"I've done something *terrible*," Louise said, "and I don't know how to get myself out of it." She sat at the head of her bed, rummaging in her nightstand drawer. "I don't know if it's connected to what happened tonight. Maybe."

"What? What have you done, Louise?"

Louise patted the bed, and Roxy sat down. The older woman took yet another deep breath, then reached further into the nightstand drawer. She pulled out a phone. She put it on the bed and removed her hands quickly as though she might catch a horrible disease from it.

"Your phone," Roxy said, waiting for an explanation.

"No," said Louise, her voice cracking. "Not *my* phone." She whispered, "Richard Lomas' phone!"

Roxy gasped. "How did you get that?!" Her voice was loud with surprise.

"Shhhh!" Louise said furiously. "Oh, gosh." She shook her head, and then covered her eyes with her hand. "I made a *huge* mistake."

Roxy's heart started thumping so violently she could feel it in her temples.

"When I found him...I...I don't really know what happened. I saw his phone on the ground, near his hand. His cold, dead, outstretched hand." Louise was nearly in tears. "He had a bunch of flowers with him, too. I don't know why. I just took them both. I threw away the flowers, but I slipped the phone into my pocket. I don't know what I was thinking. I was just...in shock, I guess."

"Oh."

"And then I didn't tell Detective Johnson because I didn't know how, and every hour since then I've resolved to, but still I haven't. It's just got harder and harder, and now we're here...I can't possibly tell him after all this time.

I look so guilty. Oh help, what have I done?!" Louise leaned over and took both of Roxy's hands in hers, her eyes wide, imploring Roxy to understand.

Roxy shook her head. The situation was a real mess.

"I considered not telling him at all," said Louise. "But the thing is...there's *evidence* on this phone."

"Really?" Roxy said sitting up straight. "What kind of evidence?"

"Take the phone yourself and read the text messages," said Louise. "We're going to *have* to turn it in. It might make all the difference in the investigation."

Roxy was hesitant to pick up the phone. She'd already noticed that Louise was using the word "we," essentially drawing Roxy into her predicament, but she was too curious about what was on the phone to let that stop her. She wasn't about to allow the chance of finding evidence pass her by because she felt a little uncertain.

Roxy picked up the phone.

"One particular thread of messages is of note," Louise said. She looked away and up at the ceiling of her room.

Roxy tapped the phone and there, the first contact was *Elijah Walder*. She let out a little gasp. "Elijah? As in Elijah, Elijah?"

"You got it," Louise said.

Roxy clicked into the conversation and immediately scrolled up to the top, to see it all in chronological order. It was full of messages that showed Richard Lomas and Elijah had been in constant contact for a period of time.

I've sent you the proposal by email, a message from Lomas to Elijah read.

When are you next in the area? Elijah had responded.

"What does it mean, do you think?" Roxy wondered out loud to Louise. "The proposal? Obviously, they were doing some kind of business together, but what? Do you think Elijah was involved in trying to get Evangeline to sell the guesthouse?" Her mind turned over, thinking back over all the times she'd been around the baker. She didn't remember ever seeing him try to influence Evangeline's decision or even discuss the deal with her.

"No," Louise said. "Keep scrolling."

"He was thinking of selling the bakery?" said Roxy as she read.

"Yes. But then things got a little hairy."

Roxy read on.

That price is an insult, Elijah had written. *This is my family business. It was passed down from my grandfather. I would expect much better compensation.*

Lomas had written back, *I'm not interested in your business. Not even in the building. Only the land upon which the business and building are situated.*

NO DEAL, Elijah had texted back furiously.

The last message in the thread was one from Richard: *We'll see about that. I have my ways and means. You having a little tantrum won't stop me.*

CHAPTER TWENTY-SEVEN

ROXY READ THE text messages over and over before she handed the phone back to Louise. "So...do you think it was Elijah who snuck into your room just now? Do you think he was going to hurt you?"

"Yes...no..." Louise said, looking a little lost. She put her hands up to her face. "Oh, I just don't know."

A tense, pregnant silence stretched out between them as they both considered what might have happened.

"Well, you'll have to hand this cell phone into Detective Johnson," Roxy said. "But...let's wait a bit, a few more hours won't make any difference now. You just focus on how you're going to transform this place. You've had enough trauma and drama as it is. I'm going to do some investigating of my own. We'll hand the cell phone in after that."

Back in her room, there was no chance now that Roxy would get any sleep. She lay on the bed for a while, tossing and turning, but eventually gave up. She rose and opened her linen curtains. The sky was just beginning to edge out of darkness.

She wished she had someone to talk to, someone to bounce her ideas off. She didn't want to trouble Louise any more—she'd been through enough already. Besides, even with this information on Elijah, she couldn't entirely rule Louise out as a suspect. Neither could she rule out Nat or Evangeline. Sam would have made a good confidante, she was sure, but she was still a little suspicious of him too. Plus, she had to admit to herself, she had a crush on him that didn't help her keep a clear head.

What about Sage?

Sage was usually up at dawn to perform her rituals, "Before the rest of the world gets up and clogs the energy space with their vibes," she had told Roxy. She was busy with programming and tarot readings during the day, but in the serenity of the early morning, she was alone and available.

Before Roxy's mind was made up, her body got into gear. She rushed over to her wardrobe and picked out some jeans, a shirt, and a cardigan. "Bye, Nef," she said as she slipped her sneakers on. "See you later, lovely girl."

She crept down the stairs, wincing at every creak, and let herself out of the front door into the cold morning air. She looked over at Elijah's bakery and gave a little involuntary shiver. She went out onto the cobblestones and looked back at *Evangeline's*. Below her own rickety balcony was Louise's room. Roxy looked at the open window and saw the thick old-fashioned drainpipe next to it. That, and the ledges that were built between the floors as part of the architectural style meant that it would be easy for someone to climb up or down.

Roxy pulled her cardigan around her to keep herself

protected from the cold air then headed out of the cobbled alleyway and onto the street.

A black car pulled up to the curb next to her. Johnson stepped out of it, his face creased with barely concealed rage as usual. Roxy gulped. She had every intention of telling Johnson about the phone, but not now. Now, she wanted to avoid him.

"You," he said.

Roxy tried to find a smile. "Good morning, Detective Johnson."

He curled his lip. "A little birdy tells me you're sneaking around, doing *detective work.*"

Roxy's heart stopped.

He edged up horribly close to her. "Listen up, lady. I'm the detective, you're just a guest in our city. Stay in your lane, okay?" He stepped back a pace. "And I sincerely hope you're not out here at this early hour doing any *investigating.*"

"Oh, no," Roxy lied. "I'm going to see Sage, for...some spiritual help. I'm not feeling so good."

"You'll be feeling a whole lot worse if you keep meddling," he said. He waved his hand, dismissively. "Keep moving. Go on, go."

Roxy scurried across the road, then headed up a stairway around the side of a store and up to Sage's apartment that was located on top. She looked down at the street to see Johnson staring up at her. An ice-cold shiver ran through her, and she quickly turned away. She had wanted to see if he was going into the guesthouse, but she couldn't bear to watch. Anyway, she suspected he would remain there staring at her until she was out of his sight.

Roxy took a deep breath and knocked on Sage's door.

As she waited for Sage to answer, Roxy wondered if she was doing the right thing.

"A visitor through the midst of esoteric time," Roxy heard Sage say through the door.

It opened, and Sage stood before her, looking quite different from normal. Her long mermaid hair was gone, a short afro in its place. She had on soft white robes but was without her characteristic jewelry. Her brown eyes seemed to penetrate deep into Roxy's soul, however. She didn't break into her usual warm smile. She didn't even speak further. She just nodded and stepped to the side to let Roxy through.

"Oh, um, thanks," Roxy said in a quiet voice, then berated herself for speaking at all. There was an atmosphere between them, a different ambiance from usual, but Roxy couldn't quite put her finger on what it was or why it was there.

Sage led her through the plain, ordinary hallway, with its white walls and wooden floor, and into a back room. Roxy gasped. It was like stepping into another world.

CHAPTER TWENTY-EIGHT

THE ROOM WAS draped with silk hangings, in rich shades of orange and crimson and deep pink, which should have clashed, but somehow looked wonderful together. The smell of incense hung thick and sweet in the air, as white smoke unfurled in a graceful dance above four incense burners placed in each corner. Three white candles were burning in large glass jars, their flames flickering. They sat atop a white-clothed table in the center of the room. A clear bowl full of water sat in front of them. Cushions were laid out on the dark wooden floor, orange and deep red and pink like the drapes, and a deck of tarot cards were spread in an elaborate formation in front of them. The whole effect was mesmerizing.

"Wow," Roxy said under her breath.

Sage sat on a crimson cushion and gestured for Roxy to do the same. When she turned to look at her, her eyes were bright. "It is no coincidence you have come here now, at this time. This is no ordinary visit. I can feel the difference. Spirit has carried you here."

Roxy didn't quite know what to say so she looked down at her lap, mumbling hesitantly, her gaze flickering up to Sage's face and down to her lap again. "Well...I came here to run something by you. Something about the murder. Some information I've found out."

Sage simply nodded.

Roxy decided to face Sage squarely and proceeded to tell her everything that Louise had told her. She also told Sage about the text messages between Lomas and Elijah. Sage listened intently. Once Roxy was done, Sage stared at the candles. She closed her eyes, and took a deep breath, exhaling with a long outward breath. She stayed still for such a long time that Roxy wondered if she had fallen asleep.

Roxy cast her eyes over the tarot cards on the floor. She still didn't know if she believed in them or not, but surely trying them out couldn't hurt.

Sage opened her eyes. "Let us consult the cards," she said.

Roxy flinched, wondering if it was a coincidence, or if Sage was reading her mind. "That's just what I was thinking!"

Sage raised an eyebrow. She scooped up all the tarot cards and began to shuffle them. First, she did so in her hand then she placed the deck on the floor face down. She pushed the deck over and spread the cards out before moving them around the floor until they were well mixed.

"Right," Sage said, rocking back on her heels. "Ask your question."

Roxy tried to get into a positive mindset and not let doubt take over. "Okay...How is Elijah involved in the murder of Richard Lomas?"

"Point to three cards."

Roxy did as she was told and Sage laid the three cards in a row face down. "Ready?" she said.

Roxy gulped, not sure that she was. The seriousness of the situation was beginning to kick in. She was in a strange city, had placed herself in the middle of a murder investigation, and here she was using tarot cards to check her suspicions. The whole thing was just so, so far out of her normal experience, and yet, here she was. It was happening. It was real. "Yes," she said.

"This card represents the past," Sage said. She turned the first card over. "The Seven of Swords." There was a picture of a man carrying swords in his arms, sneaking away, as if he were stealing them. "Deception," said Sage. "Someone is trying to get away with something, undetected." She rolled her eyes and laughed. "Really, universe? You don't say!" She immediately got serious again. "Someone has false motives and has been pursuing an agenda of their own. Someone has been keeping secrets and deceiving others."

Roxy's heart beat a little faster. Maybe these cards really *did* work! Were they talking about Elijah? It seemed the tarot cards were just as ready to condemn him as his text messages.

"Right, the next card represents the present," Sage said. She flipped it over and raised her eyebrows. "Ace of Swords," she said, as if in a trance, "Communication needs to be clarified. Persevere in your quest for an answer even if it is not the one you wish for."

Roxy's eyes popped. She *didn't* like the idea of Elijah being the killer. After all, he was part of the little group she had become quite attached to. He made the loveliest beignets. He seemed kind and, though a little outlandish, good-hearted. Sam and Elijah were great friends and excellent music partners, but what was really known about him?

"Now for the final card," Sage said. "This determines the future." She flipped it over. "Death."

Roxy gasped. "Another murder?"

"No," said Sage. "It means total transformation. The complete and dramatic end of something. Starting over."

Roxy let out a deep breath and looked at Sage. "So... do you think this means Elijah is the killer?"

Sage pursed her lips together. "It's impossible to tell, honey. Some people say you can get yes and no answers from the cards, but that's overly simplistic. They're much more complex and layered than that. You have to mix the meanings in with your intuition. What's your gut telling you?"

Roxy paused. "I don't know," she said. She had all sorts of feelings and impressions swirling around, but any time she tried to fix her mind on Elijah being the murderer, another possibility popped up. Nat. Mara. Evangeline. It was impossible to know. "I just don't know." She peered at Sage, who was now staring intently at the incense as it swirled and danced up to the ceiling. She wondered just how much Sage knew—how much secret knowledge her spiritual powers truly afforded her. "Do *you* know?"

"I wish I did," said Sage. "Life is full of mysteries. I spend my time on this earth trying to decode them, but some are complex. They only reveal themselves when they desire it."

"Well, I hope they desire it real soon," Roxy said, thinking about the intruder Louise found in her room, "before someone else gets hurt."

Sage nodded. "I'll put a protection spell over the guesthouse to keep y'all safe. While that can help, it depends on the forces at play, and right now there are some real strong ones out there. I can feel them, dark ones, greedy ones, ready to harm for their own benefit."

Roxy felt a little panicked. "So what can we do?"

"Work fast," said Sage. "My role is to liaise with the spiritual forces present. I'll work with them as much as I can to bring justice, but we need feet on the ground. Practical work. Get out there and find the truth."

Roxy breathed. "I'll certainly try."

Sage smiled for the first time that morning. She reached out and squeezed Roxy's hand. "The spirits are on your side, sweetheart."

CHAPTER TWENTY-NINE

A S ROXY LEFT Sage's magical, mystical apartment, her mind went back to that first wonderfully cozy evening when they all holed up in *Evangeline's* dining room, eating spicy Creole food and listening to Elijah and Sam as they filled the place with the sounds of jazz.

Sam and Elijah seemed so close. They were truly in sync that night. Sure, they had performed some set pieces, but they had jammed together afterward, and it had flowed as easily as the wine.

If Elijah were the killer, as Roxy was grudgingly beginning to admit may be the case, surely Sam would be devastated. They were like brothers.

She meandered back toward the cobbled street that housed *Evangeline's* and paused for a moment. She looked at the bakery to her left and *Evangeline's* to the right. The short distance between them had once seemed so quaint and intimate. Now the distance felt sinister, a huge black shadowy presence between them, one that possibly divided a murderer from his prey. Roxy shivered involuntarily, not from the cold, but from the mental image of Elijah sneaking out in the dead of night and climbing the pipes to Louise's room.

At that moment, Nat came out of the front door with a rug and began to shake it out. She looked up and jumped when she saw Roxy. "Blooming heck, Rox," she said. "You gave me one heck of a fright. What are you doing out and about so early?" Her face creased into a frown.

"Oh...," Roxy stared at Nat and wished she could explain. Everything was jumbled and muddled in her head, and it was starting to give her a headache. "I went to see Sage."

"Oh right." Nat went back to shaking out the rug, banging it against the railings and sending clouds of dust flying everywhere. She gave a happy smile. "So, Louise is taking over the guesthouse, and I get to stay on. Isn't that great?"

"Yep," Roxy said.

"Will you stay?"

"I...I don't know yet." Roxy was wary as she spoke to Nat. She didn't feel free to relax and chat normally. Anyone could be the killer. A thought popped into her head. "Do you know where I'd be able to find Sam?"

"He'll be at his laundry," Nat said. A teasing smile played at the corner of her lips. "Why?"

Roxy tried very hard not to blush. "I wanted to ask him..." There was a mischievous glint in Nat's eyes, so Roxy quickly made something up. "I wanted to ask him if he'd seen my...my...I think I left some money in one of my dress pockets. I want to see if I can rescue it before it gets put through the wash."

"Okay, if you say so," Nat said with a grin. "Well,

the laundry isn't too far away. A couple of blocks. Go out of the front entrance, turn left, and walk on until you get to 24th Street. Take another left, and it's down there a couple of minutes. *Sam's Laundry*. You can't miss it."

Roxy took off immediately, keen to get away from Nat but also because she didn't want to think too much about her decision to speak to Sam about what she knew.

The directions were easy to follow, and before long she was standing on the steps of the laundry. She could see clothing and linens turning over and over in the machines inside.

She entered and a little bell tinkled. The temperature was several degrees higher inside the laundry, a pleasing contrast to the cool outside.

"Hello," she said. Sam was behind the front desk attending to some paperwork. He didn't move. Individually, each of the machines made only gentle whirring noises, but together they created a distinct thrum, and she realized she'd have to raise her voice to make herself heard. "Hello!" Sam looked up this time, and a huge smile spread across his face. Roxy felt heat rising to her cheeks, and she had to look at the floor for a moment.

"Hi, Roxy. What a great surprise!" he said, standing up and showing his Southern manners.

"Hi, Sam." Roxy cleared her throat, reminding herself that she was here on a serious mission. There was no time to be embarrassed or to pay attention to how her legs felt. It was as though they were turning to jelly.

"To what do I owe the pleasure of this visit?" he asked. He brought out a chair from behind the counter and placed it in front of her. "Please, take a seat."

"Thank you." Roxy sat down, and taking his cue from

her, he did, too. She forced herself to look up into his dreamy blue eyes. "This isn't a pleasure visit, I'm afraid."

Sam didn't blink. "That's a shame."

"I'm going to be 100% straight with you," said Roxy.

"Good! It's about time." A smile played at the corner of his lips.

"What?"

"Oh, come on. We both..." he trailed off.

Roxy was utterly bewildered.

A look of panic sprung into Sam's eyes. "Erm...I mean to say, you know...erm...you'll be staying on at the guesthouse, won't you?" He began to talk very fast. "I mean, you keep saying you don't know, you don't know, but I think we both know you will."

"Oh," Roxy said. "Well, yeah, I think I will. For a while anyway." She laughed awkwardly. "You got me there, skipper." What was she saying? *Skipper?*

He looked immensely relieved. "New Orleans is like that. Once it gets its hooks into you, it doesn't want to give you back. I grew up here, of course. I tried going away to college, but I came straight back after I graduated and opened my first business. My father was furious. He wanted me to go into investment banking in New York."

They settled into a comfortable silence. The whir of the machines went on. Roxy liked the sound. The moment felt cozy and intimate, but she knew she had to broach the subject of Elijah sooner or later. She opened her mouth to speak.

"Sam, I..."

"Roxy, I..."

They spoke at the same time. They laughed.

"Go on," he said. His eyes were sparkling. Roxy got the distinct feeling that he thought she was going to ask him on a date. In truth, she didn't want the moment to end. She felt this pleasant, electric tension between them, but she had no plans to invite him out. She just didn't do that kind of thing.

Instead, she took a deep breath. "I have reason to believe that Elijah might have been involved in Richard Lomas' murder."

SAM'S OPEN, EXPECTANT expression changed immediately. It crumpled into a deep, concerned frown.

"What?" he breathed. "No."

"I'm so sorry. I know you won't want to believe that, but...there's a lot of evidence that points in that direction." Roxy explained about the phone, and the break-in, and the conversations that had been going on between Elijah and Richard.

Sam started pushing paperwork around unnecessarily. He shuffled his papers and stacked them. Then he unstacked them again. Roxy doubted he even registered what he was doing.

"Well, I think you're wrong," he said, his voice hard. He frowned and rubbed the back of his neck.

Roxy felt tension—now the utterly wrong kind of tension—course through her body. "I wish I were, Sam, but..."

"But what?" he said. "Honestly, Roxy, I think you should let this go. Detective Johnson is..."

Suddenly Roxy felt quite angry. "Detective Johnson is *what*?" she interrupted, surprising herself with the steel in her voice. "An idiot, if you ask me."

"So you know better than him about investigating, do you?"

"You've sure changed your tune!" Roxy snapped. "You said he might be corrupt."

"Well, maybe," Sam said. "But the alternative isn't for us to go around playing cop."

"Playing cop?!" Roxy said. "Excuse me for caring. I'm trying to ensure Evangeline isn't the subject of a miscarriage of justice!"

Sam leaned back in his chair and tapped his fingers on the desk in irritation. "Okay, let's say Johnson is corrupt and will pin the murder on whoever he wants. You think you can stand up to him and the whole police department?"

"Well, no, but..." Roxy floundered.

"Look, Roxy, you're not from this town," Sam said. His voice was a little kinder now. " You don't know what goes on behind the scenes."

Roxy felt a horrible knot in her stomach. "I'm just trying to..."

"Well, don't," Sam said. "Don't try. I know you mean well, but you're a visitor to this city, a tourist. Let the police sort it out. If Evangeline does get charged with Lomas' murder, I'll get the best lawyers on the case. *That's* what's going to help. Not this. Not you."

Roxy swallowed, tears threatened to well, but she held her head high. "I think you're only saying this because you don't want to face the fact that Elijah might have done it."

Sam shook his head. "Louise needs to hand in that

phone and prepare herself for the consequences. She could go to jail for keeping it. It's theft at best. Obstructing the course of justice at worst."

"But she was in shock!"

"Do you think Johnson will give a rat's behind about shock?"

"No, but..."

"This is not cool," he said. "Not cool at all. Louise has got herself in too deep. And now you're doing the same. This is going to blow up in your faces. Johnson might even put *you* in jail for knowing about the phone and doing nothing about it."

Roxy had been so wrapped up in her investigation, she hadn't even thought of that. His words were like a bucket of ice water dumped over her head. "He wouldn't," she said, but her voice wobbled. She imagined herself in jail with a bunch of tough women. From a steady job with a steady boyfriend, renting a nice apartment with savings in the bank...to that? Maybe this move had been a terrible idea after all. Maybe she was crazy even being in New Orleans, let alone getting herself mixed up in all of this. "Johnson wouldn't be that cruel," she said, although she suspected that he would.

"Look, Roxy, I don't mean to be harsh, but you have to be realistic. Both you and Louise have come into town and gotten yourselves wrapped up in a serious issue, an issue that could have big implications. Life-changing implications. I know New Orleans is a mystical place, but don't get caught up in the hype of Mardi Gras and Sage's spiritualism and think that magic will fix this. It won't. Despite the wonder of this city, it isn't immune from the harsher aspects of life. It won't give you a happy-ever-after ending just because. Reality is dirty and gritty and messy here, just like everywhere else."

Roxy didn't know what to say. She felt heavy all over. Her limbs were like lead. "Right," she said, still trying to inject a little sass into her voice.

Sam sighed. "I'm not trying to be unpleasant, Roxy," he said, his voice softening again. "I just want you to be realistic."

Now, Roxy felt patronized. She shot him a glare. "You just don't want to consider that Elijah might be a murderer," she repeated.

"I don't know about that." Sam shook his head. "I certainly don't think he is, but maybe I'm wrong. I hope not. But the truth will out. The police will find out who did it. It won't be tourists solving this, digging around like they're on a murder mystery weekend."

"Stop calling me a tourist!" Roxy snapped.

"But that's what you *are*," he said softly. "You've only been here a few days. You don't really know New Orleans yet. She's a mysterious, unpredictable old girl."

Roxy, her eyes gleaming furiously, stood. "I'm going back to *Evangeline's*. I'll take my washing, if you don't mind."

"Don't you want me to drive it over? I have laundry for the others, too."

"I'll take it all," Roxy said icily.

"You sure? It's a big pile."

"Fine with me."

"Come on, don't be like that. I'll take you."

"No, thank you."

Sam sighed and went into the back room. He came out with several parcels of washing, all wrapped up with paper and string. "Here you go." He put them on his table.

Roxy stacked them and picked them up carefully. She just about managed to carry them all and started forward, peering over the top. One parcel fell off, but Sam caught it and popped it back on. "Look," he said, when they were so close she could smell the deep, alluring musk of his aftershave. "I didn't mean to make you feel bad. I just..."

Roxy put on a big smile. It was like a weapon. "You didn't make me feel bad. You made me feel more certain," she said, making for the door. "Bye, Sam."

"WE'RE PULLING OUT all the stops tonight!" Evangeline said. "Louise is taking over my business. We're celebrating!" Evangeline's eyes were bright, but her voice was brittle and Roxy suspected that Evangeline, despite her brave face, wasn't as happy as she seemed. Old age was forcing her to hand her guesthouse over, and Roxy knew that Evangeline would be feeling burning shame and grief at her losing her independence, her livelihood, and her beloved building.

"Come and help in the kitchen," Nat had said, catching Roxy as she came back from her angry visit to the laundry. "We're cooking up a storm!"

Roxy was still piled high with parcels and decided to take them to her room. She'd distribute them later. Nefertiti lazily looked up when she came in. Roxy tickled the cat under her chin as she lay curled up in a chair before rushing down the stairs to help. Roxy felt so mixed up and confused that she thought a good cooking session with

Nat and Evangeline, both fierce, no-nonsense women, would make her feel better.

The warm aroma of Creole spices drifted from the kitchen around the ground floor and up the stairs, immediately making Roxy feel at home again. *Forget Sam, and forget the murder investigation for now.*

As soon as Roxy stepped into the kitchen, which was thick with steam and spice, Evangeline called out, "It's beignets or nothing for breakfast, cher. This kitchen's occupied all day."

"I came to help," Roxy said. She'd gotten up so early, it was hard to believe that it wasn't yet ten o'clock.

"Aha!" Evangeline said. "Another pair of hands. Suits me."

Nat grinned and held out the plate of beignets to Roxy. "And you can't eat as you go, so have your fill now."

Roxy took one gratefully. Despite her fast metabolism, she was sure she'd get to be the size of a house if she lived in New Orleans permanently. She took a bite. "So what are we making?"

"A Creole feast!" Nat said excitedly, taking a pan from a cupboard and whirling it around.

"Stop that, or you'll put someone's eye out!" Evangeline snapped at Nat. She was chopping copious amounts of onion and garlic at lightning speed. "Let me tell you what we're making, cher: a little turtle soup to start, then a crawfish pie..."

"My *absolute* favorite," Nat said.

"Next, our main dish." Evangeline swelled with pride. "Barbecued shrimp with Eggs Hussarde, collard greens, smothered okra, potato casserole on the side, and a jalapeño shrimp cornbread."

"In little ramekins," Nat added happily. "They look *so* cute."

"Wow," said Roxy. "That sounds like quite a spread."

"You betcha, cher," Evangeline said. "It's a mashup of my grandmomma's classics. You won't find that combination anywhere else, not in New Orleans, not in the whole world."

"I can believe that," Roxy said. She felt her mood lift.

"And to finish, New Orleans bread pudding with whiskey sauce," said Nat. She was practically bouncing around the kitchen. Roxy guessed her mood was partly to do with the feast, but mostly because she wasn't facing the threat of deportation any longer.

"Now, as a clever girl, you'll already have guessed that we'll be on our feet all darn day," Evangeline said. "And there's plenty to do. Want to chop a mountain of onions?" Roxy wrinkled her nose.

"Well then, you know how to purge crawfish?"

Roxy giggled. "Nope. Absolutely not."

"I could do it at four years old," Evangeline said. "Every good N'awlins girl can. Nat, show her."

Nat took Roxy by the hand and dragged her into a small back room that had an outside door. She pointed at a large bucket of squirming crawfish. "I hope you're not squeamish!" she said.

Roxy hadn't seen crawfish before. She looked at their shiny black shells and long red pincers. They waved at her, and she did, in all honesty, feel a little nervous of them, but she wouldn't let on to Nat. She pasted a big smile on her face. "I'm ready."

"Good. You have to purge to get all the mud out of them," Nat said, getting out a big basin. "Right, tip all the crawfish in there."

Roxy did so.

"Next we pour a bunch of salt over them." Nat grabbed a bag of salt from the side and sprinkled liberally. "Then hot water. Fill up that jug there."

Roxy filled the jug with hot water.

"Go ahead, pour it in the bucket."

Roxy poured, and the water began to turn brown.

"Ew," Nat said. "See all that muck?" She kneeled and began to stir the crawfish around the basin with a metal spoon. The crawfish squirmed and splashed in the water. Nat looked up at Roxy and grinned. "New Orleans doesn't look so glamorous now, huh?"

Roxy laughed.

Nat poked around with the spoon. "We have to fish out any dead ones. Evangeline will go bananas if they end up in the pot. Oh, look, there's one," she said, scooping it out. She flicked it in the trash. "Now we gotta drain them."

Soon they were back in the kitchen over a boiling pot of water. Nat added garlic powder, cayenne pepper, sticks of butter, oranges, lemons, and a whole load of powder called "Crab Boil."

Evangeline stood with her arms folded, casting a watchful eye over their progress. "Let that cook a little."

Roxy stood holding the large strainer of wriggling crawfish, as Evangeline poured some hot sauce into the bubbling mix.

"You're gonna burn our mouths!" Nat protested.

Roxy coughed as the mixture sent its spicy steam into her face.

Evangeline laughed at her. "A little spice is good for the soul, cher. Now tip in them crawfish, and let's get this pot goin'."

CHAPTER THIRTY-TWO

A LL DAY THEY cooked. Roxy grabbed a grilled cheese sandwich for lunch, and the time flew by as she thoroughly enjoyed herself. Before long, the day turned into evening, and most everything was ready.

"Now you two, go put on your glad-rags while I finish up here," said Evangeline.

Roxy headed upstairs and fed Nefertiti. She couldn't wait to have a hot shower, but before she did, she flopped down on the bed and kicked off her shoes. Her feet were aching, her whole body was aching.

"Oh, Nef-nef," she said, sighing happily. "Do you really think New Orleans will become our home?" Nefertiti was far too interested in her bowl of food to reply.

Roxy's earlier rush of anger toward Sam had blown itself out. All that chopping, stirring, boiling, and cleaning had purged her of it. She could even concede that he was probably right. She should just enjoy her time here and leave the investigating to the pros. If Evangeline wound up in court, of *course* Sam would pay for the best lawyers and get her off.

Why had Roxy ever felt any of this was her responsibility? She looked back on it all and felt a little embarrassed. It was as if she had been a child playing detective.

It had felt like an adventure, but Sam was right. Roxy wasn't an investigator. She was a call-center operator. Actually, she wasn't even *that* anymore. As he said, she was a tourist, just a visitor passing through.

Roxy felt her mood about to take a nosedive. Her mind started to fill with the same old anxieties and questions about where she would go, what she would do, and how she would survive.

"Nope," she said out loud. "Not today."

The evening was going to be wonderful. They would feast, Sam and Elijah would play their wonderful jazz music, and the whole world would come to a standstill for a while. They couldn't escape reality completely, but they could lock it out of the guesthouse for a few hours.

Roxy decided to look on the bright side. She took a long hot shower and padded around the room in her slippers, humming happy tunes to keep her spirits up. She managed to remember one from the parade that they'd pumped out of the speakers over and over again, and it made her feel cheerful and relaxed.

She planned her evening. She would put on a little makeup and some jewelry and if she paired that with one of her freshly laundered dresses, she might feel like a million bucks. Roxy walked over to the chair where she had left the bundles she'd brought back from Sam's. She carried them to the bed and immediately noticed she had a problem.

The outsides of the parcels weren't labeled with names, but rather with numbers. So whose was whose?

Roxy couldn't tell. She pondered for a moment. There was nothing for it. She'd have to open each parcel to find out to whom it belonged.

Roxy slipped the string that bound the bundles to the side, and opened them one by one, sifting through the clothes deliberately. It wouldn't do to mix them up. One parcel contained a pair of pants and as Roxy picked it up, she felt something hard and smooth and flat in the pocket. Slipping her fingers inside, she pulled out a laminated card. Her heart started thumping.

No way.

It couldn't be possible.

Roxy stared at the card.

"Oh, my goodness," she said. The world was spinning. "Oh, my gosh."

As Roxy sashayed down the stairs, she felt rather glamorous. She was wearing her red dress and her big, gold, hoop earrings while on her feet were espadrilles, their red straps crisscrossing her ankles and up her slim legs. She didn't normally go in for standout pizazz, she was modest in her choice of clothing, more of a wallflower, but tonight she felt a sense of confidence she'd never felt before. Her uncertainty and confusion were gone; determination burned deep in her soul.

"Oh wow, you look gorgeous!" Nat said as they met in the hallway.

Nat wore her regular clothes, only with a bit more bling; on her feet were shiny bottle-green boots with sparkly laces. "*Love* your boots," Roxy said.

Nat grinned. "Thanks! They're my favorites." She wrinkled her nose and smiled.

Roxy gasped as she walked into the dining room. It had been completely transformed since breakfast. One long, grand dining table covered with huge, heavy, white tablecloths bisected the room. There was so much silver, china, and crystal that Roxy wasn't sure how the table legs didn't buckle. White plates lay on gold placemats, and down the center sat candelabras, white candles flickering. Between the candelabras were silver platters upon which the food they were about to feast on lay under silver covers.

"This looks amazing!" Roxy said.

It smelled heavenly, too, that very specific New Orleans smell of deep, rich spices, meat, seafood, and baked bread, all rolled into one.

Sage had already arrived. Even though she was a vegetarian and the feast most decidedly was not, Sage would not miss it for anything. She wore a long flowing dress in a deep-sea blue. It was covered in lace and had draping sleeves and gorgeous little blue beaded details. Her natural hair shone with bouncy coils, and a wreath of blue flowers was woven into them.

She smiled serenely at Roxy.

"You look..." Roxy was practically speechless. "You look...like a sea goddess!"

Sage laughed in such a deep, throaty way that Roxy felt the whole room warm up. "What a lovely thing to say!"

Soon everyone else arrived—Sam in a regular black tuxedo, Elijah in an *ir*regular tuxedo, one with a loud orange African print. Louise wore a tight, bright yellow dress that accentuated her ample curves, and Evangeline, a pretty floral frock.

Nat looked around at them all and laughed, "Wow, we make quite a picture!"

"I'll say!" added Roxy. She and Sam shared a warm look over the table, letting each other know that they weren't still mad with each other.

"Come on, people, this ain't some fashion show!" Evangeline said. "Let's eat!"

CHAPTER THIRTY-THREE

THE MURDER, THE guesthouse handover, and the drama were all forgotten as they sank into the heartiest cuisine New Orleans had to offer. Plenty of wine washed it all down, and laughter echoed around the dining room.

After a long day, Roxy was hungry and eager to try everything but was a little wary of the soup. It was the first time she'd eaten turtle. Evangeline saw her clutching her spoon and looking down at her bowl nervously.

"There are seven kinds of meat on a turtle, cher," Evangeline said. "Some folk say that it tastes of turkey, fish, veal, or pork, depending on the part you get. Nat and me, we take out the fish parts and leave the rest. That's how I learned it from my grandmomma. Give it a taste and see if it isn't one of the best things you ever did eat."

Roxy forced a smile. It did *smell* delicious, which made tasting it a little easier. "Here's goes," she said. She sipped a little off her spoon. "Ooh, it *does* taste like pork! It's lovely!"

Evangeline nodded proudly, "You bet, cher."

Next, they had crawfish pie, Nat's favorite. The crawfish they'd cleaned earlier had been mixed with vegetables and stuffed into a pot pie. Each of them got a hearty slice.

As if that wasn't enough, the Eggs Hussarde that came afterward was a truly special dish. It comprised a poached egg blanketed with hollandaise sauce and draped over bacon and mushrooms. The bacon and mushrooms had been soaked in their own rich, red wine sauce and all sat on top of an English muffin. To the side, there were large barbecued shrimp, browned with burnt sugar, alongside collard greens, okra cooked with crushed tomatoes, and potato casserole with melted cheese. A small ramekin filled with jalapeño shrimp cornbread completed the dish.

Roxy was so full from the earlier courses it took her a little time to get through this one, but she persevered because it was so delicious. As she ate, she listened to the sounds of friends enjoying themselves—the clink of glasses, the peals of laughter, the sounds of animated chatter.

Dessert followed, and once they were all done with their bread pudding in whiskey sauce, Evangeline clapped loudly. "Everyone, please listen," she said. Her expression and voice were serious, in sharp contrast to just a moment before. The place fell into silence.

"Now is the time," Evangeline said, "to hand over the ownership of my darlin' buildin'." She reached down into a bag that was under the table and pulled out a contract. Tears welled in her eyes. Then she coughed, pulled herself up straight and said, "No time for nonsense. We're here to do business. Louise, please join me."

Adrenaline pumped through Roxy's body. She looked at everyone at the table. They were all fixed on the scene between Evangeline and Louise. "I don't think you want to do that," Roxy said, her voice low.

"I don't?" Evangeline said.

Louise and Roxy's eyes locked for a moment. Louise squinted.

"What are you saying, honey?" she said. Louise's voice was low and syrupy sweet.

"I'm saying that there's more going on here than we truly know." Roxy didn't flinch under Louise's sharp gaze, but she was watchful. Louise, Evangeline's contract in her hand, was like a snake waiting to pounce.

"Hmmm, you're probably right. Evangeline, I think you'd better call the police," Louise said, her eyes still narrow and fixed on Roxy, her chin lifting. "I think we have a murderer in our midst."

"We certainly do," Roxy said. The atmosphere was tense. The two women seemed to be in a standoff, like a bull and a matador.

"What?" Evangeline was wild-eyed. "Who?"

There was silence, but then Louise dramatically swiveled her eyeballs to another part of the room. "Elijah!" she said. She looked down her nose at him in triumph.

"What?!" Elijah said. He exploded out of his chair, his wiry frame shaking with adrenaline and indignation. "What are you talking about?"

"We should leave this to Detective Johnson," Sam said forcefully. "This is *not* our job."

"Huh," Louise scoffed. "You're probably in on it, too!" The giggly, flirty Louise of before had vanished.

Evangeline turned to Elijah, who was still on his feet. He was jiggling up and down with frustration. "Elijah, is this true, cher?"

"Of course it isn't!"

"Then why did you hide the fact that *you* were talking to Richard Lomas about selling your building?" Louise spat. "Did you think your secret would be safe forever?"

Evangeline gasped. Elijah crumpled back down to his seat and threw his head back, dragging his hands down his face. "Listen, I didn't tell you because I didn't want to influence your decision one way or another, Evangeline. And I didn't want to worry you. I was hoping to sell my building and move the bakery elsewhere in the city. But Lomas didn't offer me enough money, and I turned him down."

"But why didn't you tell us?" Evangeline cried. "We're your friends!"

Elijah looked embarrassed, "I thought you'd think badly of me for chasing the money and not protecting the buildings."

CHAPTER THIRTY-FOUR

"A LIKELY STORY," Louise scoffed.

Nat shook her head. "Elijah, how could you hide something like that from us?"

Roxy looked over at Sage whose eyes were closed. She looked peaceful, a small smile turning up the corners of her lips. Roxy wondered if she was meditating and had escaped to another place, maybe to a beautiful meadow where lambs were roaming free and butterflies fluttered over wildflowers.

But Roxy couldn't escape. She had to face reality. Terror of what she was about to do gripped her throat. Her hands trembled in her lap as she surreptitiously dialed 9-1-1 on her cell phone under the table.

"Look, I'm sorry for what I did, but I didn't *kill* anyone!" Elijah exclaimed.

Sam got up and put a strong arm around his shoulders. "Calm down, buddy." Then he faced the others and spoke firmly. "This has to stop, and it has to stop NOW. None of us knows what really happened. We're all jumping to conclusions and getting ourselves riled up. We should all go home and just go to bed. The police will sort it out."

"Ha!" Louise said, getting to her feet. "You think I can sleep at night?" She pointed at Elijah. "That *man* snuck into my room last night. He would have surely killed me if I hadn't been awake!"

"He was in your room?!" Nat said with a gasp.

"No, I wasn't!" Elijah looked as though his eyes would pop out of his head.

"No," Roxy said quietly. "He wasn't."

Louise looked confused. "But Roxy, you were there when..."

"When you *lied* to me," Roxy said.

"Huh?"

"Speak the truth, sweet love," said Sage, still not opening her eyes.

"I intend to." Roxy drew the card she had found in the laundry from the pocket of her red dress and laid it on the table. "This is Louise's work ID card. Except your name isn't Louise, is it? It's Emma Warren."

Louise stood dead still, stunned.

"And you work for..." Roxy pointed to the card. "Tobin & Partners, a huge property development company in Dallas. I looked it up online."

"Lies!" Louise shouted.

Evangeline snatched the card up. "Let me see that."

Nat ran from her side of the table over to Evangeline. "Me too."

Roxy looked right at Louise. "You lied to me, to all of us. You were here all along to buy this guesthouse. You don't want to keep it and do it up nicely to preserve New Orleans heritage at all. You want to tear it down and build shiny new apartments, then sell them off for a huge profit, just like Richard Lomas wanted to."

Roxy felt a wave of anger run through her. "You tricked everyone. You made up all that stuff about your marriage failing, and that you were simply taking a break here. You pretended to be one of us. You lied and lied and lied. Even your name is made up! All for money. And then when Richard Lomas looked like he was going to beat you to a deal with Evangeline, you killed him. You lured him to the cemetery that night after the boat ride and shot him in cold blood.

"How could I have done that? I was drunk. Elijah had to escort me home."

"It was all a pretense. My guess is that Lomas told you he was negotiating with Elijah as well as Evangeline, and you seized your moment. You shot him *and* stole his phone so you could frame Elijah."

Suddenly, Louise recovered from her shock at being accused. She sneered. "All right. You're right about who I am, and that I wanted to get my hands on this guesthouse. But lying isn't a criminal offense. And you can't prove I killed Richard Lomas because I didn't."

Evangeline looked up at Louise, hate burning in her eyes. "Well, you're not gettin' this guesthouse now, let me tell you that. You're a liar and a cheat, and possibly a murderer, too."

Louise's face crumpled. She looked like she was in pain. She wandered away from the table toward the kitchen. "I felt *terrible* about lying to you. Not at first, but as it went on, and I could see you were all becoming *fond* of me." She let out a little sob. "I... I'm not sure I even want the guesthouse anymore."

Evangeline couldn't stop staring down at Louise's ID and shaking her head.

Then, quick as a flash, Louise darted into the kitchen.

"What's she doing?" Nat cried.

Evangeline got to her feet. "You get out of my kitchen!" She marched toward it, but before she could make it through the doorway, Louise was back.

She had gone into the kitchen tremulous and upset but now appeared completely deranged. Her eyes were wild and the whites of her eyes were showing. Her hair was messed up, and she pulled at her sunshine yellow dress with her free hand like she wanted to rip it off. It was as though the exposure of her identity and motives had unhinged her completely.

Everyone gasped.

Louise had a huge carving knife in her hand.

CHAPTER THIRTY-FIVE

E VANGELINE, THE KNIFE a few inches from her chest, took a step back.

"You'll sign that contract, and you'll sign that contract now," Louise spat at her. "And no one here will *ever* say anything or contest this sale unless you want to end up like Richard Lomas. Six feet under."

"So you *did* kill him, then?" Roxy said.

Louise laughed. "Yes, Roxy, sweetie," she said in a cajoling voice. "I did."

"You're crazy, woman," Elijah said. "Give it up. You can't seriously think you're going to get away with this. We'll go to the police en masse and tell them all about you. You'll be slammed in a cell by the end of the night."

"Hah! Not if you know what's good for you. Property development is a murderous, duplicitous industry of scum. It's teeming full of lowlifes, and I know most of them. They wouldn't think twice about picking you off one by one."

Evangeline's hands were trembling, but she kept her

head high. "You will never *ever* get this guesthouse. Over my dead body."

"That can be arranged." Louise lunged over, grabbed Evangeline, and held the carving knife in front of her. "Don't test me, old lady."

Sam, furious, barreled toward her. "STOP!"

"Don't move!" Louise said. "Nobody move!" She pressed the carving knife against Evangeline's straining neck. The elderly woman's veins bulged as did the one down the center of Louise's forehead. The atmosphere in the room was electric as the situation sat literally on a knife's edge. "We're not far from a really serious *accident* happening here."

Sam froze. Everyone did. Everyone except Nefertiti.

Unbeknownst to everyone, the fluffy white cat had silently padded downstairs. She brushed against Louise's leg, startling her. Louise flinched, and Sam, showing lightning reflexes, reached over and wrested the knife from her hand. As he did so, Roxy lunged at Louise as hard as she could. Despite Roxy's slight build, the force of her knocked Louise over. Roxy pinned her to the ground. Louise wasn't through yet, though. She wiggled and squirmed just like the crawfish Roxy and Nat had purged earlier. Roxy couldn't keep her down. Sam bent over to help, but Louise unleashed a mighty kick at his leg, and he doubled over in agony. As Roxy checked to see if Sam was okay, Louise twisted out of Roxy's grip and ran back into the kitchen. The gang of friends scurried after her.

Inside the white subway-tiled kitchen, Louise rushed over to the huge black range. She seized a 12-inch chef's knife from the counter. She waved it in front of her, threatening the group, the point of the gleaming knife glinting in the light. "Don't come near me!" she yelled.

A lock of hair fell into her eyes, and she pushed it back roughly before grabbing a bottle of oil and pouring it into a nearby pan. With the knife shaking in her hand, she shouted, "If you're not going to give me the guesthouse, I'm going to burn it to the ground. Just you watch."

"No, don't!" Roxy screamed. She took a step forward. Louise thrust the knife toward her and grabbed her wrist, pulling her in. Now *Roxy* was being held hostage. Roxy could feel the edge of the knife against her skin.

"If any of y'all come near me, your darling Roxy will get it, do you hear?" Louise spat.

With her free hand, she got ahold of a lighter and lit the gas burner. She placed the pan of oil on top. It shot up in flames. Louise cackled like a witch. She stood in front of the range, between the flames and the assembled group. "Now, we're all just going to have to wait, aren't we? Soon this wooden dump will be burned to the ground and maybe us along with it." She flashed an evil grin at Evangeline. "Insurance can't make up for lost heritage, can it?"

Louise was pressing the edge of the knife into Roxy so intently that she knew she couldn't move an inch. Louise wouldn't hesitate to harm her. Roxy didn't doubt Louise's words on that for a moment.

"Just give it up, Louise," Sam said in an authoritative voice.

She laughed at him, and casually leaned back against the edge of the range, her hand still holding the knife against Roxy's body. The flames were getting higher, the pan was starting to smoke.

Evangeline snorted. "You sick, sick woman."

Louise sneered. "You stupid, stupid woman. People like you deserve to get conned."

"You drop that knife right now, or I'll blast you into infinity." A voice boomed into the kitchen from outside.

"Detective Johnson!" Nat called out.

All the color drained from Louise's face, but she maintained her bravado and tightened her grip on Roxy. "Why should I?"

"It's over, Emma Warren," Johnson said, pushing through the kitchen door with his shoulder, gun cocked.

Louise began to laugh again, "Hahahahaha... aaaaargghhh!" She dropped the knife and pushed Roxy away from her. She half-turned from the range, slapping at her back. Her dress had caught on fire. Flames flickered from the bright yellow fabric at the back of her dress as it melted away, exposing Louise's reddened, hot flesh.

Sam, Elijah, and Nat lurched at her in unison, but Louise refused to submit that easily. Slapping her back with one hand, she tipped the oil onto the gas flame with the other. *Whoooosh!* A gigantic wall of fire shot into the air. The others raised their arms against the blanket of fearsome heat as Louise darted across the kitchen floor toward the back hallway, almighty crashes sounding as she pushed pots and pans to the ground behind her. She was running to the small back room where Nat and Roxy had purged the crawfish earlier.

"There's a back entrance there!" Evangeline hollered, grabbing a fire extinguisher. "Someone go round the outside, quick!"

Evangeline needn't have worried. Johnson's officers were already stationed there. A few moments later, a female police officer recited Louise her Miranda rights, while Louise screamed all kinds of expletives at her.

A silence settled over the six friends as they went to the front of the guesthouse to watch Louise being escorted into a waiting police car.

Elijah was sweating, red-faced, and angry, Sam looked nonplussed. Nat frowned, Evangeline's arms were crossed, while Sage stood serenely. Next to her, Roxy was quiet and thoughtful.

"Well, that's that taken care of," Johnson said as the cops shut the door on Louise. He turned to Roxy, looking slightly uncomfortable. "The tip-off you gave us this afternoon has led to a successful arrest."

Roxy brightened when he spoke. She grinned and dared to be a little bold. "Are you thanking me, Detective Johnson?"

Johnson was deadpan. "You have done your duty as a citizen."

"I'd take that as a yes!" Evangeline said. "It's the best you're gonna get!"

"What do you mean the tip-off?" Sam asked.

"I found Louise's real ID in the clothes I brought back from your laundry," Roxy said. "So I contacted Detective Johnson and set this little drama up. I hadn't anticipated she was going to turn quite so feral, though."

"Well, my trust issues just got much worse," Nat said with a sigh.

Sam looked at the detective. "Do you have enough evidence to charge her?"

"Per the plans we set up with Ms. Reinhardt this afternoon, we've got the confession recorded," Johnson said. "We'll search for the firearm used to commit the crime, and look for DNA evidence, but we've got plenty on her so far. Even if the murder case falls through, we could charge her with arson, attempted murder, you name it. She crossed a lot of lines back there. You were all in a lot of danger."

"Nonsense," Evangeline said. "Just a little skirmish, is all."

Johnson rolled his eyes. "Still as stubborn as ever, I see."

"Hurry up and search her room, would you? And get the heck out of my guesthouse," Evangeline said, shaking her head and flicking her hands as though Johnson were an insect whose presence on the premises wouldn't do *Evangeline's* reputation any good.

"Gladly," Johnson said drily.

CHAPTER THIRTY-SIX

LATER THAT NIGHT, Roxy was in her room with Nefertiti curled up on the bed beside her.

The day had been a rollercoaster. Her tarot card reading with Sage seemed like such a long time ago. Since then she'd argued with Sam in the laundry, spent the bulk of the day on her feet cooking, found the badge that clued her in to Louise's real identity, contacted Detective Johnson with her suspicions, confronted Louise at the dinner, wrestled her to the ground, had her life threatened, and watched a murderer get arrested.

And, after it all, she *still* didn't know where she would live, or what she would do. The case had been an excellent distraction, but now she had nothing to do, nothing to look forward to...no plans, no direction.

Exhausted, she had a little cry to let out all the tensions of the day, until there was a soft knock at her door.

Roxy quickly wiped her tears and cleared her throat. "Come in," she croaked.

In came Evangeline, a look of concern on her face. She was followed by an equally serious-looking Sam.

"Oh," Roxy said, taken aback. She was sure she looked an absolute mess, her eyes ringed with mascara that had run, her red dress all crumpled and askew. "Hi." She tried to smooth out her hair and ran her fingertips under her eyes. Hopefully, the dim light hid the worst. "Sit down, go ahead."

Evangeline sat on the bed next to her while Sam dragged a chair over.

"We've come with a proposition," Evangeline said.

"Okay...?" Roxy felt a little nervous.

"Don't look so scared," Sam said, with a gentle laugh. "It's nothing too terrible. At least, I hope not."

Evangeline spoke. Her green eyes were soft and gentle. "We've really enjoyed havin' you here, cher. You're a wonderful person, friendly but not too much, willin' to roll up your sleeves and get your hands dirty. And you solved the murder. That takes some moxie. I was goin' to ask you, well, I know you said you were startin' a new life. Do you...would you...will you become part-owner in this ole place with Sam and take over the day-to-day runnin' of the guesthouse from me?"

Roxy's mind went into a spin.

"Nat'll stay on, of course," Evangeline said. "Sage'll do the website. I can even teach y'all how to *really* cook if you want. I can't stay forever, but I don't have to go rushin' off right away. Sam'll do the repairs and the laundry still, and Elijah'll bring all the bread and pastries, as usual."

Roxy stared at them.

This couldn't be happening, could it? Something so

good that was such a blessing? Things like this didn't happen to her. Life was a struggle!

"But I can't afford to buy it from you," she said.

"That's all right," Evangeline replied. "It's all settled. Sam's goin' to buy it and give you half. You'll be the manager with a steady paycheck and a stake in the property."

"Gosh." Roxy settled back onto the headboard and stared into space as she processed this information.

"Unless you have other plans, cher," Evangeline said gently. "I guess the world is your oyster now. You could go anywhere. Start afresh wherever you wanted."

"Though it'd be nice if you stuck around." Sam's voice was deep and full of meaning. "Real nice."

Roxy looked up. Sam was looking right at her, his eyes sincere.

She avoided them for a moment, pushing back the wave in her chest that was threatening to break. Instead, she pushed her fingers into Nefertiti's long fur and stroked her soft, soft belly.

Roxy allowed her thoughts to roam for a second or two. She imagined herself traveling out of New Orleans by bus, her bags packed, Nefertiti in her little carrier, as she rode away from all the new friends she had made. Where was she going? She didn't know. But as she imagined herself looking out of the window at this city she'd come to love, she felt a tug at her heart. Not a little tug, like a sentimental but necessary goodbye, but a gigantic pull, like someone had lassoed her with a thick rope and wasn't about to let go.

Her senses were alive. The colors of Mardi Gras flashed before her eyes and she heard the noises of the parades in her ears. She could smell the Cajun spices that lingered in the air around her like spirits urging her to stay. Perhaps *this* city, with all its magic and mystery and chaos was the place she'd finally make her home. It seemed so unlikely, but she had discovered that she was a little fiercer and a little wilder than she knew. New Orleans had brought all that moxie up to the surface.

"We'll give you some time to think about it, cher," Evangeline said, giving her a motherly pat on the knee.

"No," said Roxy.

She thought back to that wild, devil-may-care moment in her apartment. That split second when her spirit had told her, *WE'RE OFF!* no matter what her fearful mind countered with. This moment was different, though. The feeling didn't sweep over her from outside, gripping her soul with determination. This time, it bubbled up from somewhere deep within. To come to New Orleans had been a whim. To stay was a *conviction*.

Roxy looked Evangeline and Sam in the eyes and smiled. "I'm going to accept your offer with many thanks. I shall be delighted to stay."

CHAPTER THIRTY-SEVEN

TIME WHIZZED BY and before Roxy knew it, the night of the Grand Opening rolled around. She had changed the name of the guesthouse to the *Funky Cat Inn*, a nod to the jazz traditions of the city and the music she planned to provide regularly, and she and Nat had spent weeks reimagining each room from scratch. They'd headed to the New Orleans Public Library and checked out numerous books on traditional buildings with pictures of sumptuous decors for inspiration.

They'd hit flea markets with Sam's laundry van (and his generous cash injection) and filled it up with all manner of French antiques and some amazing reproductions that they put to use in the communal and private rooms of the guesthouse.

Sam had also gotten to work. He had rewired the building and arranged all the structural repair work necessary. New windows had been installed and the balconies fixed. By the time he had finished, the *Funky Cat Inn* was up to code and then some.

On one of their trips to the flea market, Roxy finally broached the elephant in the room with Nat. "Where *does* Sam get all this money from? Surely the laundry business doesn't make enough for him to splash this amount of cash around?"

Nat raised her eyebrows. "We don't ask about that. I think he has family money, and he's a little embarrassed about it, but that's just a guess. Like I said, we don't talk about it."

"Why not?"

"He gets very cagey," Nat said. "So we don't push it. He grew up around here, his family goes way back, generations, and Evangeline always said that was good enough for her."

That was the last they talked of it.

The dining room where tonight's event was to be held had been transformed. They'd split it into a grand lounge on one side, the dining area on the other. The whole place was painted a gorgeous, soft, pale blue. The room was now furnished with a mixture of champagne and pastel blue fabrics, mahogany side tables with ornately curved legs, lamps, gilded mirrors, and an abundance of interesting knickknacks and ornaments. They even had an enormous chandelier glittering overhead.

The bedrooms were sumptuous too, and Nefertiti looked more regal than ever curled up on one of the Louis-style four-poster beds. Her bright eyes matched the blue of the bedspreads exactly. She was the perfect accessory. Sage had taken a wonderful picture of her for their new Instagram page.

Sage had a great eye for photography. Her pictures of the food and the décor were so gorgeous that their social media follower counts were climbing every day. There had been a write-up in a local paper too, and slowly word was spreading that the *Funky Cat Inn* was the place to stay in New Orleans. Roxy trembled with anticipation when she thought about it.

Roxy felt she was in a permanent state of exhilaration. She had become so consumed by the whole process of turning the guesthouse from a vision in her head into a reality all around her that she often couldn't sleep. She'd never felt so accomplished.

"A boutique luxury, yet traditional, New Orleans experience" was the phrase she kept repeating to decorators, antique dealers, and just about anyone who would listen. It encapsulated precisely her goal for the new hotel.

Roxy rushed around on the day of the Grand Opening, but eventually, there was nothing more to do so she took herself to her room to get ready. She'd bought herself a new dress. She'd never have picked out something so show-stopping before, but being the new proprietor of this fabulous place and with some encouragement from Nat and Sage, she'd come to believe that a silver-sequined, figure-hugging dress wasn't *too* over the top. Okay, well maybe it was, especially when paired with an abundance of silver and crystal jewelry loaned to her by Sage and which now sparkled in her ears and around her neck and her wrists, but *why the heck not?* Wasn't life for enjoying, after all?

They were expecting a big turnout, but Roxy couldn't help drumming her fingertips on the arm of one of the couches as she finally sat down and waited for her guests to arrive. The time seemed to tick by so, so slowly. They'd printed flyers and passed them out just about everywhere. Elijah had distributed them with every beignet purchase made at his bakery, Sam had wrapped one inside every laundry parcel, Sage had left a whole bunch at the botanica, and Nat had spent all her days off on the street at the end of the alleyway handing out details of the event to passersby.

They'd even sent an invitation to Mara Lomas, a kind of peace offering. After Louise had been arrested, Mara had come back around to the guesthouse in tears, saying to them how ashamed she was of her behavior. They'd tried to console her by telling her that she had been right —it *was* one of them who had killed her husband—but the message didn't seem to get through. Mara was determined to feel guilty and she had returned to her home state to make some sense of her life. Roxy didn't expect Mara to attend the Grand Opening, but she'd written on the invitation, "We wish you all the best for the future," and she really did.

Nat came and sat next to Roxy. She patted her on the shoulder. Roxy wouldn't have dreamed of asking her to drop her "uniform," but Nat herself had said, "With all this grandeur, I feel a little silly in my Slipknot tee. Slipknot's a band by the way," she added to relieve Roxy's perplexed expression. Instead, Nat was wearing a smart, tailored trouser suit that looked awesome on her. She'd paired it with her shiny green boots with the sparkly laces, which somehow worked, and a plain white t-shirt. Her ears continued to drip with jewelry, and she had kept her tiny diamond nose stud in place. "So that I still feel like myself," she'd said.

Shortly after 6 PM, people began to trickle in. Evangeline, who had helped with the food, handed the guests glasses of wine and Café Brûlot. The tables were laid out with what seemed like thousands of New Orleans-style canapés, and Sage offered tarot readings in the lounge.

Elijah and Sam were on the music, filling the whole place with warm jazz and the cool, mellow sounds of Miles Davis along with the more upbeat tunes of Duke Ellington, filtered through the air. After a while, Nat joined them, astounding Roxy as she demonstrated the most beautiful, soulful voice Roxy had ever heard. Nat sung jazz classics, *Smoke Gets In Your Eyes,* and *It Don't Mean A Thing If It Ain't Got That Swing* and then, with a level of graciousness that she had not previously been known for, she took song requests from Roxy's guests.

As they finished a set, Roxy walked up to her. "Why didn't you tell me you could sing?" she whispered.

"Ah, it's nothing," Nat said, shyly.

"Nothing? You were fantastic!"

"Nat only gets her voice out on special occasions," Sam said. "For *special* people," he added.

"When she sings, she has a true Southern vibe," Sage said. She raised her eyebrows. "Quite unusual when you consider she's from across the pond."

CHAPTER THIRTY-EIGHT

LATER THAT EVENING, Roxy felt like a break and stepped outside into the warm night air. The stars were all out, and it seemed like even they were smiling down at her.

She found Sam out there too, his back turned to her as he looked up to the sky.

"Oh, hey," she said.

He jumped and turned. "Hi, Roxy." He grinned. "Going great, isn't it?"

"Yep!" She felt truly in her element.

"The stars are all out in celebration," he said.

"Lovely clear night, isn't it?" They gazed up at the stars for a moment in companionable silence. "You were wrong about New Orleans, you know," she said eventually. "It *is* magic."

Sam cleared his throat. "I've been meaning to say this for a while." He stared at his feet. "But you know, dumb male pride and all."

Roxy stayed silent and watched him.

"I don't think I spoke to you very nicely when you

came to the laundry, when you talked about your suspicions concerning Elijah."

Roxy had let that go a long time back. She laughed. "Well, you *were* right. It wasn't him, and at that point, it really would have been wise for me to butt out. It was only after we spoke that I found Louise's badge and got a part to play."

Sam looked down at her. "That's all true. But I could have spoken in more of a polite manner."

"Ever the Southern gentleman," Roxy said fondly. "Well, that means I'll have to be a *proper Southern belle*." She tried to put on the accent and failed miserably. They both burst into laughter.

Roxy didn't quite know what came over her. Maybe it was the champagne, or the beauty of the stars, or the deep happiness she felt in her soul, but she wanted to reach out and kiss him. She paused, though, wondering if it were appropriate. Would he kiss her back? Would he jump away and be like, "You've got the wrong idea! We're business partners, that's all!"? Her hesitation broke the spell, and she gave him an awkward smile instead. And besides, the doubts she had about him came flooding back. Perhaps those red flags meant something. Maybe he was just pretending to be a nice guy.

At that moment, Nat came bustling around the corner. "Roxy, I've been looking..." She cut herself short. "Ooooh," she said, her eyes shining. "Have I interrupted something?"

"No!" Roxy said a little too forcefully.

Nat raised an eyebrow. "If you say so. Anyway, come on inside. We're all waiting for you, Rox."

It was coming up on midnight.

Inside, everyone had a champagne glass in hand, and

there was a round of applause when Roxy made her way back in.

"Evangeline was just saying how proud she was of you, how you've transformed the place," Nat said. "They want to hear something from you now."

Roxy would have *died* in her former life if she'd had to do any form of public speaking. But now, here, considering who she was in this moment, all her nerves fell away, and she was filled with a deep sense of warmth and affection.

"Thank you all for coming," she said. "This place...it has come to mean so much to me. Not just this guesthouse, but the whole city. New Orleans is full of magic and wonder. It has changed me. When I got here, I had no idea where my life would lead. I had nothing except my suitcase full of clothes and my cat. No job. No family. No one by my side. No direction. I was painfully shy and didn't have any sort of belief in myself. But...this city has changed me. It has taught me that miracles do happen, that I have a power inside me that I've never been aware of. I'm a new person now, a better person, a more empowered person. And, thanks to your amazing cuisine, also a slightly fatter person!"

Everyone laughed.

"So I just want to say thank you. Thank you to Evangeline for introducing me to Creole and Cajun ways. Thank you to Nat, the craziest, most loveable girl I know. Thank you to Sage, for making me believe in magic. Thank you to Elijah, for showing me that it's okay to be different and that beignets are food from the heavens. Thank you to Sam, for being...a great friend. And thank you to New Orleans for helping me find myself. I am beyond grateful for this new chapter in my life." She raised the glass of champagne that Nat had thrust into her hand. "And thank you for being here to share it with me."

The crowd applauded, and Roxy looked around. The dining room was full of people, chattering, laughing, eating and drinking. She wandered into the lobby where she could survey the entire room.

As she watched the scene in front of her, she felt a huge sense of satisfaction and achievement.

"I *did* this," she whispered to herself. She almost couldn't believe it.

Her phone gave a little "ting." She looked at the screen. There was a text from Angela, her call center supervisor at Modal Appliances, Inc.

Jade and Chloe have been fired for fighting in the women's bathroom. We are two customer service reps down. Come back to work at 9 AM sharp, but no pay for the time you missed. Don't be late!

Roxy read the text several times. She tapped out a reply.

Can't make it. Sorry. Good luck, though.

She looked back at the room and watched her guests. Sam waved from across the room.

She knew what to do. She didn't hesitate. There was no grief, no loss, no love lost. She swiped her phone. There was a "whoosh."

Angela was gone for good.

NEW ORLEANS NIGHTMARE

USA TODAY BESTSELLING AUTHOR
ALISON GOLDEN WITH
HONEY BROUSSARD

NEW ORLEANS NIGHTMARE

BOOK TWO

Published by Mesa Verde Publishing
P.O. Box 1002
San Carlos, CA 94070

Edited by
Marjorie Kramer

CHAPTER ONE

"OOOOH, I'M SO excited!" Roxy Reinhardt said, dancing around the kitchen, while pots and pans of all sizes bubbled on the stovetop. Gumbos, stews, and jambalayas filled the room with rich, spicy steam as she boogied in the space between the range and the countertops.

"Me too!" Nat said, clapping her hands together.

Roxy was the manager and part-owner of the *Funky Cat Inn,* having been recently installed as such by the previous owner, Evangeline, and local investor, laundry-man, handyman, and something of a handsome dark horse, Sam. Nat was Roxy's "Girl Friday." She was also a former English nanny who had overstayed her visa.

Today they were preparing a Grand Welcome Meal.

"Who are these people again?" Evangeline asked Roxy, for the third time. "I don't understand all these new-fangled Instabook things, cher."

Evangeline was retired and living her own life now, but she still came over to help them with the food. She was an absolute master at Creole and Cajun cooking and baking, and Roxy and Nat had submitted themselves to an extended tutelage.

"They're called influencers," Roxy explained. "That means that they have a lot of followers on Instagram."

"Huh?" Evangeline said.

Nat rolled her eyes and gave Roxy a wink as she looked back from a pot of gumbo she was stirring. "Instagram is a platform where you have your own page, and you put pictures on it. If people like what they see, they follow you to watch what you're going to put up next. We have a page for the *Funky Cat*. Sage runs it."

"So why are these..." Evangeline frowned. "Why are these influgrammers comin' here?"

"It's *influencers,* Evangeline," Nat said.

Roxy laughed. "Influgrammers sounds pretty good, though! You might have just coined a new word there, Evangeline. Anyway, the influencers are coming here to stay as part of a promotion. We pay them to showcase their visit. All the pictures and videos they shoot while they are here get put on their Instagram feed, and their followers will see them. Since they have hundreds of thousands of followers, it's great publicity. This is huge for us."

Roxy had arrived in New Orleans during Mardi Gras season. Now though, spring had brightened into summer and the vivid colors and excitement of Mardi Gras were over. The city had lazily tilted into June, but with the imminent arrival of the influencers, the atmosphere at the *Funky Cat* was ramping up to a level never experienced in the building's entire 102-year existence.

Evangeline sighed, shaking her head with bemusement. "Back in my day, people simply bought an ad in a magazine or two."

Well into her eighties, Evangeline bustled around the kitchen with pots and spices, her floral wraparound dresses swishing beneath her aprons as she did so. She was a flurry of bustle and action. She could still manage six pans on the flame at one time, and ordered Roxy and Nat about the place as if she still owned the kitchen, which, when she was in it, she did.

Nat picked up a large sack of crawfish and carried it into the back room to begin purging them. "Times have changed, Evangeline, and we've gotta keep up if we want the *Funky Cat* to be a success."

"It only has six rooms!" Evangeline cried, rearranging bags of spices on the counter. "How much of a success can it be?"

Roxy felt awkward. She didn't want to talk about how much more upscale the boutique hotel was now or how expensive the rooms had become since Evangeline's time as owner; it would be rude and embarrassing.

"Well, the room rates are just a touch higher, so we need a new, more affluent demographic, that's all. Now, shouldn't we get started on the jalapeño cornbreads? Where have those ramekins gotten to?"

They were really going to town on the welcome meal for the influencers. It was to be a five-course affair.

"Do you think they'll be able to eat all this lot?" Nat wondered out loud as she wandered back into the kitchen a few minutes later. She was carrying a pot of newly purged crawfish with a grin on her face. "For course one, we've got a chicken gumbo with Cajun spices." Nat ladled up a spoonful of the gumbo and let it slowly pour back into the pan. "Followed by miniature crawfish and cheese pies, followed by Shrimp Creole. That's shrimp cooked in tomatoes, peppers and hot sauce, with white rice, Roxy," the young English woman said gravely.

Nat was a *Funky Cat* treasure. She helped Roxy with anything that was needed at the boutique hotel, from cooking to serving guests, from checking them in to cleaning their rooms. And her talents extended even further. Nat possessed a voice that was so smooth and creamy that Roxy had hired her on the spot to sing for guests.

Now, Nat's black nail polish gleamed in the lights of the kitchen. Her excitement about the upcoming meal really *was* something. Getting the cynical, skeptical Nat to be joyous and upbeat about anything was a true feat. But then, what was coming was a bold, new experiment for the small hotel.

"Yum, and I'm preparing dessert—warm bread pudding with caramel and whiskey sauce," Roxy said.

"Don't forget the cheese course!" Evangeline cried out from where she was stirring a huge pot of broth.

"I'm not sure they will be able to eat it all, but I do know that thousands and thousands will be watching via their Instagram accounts, and we have to give a great impression, not only of the *Funky Cat*, but of New Orleans," Roxy finished.

The city was the first place Roxy had ever felt truly at home. It was hard to explain, but New Orleans had gotten into her bones somehow. There was a *heat* about "N'awlins" as the locals called it, perhaps from the spices, perhaps from the carnivals and the magic and the spiritualism that lurked about the place, perhaps from the music that floated from basements and businesses at any time of the day or night. Whatever it was, the essence of it had found its way into Roxy's very soul, lodged itself there, and wasn't about to leave any time soon.

As she chopped onions and garlic for the Shrimp Creole, Roxy sighed happily to herself. Things were *finally* falling into place in her life, and she felt cozy and warm and safe. Just then, they heard the sound of the front door knocker being rapped. Hard.

Roxy frowned, her knife paused over an onion. She was expecting Sam, but he'd have simply walked in without knocking. Roxy wiped her hands down her apron and hurried out of the kitchen, through the dining room and into the hallway. The influencers weren't due for a good three hours. She hoped this wasn't one of them arriving early. She wanted to be dressed in her best and have the food ready before they got even so much as a glimpse of the *Funky Cat* or its proprietor. A little flustered, she pulled open the door. Her heart sank.

A very tall, slim woman with huge sunglasses and long, black hair that cascaded in waves down her back stood on the doorstep. She wore chunky high heels on her feet, skinny jeans, and a leather jacket with a fur collar that looked very expensive indeed. Behind her, six Louis Vuitton suitcases and two holdalls were piled up in the courtyard. Without so much as a greeting, the woman walked assuredly past Roxy and into the *Funky Cat* lobby.

"Oh, hello," Roxy said, stepping back to give the woman room to pass. *Who was she?* The woman had walked in like *she* owned the place, a demeanor that Roxy suspected was her visitor's default setting. Then she remembered who the woman was!

"Good afternoon," the visitor said, pushing her sunglasses on top of her head. "I am Ada Okafor." The woman eyed Roxy. "But I expect you knew that. I'm early,

I know. I'm always early. The early bird catches the worm. Snooze, you lose." She flicked her wrist and poked one forefinger into the air.

Roxy recovered quickly. "Great to meet you. I'm Roxy Reinhardt, part-owner and manager of this hotel." Roxy stuck out her hand, but Ada didn't seem to notice so Roxy gestured down at her apron, embarrassed. "Yes, um, I'm afraid we aren't quite, um, ready for the grand welcome we wanted to give you." What was happening to her? All Roxy's confidence and excitement had evaporated at the sight of this officious, elegant woman.

"It's fine," Ada said, though her mouth twitched. She didn't look impressed. "I will go to my room and do some editing on the mag while you," she looked Roxy up and down, "pull yourself together." Ada Okafor ran a travel magazine for rich Nigerians who wanted to jet-set around the world like she did. She had a huge international following on Instagram in the luxury travel market.

Ada looked around. "But who will carry my bags?"

CHAPTER TWO

THREE MONTHS EARLIER, the *Funky Cat Inn* had been a guesthouse known as *Evangeline's*. It was a large, grand house built in the French architecture style so common in New Orleans. But when Roxy arrived, the building had long since begun to crumble and fall into disrepair. It was covered in cobwebs. The balcony on the third floor was so rickety that no one dared step out on it. The once-vibrant pink façade had peeled and faded in patches until it was blush in one corner and almost white in another. Bookings were down, and one guest turned out to be a murderer. But then Evangeline retired, Sam infused an injection of cash, and Roxy had taken over. Now the place was transformed.

Roxy's do-over had started with the exterior. No one was going to be staying with her if the place looked like a flamingo on its last leg. She had gotten busy with a stepladder and used up can after can of bright pink paint until the first floor dazzled. She stopped there because she wasn't a fan of heights, and instead hired a professional who brought his ladder and took over. Now the outside of the building had been restored to its former brilliance. It stood out like a beacon among the black, white, yellow, and red buildings around it.

Roxy had bitten her lip as she watched the painter from the cobbled, narrow street below. Hiring someone had seemed an extravagance. To save money, she had done most of the work around the hotel herself with the help of Nat and Sam, but she knew she must recognize her limits. It would hardly help to save money on a painter if she fell off a ladder and broke her leg. But still, her poverty-stricken background and her thrifty ways made spending money on the renovations hard for her.

Sam had been a huge help. As well as being both an excellent handyman and the owner of a nearby laundry, he was also an awesome sax player, a car enthusiast, and apparently an all-round decent guy. Sam's most important role at present, however, was that he was the main investor in the hotel, both buying the building from Evangeline *and* paying for its renovations. He had given Roxy a budget, and she had made sure to keep well within it.

The form of Sam's relationship with Roxy had an unresolved quality around it, though. Roxy knew she had a crush on him, one that she was trying to quell. She suspected he was attracted to her too. Over the weeks and months of renovating the building together, they'd built a friendly, but platonic working relationship, their mutual attraction only slightly impinging upon it now and again. Neither had made a move on the other, either because they were too scared or too busy. Roxy wasn't too sure which it might be, and now she felt it best to keep things as they were. It didn't do to mix business with pleasure in her book. She didn't want to destroy a good thing. And now, as part-owner and manager of the *Funky Cat*, she most definitely had a good thing.

Where Sam got his money from was a second unre-solved question that had caused Roxy some sleepless nights. The laundry business was doing great, sure, but the cash needed to buy the hotel? That was more than a laundry business owner could be expected to shell out. *And* he owned a Rolls Royce!

"Where does he get his money from?" Roxy had asked Nat one day.

Nat had shrugged. "He doesn't say. We don't ask."

It was all a bit of a mystery.

Roxy's life gave her no time to ponder the question, however. After the *Funky Cat's* exterior was made over, she turned her attention to organizing the area out front in the courtyard. The hotel faced onto *Elijah's Bakery*. The owner, Elijah was a great friend and a wonderful baker. Daily he provided the *Funky Cat* with fresh bread, delicious pastries, and, of course, beignets. Elijah also played the piano and rounded out the jazz trio that performed at the *Funky Cat* alongside Nat and Sam.

Elijah was a snappy dresser. When he wasn't work-ing, he was kitted out in bright shirts and gleaming, patent leather crocodile shoes. He loved a stripe pattern or an African print. But when it came to his business, his personal style didn't translate. While Elijah might have been a master baker, he was *not* a master decorator. The façade of his building looked like it hadn't been updated since the 1980s. It was entirely black and white and gray. Roxy, with some effort, had persuaded him to paint it, and he'd chosen a pale pink and mint-green color scheme. Now the two businesses that sat opposite each other were also a match for one another. The buildings were even color-coordinated.

"I can't believe I didn't do this years ago!" Elijah said to Roxy when they stood back and surveyed his storefront. A huge grin spread across his face, and he gave Roxy a high five. He bought new cast iron tables and chairs for the outside, and Sam had given him a special deal on linen tablecloths and napkins to finish off the bright, clean look. Now the bakery was doing better than ever with clientele drawn to it by its elegant, comfortable surroundings and the smell of fresh coffee and beignets that emanated from it.

Roxy and Elijah had become firm friends as they strived to build successful businesses while staying true to their values. They both believed in offering a great product at a great price with friendly service, hard work, and decency being their driving forces. They could often be found outside Elijah's bakery nursing coffees, their heads together as they discussed the finer points of running a business.

Finally, there was just one thing left to do to the outside of the *Funky Cat*: they needed to add the finishing touches to the courtyard. First, Sam came along with a pressure washer and took out years of encrusted grime from between the cobbles. Then it was on to the decoration. Roxy had decided to incorporate as many plants as possible into the design of the new courtyard, and her friend Sage was just the right person to help her.

Sage was a spiritualist, New Orleans born and bred, with an ancestral line of African American spiritual women stretching back behind her into history. It was in her blood. She stood in the newly cleaned courtyard in her flowing robes, a deep emerald green this particular time, and put her hands out. "I'm letting the spirits come to me," she said. "You need to place pots around. They should be filled with basil and white sage and rosemary and lavender. Here, here, here, and here," she said to Roxy, pointing at four spots in the space in front of the hotel. "They will ward away evil spirits, and I will invite angels and other benevolent spiritual beings to bless and protect this space."

Roxy wasn't entirely sure she believed in all that, but she guessed it couldn't hurt. Besides, it would make the entrance to the *Funky Cat* smell wonderful. She placed huge pots of herbs just as Sage had directed and hung baskets overflowing with brightly-colored blooms from the exterior walls. Finally, Sam hung a sign with the name of the hotel emblazoned across it under a rendering of a cat that looked rather like Nefertiti, Roxy's long-haired white Persian. The cat on the sign was wearing a trilby hat at a jaunty angle and holding a saxophone.

The courtyard now looked so good that Roxy was satisfied that the standard of the outside of the hotel matched that of the inside. The interior of the building had come a *long* way in the time since Roxy had taken over and in the process of restoring it, she had uncovered yet another useful talent of Nat's—restoring or repurposing worn neglected furniture and decorations.

"It's called 'upcycling,' Rox, and you can do it with just about anything if you have the right eye and the tools," Nat had said. "Beauty on the cheap." The hotel had benefited from her passion enormously.

They'd transformed the dining room into a grand eating area and the lounge into a sumptuous, decadent sanctuary for relaxation and rest. They had furnished the rooms with a mixture of real antiques and upcycled items in a variety of dark woods, silver, and gold, with occasional touches of powdery blue. The bedrooms had had a similar treatment. But Roxy still worried that there wasn't enough color, so she and Nat went through, adding splashes of flamingo pink and royal blue and gold—a cushion here, a toothbrush holder there, until there was a heightened vibrancy to each room.

"It's so fantastic, Rox. You're gonna be on TV soon, I just know it," Nat said to her soon after they opened.

Word-of-mouth recommendations about the *Funky Cat* spread quickly. After her Grand Opening event, as news of Roxy's relaunch of the hotel became known, business picked up. Roxy had seen a dramatic increase in bookings and the hotel was now at full capacity nearly every night.

"Oh, I don't know about that, but it is pretty amazing, isn't it?" Roxy had felt her confidence grow in leaps as the days passed. The Roxy of old—anxious, wallflower Roxy —seemed to have gone. An energetic, confident businesswoman had replaced her. Roxy was mostly fine with her transformation, but occasionally doubts emerged. She knew that despite her efforts and the professional demeanor she strived to project, there were times when she wasn't quite as together as she appeared. Now though, it was showtime. Whatever the next few days had in store for her, Roxy had a responsibility to be calm, unflappable, and in charge. The game was most definitely on.

CHAPTER THREE

NAT RETURNED TO the kitchen red-faced and scowling. "What did that woman bring with her, the entire contents of Harrods? She told me she'd just been to England and had 'stocked up on essentials.' *Essentials?* She thinks all these Burberry trench coats and designer dresses are essentials? Really!" Whenever she was angry, Nat's British accent became more pronounced, all clipped tones and short vowels. "And not only did I have to carry all those bags upstairs, but I also had to get a load of the clothes out, hang them up *and* check for damage and creases."

Roxy was surprised Nat had played along with Ada's requests. "Doesn't sound like you, Nat."

"I know." Nat flopped on one of the stools they kept in the kitchen and pushed her short dark hair back from her face. "Normally I would have told her to jog on. I mean, I'm not her personal assistant, am I? But I knew I had to do it. Imagine, what if she had been secretly filming and I told her I wasn't going to help? It wouldn't make a good impression, would it now?"

"Right," said Roxy biting her lip. She was already wondering if they had gotten themselves in too deep with this Instagram promotion. They'd had plenty of guests before, but those were nice *normal* ones. Perhaps naïvely, she'd thought the Instagram influencers would be the same. "Thanks for taking one for the team."

Nat rolled her eyes and hopped off the stool. She began to drench the bread pudding Roxy had prepared earlier with caramel and whiskey sauce. "Well, the next few days are going to be *fun, fun, fun,* aren't they?" she said, pulling a face and clapping her hands. "Just four more guests to go. Let's hope they're not all as demanding as Ada. We'll not cope."

To Roxy and Nat's relief, Ada didn't make as much work for them that afternoon as they feared. She called down to reception for soda water but stayed quiet the remainder of the time. There was a lot of work to do in the kitchen, and Roxy, Nat, and Evangeline did not need distractions.

When everything was prepared and laid out for the evening meal, Roxy hurried to shower and change. Since transforming the hotel, she'd had part of a downstairs storage area turned into two rooms—a bedroom and a bathroom. These were now her private quarters. The room at the top of the house where she'd first stayed as a visitor had been transformed into a wonderful penthouse-style suite. That's where they were going to put Lily Vashchenko, one of the other influencers. She had the most followers, but now Roxy wondered if she should have put Ada Okafor in there.

Roxy went into her room and slipped off her shoes.

She padded in her socks over to the bed where her fluffy white princess of a cat Nefertiti was curled up, purring away. Roxy tickled her under her chin. "Hello, my love," she said. "You look so cozy there."

Nefertiti looked up at her, gave a little mewl in appreciation and closed her eyes in what appeared to be ecstasy as Roxy rubbed her cheek.

There was nothing Roxy loved more than curling up with a good book and Nefertiti on her lap. But there was little time for that these days, what with all the hotel work going on, and there was absolutely no time for it now! She took a lightning-fast shower and slipped into a crisp, pressed, white shirt, tight jeans, and silver pumps. She heard a knock on the front door and quickly looked in the mirror before smoothing her hair.

As she came out of her room she was immediately faced with the next couple of guests, two young men in t-shirts, jeans, and hoodies. Unlike Ada, they had their cameras at the ready.

"So we've just arrived at the *Funky Cat*," one of the men was saying. Roxy recognized him as Michael O'Sullivan. He had dark hair, thin lips, and a serious-looking face. "Isn't it looking grand?"

The other man jumped in front of the camera, pulling a silly face. "Woohoo! Far too grand for the likes of me!" Roxy knew he was Dash Davies, recognizing him from his unruly red hair, wild grin, and bright t-shirt. He was known for always wearing some wild color or other. Together the two men made up the Instagram and YouTube star duo *Michael & Dash*. They toured the world in a variety of styles, from budget to luxury, and while Michael compiled the serious reviews, Dash always had a trick up his sleeve to make things interesting and,

Roxy suspected, boost views. He posted videos with such titles as *The Ice Bucket Challenge...In Greenland!* Or *Man Downs 100 Pints of Lager in London!*

"Hey there!" Roxy said with a huge smile. Her heart was pounding. She knew she was on camera, and despite the position she was now in, she still wasn't at all used to fame, notoriety, or even people noticing her. She'd only recently allowed Sage to include pictures of her on their own *Funky Cat* Instagram profile. "The stars of *Michael & Dash!* So glad to have you guys here! My name's Roxy, I'm part-owner and manager of this hotel. I'll be your host during your time with us."

Dash bounded forward and wrapped her up in a hug. "We're totally pumped to be here!" he said into her shoulder, a little too loud for comfort. Then he backed up. "Me and Mike have been..."

"*Michael,*" his partner said.

"Oh sorry, I forgot." Dash slapped his hand to his forehead. He looked at Roxy and grinned. "I do have a tendency to be overly familiar. Excuse me. *Michael.*" He gave a little bow and discreetly rolled his eyes at Roxy as he straightened up. "So, anyway, we were saying, we're so totally excited to come to New Orleans to get our dose of the culture. We want to eat ourselves silly on all that Creole goodness. I'm planning to put on at least ten pounds. Can you hook me up, Rox?"

Roxy laughed. "I certainly can. *And,* if you turn the camera around, you'll see someone who'll make sure of it." She pointed out the door. "That's *Elijah's Bakery,* and he makes the meanest beignets—they're square donuts—the world has ever seen. We stock up on them for breakfast."

"Sounds like a plan, Roxy!" said Dash. Then he grabbed his case. "Right! Where's my room?"

"Come with me!" Roxy said feeling excited now. While Michael was quiet and serious—maybe a little pompous—Dash's energy was contagious.

But they didn't get very far. Before they'd ascended four steps, there was a cheery "Hello!" at the door.

CHAPTER FOUR

ROXY TURNED TO see an older woman in her late 60s, her gray hair cropped short, rather like Roxy's. She wore a big smile and an equally large backpack. Compared to Roxy's earlier guests, she cut a more quiet, modest figure. She was dressed in cargo pants, a plain gray t-shirt, and hiking boots. In her hand, she carried two trekking poles. For one horrifying moment, Roxy couldn't remember her name before it came rushing back to her. "Sylvia Walters!" She was a travel influencer from Maine. Most of her followers were women aged 65 and over.

Sylvia had obviously done her research. "You must be Roxy Reinhardt."

"Indeed I am." Roxy came down the steps and shook her hand. "I can show you all up to your rooms. We're ready for you."

"No personalized service?" Michael muttered. He spoke softly, but loud enough for Roxy to hear.

Everyone went quiet.

"Michael!" Dash hissed, giving him a little shove on his shoulder.

Unfortunately, the shove was a little *too* hard, and Michael fell down the four steps they'd just climbed. The camera crashed to the ground, and Michael stumbled, then over-corrected, finally splaying out at the bottom of the stairs.

"Ow!" he said.

Roxy and Sylvia gasped.

Dash hurried down the stairs. "Oh my gosh! I'm so sorry! I didn't mean to..."

"Shut up!" Michael said, pushing him away roughly. "You could have seriously hurt me."

"Are you okay?" Roxy asked, peering at him.

"Who cares about me?" Michael barked, reaching out for the camera that had crashed to the ground when he fell. "It's this I'm worried about." He took a look and nodded. "Thank goodness. Still intact and still recording." He turned the camera back to himself. "Well, I just took a dive, but I'm fine now. See you guys in a little while." He pressed a button and the red recording light flicked off. "Hmph. Let's carry on."

Dash looked embarrassed. "I'm real sorry, bud."

"I wouldn't worry about it too much," said Sylvia. "Drama always commands attention. You might even turn into a meme!"

Roxy saw Michael's facial expression darken, and she jumped in quickly before the conversation turned into an argument. "Let's get you up to your rooms, everybody!"

Roxy, having felt excited just a few minutes earlier, was feeling stressed now and wondered again if this Instagram promotion had been such a great idea after all. She tried to hide her fears with a smile. Dash seemed to read her thoughts because as they turned the corner on the staircase, he patted her on the shoulder. "Don't worry, Roxy. We're not litigious."

Roxy laughed nervously. "Well, that's something." She hadn't even *thought* about that. She settled her guests into their rooms without further fuss, but by the time she returned down the stairs, she felt a little sick. What *had* she let herself in for? She popped her head in the kitchen to see how things were progressing. Nat was hard at work at the counter while Evangeline was flitting between pans like a fly.

"How's progress?" Roxy asked. She paused. "Nat, don't you need to get dressed?"

Nat stuck her tongue out. "We have it all under control, thank you. Anyway, I'm just booting it, so no rush." Roxy knew what she meant. Nat was *not* a dressing-up sort of girl. She loved her black distressed jeans and band tees and big combat boots. Roxy doubted even a million dollars could get her slipping into something slinky. When it came to dinnertime, Nat usually just changed her shoes, from the worn-down boots she wore every day to something a little fancier.

Nat had amassed quite a collection of Doc Martens over the months of working at the *Funky Cat*—purple sparkly ones, teal patent ones, silver-and-black stripy ones, and a black patent pair with red ribbon laces that tied in a huge bow. Each time she got a paycheck, she put some aside for her next purchase. The boots, while not elegant, were part of Nat. They gave her character. She also put a brush through her short, unruly hair, which transformed it into a pretty, sleek bob. Her tattoo sleeves still showed, though. All in all, Roxy had reconciled herself to Nat's appearance and just about considered her trademark look an asset, a nod to the quirky character of the *Funky Cat Inn*. She certainly sparked conversation between the guests at mealtimes.

Despite Nat's tongue poke, Roxy smiled back at her and said, "It's smelling delicious. I can't wait!" She looked around at the food preparations laid out in the kitchen. It gave her butterflies to know that much of the next few days would be memorialized in perpetuity in videos and pictures and reviews. Were they really ready? She shook her head. It was too late to think about that. At least she could rely on the food not to let her down.

Her nerves made her want to start fixing everything. She headed back into the dining room where Nat had laid out fancy white tablecloths and huge place settings with reams of cutlery for each person. Three vases of flowers graced the center of the table. Roxy clasped her hands and tapped them against her mouth as she walked around inspecting everything. She scanned every place setting, making sure each knife, fork, and spoon was just so. She tweaked the positions of the flowers. When she couldn't improve things any further, she went over to the lounge area and checked that all the cushions—blue and bronze— were in perfect alignment.

"Hello?" a deep female voice called out from the hallway.

Roxy hurried through to the entrance. "Hello, there!" she said. The final influencer to arrive, Lily Vashchenko, was in front of her. Lily was tall, much taller than Roxy, and older, perhaps in her early thirties. Waves of blonde that emerged from darker roots bounced over her shoulders. She had slanted almond eyes that were distinctly Slavic and made her look innocent but a little seductive at the same time. She wore tight white jeans and a white swishy top with silver butterflies fluttering all over it. Black stilettos with a silver heel finished off her ensemble along with big silver jewelry that pierced her ears and lay around her neck.

"You must be Roxy," Lily said somberly. She placed her palms on Roxy's shoulders and bent in to air kiss her on both cheeks. Roxy, her mouth forming a perfect "O," couldn't help but allow herself to be embraced like this. "Lovely to meet you, Lily." As Lily let her hands fall, Roxy watched Lily's rose gold iPhone warily—was she filming?

Lily saw her glance and said smoothly, "I'm not recording yet. That would be bad manners. You're new to this whole business, so I shall not put any pressure on you. I'm only going to put good things in this review, don't worry." Lily had a thick Russian accent. She grabbed the handle of her large suitcase, also rose-gold, and smiled, cat-like, the skin around her eyes creasing at the corners. "So, where's my room?" Lily tilted her head to one side and smiled with her lips pressed together. "I don't know you, but I am proud of you for running such a lovely hotel. That's such an achievement at your age."

"Thank you! Please come with me," Roxy said, unsure whether to be flattered or patronized, but she was glad to be able to tell Lily, "You're getting the penthouse suite!"

CHAPTER FIVE

AT 6 PM, ROXY called up to the guests' rooms to let them know that dinner would be served in an hour. She told them that beforehand they could relax in the lounge and have the nibbles she'd prepared: chips, pistachio and cashew nuts, olives, and champagne. Then they'd head to the huge dining table for their meal.

In preparation for the evening, Roxy changed into a purple satin dress and paired it with silver sparkling shoes and a silver necklace and earrings. Before Roxy arrived in New Orleans, she'd loved clothes and jewelry, but never had the confidence to wear show-stopping outfits. She felt like a kid playing dress-up when she tried. She also hadn't had the budget for anything but basics. She'd stuck mostly with jeans, plain skirts, sweaters, and tees. But now? Now, she had a newfound confidence and she was making the most of it! Nat had shown her the best thrift stores in the city, and Roxy had become an exceptional bargain hunter, kitting out her wardrobe with the kind of outfits that befitted her role at the hotel but on a very small budget. There was nothing else for it in her opinion, New Orleans and her position simply demanded glitz and glamor.

Roxy didn't have time to do anything special with her hair, not that there was a lot she could do with it—it was a pixie cut after all—so she simply finger-combed it, and with a flick of mascara and a slick of lip gloss, she was ready to go.

Roxy had laid out glasses on a tray on top of one of the coffee tables, a couple of bottles of champagne resting in ice coolers beside it. After calling her guests, she had hovered, ready to greet them with a glass of bubbly, conscious that each and every moment was a video and review opportunity. She didn't want to give the influencers the slightest chance to produce anything negative.

While Roxy waited, she wondered if they had *already* made any less than favorable content for their Instagram accounts. She had an overwhelming temptation to whip out her own phone and check, but she resisted. It wouldn't look very professional if the influencers sauntered in ready for the finest New Orleans had to offer and found her glued to her phone like a teenager so it stayed in her little glittery cross-body bag, firmly on silent.

Sam arrived first. He brought his saxophone with him and looked suave and sophisticated in a gray tux. "Hi, Rox," he said, setting his sax at the back of the room behind one of the luxurious couches. "Everything ready?" His eyes were lit up with excitement on Roxy's behalf.

"I hope so!" Roxy said. "I'm a bit nervous. Their arrival wasn't entirely without a hitch, but I think the meal will go well."

"You'll be absolutely fine. You'll do great, in fact. You've worked so hard on this place and..."

"With *your* help," Roxy interrupted. She knew she'd landed on her feet thanks to Sam and Evangeline and felt a little guilty about it, though she didn't quite know why.

"It's been an absolute privilege to help," Sam said firmly in his lovely low voice. "I didn't want to see this place turned over to a developer, torn down, and turned into shiny new apartments any more than you did. This is my heritage. Yours now too."

"I know," Roxy said. "But thank you all the same."

"You're welcome. Now I won't hear any more about it," he said briskly. He bent over the ice bucket containing the champagne. "May I pour you a glass, Ms. Luxury Hotel Manager?"

Roxy laughed. "Please do. Though I won't have much, or I'll be spilling my secrets to the world via Instagram video."

"Ha!" Sam said. "The deep dark secrets of Roxy Reinhardt. Are you part of a criminal underworld?"

"Busted," Roxy said with a smile, taking the glass of champagne from him. "Don't blow my cover now. Or I'll have you..." She raised her eyebrows, and her glass, in a meaningful way, "dealt with."

"Ooh hoo!" Sam said. "That's me told." They stared at one another over their champagne for just a little longer than necessary before a door closing behind them eased the tension.

Sage and Elijah had arrived. Sage, as ever, looked like something from another world. She'd dusted her cheekbones with silver glitter that shimmered in the lamplight, and she had a wreath of silver and deep pink flowers on her head. Magenta robes flowed loosely around her frame and brushed the ground. Silver sandals peeked out from beneath.

"Looking like a dream as always!" Roxy said to her, giving Sage a kiss on the cheek.

Sage gave a humble little bow and said, "May the golden light of blessings engulf you." Being engulfed, even with blessings, seemed rather overwhelming to Roxy, but she was quite certain Sage's intentions were kind.

With Sage came Elijah. He strode into the hotel in a dark purple suit and bright white shiny shoes with gold flecks. A black shirt with a gold bow tie completed his look. His reputation for flamboyant outfits wouldn't suffer that night.

"Hey, hey, hey, it's crunch time!" Elijah said, which didn't help to calm Roxy's nerves in the least. "Time to let the *Funky Cat* spread its wings and fly!"

"Cats fly now, do they?" Sam said.

"In some mediums," said Sage, gravely. She was a vegetarian and loved animals. Her expertise in the spiritual realm gave her an otherworldly view of them. "On the human plane, cats' wings are clipped." She put her hand to her chest like she was in pain, feeling the cruelty toward the felines in her own heart. "But they do fly. In the astral sphere, they are free."

The others stared back at her astonished as she looked at them seriously before bursting into giggles, clutching her chest.

"You should see your faces!" she said. "I am kidding! Well, mostly." She winked at them.

"I don't know when you're kidding or serious, darling," Elijah said to her. "It's all weird and fantastic to me." He turned to Roxy, kissing her on both cheeks. "Did you get those pastries I sent over? They are specially for the influencers."

"Yep, I guessed."

Elijah had made custom cupcakes for each of the guests. Each one was decorated with the Instagram logo and the guest's name. "They look fantastic and adorable, Elijah. Thank you. Nat will deliver them to the guests' rooms along with a personalized thermos of brandy milk punch while they're eating so it's a nice surprise for them after their meal, like a sort of nightcap."

"Marvelous. You think of the finest of touches, girl-friend," Elijah said.

Before long, Roxy's important guests trickled in. Michael and Dash didn't really *do* the whole tux thing, but they came down in linen suits and snappy dark brown leather shoes. Ada, the Nigerian socialite, was absolutely stunning in a long white gown that made her skin look richer than ever. It hugged her slim body, and she looked like a million bucks. Sylvia, the influencer from Maine, looked smart in a navy blue pantsuit and Mary Janes, while Lily, the tall, slightly haughty influencer who was staying in the penthouse suite, wore a little cocktail dress in pink. It was her favorite color. Her Instagram profile was awash with it.

Roxy had decided that all her friends would sit down to dinner with the influencers, just as they often did with her guests. This mingling of friends and visitors had been a part of the tradition of the hotel when it was *Evange-line's*. It created a warm, homey atmosphere. Elijah was always on hand with a joke, and Sam could be relied on to charm the guests and provide great conversation. Sage exuded goodwill toward others and might read their fortunes, while Nat could be great fun under the right circumstances. She had been known to burst into glorious song after dinner and would take requests if she was in a particularly good mood. It was true that Evangeline wasn't the most sociable of people, she certainly wasn't a party animal or a social butterfly, but she could talk at length about New Orleans and would introduce the guests to all sorts of hidden attractions they would not have otherwise discovered. Roxy, of course, would be the consummate host.

CHAPTER SIX

AFTER CHAMPAGNE, THE influencers, Roxy, and her friends sat down at the table. Roxy had suggested offering canapés, but Evangeline had said she wasn't a fan of all that "newfangled, posh fiddly stuff." She preferred serving a good, hearty New Orleans dinner that didn't come with any fussy, fancy crudités or appetizers. Instead, the meal began with gumbo.

Normally Evangeline would have made it thick and filling, but since they were having so many courses, they had decided a lighter version would be more appropriate. Naturally, the influencers got out their phones and began to snap pictures before they tucked in. Lily Vashchenko even arranged the napkin and cutlery in a delicate arrangement next to her bowl and angled the picture so that she got some of the lounge décors in the frame. Roxy was sure it would look impressive and made a mental note to check the post on Instagram later.

After the flurry of clicking and updating of statuses had been completed, the influencers settled down to eat, all of them seeming to enjoy the gumbo a great deal. They made the right noises, even Ada, and they all complimented Evangeline. After that, they moved on to the crawfish and cheese pie course where the frenzy of picture composition and status updating started all over again.

Roxy watched them, fascinated, and wondered how animated and raucous the night was going to get. Dash, in particular, seemed to be enjoying himself. There was plenty of wine on the table, and she noticed how he repeatedly filled up his glass with one of the reds from a local Louisiana winery.

"You really should drink white wine, you know," Ada said, sniffing, "since we're having so much fish."

"Meh," Dash said with a shrug. "I don't really like white, to be honest. I'm more of a red-blooded man," he winked, "if you know what I mean."

Ada looked down her nose at him.

"You go ahead with your red," Sylvia said kindly, then chuckled. "Live on the wild side!" She had barely touched her glass of white, and her champagne flute from earlier sat next to it, still half full.

"Wine messes with my palate." Ada sipped her water with pursed lips. "I wouldn't drink such cheap wine anyway." At that, Roxy had to hold her tongue. It wasn't a cheap wine! She'd taken a deep breath and splurged out on bottles that cost over $100 each. They were drinking some of the best wine produced in Louisiana. But Roxy guessed Ada was used to everything being super high-end luxury. Roxy had heard Ada mention her father's private jet as she chatted to Lily when they were drinking their champagne before the meal.

Roxy had grown up with her single mother in a poor,

rural area in Ohio. She had never met her father. She didn't even know his name. So while drinking $100 bottles of wine in a boutique hotel might be a step down for Ada, it was an entire staircase *up* for Roxy, a life which, when she was younger, she never imagined living. People in the neighborhood where she was raised were doing well if they had a steady job, even if it was bagging at the local grocery store for minimum wage. As long as they could buy their own food and they had roofs over their heads, even if it was a trailer roof, they were relieved if not exactly content. Roxy imagined Ada walking through her old neighborhood, sniffing at the trailers and the children who played outside, some of whom had holes in their shoes. Their separate experiences of the world were completely different. But that didn't matter now. Roxy was aware of her responsibility to her guests, her staff, and the wider community. They all depended upon the *Funky Cat* being a success. Roxy shook her head to bring herself back to the present.

Next came the main course, Shrimp Creole with rice and jalapeño cornbread. It was Roxy's absolute favorite. Lily Vashchenko languidly snapped pictures of the "cute little ramekins," taking a flower from one of the vases on the table to place it in her picture while everyone raved about the shrimp.

"Fabulous food, Nat, Roxy!" Sylvia said.

Even though Evangeline had done most of the work, the elderly woman kept quiet with a secret smile on her face, knowing that she was passing the glory of Creole and Cajun cooking onto the next generation. Roxy was extremely proud and glad that she was keeping this grand old tradition alive and was inordinately grateful to Evangeline for taking the time to teach them her recipes.

"Credit where it's due. This is all thanks to Evangeline," Nat said modestly.

Dash paused, his fork loaded. "Evangeline is a lovely name," he said. "Where does it come from?"

"It's Greek, right?" Michael began before Evangeline could even open her mouth.

Evangeline winked and said, "You're right about that, cher. You've done your research. It means 'bearer of good news' so your luck might be in." She looked at Dash and smiled. "Your name's not that common. What does it mean? Apart from the obvious, of course."

"It's short for Dashiell," he said. "It's Scottish. Apparently, my ancestors came from the highest Highlands of Scotland, which probably means they were raving mad murderous warriors back in the thirteenth century or something. The name doesn't mean anything as far as I am aware, at least nothing exciting."

Nat laughed. "It does suit you, though! You're always dashing around the place. You're going to India one day, Canada the next! You dash all around the world. I'd love to do that!"

Dash leaned forward, his eyes bright with excitement. "So why don't you?" he said in an encouraging voice. "I love experiencing different cultures, different types of people. And when I make a load more money from this Instagram and YouTube business, I want to *help people*. Build schools and hospitals. I can't wait!" He breathed out, his eyes gleaming with visions of his dreams. "I think you should travel the world, Nat. It would give you a totally new perspective."

Nat looked a little awkward and mumbled something about New Orleans feeling like home before dashing from the table to serve dessert.

"This is a lot of food," Lily said, exhaling discreetly through full, pouting lips. "I can barely take another bite." Lily had only been nibbling at her food, a bite here, a taste there. Roxy supposed that was how she maintained her lithe figure.

"It's certainly very filling," Michael agreed, as Dash snapped away, taking a picture of the warm bread pudding soaked with caramel and whiskey. Soft, slightly melted vanilla ice cream made waves through the brown sauce making it look delicious and lush. It smelled heavenly, and Roxy knew from experience it tasted even better.

Nevertheless, after all the snapping and posing and updating and submitting was over, they all, perhaps with the exception of Lily, fell on the pudding, silence pervading the room as they focused on the delicious dessert.

"Mmmm, this is slipping down a treat," Sylvia said.

"We have cheese next," Nat reminded them.

Michael took the camera from Dash and pointed it at him.

"Cheese? This is CRAZY," Dash said into the camera. "Five courses...five! That's how you know this is a real luxury place. You know, the local wine is really great too." He raised his wine glass a little wildly and then lowered it to take a sip as he leaned into the camera. But as he did so, he knocked his chin against the glass.

"Dash!" Michael said, but it was too late. The damage was done. Dash's red wine had launched itself all over Ada Okafor's pristine white gown.

CHAPTER SEVEN

"OH, MY GOODNESS!" Ada shrieked, jumping to her feet. The front of her white dress was stained with so much red wine it looked like she'd been stabbed.

"Oh, oh, oh," Roxy said, rushing over to her.

"Noooooo!" Dash said, his eyes bulging with horror. "I'm so, so sorry, Ada!"

Elijah leaned over, "Never fear, Elijah is here." He started patting the stain with his napkin.

"Get your hands off me!" Ada screamed. Elijah snapped his hand back like a slapped child.

Sage didn't make a move, but closed her eyes and placed her hands, palms upwards, her fingertips touching. She was an oasis of calm in an uproarious sea.

"Dash! You fool!" said Michael. He was still recording.

Evangeline, shaking her head like a disapproving grandmother, put her arm around Ada. "Come on, cher, no real harm done, let's get you cleaned up."

But Ada wriggled away. "You get *off* of me too!" She radiated fury. "How dare you! This is *a Versace!*" she shouted at Dash. "Do you know who I am? My father..."

"Sorry to interrupt!" Sam hollered over her. "But trust me, you need to act fast on that stain. I'm a laundry guy, and I know what I'm talking about." They all swiveled their horrified gazes from Ada to Sam. "You'll have to take your dress off and pour white wine over it fast. I'll run to the laundry and get some proper stain remover. We can save your dress, but only if we move very quickly." Sam dashed to the door and disappeared.

"Finally, someone who speaks sense," Ada said, recovering some of her composure. She stood and began to strip down to her underwear in the middle of the dining room.

Roxy's eyes widened. "Let me get you a robe!" she called over and rushed to her bedroom to fetch one.

Dash still looked horrified at what he'd done. He leaned back in his chair, his hands clasped across the top of his head. His partner, Michael, was deadpan as he recorded surreptitiously, the camera resting on the table, the shining red "record" button the only sign that it was on.

When Roxy hurried back, Nat, her eyes transfixed by the sight of Ada standing in the middle of the dining room in her underwear, was pressing her lips together so tightly they were white. Her throat was bobbing up and down. She was clearly trying not to laugh.

"Oh, so it's funny, is it?" Ada said to Nat.

"The Universe has its little jokes with us sometimes, in this realm of chaos," Sage said. Her low, soft voice could make any words sound soothing, but Ada looked at her like she had two heads.

Roxy offered her robe to the Nigerian woman who immediately swiped it from her, handing Roxy her red-stained dress in exchange. Roxy took it and glared at Nat, "Come with me into the kitchen to fix this up." Nat didn't respond immediately. "Nat!"

But Nat didn't move fast enough, so Roxy grabbed her by the wrist, pulling her into the kitchen. She shut the door behind them. "What are you playing at?" she hissed while finding some white wine to douse the dress with. "Don't you know this is all going on the Internet? This could ruin us! Why are you grinning?"

"What?" said Nat, smiling. Roxy couldn't remember the last time she felt so angry. Then Nat sighed. "Oh... okay, I see what you mean. Sorry, it was just a teentsy-weentsy bit funny. She just stood in the mid..." Nat looked like she was about to burst into a fit of giggles again.

"Stop it! You're jeopardizing everything!" Roxy hissed, still furious, and, if she were honest, scared to death at what this debacle might mean for her business. "It's bad enough that this has happened, but you're staff! You can't laugh at her!"

"I didn't actually laugh!" Nat protested.

"Near enough. Look, pull yourself together. I know you don't like her, but still."

Nat stifled her giggles, "You're right. I'm sorry. How can I help?"

Just then, Ada burst through the kitchen door. She was quite a sight. Her eyes were wild and her shiny high heels and Roxy's robe made an unconventional fashion statement. "How's it going?" she growled, her arms outstretched, her hands curled like claws in front of her.

She dropped them the moment she noticed Nat, folded her arms and pursed her lips. "Not that *you* care."

"I'll just go clean the wine from the floor," Nat mumbled. She left the kitchen, avoiding Ada's withering look.

"I think your dress is doing okay so far," Roxy said to Ada. The white wine was spreading over the red stain and seemed to be neutralizing it. There was still some discoloration though, a light pink. "I just hope Sam comes back quickly."

"He'd better," Ada said. "I don't know what you're thinking, bringing that Dash prankster person here. Who does he think he is? You need to ask him to leave. In fact, my whole visit here has been a poor one. No one to greet me, no personal service. Are you sure you know what you're doing?"

A lump formed in Roxy's throat while butterflies chaotically danced in her belly. At that moment she felt she *was* in over her head, just like she'd feared in her least confident moments. And now she was in a bind. If she asked Dash to leave per Ada's request, surely it would be some huge scandal that Michael & Dash would milk for all they were worth, probably for months, on their social media accounts. It might ruin her business. But if she let him stay, what would Ada do? Ada had huge influence among affluent tourists—especially in the African and Middle Eastern markets—who were looking for luxury experiences and Roxy was quite sure Ada had the power to generate a negative buzz. Perhaps they would all turn on her and destroy everything she'd worked for. She blew out her cheeks. At least it would be over quickly.

She didn't know what to say to Ada. She was in a no-win situation. So she smiled brightly. "Let's hope Sam hurries up; we need to save this dress!" she said. "It must have cost a ton."

"It's not about the cost. It's *never* about the cost," Ada snapped. She even stamped her foot on the tiled kitchen floor. "This is a Versace *limited edition*."

CHAPTER EIGHT

"**O**H," ROXY SAID. She didn't even know it was possible to have a limited edition Versace dress. She looked up to the ceiling and down to the floor. Her thoughts started to run, and they followed a familiar theme. Had there been a time in her life when she felt more inadequate? Her owning and running a business had happened so quickly. It had skyrocketed out of nowhere, in fact. And now she wondered how she'd gotten here. It had been too easy. She didn't deserve it. Evangeline and Sam must have made a mistake. The *universe* itself had made a mistake, surely. And now it was self-correcting. Good things like running the *Funky Cat* didn't happen to people like her.

"When is that big buffoon going to return?" Ada said impatiently, her eyebrows knitted together, her eyes cold and hard.

"He's *not* a buffoon," Roxy shot back without thinking. "He's a very kind, capable, strong man, and one of our dearest friends."

Ada's expression didn't change.

"*And* he drives a Rolls Royce Phantom." Roxy didn't particularly care about that, but she knew Ada would. It wasn't her finest moment, but she hated to hear Ada talk badly and without reason about Sam. It made her feel a little better to defend him.

"Really?" Ada said, perking up before relaxing and looking nonchalant. "I rode around in one before I was five. It was my father's driver's favorite car in our fleet."

"Sam's is a limited edition with maroon paint. So, you see, you two have something in common—limited editions."

"Oh." Ada nodded. "Well, that sounds nice." She offered Roxy a small smile.

Roxy smiled back, bemused at how something so inconsequential to her made such a difference to Ada. "Oh, look," she said, pointing at the dress, "it's looking pretty good now."

Ada ran her perfectly-manicured hands over the surface. "I can still see some staining."

Sam came through the door then, panting, clutching a stain-remover pen and a spray can. "I've got what I need. Let's get this fixed."

There was a rapt silence as the two women watched him work. They both looked on intently. For obvious but different reasons, Roxy and Ada *really* wanted the stain remover to work and as if by magic, it did. After a few minutes of application, the stain completely disappeared.

Ada burst into a grin and threw her arms around Sam's neck. "Oh, thank you! You are the only decent person here!"

Roxy felt an unexpected pang of jealousy course through her, closely followed by anger laced with relief. Heat rushed to her cheeks. When she'd taken on the *Funky Cat*, she'd decided that, despite feeling *something* for Sam, she was going to keep their friendship strictly platonic. She didn't want to mix business with pleasure. She wanted to keep things just as they were, one big, happy *Funky Cat* family. But she still didn't like this over-familiarity Ada was showing Sam. It ruffled her. And she didn't appreciate her comment about him being the sole arbiter of decency. They were *all* bending over backward to help *her* if only she'd notice.

Sam gave Ada an awkward pat on the back and extricated himself from her hug. "You're welcome."

"So," Ada said, smiling up at him. "I hear you have a limited edition Rolls Royce Phantom?"

"Oh, that?" he said quickly. "That's just my guilty pleasure. Shall we go back into the dining room and finish our meal?"

"So what do you do?" Ada asked, taking his arm and leaning into him. "It's so good to finally meet someone of my standing here. I'm medically trained, at Oxford University in England, but I don't practice. My father persuaded me that I was more suited for the limelight."

"Oh, right," Sam said. He sounded genuinely interested. "I took the opposite route. I studied business at Stanford. My dad wanted me to become an investment banker in New York, but I preferred the idea of a lower profile life and came back here, my home town, to start my laundry business."

Ada laughed. "And the rest. A hometown boy with a Rolls Royce? My, what did you do? Rob a bank?"

Sam laughed and got that awkward look he always did when the subject of his money came up. "Absolutely! Don't hand me in, now, Ms. Okafor!" He clapped his hands and looked at Roxy. "Right! What's next on the menu?"

Roxy's head was all awhirl, what with the red wine mishap, the complicated emotions that she was trying not to feel, *and* the new information about Sam she was learning. "Um..."

Evangeline rescued her by coming into the kitchen. "Time for the cheese course now," she said. "Come on, Nat."

Nat came in after her. She wouldn't make eye contact with Roxy or Ada. As Evangeline, carrying the cheese boards, followed Sam, Roxy, and Ada back out into the dining room, Nat took Elijah's personalized cupcakes from the fridge and quietly began to boil some milk.

After the cheese course, they had planned for music with Nat singing, Elijah on the piano, and Sam playing sax. Sage had offered to do tarot readings. But Roxy's energy was waning, as was everyone's, it seemed, worn out by the drama of earlier. Ada was still in her robe, her dress forgotten as she focused on Sam.

"Let's do jazz and spirits another night," Evangeline suggested. "There's always time for music and magic in New Orleans."

There was a murmur of agreement and everyone dispersed for the night. After checking that everything was locked up and safe, Roxy went to her room. She changed quickly and snuggled up with Nefertiti. The day had been so overwhelming.

"Oh, Nef-nef," she said quietly into her kitty's velvety ears. "Can I really do this properly? I was just beginning to believe that I could. Is everything just going to fall apart like it always does?"

Nefertiti looked up at her and purred. Roxy shook her

head sadly. "You're just a cat. You don't even care, do you? As long as I feed you and stroke you, that's all you're concerned about." Roxy looked into the cat's deep blue eyes and at her squashed-up little nose. She felt a wave of shame wash over her. She was being mean to her cat. Roxy hugged Nefertiti to her even closer. "Sorry, Nef. I just don't know what's up and what's down right now." Roxy sighed and closed her eyes. She soon slipped into a deep sleep and dreamed of dancing wine glasses and disembodied white dresses that swooped around her like ghosts at a disco.

CHAPTER NINE

"**G**OOD MORNING, NEFFI!**"** Roxy stretched her arms over her head. She felt a lot better. She had woken early and taken a long, hot shower, scrubbing away the dress drama of the night before. She did not look at Instagram to see how the incident had been portrayed there, preferring to think good thoughts and hope that everything would turn out okay in the end.

Roxy knew that even if dinner had been overshadowed by events, at least breakfast was likely to be sedate and special in real New Orleans style. They'd have beignets, of course, and café au lait and Evangeline had promised calas and couche-couche too. Calas were a type of deep-fried dumpling made from rice, egg, flour, and sugar. They were so tasty that Roxy dared not eat even one. She knew from experience that if she did, she'd scoff the whole plate. Couche-couche was Evangeline's favorite. It was made of fried cornmeal and eggs, milk, raisins, tons of syrup, often a dash of liquor too. Roxy imagined all the beautifully curated Instagram pics of the influencers' breakfasts beaming out to their followers across the world. She smiled to herself.

"Oh my gosh! Have you seen Instagram?" Nat cried out as soon as Roxy burst into the kitchen.

"No, why? What's going on?" Roxy's heart started to beat fast.

"It's gone viral!" said Nat.

"What?" Evangeline said from her place in front of the pot. "Them people have a virus? And I breathed the same air last night?" She wrinkled her nose and pursed her lips.

"Evangeline, you *know* what it means, I've told you before. Sage told you too. It means something's spreading fast online, just *like* a virus." Nat was abrupt.

Evangeline shook her head. "Whatever you say, cher. It's all too much for an ol' chick like me."

"It wouldn't be if you just *applied* yourself," Nat said with a sigh.

"I don't want to *apply* myself, Miss Natalie," Evangeline said, a little testy now. "I'm fine just as I am, thank you very much."

Nat rolled her eyes and turned back to Roxy. "Anyway, you know, Dash spilling wine over Ada. I mean, it *had* to go viral! They're some of the biggest influencers online, and they're having a spat! The fans are going *crazy* about it. Ada's fans are messaging Michael and Dash, threatening them with legal action and all sorts!"

"Wow," said Roxy, unsure what to think and a little confused before a feeling of dread spread over her. It was like being draped in a wet coat. Nat, on the other hand, judging by her bright eyes and excited voice, made it sound like a good thing. "I mean, I thought there would be more death threats," she continued, "but Ada's crowd are the type that sends the lawyer over to deal with their problems."

"What are Michael and Dash's fans saying?" Roxy asked. She was starting to tremble.

Nat was looking at her phone, scrolling through comments. "Some of them are saying that it was an accident while others think it was done on purpose. Even more think it's hilarious. And in all honesty, I'm inclined to agree!"

Roxy felt the anger of the night before resurfacing. "Are you crazy, Nat? Don't you realize how serious this all is?"

Nat shrugged, still looking down at her screen. "What is with you? Why do you always take life so seriously? This is great! We're getting so much publicity! And you know what they say about publicity."

"I don't want *negative* publicity," Roxy said carefully, keeping her voice even. "I want to earn a professional reputation. And right now, that is not happening."

"Professional?" Nat said. "You invited Michael and Dash for goodness sake. Didn't you know things would get wild?"

Roxy had let Sage take care of setting up the influencer campaign and had taken only a cursory look at each profile before agreeing. Now, she berated herself for not paying more attention and thinking through the implications of the campaign more carefully. At the time she'd been swept up in the excitement of the idea.

"I didn't expect it to be this wild, and even so," Roxy said, "*you* need to stay professional and not be disrespectful about the guests behind their backs, or in front of them for that matter. You've made an enemy of Ada."

"Good, because I don't like her either." Nat folded her arms, thrust out her chin and tapped her foot in defiance.

"Nat, please! You're acting like a child. Come on, Evangeline, back me up!"

"Leave me out of it!" said Evangeline. "I don't work here anymore, and I certainly don't fix workplace arguments. I'm just a hired cook, that's all, cher. But aside from that, Nat, you should listen to your boss. You're bein' insubordinate, and she's talkin' truth."

Nat shook her head as she scrolled through the influencers' posts once more and sighed. "I suppose you're right. Roxy, I'm sorry. I will be extra nice to Ada at breakfast, I promise."

Roxy's thoughts wandered for a moment. She found herself thinking again about how ill-qualified she was to run a hotel and on top of that, now she was arguing with her staff. What kind of employer did that make her?

CHAPTER TEN

C ATCHING HERSELF, ROXY quickly put all her negative thoughts to one side and decided to focus on what had to be done. It would be no good for her to be angry when the guests came downstairs. She wanted to be sunny and welcoming and represent the warmth and hospitality of New Orleans. Nausea, though, churned in her stomach. The influencer campaign was starting to become something of a disaster.

At that moment, Elijah walked in. He flounced through the swinging kitchen door holding a big white box aloft in one hand as he always did. He was delivering the first batch of pastries of the day. They would be still warm from the oven. "Here we are, my darlings. Beignets for your VIPs. Tell me, have you seen Insta this morning? My, my, those followers are *crazy*."

"Argghh, not you too, Elijah! Can't you see what this could mean for my business? We're being associated with a major social media event, a *negative* social media event. That is not the kind of publicity I had in mind when I decided to do this promotion," Roxy said.

Elijah had the decency to look abashed. "Yes, you're right," he said, more gently than she'd ever heard him. "I wouldn't like it if it were my business caught in the eye of this particular storm. It'll all blow over though, I'm sure." Elijah kissed the back of her head as he left to return to his bakery across the alleyway.

Straightening her shoulders but feeling rather abandoned and alone, Roxy took out the beignets in Elijah's box and silently arranged them in pyramids on serving platters. She took them through to the dining area and placed them on the serving table. In the empty room, Roxy checked that the coffee machine was switched on and ready, and she got out the brandy and milk and some whipping cream so her guests could garnish their coffee in true Creole style. As she looked up, she saw Ada coming down the stairs.

Ada wore a floating sundress the color of the sky and had even painted her nails to match. Roxy brought the plate of beignets over to her. "I'm so sorry about what happened last night," she said to Ada. "It was very unfortunate. How are you feeling?"

"Okay," said Ada, though she didn't sound entirely convincing. There was a hard edge to her voice, and she didn't smile. "Once you get that horrible man out of here, I will be absolutely fine. Don't worry, I won't hold you responsible for the incident. *He*, on the other hand, will be speaking to my lawyers. My father will retain the best legal team that money can buy, I can assure you of that.

"Well, I'm glad you're feeling better," Roxy said as Ada sat at the table and started to scroll through her phone. Inside, Roxy was all abuzz with nervousness. She had hoped a good night's sleep would encourage Ada to change her mind about making Dash leave. "Would you like some coffee?"

Ada didn't look up from her phone. "Actually, I'd like some of that punch we had yesterday. Please make me..."

Ada was interrupted by a scream and the sound of a wall being thumped. Steps pounded on the stairs and Michael rushed into the dining area. He was wild-eyed and frantic. He wore only his pajama pants. His hair was standing up on end, and for once, he carried no camera. "Quick, quick! Come quick! Somebody, anybody, quickly!" He gesticulated wildly, his voice rising with increasing frustration—no one was moving fast enough for him.

Roxy jumped away from the table and followed him as he streaked back into the hallway and up the stairs. "What's going on?" she said, feeling her breath catch in her throat.

"It's Dash! It's Dash!" Michael said. "I think...I think..." He led her into a bedroom and pointed at Dash. Michael backed into a corner of the room. He was shaking, clutching his own arms and rubbing them up and down as if it were the middle of winter, not the middle of June. It seemed to Roxy that the temperature in the room had turned icy and time had stopped. Dash was lying on his back in the bed, his skin eerily white against his red hair. "Is he...Is he...Is he...?" Michael couldn't bring himself to say the word.

Roxy inched forward slowly, her limbs weighed down by dread. She knew the answer to Michael's question before she even reached out to touch Dash, but she just couldn't make herself believe it. "No, no, no," she whispered under her breath. She touched Dash's arm with a brush of her fingertips. It was cold.

"How...how could this happen?" said Michael, but Roxy couldn't answer him. Her voice had deserted her. All she could do was stare at Dash. Was she still asleep, and this was some kind of nightmare? Blood rushed through her ears.

Moments later, everyone in the hotel arrived, drawn by the sound of Michael's cries. Ada shrieked. Lily turned ashen. Sylvia gasped. Nat pressed her palm across her mouth. Even Elijah, alerted by the noise that he could hear across in his bakery, arrived at the entrance to Dash's room and put his palm to his forehead in horror. Everyone was shocked to the bone.

Only Evangeline had the presence of mind to act. She stood, grimly silent until, with her voice quiet and level, she said, "I think we better call Johnson."

CHAPTER ELEVEN

DETECTIVE JOHNSON LOOKED ready to burst with rage. He was an intimidating presence at the best of times, but when he arrived at the *Funky Cat* just minutes after Evangeline had phoned him, his large body was so taut that it looked as though his muscles might snap at any moment.

They had closed the door to the room where Dash's body lay. No one could bear to look at him, and they congregated in the upstairs hallway in a silent huddle. Michael had stopped crying and was pacing back and forth, shaking his head. He was almost as white as Dash was. Evangeline and Roxy stood by the window, Roxy staring out of it blankly. Sylvia sat on the stairs with Nat, her arms around Nat's shoulders, while next to them was Elijah. He leaned his elbows on his knees and stared at the floor. Lily was slightly aloof and leaned against the wall a few feet from the others. Even Ada didn't have anything to say.

Johnson exploded up the stairs. "Another death?

What is this? The Doomsday Hotel?" he raged. "This *cannot* be real."

Roxy was too stunned to speak, but Evangeline didn't have the same reserve. Her brow furrowing, she spat out, "How can you..."

But Johnson was not in the mood to be interrupted. "This is starting to look very suspicious, Ms. Evangeline, Ms. Reinhardt. Very suspicious indeed. This is the second dead body found in or around your hotel in the space of a few months. Is there something going on here that I should know about?"

A small wave of energy rippled through the group of influencers for whom reports of an earlier death was news. No one said anything, but a look here, a shift in posture there, indicated they had heard what Johnson had said and taken note. Roxy couldn't believe the audacity of the man. He was trash-talking her business in front of guests, *her* guests, the people essential to the business' success. Even for him, it was a new low.

In the past, in the face of such hostility and humiliation, she would have cowered and willed herself to disappear, but this was the *new Roxy*. Outraged, she drew herself up to her full height, which wasn't too tall in truth but was the best she could do. "Detective," she said sternly. "This is Michael, Dashiell Davies' best friend and business partner. It was Michael who found Dash's body. What do you have to say about that?"

Michael turned to the detective and stared him down with a look so penetrating it would have pierced right through anyone else. But Johnson was unfazed. "Humph. I'm sorry for your loss, but it's not my job to be your therapist," he said. "It's my job to investigate, and if there are suspicious circumstances, to find out who did this and bring them to justice." Michael looked away and closed his eyes. Unperturbed, Johnson continued, "The next step is to secure the crime scene and get forensic evidence. I will be interviewing y'all personally." He stared at Roxy and squinted. "Especially you. Don't you think it's a coincidence that all of these deaths started happening when you rocked up in town?"

"That's so unfair!" Nat burst out. Roxy was touched that Nat was sticking up for her. Nat's expired visa and her questionable immigration status meant that she usually tried to fade into the background whenever the police were around. "Of course this has nothing to do with Roxy!" Nat continued. "Why would it? She's just trying to live her life and run this hotel the best she can."

"A touching, if irrelevant, story," Johnson said.

But Nat wasn't to be dismissed. "This is a very serious situation and very stressful for our business. We would appreciate it if you didn't go around accusing us at every given opportunity!"

"Look, do you think we can focus on what's *important* here? Like the fact that my friend and business partner is lying *dead* in his bed!" Michael cried. Chastened, Nat looked down at her feet. Not chastened at all, Johnson ignored him.

"So where's the body?" he asked. Roxy pointed to the bedroom door a few feet away. "Okay, everyone," he continued. "Go downstairs and get ready for questioning. I am going to bring the forensics team in now. None of you must be in this area." They all waited for what he would say next, and he glared back at them as if they were idiots. "Well, go on then. Get a move on!" Obediently, they all trooped downstairs. All, that is, except Roxy and Ada.

Ada faced Johnson squarely and put her perfectly manicured hand on her hip. "There's no way I am going down there without changing into something more appropriate." She gestured down at her blue sundress. "This is not a suitable thing to wear after a death."

Johnson looked at her as though she were a one-eyed, many-limbed alien. "Excuse me?" he said in a tone that would shut down anyone else.

"My father has links with the Chief of Police and Prosecutions in Nigeria," Ada said. "I will not be told what to do by some provincial, small-town detective."

Roxy felt herself shrink a couple of inches. Johnson's eyes gleamed nastily.

"Ada," Roxy said in a half-warning, half-laughing tone. Was an influencer with a fan base of nearly three-quarters of a million about to be thrown in a New Orleans city police cell? An influencer who was only here because Roxy had invited her? She half-expected Johnson to charge Ada with obstructing a police investigation.

"I think you should stop right there, Miss," Johnson said, side-eyeing Ada and squinting as he assessed the creature before him.

But Ada did not stop. "I think you are a bad boy," she said, wagging her finger at him, "a very bad boy, throwing your weight around and accusing people. I know your kind. My father was targeted by your types when he became successful in business. His competitors wanted him out, but we Okafors do not bow to such pressure. There is nothing wrong with me going upstairs and changing my clothes. Or do you think that I might grab my Gucci handbag and kill someone on the way down? Or hide evidence in my Louis Vuitton carry-on? Types like you are absolutely ridiculous. Surely, if you let me go upstairs to change, that is not too much to ask? I will be back down within five minutes."

Johnson raised his chin. Ada's finger was still extended. They were like two bulls in a standoff. For a moment, there was a tense silence. They glared at each other.

Johnson blinked first. "Do whatever you want," he growled. "I don't have time for this."

Ada's eyelashes quivered on hearing these words. She turned to float upstairs like a queen ascending a grand staircase, her head held high, dignified and victorious. Roxy's jaw almost dropped to the floor. It seemed the detective had met his match!

CHAPTER TWELVE

J OHNSON'S EXPRESSION WAS impassive, but as he tore his eyes away from Ada, he noticed that Roxy was still there. He gave a little jump, and his face turned an even deeper shade of purple. "What is it now?" he barked.

Roxy gulped but gathered herself to speak. She wanted to sound confident. She still didn't find confrontation easy, but she was getting braver at dealing with it. "I wanted to let you know we're in the middle of an Instagram campaign."

"A what?" he said.

"It's a marketing thing," Roxy explained.

"And what makes you think that interests me in the slightest?" he said. "Move. Go away. I need to enter this room, and I don't want you contaminating evidence."

"I need to let you know that," said Roxy, taking her cue from Ada and holding firm—just, "well, it's that my guests might photograph or video things. The people here are famous to their Instagram tribes. Between them, they have hundreds of thousands of followers. They make their living by producing videos and beautiful images. People watch them online. I wondered if it might interfere with the investigation." Roxy kept her voice even, but it was quivering a little.

Johnson looked incredulous. "Right," he said. "So the crazy modern world has finally infiltrated New Orleans, has it?" He sighed. "Today is a sad day, Ms. Reinhardt." He looked at Roxy disapprovingly as if she were personally responsible for this invasion. "I know nothing of this, and I don't *wish* to know anything of this. Just make sure to tell them that until I say so, there is to be no more photography or video. If they don't comply, they will be charged, and I will slap the handcuffs on them myself."

Roxy felt a shiver go through her. There was something about this man that got under her skin and made her want to run away as fast as possible in the other direction.

"Okay," she said. She managed to manufacture a smile. "I'll go and tell them now."

When she got downstairs, everyone except Michael was nibbling on beignets and sipping the brandy milk punch that Evangeline had made "for the shock."

"I can't believe that guy!" Nat said when she saw Roxy. "Who *does* he think he is? Why *does* he have to be so rude?"

"Will you pipe down, cher?" said Evangeline. "He's just doin' his job."

"No, I will not *pipe down*," Nat shot back. "Anyway, I don't see why you're defending him. He's not exactly your greatest fan, is he?"

Evangeline sipped her punch and let out a deep long sigh.

"Johnson says that nobody is to record. No pictures, no video," said Roxy to the room.

Michael looked up from where he sat curled silently in an armchair. "How dare he," he said, quiet and deadly. "He can't tell us what we can and can't do in the wake of a tragedy. In any case, it's too late. I was recording an Instagram video when I went into Dash's room. The whole world knows about it already."

Roxy took a second to register Michael's comment before the full implications of what he was saying hit her. She put her hands to her head. "No, no, no," she whispered. If it weren't for the guests on every side of her, she would have crawled into a fetal position and rocked back and forth at this news. When she had considered the wisdom of the influencer campaign, the worst she imagined was a few bad reviews. She never considered the possibility that an unexplained death would be beamed from her hotel live across the whole planet.

Just then, there was a series of knocks at the door that turned into a rain of hammer blows. Roxy practically jumped out of her skin. She flinched so hard that she elbowed Evangeline, who was standing next to her causing her to spill her punch on the floor.

"Oh sorry, sorry," Roxy said. "Who could that be?"

"It's probably the forensic team," said Lily. She looked coolly at Roxy. "Would you like me to answer?"

"No, no," said Roxy. "It's my responsibility." She felt like she was living a nightmare: an influencer dying in her hotel that was full of other influencers recording everything as a testimony. And she'd thought the Versace dress incident was bad enough.

Roxy walked into the hallway and with a sharp exhale opened the door. She expected to see people in white suits standing on the step with bags full of investigating equipment. Instead, the scene that greeted her when she swung open the heavy wooden door was far worse than that.

"Arghh!" She was blinded by a flash. Then another flash, then another. *Flash, flash, flash!*

"Roxy Reinhardt?" a woman shouted. A microphone was shoved into Roxy's face. A crowd of other men and women—all waving phones, cameras, notepads, pens, or microphones—pushed and jostled in front of her.

"Uh... yes?" she said, blinking. Roxy turned her head to protect her eyes from a flash only to be assailed by another. She was so stunned she couldn't move. She stood on the doorstep of the *Funky Cat Inn* protecting her eyes with her hand and noiselessly opening and closing her mouth like a goldfish as the frenzy in front of her refused to abate.

Suddenly, Roxy was grabbed from behind and pulled back into the hallway. Nat slammed the door shut and pressed her back against it for good measure. Only then did Elijah loosen his tight grip on Roxy's shoulders.

"Reporters!" Roxy cried. A couple of angry tears streamed down her face. She wiped them away furiously. "This is too much!"

Evangeline joined them. She shook her head. "No time for tears and shoutin', cher," she said. "We've got to make sure those reporters don't start puttin' cameras at the windows. You know they're goin' to be lookin' in from every angle.

"She's right, Roxy," Elijah said. "This is the hottest story out there right now, and I guarantee it's only going to get worse. My brother worked for a politician caught in a scandal and what those reporters will do for a story would make your short li'l blonde locks curl."

"But how can that be?" said Roxy. "We found him dead barely ten minutes ago."

"It was live on Instagram," said Nat. "This is a huge story."

"One that's only goin' to get bigger," said Evangeline. "A virus, isn't that what you called it? The news will spread like wildfire. He was a celebrity of sorts, right? This isn't gonna go away, cher. You need to face it."

Roxy felt trapped. She could hear the clamor of reporters outside. "But what about when we want to go out?" she said. "What if they push their way in?"

"For now we're stuck inside unless the police decide to help us out on that score." Evangeline threw her eyes up to the ceiling. "And I doubt *that* very much."

Roxy felt sick to her stomach.

Evangeline was not generally a hugging type of person, but now she put her arm around Roxy and patted her shoulder. "None of this is your fault, cher," she said kindly. "Don't be too hard on yourself, and don't get caught up in too many emotions, y'hear? You need to stay strong for the guests and make sure that everyone is okay. The world is watchin'. We can turn this around. Guests remember what you do when there is a problem much more than when everythin' goes well. Lemons to lemonade, cher."

"She's right, Roxy. Give the world an excellent impression of the hotel, despite being at the center of a crisis. You can do it. We've all worked too hard to give up now." Elijah snapped his fingers and sashayed in a tight circle around the lobby, his head rocking from side to side.

As she watched him, Roxy instantly felt better. Evangeline was right. Roxy had read in *The Hotelier,* the #1 industry magazine, that the level of service a hotel provided when a guest had a problem and was upset created the strongest impression. Well, the *Funky Cat* certainly had a problem now and her guests were certainly upset.

Summoning the strength from somewhere, Roxy clapped her hands together with a burst of energy. She was being looked to for leadership. "Let's show them that we can handle a crisis, the *worst* kind of crisis. Come on, people!" She didn't feel quite as confident as she sounded, but she was determined to take another crack at turning the situation around. She was going to take charge. She was going to *do this*.

CHAPTER THIRTEEN

W HILE DETECTIVE JOHNSON
questioned the guests and staff, the forensics team were let in to the hotel and got to
work. Johnson gave the press a stern warning not to come
inside, and almost blocked Sage too, but eventually let her
in. She, together with Nat and Elijah, worked to cover up
the windows with trash bags secured with white strips of
tape. This made Roxy feel sad.

"My gorgeous boutique hotel looks like it's in the
middle of a war zone or in the path of a hurricane that's
about to pass through," she said.

"Yeah, it looks and feels completely and
utterly *wrong*, but it's necessary," Elijah said. When the
chips were down, Elijah, for all his flouncing, custom
cupcakes, and proclivity for partying could be pretty
practical. "It won't be for long. We'll all be here to tear it
down when this is over, and those horrible reporters have
gone away."

Unable to leave, the guests and staff played board
games and charades, and Evangeline kept everyone's

spirits up with a never-ending supply of punch and café au lait. She rustled up po' boys and salad for lunch. Eventually, they all dispersed for an early afternoon nap, leaving Roxy alone in the lounge.

She sat down in a squishy armchair, her chin propped on her fist. There was a little squeak, and she looked down to see that Nefertiti had decided to join her. The fluffy white cat wound her body between Roxy's legs, the softness of her fur soothing her owner like a blanket. Roxy bent over to pick her cat up and plop her in her lap.

"Nef-nef, I'm trying to be brave. I'm trying to keep my spirits up. But it's hard, you know?" She stuck her nose into Nefertiti's fur and lay her cheek on the cat's back. It was like lying on the softest of soft white pillows.

"Come on, girl. Let's tidy this place up." Roxy stood and, with a mewl of protest, Nefertiti was dropped to the wooden floor.

As Roxy was picking up the used plates, Detective Johnson appeared. He looked grumpy and was chewing on a pen.

"Would you like something to eat, Detective?"

"Uh, no," Johnson said. As an afterthought, he added, "Thanks."

Roxy waited for him to say something, but when Johnson continued to chew on his pen, she asked, "Are you done here now? Can we get on with things?"

The detective sighed. "Yeah, seems no one saw or heard anything. According to them, they were all in their beds until morning. We'll see what they have to say down at the morgue about the cause of death, but you can go about your day. Just don't let anyone leave town until we know more about what happened here." Johnson appeared distracted. He made to leave, before turning back to face Roxy. "Tell me," he said wagging his pen at her. "There was a half-eaten cupcake on a plate beside the deceased's bed. And a thermos with the dregs of something milky inside it. There was a faint whiff of liquor. What was that?"

"We gave the influencers personalized cupcakes and brandy milk punch as a nightcap last night."

"And was that the last thing the deceased would have eaten?"

"I guess."

"Who was involved in preparing it?"

"Elijah made the cupcakes and N–Nat..." It suddenly dawned on Roxy where this line of questioning was going. She cleared her throat, "Nat made the punch and delivered it along with the cakes to the guests' rooms."

Johnson eyebrows shot up, and he tapped his pen against his lips, a small smile forming.

"Surely you aren't suggesting that the nightcap had something to do with Dash's death?" Roxy asked in a here-we-go-again voice. "Or that Nat or Elijah were involved in some way?"

"Let's wait for the post mortem results before speculating, shall we, Ms. Reinhardt?" Johnson wagged his pen at her again, but his skeptical expression told Roxy that he clearly wasn't following his own advice.

By the time Johnson and his forensic team had left and Dash's body had been removed, it was evening. After checking that everyone was all right, Roxy decided to go for an evening jog. She thought it might clear her head. The press corps was still on her doorstep, but those who had hung around the back seemed to have given up. Roxy slipped out of the back door. When she set out, the sunlight was just beginning to fade, leaving a purply haze that felt a little eerie. As she ran, her feet rhythmically pounded the sidewalk while her mind wandered.

Roxy had grown up with a mother who put her down, who had never believed that Roxy was destined for any kind of happiness or success. In her head, Roxy could hear her mother's voice.

Why did you believe that you could have a good life, that things would get better, that you could be successful? Can't you see that everything you touch turns to dust?

Roxy knew that if her mom was with her right now, she'd get a knowing look followed by, *"Roxy, why did you even try to do that? You never finish anything you start. You should have played it safe."*

But Roxy had not wanted to play it safe, not any longer. She had wanted to break with the past. She had tried her best to turn the *Funky Cat Inn* into a thriving business, tried to create, tried to succeed. And it had gone well for a while. But now look what had happened. Things were turning out worse than she could ever have imagined. Would she have been better to play it safe in the first place, like her mother would have said?

But it was too late to be second-guessing herself now. Evangeline had handed management and partial owner-ship of the *Funky Cat* over. Roxy had staff and suppliers who were relying on her. The Instagram campaign was underway. There was no way out but through. She needed to step up.

Back at the *Funky Cat*, after a shower, Roxy fell into a fitful sleep, waking up several times in the night, horrible thoughts riding around her head and trampling all over her soul. Images of Ada wagging her finger and Johnson arguing swam in front of her eyes while the sound of Michael crying for help rang in her ears. It felt like someone had reached into her chest, grabbed her heart, and squeezed. But amid the chaos, she saw her friends—Sam, Nat, Elijah, Sage, and Evangeline—urging her on, telling her not to give up. Even Nefertiti made an appearance.

CHAPTER FOURTEEN

THE NEXT MORNING, there was no time to be dragged down by the trauma of the previous day. Roxy knew that it was her responsibility to make sure at the very least that the influencers were all right *and* that no further negative impressions of her hotel were going out into the world. She planned to make sure the reputation of the *Funky Cat* wouldn't be torn to shreds on her watch if she could possibly help it.

She got up, washed her face, and smiled at herself in the mirror. "I can do this," she said to herself. "I can, I can, I will, I must." She felt a little blip of depression catch her heart, a little reminder of the obstacles facing her, but she decided not to pay it any attention. She needed to be strong now, and strong she was going to be.

First things first, Roxy checked on Michael. He didn't come down for breakfast, and as Roxy went upstairs with a coffee and a plate of beignets, she had horrible visions of finding him in the same condition he had found Dash the previous day. Fortunately, that did not turn out to be the case. When she found him, Michael was sitting at the window in his room, staring out at the city. It was a gray morning, which obviously wasn't helping his mood.

"How are you doing?" asked Roxy, not knowing what else to say. She knew it was a dumb question, but it was hard to know what to say to someone whose best friend had just been murdered.

Michael said, "Oh fine, fine," in a dreamy, distracted voice. He seemed worlds away.

"Did you sleep all right?" she asked, setting the beignets and coffee next to him on the table.

"Terribly," he said. "All I could see was Dash's dead face looking back at me. I can't sleep here again."

Roxy nodded. "I understand. Why don't we get you to another hotel?" she said. "Maybe you'd be better staying at somewhere larger, more anonymous, and with more people around."

Michael looked at her for the first time since she entered the room. "That makes sense," he said flatly.

"If it weren't for Detective Johnson's orders you could go back home. You probably don't feel like being in New Orleans right now."

Michael shot back, "Do you want me out of the way? Do you want me to leave so as not to inconvenience you anymore?"

"No, no!" Roxy said, horrified. "I was just thinking about your well-being.

Michael shook his head. His shoulders slumped. He leaned against the window. "You see? I just can't stay here. I keep wondering who would have done that to Dash and why." He got out his smartphone and showed it to Roxy. "That horrible detective released a statement to the news. Dash was poisoned. The police are treating his death as suspicious. Why would someone poison him?

And how? We all drank and ate the same things at dinner, didn't we? It just doesn't make any sense."

Roxy cringed inwardly on hearing this news and felt an ice-cold hand clutch at her heart. Was her food responsible? Was it the nightcap? Was there a murderer staying in her hotel? Would suspicion fall on her and her friends, *again*? She shook her head. "You're right. It doesn't make any sense."

Michael looked at her with a disbelief that he did not even care to veil. Roxy looked back at him, bewildered. "You don't think I...?"

"Sorry," he said. "No, I'm not sorry. I don't know if I'm sorry! It's just...anyone could have killed him. How am I supposed to know? How am I supposed to tell who's innocent and who's guilty?" He burst into tears. Great big sobs. "I'm so sorry, buddy!" he said through his wailing cries as he looked out of the window. "I'm so sorry!"

Roxy felt her heart might break listening to him. She rushed to kneel down in front of him and put her hands on his knees. It was an intimate gesture as if they were very good friends, but his cries reached deep into her heart and brought out all her compassion. "I am so, *so* sorry," she said. "But there was nothing you could have done. None of this is your fault."

"But it was!" he said. "It is! I was the one who convinced him that we should do this job here at your hotel. He didn't want to. This isn't his style. He wanted to go for the Hilton project. He wanted to focus on that. He was saying we should do a showreel to impress them and even stay and shoot in Hilton Hotels ourselves on an unpaid basis to prove what we can do and get the job that way. But I told him no." Michael choked back a sob. "I told him, let's focus on our own indie stuff and not go running after a big name brand. And now look what's happened! It's all my fault, and nothing anyone can say will change my mind."

Roxy couldn't fathom what Michael was talking about, but she didn't feel it was the right moment to probe. She waited for him to continue speaking. She was willing to sit there and listen to him for as long as he wanted, but he shook his head and said, "I need to get out of here."

"I'll help you," Roxy said. "You want me to get you a reservation? Or parking? Or...? What do you need from me? I'm here for you." This was far beyond customer service. This was human to human. Roxy's heart was so heavy with compassion for Michael. She could not even begin to imagine what it must be like to have your best friend die, let alone find them dead, possibly murdered. She thought of what it might be like if she found Sam, Elijah, or any of her friends the way that Michael had found Dash, but her mind just wouldn't go there. She couldn't, wouldn't imagine it.

He said, "No, I'll take care of everything. All I need is for someone to get me over there so I don't throw myself in front of traffic."

That took Roxy aback. "I will go with you," she said quickly. "Tell me when you're ready."

"Now," he said, beginning to tap away at his phone. "I'm ready now."

"I'M JUST MAKING the booking," Michael said. "I'll go to the Hyatt. Then I'll see that awful detective and give him a piece of my mind. Why is he talking to the media before talking to me? I was Dash's business partner and his friend and..." He trailed off.

"I understand," said Roxy again. "Just remember that when we go out, there may well be reporters looking for you and perhaps me. We're two of the people who'll face the most press interest—me as the owner of the hotel and you as Dash's partner."

"Oh, man, I'd forgotten about that," said Michael. "I haven't thought of the outside world since the moment I found him. But I know my fans, Dash's fans, are out there, waiting. They need to hear from me, not a bunch of random reporters. It might seem crazy to go back on social media straight after this, but honestly, some of the fans are...well, they're like family. They need to hear from me." His face crumpled, "But I'm not strong enough yet." He sniffed and wiped his eyes.

"If they really care about you, they'll give you all the

time you need and will totally understand how you feel," said Roxy. "Just do it when you're ready."

Michael gave her a small smile. "Thank you so much for understanding, Roxy," he said. "I'm very hard on myself at times. It's wonderful to have a friend like you. Dash was..." His voice faltered.

Roxy felt her heart swell with warmth. "It's nothing," she said. "I'm glad to have met you. I just wish it had happened under better circumstances. Let's do what we can to get justice for Dash now. I promise I will fight to the end for him."

Roxy thought they should take a vehicle to the Hyatt. They could go in Sam's work van. They could hide in the back. But shortly after Sam said he was on his way, he called Roxy's phone. "The street's jammed with reporters and their cars," he said. "All over the place. They're parked in the middle of the street, everywhere."

"Have you tried the back entrance?"

"Yep, there's reporters there too."

"Let's just face them, Roxy," Michael said. "They want their pound of flesh, so let's give it to them. How bad can it be?"

Roxy thought it could be pretty terrible actually, but she said, "Okay, but no talking to them, promise?"

Michael nodded.

So with Sam unable to make it through the throng, Michael and Roxy had no choice but to walk through a sea of reporters. They had to push their way through. There wasn't a single foot of space and none of the journalists would give an inch. Microphones were shoved in their faces. Questions were shouted in their ears. Someone even tried to wrestle Michael's case out of his hand. In response, Michael elbowed the man in the chest to push him away. "Leave us alone!" Michael shouted.

Roxy winced. She pictured Michael looking like a crazy man on the front page of the newspaper. Perhaps they would even start to make up a narrative about Dash's killing, implicating Michael as the culprit. Trial by press, isn't that what they call it? Terrible. She didn't want to even think about what they'd print about her and her hotel.

Eventually, after much pushing and shoving and stonewalling, the pair arrived at the Hyatt. Thankfully, the reporters were barred from entering while Michael and Roxy were let through. The hotel locked the doors from inside once they'd passed into the lobby. Frustrated to have their quarry elude them without responding, the reporters piled up outside, banging on the glass. "We're going to call the cops on you!" a security guard shouted to the journalists, but it made absolutely no difference. The reporters were like a pack of wild wolves desperate to sink their teeth into their prey.

"Oof, this is what it must be like being part of a boy band. Thank you so much for coming with me," Michael said to Roxy breathlessly. They were both red-faced with exertion and adrenaline. "Those reporters were crazy. How are you going to get back?" Michael said.

Roxy looked out the door. "I think I'll have to get a police escort," she said with a sigh. Overhearing her, a young, bright, overly enthusiastic concierge said, "I can arrange that for you, miss."

"Thank you," Roxy replied hoping against hope that it wouldn't be Johnson who came to get her.

Michael's phone beeped, and he fished it from his pocket. His face clouded over as he read it. "I just got a message," he said. "It's Dash's family. Well, his mother and brother. His father died a long time ago. They're staying here until the case is solved. They're coming down from Missouri." His face was strained.

"Oh, I see," said Roxy. Then she ventured, "Is everything okay?"

"No, not really," he said. "They are not nice people, Roxy. They hate me and have wanted me out of Dash's life for a long time. They didn't trust him to live his own life, they wanted to dictate everything he did. But they didn't know him, they didn't *care* to know him, not the *real* him. They didn't understand what he wanted or what he loved. They just wanted to control him and have him conform, be a good, hometown boy who's great to his momma. He was never going to be like that, he wanted more from life, but they kept on trying."

Roxy gave a sad little smile. "He was about the furthest thing from a conformist you could imagine, wasn't he?"

"Tell them that when you see them," Michael said bitterly. "They thought he was being led astray by me." He gave a sad smile too. "It was probably the other way round, wasn't it?"

Roxy returned Michael's smile. "I think so, yes."

"Anyway, they're planning to stay at your hotel." He widened his eyes meaningfully. "Good luck."

CHAPTER SIXTEEN

UNFORTUNATELY FOR ROXY, it *was* Detective Johnson who drove her from the Hyatt back to the *Funky Cat*. He took the opportunity to drive her in a marked squad car complete with flashing lights and the occasional blast of the siren in order, she suspected, to make a spectacle of her and give her a stern warning.

"I heard that you've been saying that Dash was poisoned," she said to him.

"Yeah, that's right. At *your* hotel." Johnson kept his hands on the steering wheel but leaned over meaningfully, taking his eyes off the road and the reporters for a second to glance in her direction.

"Does that mean we can expect to be graced with your presence some more? Will you be coming to question us again?"

"And poke around your kitchen. We're waiting on the full toxicology reports, but your place was the last one where the victim ate or drank anything."

"Only along with everyone else!" Roxy said, her

indignation overcoming her shyness. "And the rest of us are fine."

"Means nothing, we have to investigate thoroughly. The victim's food may have been messed with. And I want to talk to that flibbertigibbet again. The one from across the road."

"Elijah."

"Yeah, him. And that goth. The one with the tatts."

"You mean Nat."

"Yeah, her. I want to talk about them nightcaps. You likely have a murderer in the house."

Roxy frowned. She didn't like the sound of this at all.

Johnson was prattling on in the seat next to her. "Now, don't you go around investigating like you did last time, y'hear? I'll slap cuffs on you faster than you can say Miss Marple, if you do," he threatened. "We need to treat this very carefully, what with the press interest and all."

They lapsed into silence and neither of them said much else for the rest of the ride. Roxy stared out at the reporters clamoring at the patrol car's windows, fighting the misery that was weighing her heart down as they crawled along the street. What had her life become? Riding in police cars, chased by hordes?

It was only when she got back to the hotel and into the kitchen where Nat and Evangeline were clearing away breakfast that she realized her insides were turning over with hunger. She hopped onto a stool and ate beignet after beignet while watching Nat load the dishwasher.

"Johnson wants to talk to you again. He says Dash was murdered and that it was probably one of us. You were the last person to serve Dash food."

Nat looked at her quizzically.

"The nightcaps," Roxy explained.

"Oh right, well I'm totally in the clear. Unless some-one's put rat poison in the punch when I wasn't looking, they were regular old brandy milk punches."

"Yeah, I know you didn't do anything," Roxy said mournfully. "But someone did. And probably someone who was here that night." Hopelessness was starting to wash over her like a tide on a beach. She kept pushing the emotion away but it kept returning. Each time it got a little bit stronger and pervaded a little bit further into her soul.

Nat regarded Roxy with a worried expression. "Look, I'm really sorry if anything I've done has made things diffi-cult for you." She winced, then paused from loading the dishwasher, and turned to lean against the side. She gave a deep sigh. "I know I should have been nicer to Ada. About Ada...it's just that...well, everything is changing. I've never been a person who is good with change. Do you know what I mean?"

"Oh, I've forgotten all about the dress incident. That seems like an age ago now and, well, we're both in the same boat," said Roxy. "I don't like change either."

"What do you mean?" Nat said. "You seem to revel in it. You're sure fancy enough around this place, always wearing your lovely sparkly outfits, smiling like it's Mardi Gras."

"You're plenty good enough as you are," said Roxy, smiling. "Isn't that right, Evangeline?"

"I don't know what you're both talkin' about," the older woman said. "You young ones and all your soul-searchin' are a mystery to me. Back in my day we were hired for a job and we did it, no questions asked, no navel-gazin' required."

"That's all very well for you to say, Evangeline," said

Nat. "You don't live in the age of social media. Everything is about identity now. Everyone has to have their own personal brand. It's not easy. It brings with it a whole bunch of insecurities and worries that we are not matching up to everyone else." She popped her head out into the dining room to check that there were no guests there. She lowered her voice to a shouted whisper. "Like Lily Vashchenko. She's just so perfect! Her home is immaculate and beautiful. She always has the best outfits on, and her hair is amazing. And that's before we even consider her social media content! How are we supposed to match up to *that*? That series she did on other people's kitchens was tremendous."

Evangeline shook her head. "Why would you want to look at pictures of other people's kitchens for goodness sake?" she said. "How do people even have the time?"

Nat sighed. "You just don't get it."

"You're right about that, cher," Evangeline said. "I don't. And I have no wish to."

Roxy continued to munch away at beignet after beignet, amused at the conversation but feeling heavy-hearted still. "He wants to poke around the kitchen some more too," she said.

"Who does?" Evangeline asked.

"Johnson."

"Hmph! It wasn't my food that poisoned that Dash fella!" Evangeline grumbled.

"No, I'm sure it wasn't. We'd all be dead if that were the case, but maybe whatever poisoned him was put *in* the food. He's right, it's not outside the realms of possibility that someone tampered with it." Roxy put her half-eaten beignet down, her stomach finally signaling that it had had enough. She pushed herself from her stool.

"I want us to do something," she said. "Moping around is not helping. One of us may be the murderer, but the rest of us are innocent. I have to keep things positive. I can't give up."

"There's the evening with Sage coming up. She's bringing her crystals and cards and whatnot," Nat said.

"I know, but that's not until tomorrow. I want to do something *now*. I have to shift this energy that's weighing me down."

"Once I'm finished up here, I was looking at hitting a couple of flea markets," said Nat. "I want to find some more furniture to upcycle."

"But everything's done!" said Roxy. "The hotel décor's complete."

Nat got a mischievous glint in her eye. "It'll never be done. Not if I've got anything to do with it," she said. "I have a great idea for a piece in the dining room that's going to take the luxury quotient to a whole new level."

Roxy smiled. When Nat put her heart and soul into things, it was always a fun time. "Come on, share with the class, then."

"Nope," Nat said with a cheeky grin. "You'll have to wait and see."

"Why don't we ask Lily Vashchenko to come along with us? She's turned upcycling around. It used to be something you'd do when you were broke. Now it's a virtue signal," Roxy said. "Isn't she the upcycling Queen?"

Nat pouted. "No! I am!"

"Okay, okay," Roxy said, her palms up. "You *do* know what you're doing, I'll give you that. But you don't have nearly a million Instagram followers just yet, do you?"

"Nope, and I never will," said Nat. "The idea of being

famous makes my skin crawl, *especially* considering what's going on right now."

"Very sensible, cher," said Evangeline. "More trouble than it's worth. You run along now, I'll finish up here."

"Thanks, Evangeline!" said Nat. She ran out of the room at a sprint, anxious to be on her way.

Lily Vashchenko was delighted by the invitation to visit the flea market. At least she smiled, enigmatic and cat-like as usual. "I wonder if I'll find any unique New Orleans pieces," she said. "The architecture around here is very interesting. Perhaps I'll find something wonderful to put in my own home."

Roxy called up to Sylvia's room to see if she wanted to join them, but there was no reply.

"I think I saw her going out the back with those pole thingies of hers," Nat said. "What does she need them for anyway? It's not like she's going to be climbing any mountains."

"They'd be good defense in the event she comes upon any rabid reporters though," Roxy responded. Nat nodded in agreement.

The three of them assembled in the lobby and Roxy peered through the front door spyhole. Most of the reporters seemed to have given up and dispersed. "They probably followed Johnson to the station after he escorted me back here in a squad car. He's the only one talking to the press about what happened. Come on, there's hardly anyone outside. Let's go before we change our minds!"

CHAPTER SEVENTEEN

ROXY, NAT, AND Lily set out together on foot. There were still dribs and drabs of reporters on the sidewalk, but Roxy told Nat and Lily, "Walk straight past them, don't answer any questions. Don't even look at them. Just pretend like they're not there."

They only planned to walk as far as Sam's laundry. They took a couple of back streets and managed to lose most of the reporters that trailed them. By the time they reached their destination, there was only one still following them, and he was content to stand at the street corner and watch.

"Sam!" said Roxy, with relief, as they burst into the laundry, the constant whirring of the machines making a loud hum. It was hard to make herself heard. Sam was loading a machine, but he stopped when he saw the trio come in.

"Hey! How are you?"

"Um, well, it's been quite a day so far," she said. "I

took Michael to the Hyatt, and the press chased us, and I had to have a police escort home and now..."

"Are you okay?" His eyes were soft with concern, and he came toward her as if to hug her, but then thought better of it and backed away.

Roxy felt heat rise to her cheeks. "Oh fine, fine," she said. "Don't worry about me. I'm just concerned about Michael and the rest of the guests, and now Nat and Elijah because Johnson is taking a hard look at them because of the nightcaps, and oh well, we just wanted to get out and lose ourselves in a crowd. We want to go to the flea market. Do you think you could take us in your van?" She was babbling and she knew it.

"Oh," Sam said, wincing. "I'd be happy to, but I've just sent one of my guys out in it to collect an order. I guess..." He looked a little embarrassed. "We can go in the Rolls?"

"That would be fabulous," said Lily immediately.

"Fine with me," said Nat.

Roxy thought they might be a little conspicuous, but she grinned at him nonetheless. "You can take us by horse and buggy if you like. Just so long as we get there."

Sam grinned back, and the atmosphere between them lit up, so much so that Nat had to wave her arms between the two of them to break it up.

They went out the back entrance to the parking lot. Lily's slanted almond eyes widened when she saw Sam's maroon Rolls Royce. "Wow," she said, a rare enthusiasm animating her voice. "Now that's a real car. The laundry business must pay better than I thought."

Sam avoided eye contact with her and shoved his hands in his pockets. "Um... well..."

But Lily wasn't paying enough attention to realize how shifty he was being. She had her iPhone out and was snapping selfies of herself against the car at every angle. "This will look good with my fans," she said. "A Rolls Royce. That's style."

When they got inside, Lily admired the cream leather seats and ran her hands over the surface of them. "Goodness," she said. "If I capture the Hilton deal, maybe I will be able to cruise in one of these myself."

Something clicked in Roxy's brain. *First Michael, now Lily.* "The Hilton deal? What is that?"

"Oh, it's a huge contract," Lily said. "They're looking for an influencer to partner with for an enormous advertising campaign. It should last the whole of next year. I'm putting together a portfolio to impress them, and this visit with you is part of that. They're going for the young, upcoming luxury market. That's my target, and what you do fits in pretty well, which was why I was so keen to visit you," she said with a smile.

Roxy's palms began to sweat. *The Hilton deal.* The same deal that Dash and Michael had been going for! Lily, Michael, and Dash had been competitors. As they drove, Roxy looked at Lily out of the corner of her eye, studying her intently. Was she capable of murder? She seemed nice enough. She wasn't effusive or gregarious, rather cool, even unapproachable at times, but Roxy knew that appearances were not necessarily all that they seemed. Perhaps Lily had had something to do with Dash's death. Perhaps Dash and Michael were nearer to closing the deal than she was and she knew this. Perhaps Lily had picked Dash off. Perhaps, Roxy thought, she should find out.

Then she remembered Johnson's warning. He had seemed deadly serious. She was *not* to investigate. He had ordered her. Roxy reflected on what Lily had told her as she leaned back in her seat. Her theory made sense, but it seemed barely credible to conclude that this elegant, successful woman would murder someone for money. Roxy couldn't believe it and eventually, exhausted by events of the day and lulled by the sublime, if incongruous, ride to the flea market in Sam's Rolls Royce, she put the thought out of her mind and fell asleep.

After the flea market, Sam dropped Roxy, Nat, and Lily off back at the *Funky Cat*. The trio clambered out of the Rolls with their flea market finds. Nat had found a small, broken old table and a sculpture of a woman with a bow and arrow that was so chipped, Roxy couldn't conceive how on earth Nat was going to turn it into something that was even half-decent. All the reporters had gone now and Sage met the three women at the front door.

"Greetings to all," she said, her voice trembling. "Dash's family members are here. They are in the dining room."

It took a lot to rattle Sage. She'd done years and years of spirit and mindset training to make sure that she stayed tranquil and "aligned with the spirits," even in the most difficult of circumstances. Now though there was a look of fear in her eyes, and she was breathing a little more deeply than usual, as if she were trying to calm herself.

Roxy wondered what on earth could have upset Sage so, but her attention was dragged away by the need to face

Dash's family. Roxy took a deep breath and plastered what she hoped was an appropriate expression on her face, sympathetic and kind, but "in charge." She walked into the dining room with her head high and her stride firm.

There, sitting on one of the most luxurious couches in the lounge was a plump, attractive-looking, middle-aged woman, and a sickly, pale young man of about twenty-five.

The woman stood up with a smile that seemed rather broad under the circumstances, her hand outstretched for a handshake. "Hello, you must be Roxy Reinhardt," she said with all the formality of a businessperson closing a multi-million real estate deal. Roxy was taken aback. The woman didn't come across as a mother whose son had just been poisoned. Her hair was blown out, her long nails were bright red, and her lipstick matched her fingers. She wore high heels. There was a designer logo on her purse.

As Roxy scrutinized the woman carefully and slowly, a barely discernable sadness in her eyes became apparent. Her polished exterior, to Roxy at least, was a façade, one that was brittle and which Roxy suspected could break down at any moment.

"My name is Kathy, and I'm Dash's mother." Her smile fell for a moment before she pulled it back into place. "This is my younger son, Derek."

The young man next to her did not stand up and had none of his mother's charm. He was wearing a hoodie pulled too far forward; it partially obscured his face. When his mother spoke, he stayed seated in his chair and peered out from under too-long bangs, fiddling with a model airplane in his lap.

"My little Derek is pretty shy," the woman said, proudly. She looked at her son affectionately as if he were ten years old. "We are going to stay here until Dash's... killer...has been caught. You won't get rid of us for quite a while probably." She started laughing, but in a moment, her laughter turned to sobs. Composing herself quickly, she gave a huge snort and wiped her eyes. "Sorry, you'll have to excuse me," she said. "It's a difficult time."

"Of course it is," said Roxy kindly. "Please, *please* do stay for as long as you'd like, and ask me if you need anything. Has Sage shown you up to your rooms yet?"

"Yes, she has. Thank you," said Kathy.

"I'm staying in Dash's room," said Derek, suddenly coming to life. "To be close to him."

"He knew where it was and everything," said Sage. She had a strange look on her face. "Something must have called out to you, Derek," she said.

"Now I just have one thing to tell you," said Kathy. She maneuvered herself close to Roxy and lowered her voice. "You've got to understand that that horrible Michael was a terrible influence on Dash. He got my son involved in all sorts of shady things. I'll tell you the story of how they met...Well, maybe not now, maybe another time, someplace private, but let's just say that Michael, well, he's not *good news*. I'm glad he's not here. I couldn't stay here if he were. I wouldn't be surprised if he were involved somehow in my son's death. After all, they split the business fifty-fifty. Michael stood to gain a lot if Dash weren't around.

"I...I...I... Well, perhaps you should be telling this to the police, not me," Roxy said, waving her hands in front of her. "I'm not an investigator. I hear what you're saying, and I'm so sorry for your loss, but if you want to speak about the case, I think you'd better talk to Detective Johnson."

"I will," said Kathy. "Soon. I'm just warning you, don't get involved with Michael, and don't listen to any of his stories. He's not a good man. Trust me." Her blue eyes pierced through Roxy. "Just trust me on that."

CHAPTER EIGHTEEN

"**D**ASHIELL WAS MY darling boy," Kathy Davies said the next morning. It was Sunday, and she was standing in front of the congregation in a packed church, St. Joseph's. Kathy, showing phenomenal organizational skills, had organized a memorial service for her son in just a few hours and the viral communication properties of Instagram had done the rest. Every seat was taken, and all the aisles were chock full of people in bright t-shirts, just like the ones Dash used to wear. The shirts had been Michael's idea. The press had been banned, but reporters congregated around the door outside, like bees around a honeypot.

"He was a good soul and a good boy," Kathy continued. "He had a bright future ahead of him. He was going to quit playing around on YouTube and Instagram, jaunting all over the world. He was planning to settle in his hometown, and live close to his momma." The crowd murmured at this news but quickly settled down.

"It's lies," Michael whispered furiously to Roxy as they sat next to each other in one of the hard pews. "All lies. He couldn't stand her. All she wanted was to control him, just like she controls Derek."

Roxy listened to Michael's words, but she was still a little wary of him after what Kathy had said. She truly didn't know who to believe.

"But he wasn't quick enough to make that decision and look what happened," said Kathy. "I don't want any of you to make the same mistake. If you have a family who loves and adores you, go *home* to them. Don't go running around the world chasing butterflies, and putting yourself in danger. You might just end up...," her eyes welled with tears, "in a casket."

Another murmur rippled through the crowd. Michael got up and stormed toward the entrance. Roxy followed him. She had to push and shove through the sea of bright colors to make it through. When she got outside, it was like she'd been underwater and had finally surfaced, gasping for breath. Around her, fans who had been unable to fit in the church milled around. Roxy and Michael hid among them, catching their breath until a group of reporters spied them and came rushing forward. It was an ambush and not a little scary.

"Get away from me!" Michael hollered.

Roxy looked around, trying to find a spot where they'd be left alone, but there wasn't one. There was only a large cemetery to the right, where reporters hung around on the paths between the gravestones, and a wide row of stores to the left. The street in front of the church was blocked with vehicles.

"Come on," Roxy said. She grabbed Michael's hand, and they took off running through the vehicles and into the streets beyond.

Soon they let go of each other's hands and flew

through the backstreets of New Orleans independently. They heard the pounding of footsteps as journalists ran behind them, trying to catch up, but the pair kept running and running until Roxy felt a pain in her side.

Finally, they reached the *Funky Cat*. The courtyard was deserted. The front door to the hotel was locked, even though Roxy knew Nat was in there with Evangeline and Sage and Elijah. They were preparing for the influx of fans they were expecting after the service.

Roxy hammered on the door, hoping there were no reporters close behind. No one answered. She scrambled to get her phone out of her pocket and called Nat. "Let us in!" It would take too long to go around the back.

Within moments the door was open. Michael and Roxy darted inside.

"That woman!" Michael said as soon as he had gotten his breath back. "She's crazy! Seriously, Dash and her didn't get on. He respected her because she was his mother, he went to visit and was kind to her, but man, if she'd had her way, he'd be living his life in a prison of her making. Did you see Derek? He's like a shell, like a ghost of a person. She dictates his whole life. She won't even let him have a girlfriend. Dash said Derek had one once, and she sabotaged it so bad the girl left town and never came back."

Roxy shook her head not knowing what to say. Family troubles weren't her forte. They made her uncomfortable.

"And did you *hear* what she said about dreams, oh excuse me, *chasing butterflies*? Don't do that, or you'll end up dead? That was the total *opposite* of how we lived life. Dash and me, we lived *only* for chasing our dreams."

Michael fell down onto one of the chairs in the lobby, his legs splayed, his hands dangling over the arms of the chair. "Maybe she's right, though. If we hadn't been following our bliss, none of this would have happened. If we'd stayed home like good little boys, gotten regular jobs, and stopped reaching for the stars, Dash might still be alive. Maybe following your dreams *is* dangerous."

"I don't think so..." said Roxy. His declaration had her thinking. If *she* hadn't gone for her dreams, leaving her life behind to come to New Orleans and taking up management of the hotel, she certainly wouldn't now be mixed up in a murder investigation. But then again, she wouldn't be having the adventure of her life either, wouldn't be making great new friends, wouldn't be learning, living, and loving it. She'd be stuck in a dead-end job with a succession of dead-beat boyfriends, most likely.

Michael shook his head. "No. Dash never believed in living smaller than you dreamed. He'd have preached, 'Go out there and get it, whatever it is!'" He thumped the arm of his chair. "I should keep his legacy alive." But then he shook his head. "No. No, I shouldn't. He's dead now. Who'd take life advice from a dead guy?"

"Let me ask you a question," said Sage.

Roxy jumped and turned around—she hadn't realized Sage was there. She was standing in the doorway in flowing blue robes and a serene expression.

"Sure," Michael said, his face a picture of torment.

"If you could speak to him now—to Dash," a mystical look crossed Sage's face, "do you think he would regret the way he lived? Do you think he would wish that he had bent to his mother's wishes?"

Michael thought for a moment. "No, I don't think so, not at all."

"Do you think he'd still believe in chasing one's

dreams, spiritual expansion, achievement, and fulfillment?"

"Yes," Michael said, his eyes brightening a little, and his face settling, more relaxed. "Yes, I do."

Sage said nothing more. She turned and went back into the dining room without a word.

After a few moments of silence, Nat came over to Roxy and said quietly, "I think you're going to have to help us. We're really behind."

"Okay," said Roxy. "Michael, I need to help with preparing the food for our guests. They'll be here for the wake soon. Are you okay with me doing that? Do you want me to stay with you? Is there anything you need?"

"I'll come and help," he said.

"Oh, you don't have to," said Roxy.

"I *want* to," Michael insisted, and Roxy could see that it would help, so she let him.

CHAPTER NINETEEN

THEY SET ABOUT finishing up preparations for the wake. A buffet comprising some of the best food New Orleans had to offer—gumbos and jambalayas, rice and vegetables seasoned and spiced to Creole perfection—was laid out. Tiered cake stands were stacked high with Elijah's pastries, and coffee stations stood at the ends of the tables along with condiments, cream, liqueurs, and spirits. To create the right atmosphere, Nat would sing some light, soulful jazz and a few of Dash's favorite tunes accompanied by Sam on his saxophone.

"It looks fabulous," Elijah said.

Roxy looked around. "It does, doesn't it? We're doing Dash proud." She looked at Elijah and leaned in. "Look, Elijah, are you worried about Johnson investigating you? He means to look carefully at your cupcakes."

Elijah laughed. "I'd like to see him try!"

"But seriously, Eli, Dash ate your cupcake. It was the *last* thing he ate."

Elijah shrugged. "I've been making pastries since I

was knee-high to a grasshopper. I've not poisoned anyone yet. And besides, everyone got one. They'd all be dead if I messed up."

"That's what Nat said."

Elijah clasped Roxy firmly by the shoulders and looked into her eyes. "It'll be fine. You don't seriously think Nat or me interfered with his nightcap do you?"

"No, but..."

"Well, then. The police will catch the real killer and everything will go back to the way it was. You'll see."

Roxy wished she had as much confidence as Elijah clearly had.

"Look, I've got to go back across to the bakery. You can send the overflow there if you become overrun." He drew his wiry body up to his full height and clapped his hands like a male flamenco dancer. "It's time to *partay*!"

"Elijah, please. It's a wake," Roxy said.

"Trust me, Rox, it'll be a party." Elijah turned with a flourish and returned to his bakery to await the crowd.

Elijah was right. Before Roxy knew it, everyone from the church had descended on the *Funky Cat*, and she and the others were rushed off their feet serving guests and replenishing the buffet. They were deluged with so many people that many of them overflowed onto the cobbled street outside while others crammed into Elijah's bakery. Weaving and bobbing through them all, Elijah carried trays of pastries high above his head, serving them to anyone who wanted one.

The light, soulful jazz Nat had planned to sing gave way to a blistering rendition of *Chattanooga Choo Choo* when a guest showed up with a trumpet. The crowd contributed improvised train sound effects and even a beatboxer joined in! Dancing and toasts and stories and jokes, all in memory of Dash Davies, continued into the late afternoon. "I told you," Elijah said to Roxy afterward.

Three hours later, as the event started to wind down, Roxy noticed an empty spot on one of the couches. She took the opportunity to flop down into it, exhausted. She'd been running around with food and drinks, meeting her guests' wide range of needs for the entire time. She had had to eject some people out of a bedroom at one point. They were admiring it, but still.

As she plopped down, she happened to sit between Sylvia Walters and Ada Okafor, who didn't seem to be making much of an effort to talk with each other.

"Hi, Roxy," said Sylvia. "You look exhausted." She was wearing a navy t-shirt and khaki cargo pants. A bright orange neckerchief was tied around her head. She pointed to it, "Out of respect for Dash."

"That's nice. Yes, exhausted," said Roxy. "But it's all worth it to honor Dash."

Ada was sitting on the couch like a movie star. She was wearing a long, vivid, pink gown that trailed to the floor, there was a glass of champagne in her hand, and again her nails were perfectly manicured to match her outfit.

"It is very sad," she said to Roxy. She even sounded like she meant it a little.

"Yes," Roxy said. She looked around the room. "He seems to have led a very full life, though. His message certainly spread far and wide."

"Indeed. I was not a fan of his silly nature, but never

mind." Ada's face was totally expressionless, and she sipped her champagne in a very serious manner.

Roxy looked at her out of the corner of her eye. She knew that Ada had felt humiliated by the dress incident even though Roxy was sure that Dash had spilled his wine by accident. Nevertheless, it had happened in front of her fans, all of *his* fans, and perhaps any of Nigerian high society who happened to be watching. Had Ada been unhinged enough by that to kill him?

Roxy wanted to ask a probing question but wasn't sure whether to. She thought for a moment. "You two weren't the best of friends, were you?"

"He spilled red wine all over my white Versace. You wouldn't be happy, either. It was a limited edition, you know."

"Yes, so you said." There was a pause during which Roxy held Ada's gaze as she wondered about the possibility of Ada being a murderer.

Ada suddenly jumped. She put her hand to her chest. "You're not implying that *I* had anything to do with his death, are you?"

"No, no, of course not!"

"I am a very religious woman, Roxy," Ada said. "Just because a person believes in Louis Vuitton it does not mean she cannot believe in God also. I am very forgiving and would never harm anyone, much less for a prank. I am medically trained, remember."

"Sorry," said Roxy. "I didn't mean anything by it."

"I should hope not."

The atmosphere felt so uncomfortable that Roxy had to leave. "Well, you'll have to excuse me, I have to go check on the next crawfish boil," she said.

She didn't know why, intuition perhaps, but as soon

as Roxy reached the small room at the back of the kitchen, she checked Ada's Instagram profile. She whipped out her phone and loaded the page. There was a gorgeous picture of Ada posing at her dressing table in her room at the *Funky Cat*. Roxy wondered how she had done it—it was so good, it looked like a professional shot. The caption simply said, 'Condolences.' Ada wore a grave expression, but she looked like a model posing for a designer brand rather than someone about to attend a funeral service. It seemed to Roxy to be extraordinarily inappropriate. That there was no picture or mention of Dash, merely compounded her confusion.

Roxy scrolled through the comments. Some said, *RIP Dash,* but many more were commenting on how beautiful Ada looked and the exquisiteness of the dress she was wearing. One even said, *Condolences. Ha ha ha! He deserved what he got after what he did to you.*

Roxy noticed something else too. Ada had tapped the red heart next to each and every comment. She had "loved" them all, even the nasty ones.

CHAPTER TWENTY

"PHEW, IT'S A busy day," Roxy told Nat.
"You're telling me," Nat replied. They had cleared the debris from the morning's wake and were now preparing for the evening entertainment.

Roxy had planned what she was calling an "Evening of Love and Light" for the influencers. Whenever anyone came to New Orleans, they always wanted to know about the spiritual influences and who better to introduce them to New Orleans's mystical realm than Sage?

"Sage has persuaded Dr. Jack at the botanica to bring along a selection of magical supplies and a pile of crystals of all types," Roxy told Nat. The Englishwoman looked up at her boss, her lips pressed into a thin line. Nat was on her hands and knees in the dining room sweeping under a corner unit with a hand brush. Nat didn't say anything, her silence speaking for her.

"What?" Roxy cried. "I loved crystals as a little girl. I desperately wanted a 'Grow Your Own Crystals' kit for my birthday one year. Of course, I didn't get it." Roxy was laying the table for the evening's dinner. "Did you know that if you drink the water that crystals have been in, you absorb their powers?" Nat rolled her eyes. "At least that's what Sage said," Roxy finished.

"I think she was having you on."

Before the evening began, however, Roxy, Sage, Elijah, and Sam headed over to the Hyatt to check on Michael. He'd spent most of the afternoon following the memorial service sitting in a corner of the kitchen at the *Funky Cat,* avoiding his fans, his mood successfully repelling them for the most part. He'd gone back to the Hyatt for a nap.

"I'll take him his very own goodie bag of botanical items," said Sage. "The poor soul is in a bad place. He needs the spirits now more than ever." She found a basket in the kitchen and made up a hamper of sorts with candles, an oracle deck, sparkling pastel crystals, colored stones, a notebook with 'Magic' written on the front, some beaded necklaces, and incense.

When they arrived at his room, Michael opened the door with groggy eyes. His face was so swollen with misery, he looked like he'd been in a boxing match. When he saw them, he pulled a robe around his body defensively, the untied belt trailing on the floor.

"Hello," he said flatly.

"Hi there," said Roxy kindly. "If you need some time to yourself, we can leave. We just wanted to check on you."

Sage smiled. "And we brought you a gift, honey."

Sam smiled too. "I have nothing to give you, but a friend in need is a friend indeed and all that. I'm here for you, buddy."

"And I'm here in the event you wish to rock 'n' roll,"

Elijah said, pulling a dance move. "Otherwise, I'll shut up."

Michael looked at them all and gave them a small smile. "Come in."

Roxy expected the room to be a mess with clothes strewn everywhere and half-eaten room service cluttering the table-tops. If she were to face the loss of a good friend, Roxy suspected that she would descend into chaos, but the room was the opposite of what she expected—it was as neat as a pin. Even the coffee cups and sachets on the side table were in perfect alignment as if Michael had spent time arranging them to be just so.

"Sit, please," Michael said, gesturing at the chairs by the window. He sat down on the bed. Elijah and Sage remained standing. Elijah was too full of energy to sit down while Sage stood tall with all the poise and elegance of a statue, her light gray robes flowing around her. Sam and Roxy sat on the chairs Michael had pointed to. Sage handed Michael the basket she had brought with her. "Michael, honey, this is the least we can do for you. Remember, it is in moments of deep pain that we are the most connected to the spiritual world. Shamans, they're spiritual doctors, will eat burning hot chili peppers without water. They incur great pain as they do, but they believe that in this way they can most securely contact the dead and any other spirit they want to connect with." It was not an approach Roxy would have taken, but Michael was enthralled.

Sage continued. "Alchemy is the ability to turn tragedy into victory. This is a tragedy for *us,* but know that Dash is on the other side, laughing and playing jokes, as usual. His spirit isn't gone. How could it be? I feel it now. Can't you, if you think of him? He's still around. He won't stay long, though. He's got to reincarnate and will soon choose where and when. He might go back to Source for a while to recharge, but then he will return in another form. But none of that technical detail matters. All I'm showing you is that his energy will go on and on. He lives forever. Like us all."

Roxy watched Michael's response to this carefully. She was skeptical of the idea about life after death, and she was ready to jump in if he responded poorly, but she also knew that to people who were grieving, sometimes these ideas helped.

"Thank you, Sage," Michael mumbled tearfully, looking at his hands. "I'd like to come tonight."

Sage's display of crystals was something to behold. It had a shining, other-worldly aura. Sage had taken one of the trestle tables that were usually put into service in the kitchen, covered it with a soft purple velvet cloth, and laid crystals all over it. They caught the light of the lamps around the lounge and twinkled and sparkled in the early evening light.

Roxy hovered by the table, staring at the crystals for ages. One, in particular, caught her eye. There was a heart-shaped pink stone in the middle of it. Other pink and clear stones radiated from the center in beautiful swirls.

"That one's for finding a happy romantic relationship," said Sage, coming up behind her. "Is that something you'd like?"

Roxy was quite taken aback. "Um...well, yes.... But no! I mean, I love the stones, but I don't want a romantic relationship right now." She became acutely aware of where Sam was at that moment. He had just arrived and was on the other side of the room rigging up some fairy lights.

"Oh, right," Sage said, a little smile tugging at the corner of her lips. She flicked a glance in Sam's direction. "I understand. Well, when you're ready, I'll help you make a crystal grid. It'll help you generate one. A romantic relationship, I mean."

"That won't be any time soon, I can assure you!" Roxy said. "I'm much too busy." She laughed a little too loud. "But what about doing a crystal grid to ensure justice for Dash?"

"Aha! You read my mind, honey," Sage said. "When Michael arrives, I am planning to share it with him. Because he was close to Dash, if he's the one to put the crystals in place, it will have a stronger effect. Also, if..." She trailed off.

"If what?"

Sage drew closer and lowered her voice. "If he's *not* who he seems to be, he'll resist making the grid. He'll be *terrified*, and it'll show. Trust me."

CHAPTER TWENTY-ONE

ROXY FROWNED. "DO you think he might have...?"

"I don't know," said Sage. "My intuition is all over the place. Unfortunately, it picks up a lot of little things, like jealousy, or overprotectiveness, or anger, or sadness, or simple nastiness. These negative energies clog up my radar. I can't just hear 'Murderer! Murderer!' loud and clear in my head. I wish I could."

Roxy sighed. "I wish you could too..."

Just then Dr. Jack came over. Roxy had heard a lot about him, interesting anecdotes, but she had never met him before. He was the owner of the botanica, the magical supplies store that she had visited a few times with Sage.

"Hello, Roxy."

"Dr. Jack, I'm so pleased to meet you. Thank you for closing up your botanica so you could attend this evening."

"Oh, I haven't closed it, my dear. My assistant, Leroy, is manning the fort. We have a commitment to stay open late. We are *always* open late." He leaned in conspiratorially, "For the witches, the nocturnal ones, you know." He winked and tapped his nose.

Roxy broke into a smile. Dr. Jack was delightfully eccentric. He wore a rose pink felt fedora, mirrored sunglasses, and a purple leopard-print scarf. A royal-blue trench coat was draped over his trim body, and he wore a white shirt underneath a black velvet waistcoat and purple corduroy trousers. Simple black shoes completed the outfit.

"Did I just hear you two lovely ladies talking about justice?" he said, rubbing his short, gray beard. He spoke very softly.

"That you did," said Sage, smiling at him.

Roxy watched them both. The heart-shaped pink crystal popped back into her mind, and she mused how Dr. Jack and Sage would make an awesome couple.

"Justice is the most important topic facing us on this planet at present," he said. "Because we've rather failed on that front, haven't we? When one person can die of a preventable disease in childhood, and another can live in a luxurious mansion and go on to inherit huge wealth, all because of an accident of birth, it feels like we've gone wrong somewhere. An ovarian lottery of sorts, don't you think?" Dr. Jack looked at Roxy for confirmation.

Roxy nodded, a little stunned at the diversion the conversation had taken. Being around folks like Sage and Dr. Jack was like riding a roller coaster. From romance to murder, to witches, to justice, to privilege, you never knew what would pop up next! "You're right. Although Sage and I were really just talking about making sure Dash's killer is found." Then, feeling a little foolish, but also quite brave, she asked, "Do *you* have any means for finding out who could have killed him?"

"Spiritual technology to divine the identity of a killer?" he said. "This is not my specialty, I'm afraid."

Roxy felt she'd landed on another planet. *Spiritual technology? What was that?* But there was no time to ask as Evangeline and Nat came out with the cold canapés. This time, Roxy had successfully persuaded Evangeline to go along with her idea for "newfangled, posh fiddly stuff," and Evangeline had rather enjoyed making small versions of her crawfish pies, crab boulettes, and Cajun pork belly tacos. As she moved about the room, Nat's expression was inscrutable—she was *not* a believer in or fan of anything remotely magical. As far as she was concerned, crystal grids and spiritualism were mumbo-jumbo nonsense, but she knew better than to say so.

"Roxy!" Nat said. "You're not even dressed!" Nat had a trademark band tee on, but she had changed her boots. They were pink and matched the color printed on her t-shirt.

Roxy had gotten so caught up in the crystals and conversation that she'd forgotten to get ready. "Oh, my gosh!" she said.

Roxy dashed off to her room, fed Nefertiti, and dressed. She grinned as she pulled her outfit out of the wardrobe—a dress covered in gold sequins. She'd spotted it in a store near Sam's laundry but hadn't had occasion to wear it. It was a *very* bold choice. But what night could be better to debut it than an "Evening of Love and Light?"

She paired it with gold sparkling shoes, gold earrings, necklace and bangle, and a pearl bracelet. She even put a vine of golden flowers in her hair. Glittering from head to toe, she stepped back into the lounge. Predictably to everyone except Roxy, who was immune to her own beauty, all eyes turned to her. Some eyes, like Sam's, lingered.

"Wow, you look simply devastating!" Elijah said. He kissed her on both cheeks. Elijah was wearing a purple suit covered in green and blue skulls. It was quite the loudest outfit Roxy had ever seen.

"Thank you, you are too sweet," she said. "Now, I don't know about you, but I'm ready for some magic!"

Ada swept into the room looking as beautifully presented as usual. She was wearing a diaphanous tangerine gown that reached her ankles, and once again, her nails matched her outfit.

"Good evening!" Roxy said cheerfully.

Ada gave her a tight smile. "I am going out. I don't believe in crystals and those types of things. I came to New Orleans for the architecture, not some crazy, weirdo, woo-woo nonsense. It is incompatible with my spiritual beliefs."

"Okay, no problem!" Roxy said sunnily, clasping her hands tightly, determined that nothing would bring her down. "No problem at all. I hope you have a wonderful time."

Kathy, Dash's mother, on the other hand, was *not* so reluctant. She made a beeline for Sage's crystal table. Taking the glass of champagne Roxy offered her, she said, "Oh, I love all this stuff. Church on Sundays, psychic on Wednesdays, that's my routine."

Ada sniffed and left.

Kathy's son Derek wasn't so keen on the evening's planned activities, either. As soon as he wandered into the room, he headed right out again, still playing with the model airplane he'd had when he'd arrived. "Bye," he mumbled, turning paler than ever when he saw what was laid out. As he left the room, Nefertiti, who had been sitting in the lobby, wandered lazily in. She jumped onto an armoire and parked herself down to watch the proceedings. Her eyes were alert, watchful.

"Derek's going to see Father John, the priest," Kathy said, her voice full of empathy. "He's struggling with... well, everything. I try to help him as best I can, but I'm struggling too. And there's only so much a momma can do. Besides, we're thinking about holding a celebration of life for Dash, something less formal than the memorial service. He's gone to talk arrangements with the priest."

Roxy gave her a sympathetic smile.

Soon afterward, Sylvia and Lily came down together, deep in conversation about Pinterest and their "conversion rates." They seemed to have become fast, if unlikely, friends and stood a little aloof from Kathy after nodding to her from the other side of the lounge. Michael hadn't yet shown up.

After he'd fixed the lights, Sam decided to stay for the evening. Crystals weren't really his thing, but he was open-minded and loved to learn about anything and everything, and as Roxy's friend, he wanted to support her as much as possible. Evangeline and Nat stayed out of sight in the kitchen mostly, Nat especially, although Evangeline could be seen peeking around the kitchen door from time to time, eager to view the scene.

And so the small crowd of Kathy, Sylvia, Lily, Sam, Elijah, Roxy, Sage, and Dr. Jack hung around drinking champagne, chatting, and admiring the crystals until Sage caught their attention.

CHAPTER TWENTY-TWO

"WHO WANTS A reading?" Sage said.

"Ooh, me please," said Sylvia immediately. She was clutching onto the frothy blue scarf wound around her neck, a point of elegance that elevated an otherwise bland outfit of beige button-down shirt and brown slacks. Roxy looked at her with new, appraising eyes. Sylvia had seemed more down-to-earth than this enthusiasm for crystals suggested. "I've never done anything like this before. Is it okay if I record it for my channel?" Sylvia added.

"Of course," said Sage. She paused and watched Sylvia for a moment as if she were reading her. "I warn you, though. It may get personal. Very personal."

"That's okay," Sylvia said. "My followers know just about everything about me anyway. I'm pretty much an open book."

The group sat down in the lounge. Sage and Sylvia sat in the center. Earlier, Roxy had arranged two chairs on either side of the coffee table for this very purpose. The atmosphere in the room became serious, and as they prepared themselves, a sense of gravity and purpose swept through the lounge like a draft.

Sage whipped a deck of tarot cards from a pocket in her robes and began to shuffle them. She closed her eyes. Nobody said a word as she concentrated. "I have a feeling we need to delve into the past, to bring something to light that needs to be cleared. Then, and only then, will the future be revealed."

Sylvia gulped. Her eyes flitted around the others sitting around the room. "Okay."

Roxy leaned forward. "Are you fine with doing this, Sylvia?"

Sylvia sat a little straighter in her seat. "Yes. Yes. It's no problem."

Sage spread the cards face down on the table in a long line. Dr. Jack hung back next to Roxy, looking on intently. He was the only one who remained standing. Roxy shivered. She sensed someone looking at her from behind and turned around. There was no one there. Dr. Jack caught her eye and raised one eyebrow.

"Choose three cards," Sage said, a heavy tone giving her already low voice even more gravitas.

Sylvia reached out tentatively and slid three cards toward her. Sage packed up the rest of the deck and slid it back into her pocket. She laid the three cards out in a row, still face down. With three quick flicks of her wrist, movements so swift everyone jumped, she turned them over.

Sage gasped. "The Three of Swords, a betrayal by a lover. The Justice card in reverse, meaning justice *not* served, and the Death card, meaning the end of something, or..."

Sylvia burst into tears. "Oh my goodness! This stuff really works!"

Kathy gave Roxy a triumphant nod. "If only that Ada was here to see this," she whispered.

Roxy didn't reply. Her heart had dropped. Now one of the influencers was crying. *And* she was recording! Roxy breathed in deeply and exhaled through her nose. There was nothing she could do so she kept smiling and clasped her hands together tightly in her lap. Her mind wandered to Michael. Where *was* he?

Sage leaned forward and took Sylvia's hands. "Let it out, my love. Let it out."

"I had a horrible, abusive ex-husband." She shuddered. "And I didn't leave him. Sometimes, I thought I deserved his abuse. Other times I knew I didn't, but was too afraid to leave." She wiped her tears and laughed. "Oh, I shouldn't get so emotional. It was twenty years ago now. A little more, in fact."

Sage nodded. "It's okay to cry. The wound is raw because something about it is not resolved. There is still a healing, still a message for you in this memory. What happened in the end?"

As though the intensity of the moment was too much for her, Sylvia sat back. She dropped Sage's hands and looked down into her lap.

"I finally found the strength, the courage to leave, and took off to Europe where he couldn't find me. I had no money. No home. I slept on couches, in hostels, even sometimes under railroad bridges. It wasn't easy. I felt like ending it all at times. But eventually I came back to the US, to a totally different state, and began my life over. I've never seen my ex-husband since."

Sage nodded slowly. "What is there left to release?"

"I...I don't know."

"Maybe there's a part of the story you haven't told?" Sage pushed.

Sylvia looked bewildered. "Nothing that I can think of." She laughed, but to Roxy, it sounded a little forced. "Well, I won't underestimate a tarot reading in the future, that's for sure! I thought this was just going to be a little fun." She looked around at the others in the room, clearly hoping someone would rescue her. Her audience looked hesitant, a little awkward. Elijah was jiggling his foot vigorously. Sam rested his elbows on his knees looking very grave. Dr. Jack looked equally serious. Lily's expression was impassive, but she had turned her body away from the scene in the center and crossed her legs. Only Kathy looked eager, her eyes shining as she looked at Sylvia.

Roxy stepped in. "Perhaps that's enough of the cards for now? Maybe we could look at the crystals and talk about them."

"That's a good idea," said Lily Vashchenko in her slow, somber voice. She stood and pulled down her short cream skirt so that it hovered just above her knees and straightened her baby blue t-shirt. She walked over to the velvet-covered trestle table, her champagne glass in her hand. "I really like this one." She pointed to a crystal grid Sage had set up. "A grid is a configuration of crystals placed in a pattern that amplifies their intention. All crystals are infused with a purpose," Sage explained. "This grid comprises of peacock colored crystals—deep greens, blues, and purples. They represent healing and well-being."

"Isn't it lovely?" said Roxy, keen to raise the energy in the room.

"Hmm, I don't know." Kathy pointed at another grid

full of oranges and yellow crystals. "This one is much more to my taste."

"Crystals are about much more than pretty colors," said Dr. Jack. "Though what you're drawn to *can* indicate personal issues you may be struggling with. They can also indicate what you're *comfortable* with." He pointed to Kathy's choice. "This one is for inviting cheerfulness and joy into your life. Or, conversely, you may be attracted to it if you use cheerfulness and joy *too* much, to cover up issues or hidden motivations, for instance."

Roxy felt distinctly awkward, and Kathy gave a laugh devoid of any kind of joy at all. She blinked at him and shook her head ever so slightly. "What on earth do you mean?"

Dr. Jack nodded. "Just like that."

"HUH?" KATHY SAID. She was still smiling, but now she looked like a shark baring its teeth.

"In this society, we've become addicted to pleasure and afraid of what is uncomfortable," said Dr. Jack. "But the wise person knows that beyond discomfort and even downright pain lies truth. There are blessings and strength more than we could ever believe if we travel to journey's end."

This was all getting a little intense and complicated for Roxy. Her head was beginning to spin, and she got the impression that the evening wasn't going so well.

Sage turned to Lily. "Would you like a reading?"

Lily looked at her warily. "Oh, no, no, thank you. In fact, I have some fans in the area. I'm going to go and meet with them, actually. I'll be back later. See you!" With that, she was out the door. She didn't even bother with a jacket.

Roxy felt a teeny-tiny bit like doing that herself.

Almost immediately there was a knock on the front door and in stepped Michael. "Sorry I'm late," he said. He looked a little more like his normal self than he had earlier, very serious, but he held his head high and made eye contact with everyone.

"Kathy," he said. He nodded politely in her direction.

"How nice to see you, Michael," she said, returning his gaze only briefly. She spoke like Evangeline's whiskey and caramel sauce was spread across her teeth.

Sage looked relieved to see him. "Michael, would *you* like a reading?"

"Absolutely," he said. His eyes lit up. "And I'd like to know more about these crystals."

Dr. Jack looked delighted. "I can answer all your questions."

"Awesome," Michael said briskly. He took his jacket off. "Let's do this."

Michael sat down for his reading. This time Roxy was unwilling to watch, it felt too intrusive, so she struck up a conversation with Sam.

"How's business going?" she asked.

"Ticking along nicely, as usual," he said.

"Ticking along?" said Roxy. "I didn't think you were a 'ticking along' sort of guy. I thought you were more about expansion and trying new things. That's what you've been encouraging me to do with the hotel all this time."

He gave a small smile, a little embarrassed. "Well, I *am* working on something."

"Do tell," Roxy said.

Sam rarely spoke about himself, his goals, his dreams. He seemed to prefer encouraging others. But now he said, "I'm thinking of setting up a program for the homeless."

"Wow," Roxy said. "That sounds bold."

"Yeah, I've been thinking about it for a while now. Sylvia was lucky. She had a way to come back from being down and out, but others aren't so fortunate. I'd like to offer a path for people who want to get back on their feet."

"And how would you do that?"

"I'd get them access to good healthcare, teach them skills to enable them to support themselves, employ them in my business to give them experience, and maybe build a network of other businesses for them to work in, that kind of thing."

"That *is* bold. Big and bold," said Roxy. "What a great idea! It could be massive."

"It should be relatively straightforward," he said. "I just have to..."

"Straightforward?" Roxy cried, astounded. It sounded complicated and overwhelming to her, but Sam had an easy, can-do, confident, nothing-was-too-difficult attitude. Who *was* this enigma? How did he get to be like that? And how could she become a little more like him?

"I should probably keep quiet about the idea for a bit," he said, "until it's up and running. I have so many ideas. If I talked about them all, I'd seem a huge flake. The vast majority never see the light of day." He laughed, his broad shoulders shaking a little. "So I keep my hands close to my chest until I know I can play winning cards."

"I wish I could do that," said Roxy. "I just tend to be a mess in front of everyone, and then it somehow works out. Or not."

"You don't look a mess in front of anyone."

"I worry about what people would say if I fail."

"Any undertaking involves risk, and risk requires courage. The only people who criticize others' failures are those who don't dare to take risks in the first place. They are not worth bothering with."

Roxy blinked. She hadn't thought of it that way before. Sam was right. She felt a smidgeon of anxiety leave her, and she steepled her fingers in front of her. She might have grown an inch or so. She certainly felt happier.

Elijah sidled over to them. "Look, Rox. Have you considered speaking to those awful reporters outside? I know there's not many of them left, and the Lord knows when we were teeming with them, they drank so much coffee and ate so many of my pastries they increased my bottom line no end, but the stragglers are bothering my regulars. They're costing me business." He winced. "I thought that perhaps if you spoke to them they might go away."

"Yeah, I think you should, Roxy," Sam said. He caught sight of the look Roxy gave him. She might be small and not so brave at times, but she didn't like being *told* what to do. He raised his hands. "Okay, okay, give it some thought. Just say something, not much, a short statement, just enough for them to be pacified. It doesn't help anyone, them being on your doorstep all day."

Roxy folded her arms. She did *not* want to do that.

Sam looked over at Michael. The influencer was engrossed in conversation with Dr. Jack and Sage. "He looks all right, thank goodness."

Roxy wanted to talk to Michael and find out how he was doing—she felt a sort of duty of care toward him—but he was in the midst of what appeared to be an animated discussion. Michael was gesticulating excessively, but his expression was warm. He was enjoying himself. She knew that with Sage and Dr. Jack, Michael would be fine. "He's in good hands," she said.

Sam smiled at her. "Indeed. Even if they are a little eccentric."

Roxy laughed quietly. "Just a little."

CHAPTER TWENTY-FOUR

T HE EARLY MORNING sun poured into Roxy's room and she woke up with a newfound sense of joy. She felt totally and utterly refreshed. It was as if the good energy from the crystals the previous evening had swept away all her cares and worries, leaving confidence and optimism in their place. Nefertiti was sleeping beside her, and Roxy sunk her hands into her soft white fur. The cat woke and blinked at her. She looked as if she might be smiling too.

"Good morning, princess," Roxy said. "How are you this morning?"

"Meeeooowwww."

Roxy giggled. "Right! I have the feeling that today is going to be a good day."

Her mood didn't even dip when she thought of Dash. She remembered what Sage had said—that Dash was on the other side, watching them. She knew that Michael would honor Dash's memory in only the best ways and that Dash's message of the importance of realizing one's dreams would be spread far and wide.

They still hadn't heard from the police beyond the initial interviews. Detective Johnson had been very tight-lipped. She didn't know how the investigation was going or what kind of poison had killed Dash, nor did she know how it had gotten into his bloodstream. All of them in the hotel that night were under suspicion for murder, and there was the still unresolved question of the role her hotel's food had played in Dash's death. The forensics team had returned just like Johnson had promised they would. They had taken away samples of food from the kitchen, but Roxy had heard nothing. Even if it were found that her food had nothing to do with Dash's death, Roxy knew as well as anyone that mud stuck. But even that didn't matter right then. The sense of calm that pervaded her was too deep to feel any sort of worry at all. Everything would work out. Of course, it would.

After showering and dressing in a canary yellow sundress—something she only felt good wearing when she was feeling just as sunny inside—Roxy headed to the kitchen. There was a wonderful aroma coming from it.

"Morning, Nat!" Roxy said, cheerfully.

Evangeline wasn't working that morning. Nat had got the hang of making all the breakfast dishes now, and Evangeline liked her lie-ins.

Nat flashed her a grin, looking back from the big pot she was stirring. "Hey, girl."

"I feel wonderful this morning," Roxy said. "Like everything's going to work out. I feel like maybe taking Sylvia and Lily and the rest of them on some kind of tour. A boat trip, maybe?"

"Great idea!" said Nat. "I'd like to come too. I think we could all do with a nice little cocktail cruise to forget our troubles."

"Cocktails! You're a genius!" said Roxy. "That sounds like just the remedy. The influencers will be able to take wonderful pictures down the river too."

Nat nodded. "Glad I could help."

Roxy grinned mischievously. "So how did you like the tarot reading and crystals last night?" She chuckled. "Get any messages from the other side?" Nat was *not* into anything spiritual or magical, and Roxy enjoyed teasing her about it.

"Of course not!" Nat said. "I hid in the kitchen all evening, didn't I? Load of rubbish." There was a little pause before she said sheepishly, "But I *do* have to say that I woke up feeling fantastic."

"Me *too*!" said Roxy. "It's like...I don't know, it's hard to describe. Maybe like...like the air has glitter in it!"

Nat burst out laughing. "You crazy, girl, but I know exactly what you mean! I got up all excited. Got everything ready so everyone can have a full cooked breakfast if they want one. *And* I've been for a run." Nat lived in a unit that was situated immediately behind the *Funky Cat*. "But of course, that has *nothing* to do with *crystals*."

Roxy grinned. "No, nothing at all."

"How about Dr. Jack, though?" Nat said excitedly. "He's so wonderfully nuts. When do you think we'll be invited to his and Sage's wedding?"

"That's what I was thinking!" said Roxy. "He's exactly her type. They'd be wonderful together."

"Totally! And then Sage would be able to *live* in a magical supplies store. Wouldn't that be her dream? He told me he lives in the apartment above it."

"She would be in heaven," Roxy said. She let out a happy sigh. "I love living here. Don't you?"

"Yep," said Nat. "And it looks like Detective Johnson

isn't focused on me at all, so that's a plus. I am always really worried around him, but he's not said anything to me about, you know, *my paperwork*. I guess he hasn't noticed, or maybe he doesn't care. Perhaps murder investigations are his one and only thing. Anything beyond that, and he's not interested."

"Probably," said Roxy. "He does seem very focused. Laser-like. He hasn't contacted us with any update though, has he?"

Nat laughed. "Thank goodness. No news is good news."

"Are you going to do anything about your status?" Roxy asked, quietly. "Try to get legal?"

Nat bit her lip. "Well, to be honest, Rox, Sam told me that if I was found out, *you* could be in trouble too. You know, for hiring me, so I'm going to do something about it. It's not fair to you for me to stick my head in the sand. I'll get it sorted out, I promise. Sam said he'd help."

"I'm sure it will be okay. Can't you find yourself a handsome Southern gentleman to make an honest woman of you?"

"Oh! Perhaps that's what Sam meant! Me and Sam, can you imagine?" Nat threw her head back and laughed.

Once again, Roxy felt a little ripple of defensiveness at the mention of Sam. "You need to get out there and mingle, girlfriend."

"Ugh." Nat laughed and shuddered. "I *hate* that word. Mingle."

Roxy chuckled. "You make me laugh."

"Hello?" someone called from the dining room.

Roxy hurried out to see Sylvia. "Hi there, Sylvia, good morning. How did you sleep?"

"Great, thank you!" Sylvia said. "I feel so rested. I was just wondering if breakfast had started yet."

"Nope, but it can start just for you," said Roxy, gesturing at the table. "Both Nat and I were saying how well we slept too. It sounds a little woo, but I'm wondering if it isn't the energy of the crystals doing their thing."

Sylvia sat down. "It really could be. Sage certainly cut right to the chase with me!"

"Indeed, she did," said Roxy. "I hope the reading wasn't too uncomfortable for you."

"Well, it was at the time," said Sylvia. "But sometimes it's good to be uncomfortable. I feel renewed and happy now."

Roxy smiled. "I'm so glad to hear it. Now, tell me, what would you like for breakfast? We can do just about anything you want. The full works, if you like, or beignets that are up-to-the-minute fresh."

"Ooh, what about bacon and eggs?" Sylvia said.

"Coming right up!" said Roxy. "Why not have them with a New Orleans twist—eggs deviled with Cajun spice, and praline bacon?"

"Yum. Sounds wonderful!" Sylvia said.

Roxy dashed into the kitchen to give Nat Sylvia's order, then came back out to chat with the influencer while she waited.

"So how have you enjoyed your time with us so far?" Roxy said. "I know, of course, with...Dash, it's not quite the same. But I hope you're still getting something out of your trip."

"Oh, yes," said Sylvia. "It is tragic about that young man. He was so young, with so much life to live. And I feel for Michael and Kathy and Derek so much. I'm praying for their healing." With a sad expression, Sylvia looked down at her fingers on the tablecloth. Roxy noticed they were a little gnarled with arthritis. Sylvia lifted her head before resuming. "This is the first time I've been to New Orleans. While I love your hotel, especially the staff and food, I'd love to get out and see more of the city. I need to take more photos and videos for my Instagram account. My followers are like greedy children. They need feeding every couple of hours."

"How about we all take a cruise down the river? Nat and I were just talking about it. How does that sound?"

"Fabulous," said Sylvia, smiling. "I'm looking forward to it already."

CHAPTER TWENTY-FIVE

THE FEELING THAT everything was going to be just fine continued as everyone came down for breakfast. Lily Vashchenko glided down the staircase with a smile while Ada was a little kinder than usual. She even asked Sylvia how the previous evening had gone. Derek was, as always, extremely quiet and shy, but Kathy took care of him. She helped him order a huge breakfast of bacon, eggs, sausages, beans, rice, and French toast. Everyone marveled at how he stayed so thin.

"We're planning on a cruise down the Mississippi later. Is everyone up for that?" Roxy asked. They all nodded in agreement.

"Dash loved the water," said Kathy.

Roxy leaned over and gave her a hug. "You sound so incredibly strong, Kathy."

The older woman held her head high. "Dash would have wanted me to be. I can hear his voice now. '*Don't worry about it, Mom!*' he'd say. He always said that. I'm trying to channel his spirit instead of being a ball of anxiety. I want to be like him, fearless and brave."

Later that morning, they headed out for the boat ride. Roxy called Michael at his hotel to see if he would come along, but there was no answer. A few reporters still hung around the steps outside, so a plan was hatched to avoid them. Three of them acted as decoy and went out the front door. Once they saw Nat, Sylvia, and Derek emerge from the *Funky Cat*, the reporters immediately ignored them and returned to distractedly scrolling endlessly on their phones while the more newsworthy quarry of Roxy, Lily, and Kathy escaped via the back. They met up on the street at the end of the alleyway. The group walked along the streets of New Orleans together in a gaggle beneath a bright sun. The sky was a wonderful, creamy blue. It was a beautiful day for a cruise.

"Some of the best boat rides go from the French Quarter," Nat said. "Let's head in that direction."

So they did and found themselves a glorious steamer. The captain was standing around on the riverfront, looking bored. He looked as though he had been there a while, and no one was interested in what he had to offer. Monday mornings were pretty quiet.

It was a *very* large boat—named Marie—and far too large for their small party. Roxy guessed 200 people could have fit onto it. But there was no one else around. Nat barreled her way to the front of their group and demonstrated to them, and the captain, her negotiating chops. They had been honed in the flea markets of New Orleans. Nat skillfully persuaded the captain to allow them to commandeer the entire boat for just a small fee so that they could leave immediately and keep their party private. Roxy knew she was getting an amazing bargain, and with a nod to Nat, produced her business credit card before the man could change his mind.

"Where's the bartender?" Lily asked when they got on board.

"It's Monday. It's her day off," the captain growled.

As one, their faces fell. Their disappointment was total. They had been looking forward to their cocktails.

"No problem! I can do it. Before Instagram came along, I supported my travels with bartending. That's how I got started in this biz." They all turned to look at Sylvia, a gray-haired, cargo-panted, slightly arthritic, sixty-something woman, in surprise and not a little respect. "If I can have access to the bar, I can make us all cocktails."

Seven pairs of eyes immediately swiveled to the steamer's captain, and after a few moments pause during which he surveyed their eager expressions one by one as he considered Sylvia's request, he reached for a huge bunch of keys, one of which unlocked the bar. Sylvia immediately got to work cleaning glasses and checking the stock.

"It's a bit early for me," Roxy said when she saw Sylvia reach for some brandy. It was only 11 o'clock.

"Don't you worry, my dear, mocktails are my specialty. I'll rustle up something delicious you'll love."

Soon they were out on the open water, cocktails and mocktails in hand.

Roxy stood nearby the captain in the pilothouse. "So, why *Marie*?"

"After Marie Laveau, of course!" The boat's captain wasn't particularly polite and certainly not gracious. "Rough around the edges," Nat would have called him.

"Who's Marie Laveau?"

"Only the Voodoo Queen of New Orleans!" he said. "Her mausoleum is in the Saint Louis cemetery. You haven't heard of it?" He looked at her incredulously.

"People still go to her grave and ask her to grant them their wishes."

"Huh," Roxy said.

"You have to mark an X on the grave, turn around three times, then yell out your wish. If it's granted, you're to come back, draw a circle around the X, and leave her an offering as thanks," the captain continued. "If you don't, well, you know..." He raised his eyebrows as high as they would go.

Just a few months ago, faced with a comment like that, Roxy would have felt as though she'd entered a different world. Now that she was steeped in the mysticism of the city, she didn't blink an eye. "Oh, I'll have to visit," she said mildly.

The cruise was delightful. Jazz music wafted through the speakers, making it all the more relaxing. Nat got everyone tapping their feet and swaying as she sang along to the upbeat *Hit the Road, Jack* and the more soulful *Cry Me a River*. They got wonderful views of the city as they cruised by, and Lily and Ada and Sylvia took so many pictures and videos, that Roxy marveled at the full-time job it must be to sort out which shots would make it onto their social media accounts.

The cruise went on for a little over three hours, and thanks to Sylvia, the cocktails were colorful and became more intense (alcoholic) as the journey went on. By the time they cruised back to the dock they'd launched from, the whole party was playful and chatty. Even Derek had come out of his shell a little and was trotting up and down the top deck while his mother, frightened that he might fall in the water, told him to calm down. The group felt closer, somehow, like the water running beneath them had bonded them together.

"Great idea you had, Nat," Roxy said, as the boat cruised back to its dock. Roxy felt relaxed for the first time in days.

"What?" Nat sat on a bench looking out from the side of the boat, her eyes closed, the gentle breeze from across the river making strands of her bobbed hair dance.

"This cruise, it was a great idea. Got us all out in the fresh air. We needed it." Roxy caught sight of a man standing on the riverside. "Oh no. Really? Now?"

"What?" Nat repeated.

"It's him."

"Who?" Nat stood and turned. She shielded her eyes from the sun as she looked toward the dock they had left from. Standing there waiting for their return was Detective Johnson.

Roxy disembarked first. She felt it was her duty as the owner of the hotel and organizer of the trip.

"Come here," Johnson ordered, as soon as she stepped off the boat. Roxy bristled. It felt like a very hard reintroduction to the reality of life on the ground after their relaxing cruise on the water. Johnson held his hand up to the others who were readying to leave the paddleboat behind Roxy. "Ms. Reinhardt only. Everyone else must wait."

Roxy's heart thudded in her chest as Johnson led her away.

"What's wrong?" Roxy said.

"Michael O'Sullivan was attacked last night. Beaten up and left unconscious. He was on the way back from an evening at your hotel, I understand." Johnson looked at her. He squinted, deliberately lowering his head to study her.

"Oh, my gosh! Is he okay?"

"Yes, he is. He went to the hospital for some treatment and is now being monitored for a concussion, but he'll be fine. I need all your guests to come to the station for questioning. I have squad cars standing by the curb. You need to explain to them all what's going on."

"Do you...do you think it has anything to do with Dash's death?"

"I don't know. Probably."

Roxy closed her eyes in despair. What had she gotten these people *into*? And which one of them was a murderer?

I F ROXY HAD felt like a billion dollars when stepping out of the *Funky Cat* earlier that day, she felt like less than a dime coming back in. It was still only late afternoon, but it felt like so much time had passed, it should have been late at night. Before they left the police station, Johnson had assembled the group in the lobby. Roxy, Nat, Kathy, Derek, Sylvia, Lily, and Ada stood before him. Various expressions of anger, boredom, and exhaustion stared back at him. "Now, you are all free to go, but I will be keeping an eye on you. No one must leave the city, and," he glared at Roxy, "no meddling, d'ya hear me?" The group nodded and, grumbling just a little, turned to trudge their way out of the station and back to the *Funky Cat*.

"Well, we are certainly seeing the sights of New Orleans today," Sylvia said cheerily. "Now we've seen the inside of the local police station!"

Roxy closed her eyes momentarily. Could this Instagram promotion campaign get any worse?

When they arrived back at the hotel, Roxy and Nat

headed straight for the kitchen to make po' boy sandwiches. They were all ravenous. It was in the kitchen that they found Sage. She was wired. Roxy had come to know this was Sage's "business" energy. When she was coding for her clients or working on the marketing for the *Funky Cat*, she was as sharp as a razor. She buzzed around getting things done at the speed of light. It was such a clear distinction from her usual, peaceful, floating energy and unquestionably and wordlessly telegraphed what she was doing.

Sage was munching on a beignet while tapping furiously away on her laptop with the other hand. "Client's got a major issue," she said through a mouthful. "I'm going to be gone for the rest of the day. You don't need me for anything, do you?"

Roxy *did* need her. There was something so reassuring about having Sage around. The African-American woman felt like an ever-loving mother figure who could comfort Roxy and make her feel safe. But Roxy didn't know how to say that. Plus, she was the proprietor of a hotel. She needed to be strong. An adult. "No problem," Roxy said with a forced smile. "Go ahead. We'll be fine."

"Do you know what happened?" Nat asked Sage.

"No...what?"

Nat explained what had happened to Michael.

Sage frowned. "But Dr. Jack and Michael walked back together from here last night. How could that have happened?"

"Apparently they separated at some point and Michael walked on to the Hyatt alone," Roxy said. "That's when he was attacked, according to Detective Johnson."

"Oh," said Sage. "What *is* going on right now? The

energies are very, *very* strange at the moment. Up and down, up and down, up and down, and all over the place."

"I'll say," said Roxy.

"Well, I really must be going," said Sage. "I'm so sorry, I know this isn't a good time for me to jump ship, but I'll send healing energy through the building and into the air so that you will all feel more grounded and at peace."

Roxy smiled, not knowing if Sage was amazing or absolutely crazy.

Sage paused for a moment, closed her eyes, and waved her hands back and forth. Then she said a quick, "Goodbye! I leave you in love!" and was gone.

Nat and Roxy continued to make po' boys in silence. The atmosphere in the kitchen was a little lighter, but still quite somber. Nat turned on Evangeline's old-fashioned radio, and it crackled into life. The station played authentic Deep South jazz music, and the sounds of a double bass solo bubbled into the room, bringing some warmth with it.

After being grilled by Detective Johnson, no one was feeling particularly sociable, so Roxy and Nat took the roast beef po' boys, chips, and salad to the guests' rooms and returned to the dining room, where they sat down to eat. Roxy poured herself some coffee and offered Nat a cup. Nat shook her head.

"So who *wasn't* here last night when Michael and Dr. Jack left?" Roxy mused.

"Well, Ada left earlier so she wasn't here at all," said Nat. "I think we need to keep a proper eye on *her*."

"Yes, I know you don't like her," Roxy said, a little more sharply than she meant to. "But I don't see a real motive for harming Michael, let alone killing Dash."

"Oh, come on. Dash *humiliated* her."

"I don't think she'd kill for that," said Roxy. "Anyway, I think it's much more likely to be Lily. She wants to win the Hilton Hotels sponsorship, and Michael and Dash were after it too. Imagine if she took Dash out, and then last night she tried to stop Michael?" Roxy's heart skipped a beat. "Remember, she ducked out when Sage offered to do a reading for her? She said she was going out to see her fans. I didn't see what time she came back in. Did you?"

"No," said Nat. "But it can't be her. She's so elegant and fine!"

"I think she has the strongest motive so far," said Roxy. "*And* she doesn't have good alibis. She was in the hotel the night Dash was killed and she was missing for part of last night too.

"Perhaps we can get in contact with the fans she saw," said Nat, "and find out the time she was with them."

Roxy sighed. "Johnson warned me off investigating right when Dash's body was found, and you heard him in the lobby of the station earlier. We're not supposed to investigate at all. We shouldn't even be talking about it. I mean what are we thinking? We're discussing which of our guests could be a murderer! Let's talk about something else, get our minds off it."

CHAPTER TWENTY-SEVEN

SO NAT TOLD Roxy all about the next pair of Doc Martens she planned to buy. They had a white skull and red roses design and came with bright red ribbon laces that looked just *awesome* when tied in a bow. Then Nat explained how she was going to upcycle the new table and sculpture they'd bought on their trip to the flea market and that a niche goth band that she liked would be in town later in the month and could she have an evening off to go see them?

"Of course," Roxy said.

"Thank you. And now, I'm going to prep some vegetables in case anyone wants dinner later," Nat announced.

Roxy got up from the table and stretched. "I feel so tired," she said, "like all the energy's been sucked out of me."

Nat smiled wryly. "Being around Johnson will do that to a girl, right?"

Roxy sighed. "Unfortunately, yes."

"Go have a nap."

"I can't," said Roxy. "I have some admin stuff to do,

and I also need to decide if I should speak to these darn reporters that are still hanging around. Elijah's saying they are affecting his business. His regulars aren't coming around so often because they are bothered by the reporters. He asked if I'd consider speaking to them. It might get them to go away, he said, but I'm not convinced. Sam agreed with him."

"Yeah, but they've faded away now, pretty much," Nat said. "There's just a few left. It's not like it was before. We didn't even have any follow us when we went for the boat ride, did we?"

"That's because we were clever," said Roxy. "Still, it might be the proper thing for me to make some kind of statement. What do you think?"

Nat shrugged. "I have no idea, Rox. Just do what you want to do, I say." She put their plates into the dishwasher. "See you later!" she called as Roxy picked up her coffee and headed to the tiny little office that was next to her bedroom. "I'll be back in time to help you with dinner," Roxy replied.

Roxy's office had once been a much larger space, but it was rarely used and had become a dumping ground for all sorts of items that "might come in useful someday." The room had been filled with spare crockery, a broken washing machine, and bed linen that no one ever used. Papers from as far back as the 1980s had been strewn next to electrical parts that no one knew what to do with. There had even been a bicycle wheel propped up against the wall. During the refurbishment, the junk had been cleared out, and walls were put up to divide the space into a new, sleek office on one side, and Roxy's personal rooms on the other.

The office was absolutely tiny, but Roxy *adored* it. It

had a large window looking out onto the cobbled street, and she'd painted the walls one of her favorite colors, aquamarine. She had a brilliant white desk, a slimline white laptop, a white spinning chair that Nat had painted to make it look distressed, and a glossy white table lamp. The dark wooden floorboards had been polished until they shined, and everything felt *just right*.

Roxy used a computer to do the hotel accounts. Sage had taught her how, but she still wrote them down in a book too. The physical act of writing out the numbers made her feel more in touch with the financial health of the business than did tapping keys and moving a mouse around. She used an aquamarine gel pen—she had quite a few of them, all kept in a sparkly green box—and wrote everything down in a navy blue ledger.

Roxy spent a little time filling in the ledger and balancing the petty cash. She put on some relaxing music, checked her email, and updated the hotel's Facebook and Instagram pages. Before she realized it, two hours had flown by. Hearing Nat clattering around in the dining room as she laid tables for dinner caused her to pay attention to the time. Roxy looked at her watch, astounded, then got up and stretched her neck from side to side. Where *had* the time gone?

She left her office and noiselessly walked into the kitchen. She made Nat jump. "Oh gosh, you scared me!" Nat cried.

"Hey," Roxy said, blinking. She felt like she was waking from a dream. "Sorry about that. I got into some kind of zone, a business accounts and petty cash zone if you can believe that. I've literally had my head down since I last saw you. And not for a nap." She raised the cup of coffee she was still nursing, the coffee long cold.

"Rather you than me. Look, I'm going to have a fifteen-minute rest before I start dinner," Nat said.

"I think I'll do the same," said Roxy. "See you in a few."

Roxy opened the door to her room and straight away looked around for Nefertiti. Her little cat seemed to love staying in her room even though she had the freedom to roam just about wherever she liked in the hotel. It was certainly quiet and peaceful for her in there but not very interesting. Still, Nefertiti seemed to be perfectly content most of the time. Occasionally, when the sun was shining, the Persian would meow to be let out and sun herself in the courtyard, looking nothing short of regal. But now, Nefertiti was curled up on Roxy's chair, purring in her sleep. Roxy gave her cat a tickle under her chin and took off her shoes. It was only then that she noticed something by the door, a slip of paper on the floor. She'd stepped over it when she came in.

Roxy bent to pick it up and frowned.

LOOK INTO SYLVIA'S STORY. YOU'RE ONLY GETTING HALF THE PICTURE.

It was written in capital letters. The handwriting was shaky like the person was writing with their opposite hand or they were trembling. The paper was unlined and smartly folded.

Roxy walked back to her bed slowly, reading the note over and over. Was it genuine? Or was it malicious? And who could have left it?

Now Roxy was *wide* awake and the possibility of a rest was gone. She climbed onto her bed and reached for her phone.

She navigated to the browser and typed *"Sylvia Walters"* into the search bar. All she saw was a list of

Facebook profiles for women with the same name, none of them the Sylvia that she knew. Roxy tried again.

"Sylvia Walters' story"

"The truth about Sylvia Walters"

"Sylvia Walters' scam"

All of these search terms turned up nothing at all. It was only when she searched *"Sylvia Walters' secret"* that Roxy came across something, and even that was buried deep, deep in the search results. On page fourteen, in fact.

CHAPTER TWENTY-EIGHT

THE BLOG WAS called *The Musings of a Middle-Aged, Mid-Western Mom*. It didn't look very professional at all—more like a site made from a free template. The second to last entry was dated 10 years ago.

But the last post, the most recent one, the one that when she read it had Roxy's breath catching in her chest, was from just one year ago. Obviously, the blog owner had given up on broadcasting their thoughts to the world but had deemed this subject worthy of logging back in after a nine-year break.

The secrets you don't know about popular Instagram influencer Sylvia Walters.

Roxy scanned the article quickly, her eyes darting from side to side across her phone screen. The blogger wrote that she was from Sylvia's hometown, a place with a population of less than 5,000 in Illinois but wasn't specific. *But Sylvia Walters isn't even her real name. It's Helen Matheson. Don't believe me?*

There was a grainy photo of the front page of a newspaper. The newspaper had printed an image of a woman, her hands cuffed, seemingly walking out of court surrounded by police officers. The headline screamed *KILLER WIFE TRIAL CONTINUES!*

Roxy thought her heart might burst out of her chest. Killer wife? She squinted at the newspaper photo, but it was hard to see if it really was Sylvia. The woman in the picture looked larger, but Roxy supposed Sylvia might have lost weight since then. She read through what the "Middle-Aged Mom" had to say.

Well-known Instagram influencer, Sylvia Walters AKA Helen Matheson, was sentenced to 20 years in prison for killing her husband Raymond Matheson in an altercation at their home. When she was released, she took a new name and moved to a new state.

I had forgotten all about her until I saw her posts in my Instagram feed. I recognized her immediately and saw that she had written a book. I bought it. It is packed with LIES.

In it, Sylvia/Helen says she spent a lengthy time in Europe, but I'm writing to tell you that she was never in Europe. She was in JAIL. For killing her husband. And the jury found that her attack on him was NOT in reasonable self-defense.

Raymond Matheson was a good man and well-loved by his community. Sylvia/Helen's defense was that he was abusing her, but no one in our town believes that. We think she was trying to kill him for the insurance money but got caught before she could cash in. Anyone who comes into contact with this so-called "Sylvia Walters" should BEWARE. She is a liar and a convicted felon. Steer clear!

Roxy put her phone down on the bed. This was all

too weird for words. Was it true? But why would anyone make it up?

Roxy's thoughts were whizzing through her brain far too fast. All of a sudden her bedroom was too small. The walls felt like they were closing in on her. Her head was hurting. She needed coffee and she had an overwhelming urge to get out of the hotel.

Roxy slipped her shoes back on, squeezed out a pouch of cat food into Nefertiti's bowl, and headed out of her room, grabbing her coffee cup as she did so. It was in the lobby that she bumped into none other than Sylvia. She was carrying her trekking poles. Roxy gasped.

"You look like you've seen a ghost!" said Sylvia, laughing. "I don't look *that* bad in a tracksuit, do I?"

"Oh no, not at all!" Roxy said. "I just didn't expect anyone to be here. It's been quite a day. I'm a bit on edge, that's all."

Sylvia pursed her lips and nodded. "I know what you mean. It has been a day." Sylvia looked at Roxy's cup. "You know, I gave up coffee a while back to manage my stress. It's helped tremendously," she said. "Nothing after 2 PM, otherwise I get these anxious thoughts at evening time. I thought I actually suffered from anxiety and went to the doctor for medication, but before I took any, someone suggested I give up caffeine as an experiment. I've been anxiety-free ever since! You should try it."

At any other time, this would have been very interesting to Roxy, but right now Sylvia's prattling made her want to scream. Maybe in the future, she *would* give up caffeine, but for now, she just needed to be alone to *think*.

"I'm going to try that," Roxy said, pointing her finger in the air. "Maybe I'll get some decaf in the meantime."

"Good idea," said Sylvia. "I'm going for my power

walk now, down by the riverside. I'll be back in time for dinner. Want to come?"

"No, no. You go. Have fun," said Roxy.

Sylvia smiled. She waved. "See you!"

Roxy whipped out her phone and pulled up the city library website. After scrolling around the site, she texted Nat. *Sorry, can't help with dinner after all. Have to go do something. I found out something crazy. Talk later.*

Roxy put her coffee cup behind the reception table and headed out the door, not even sure in what direction she was headed. She consulted her phone for the street name and punched it into her maps app.

Roxy ran to her destination. Unable to stop herself, she sprinted so fast she could hear the wind rushing past her ears. She only slowed to a jog when her destination came into view.

The library was housed in a huge colonial mansion fronted with white pillars and white woodwork. Out of breath, Roxy slowed her pace to a walk. As her heart rate slowed, she also started to doubt herself again. What had seemed like a no-brainer back at the *Funky Cat*—delve into the library records—now felt like an over-reaction.

Still, over the past few months, Roxy had gotten a lot better at trusting her intuition. She marched into the library and up to the librarian's desk. "Hi there, good evening," she said breathlessly. "I was wondering if you have a way of looking up old newspaper content. Say from 20 years ago?"

"Sure we do," said the librarian, a kindly looking man in his 60s. "A New Orleans paper?"

"Well, no. Illinois. But I'm not sure *where* in Illinois."

The man grimaced. "Might have a problem there. What information are you looking for?"

"I want to look up reporting about a woman. A Helen Matheson. She was on trial for murder."

"Okay," the man said as if this were a perfectly normal request. "Come over here to this computer, and we'll access the database."

An hour later, Roxy walked out of the library, shivers running up and down her spine. It could have been because she was still only wearing her yellow sundress and the sun was going down, but more likely it was because she *had* located Helen Matheson in the online database. Everything the blog had said was true. Roxy had even seen a picture. Helen Matheson was clearly and indisputably a younger version of the woman she knew as silver-haired, sexagenarian Sylvia Walters.

Roxy meandered through backstreets on her way home, her thoughts mirroring her rambling walk. She was so distracted, she found herself by the river without even knowing how she got there. Roxy sat down on a bench and chewed her lip as she thought some more. If anyone could see inside her brain, they would have seen ideas and theories shooting between her synapses, like spectacular lightning bolts exploding in an electric storm.

She didn't want to go back to the hotel just yet. How would she face Sylvia with all these questions in her head? Roxy had always been great at hiding her feelings, but *only* if she was quiet and could make herself small, practically invisible. She used to be able to do that without too much effort, but now? Now, she had to be an upbeat, welcoming host who constantly ministered to her guests. Hiding her emotions in the type of situation she now found herself felt almost impossible. She was too honest.

When Roxy came to the small cobbled street that led

to the *Funky Cat*, she walked right past it. She wasn't ready to go home just yet. She would visit Sam at his laundry. There were still a couple of reporter's vans parked on the street near the inn, but she strode along, confident that the journalists wouldn't notice her as long as she walked purposefully.

But Roxy's confidence was misplaced. As she turned a corner, she bumped into a female reporter. The other woman had been walking quickly and banged into Roxy with some force. Thick black hair tumbled in waves over the reporter's shoulders, and she struggled to move freely in her tight black skirt suit and high heels. Roxy didn't recognize her and wouldn't have known she was a reporter by sight, but for the microphone that the woman wielded like a weapon in front of her bright red lips.

The woman stumbled back and looked shocked for a moment but recovered in an instant. "Roxy Reinhardt!" she cried.

"ROXY REINHARDT, THE manager of the *Funky Cat Inn*, formerly a call center operator with Modal Appliances, Inc. My name is Mariah Morales, KQNR-20 Nightly News." The woman assumed an expression of concern. "Tell me, Roxy, a murder was previously connected to your establishment when owned by Evangeline Smith. How do you explain this second death? A poisoning at that." She shoved the microphone in Roxy's face, awaiting answers to her questions, and gestured urgently toward a man with a camera. "Come on, Sheldon!" Morales hissed.

Roxy felt a huge lump rise in her throat. The microphone terrified her, and she felt adrenaline shoot through her body as, like a cornered animal, she looked for an escape route. "Sorry, I can't say anything," she gasped. A car passed and seeing Morales' microphone, the driver honked the car's horn loudly. The sound startled the reporter and for a second she took her eyes off Roxy. Seizing her opportunity, Roxy fled, hoping Mariah couldn't follow in her stiletto heels.

Propelled by a speed that she didn't know she possessed, Roxy flew down side streets and across sidewalks. People scattered to let her through. Shame burned in Roxy's pink cheeks, but her feet drove her forward and away from Mariah Morales and her menacing microphone. Why, oh *why* hadn't she been content living her quiet little life? Why had she chosen to live bigger? Why couldn't she have enjoyed the total obscurity of being a call center operator?

By the time she exploded through Sam's doorway, Roxy was angry with herself, with the world, and especially with Mariah Morales. She found Sam at the front desk, quietly doing some paperwork. He raised his head in surprise when she shot through the door.

"I'm so *sick* of this!" she burst out.

Sam laughed a little. "Hello to you too, Roxy."

"Sorry," she said, glaring at him. She looked back to see if Mariah and her cameraman Sheldon had followed her. They had. She could see Morales tottering on her high heels up the street, Sheldon jogging beside her.

"Help! The press. They're following me."

"Here." Sam parted a rack of shirts each draped in plastic. "Behind there. Be still. Don't make a noise."

Roxy slipped in between the shirts, and Sam let them fall so that they obscured her.

Mariah pushed open the door to the laundry and said, "Can I just...?"

"I'm sorry, no, you can't," Sam said walking up to her.

"But..."

"This is private property, and I ask that you remove yourselves immediately."

Mariah stretched her red lips into an especially beguiling smile. "I can assure you, sir, that we..."

"No," Sam said firmly, not swayed by her feminine wiles, attractive as they were. "Please leave right now. That is all. You are trespassing."

Mariah's expression quickly changed into a scowl. "Whatever." She flounced out, carelessly allowing the door to close on Sheldon who scurried behind her, the big camera he carried on his shoulder weighing him down.

Sam locked the door behind them. "You can come out now, Roxy." There was a rustle of plastic as the shirts parted and Roxy appeared, red-faced and windswept. "The reporters are still bothering you, I see," he said.

"Yes," said Roxy. "You saved me. Thank you. I don't know what came over me, I just ran and ran." She was feeling a little better already. The laundry was lovely and warm, and the thrum of the machines was hypnotic. They relaxed her. She flopped down on a plastic chair. She felt safe here with Sam.

"But the reporter is not really what's on my mind."

"So what's up?" he said.

"I found out some things about one of my guests. She's not been truthful, and I'm not sure what to do. Not in the circumstances. I'd like your help, your advice."

"You don't seem to like it when I give you advice. So I don't know how I can help."

"This time it's different, I'm *asking* for your advice—about this little...um, *investigation* I'm doing into my guest."

"Hmm well, you ignored me last time when I told you to stop investigating, and then you went and solved a murder!" said Sam. "Boy, did I feel like a jerk afterward."

"But you were right!" Roxy said. "It was just by chance that I solved it. It was a lucky break. But this time, I'm really out of my depth. I have to keep the influencers happy or they'll post terrible things about the *Funky Cat*, but this person, the one who's been untruthful, is *one* of the influencers! Oh dear. And it looks like I'm going to have to say something to the media eventually. Or they're just going to keep popping up in unexpected places. Oh dear, oh dear." She was wringing her hands and looking around the room as though the answer might lie among the racks of plastic-swathed laundry or in the churning washing machines.

Sam came up behind her and put his hands on her shoulders. "There, there. You just need to calm yourself a little. And never mind those journalists. They are like cockroaches. They scuttle away when you stand up to them."

The pressure from Sam's hands calmed Roxy, and she took a couple of deep breaths. "*Exactly* like cockroaches."

"You could just give a generic statement that yes, this thing happened. It's a terrible tragedy, that your thoughts are with the family, and you're looking forward to the case being resolved."

Roxy gulped and looked down at her lap. "That sounds like a press conference. Lots of journalists."

"It doesn't have to be like that," he said. "You can do it with one news crew. I guarantee all the other stations will pick it up."

The very thought of Roxy's face being beamed across the country, even the state—heck, the city, was terrifying.

Sam moved in front of her, and when she looked up from watching her fingers, which she was interlacing in different patterns in her lap, she saw him looking at her intently. The concern in his eyes caught her off guard.

"Just do it if you want to," he said. "If you don't, that's

383 NEW ORLEANS NIGHTMARE

fine too. Just don't let fear get in the way of what you want to do."

Roxy smiled a little. "Easier said than done, though, right?"

He nodded. "Generally, yes, but don't feed fear with time, that's what I always say. It's like ripping off a band-aid—it's best just to go for it."

"And what about Johnson? And the untruthful influencer?"

"Well, that's up to you too. Do what you think would be the best for Dash."

CHAPTER THIRTY

OR DINNER THAT evening, Nat had prepared shrimp étouffée and salmon cakes with rice and a Creole remoulade. None of the guests felt in the mood for a large, dress-up dinner, so everyone came down in their jeans and sweaters. The evening had turned cool. Lily Vashchenko even wore bright pink fluffy slippers with rabbit ears—and two-inch heels. Only Ada dressed up. She wore jeans but with towering stilettos and an emerald-green silk shirt.

Everyone—even Kathy—made a concerted attempt to talk about everything *except* Dash's death. They talked about the weather (changeable), what was planned for next year's Mardi Gras (nothing that they knew of, but they were sure it would be fun), the color of the dining room wallpaper (powder blue with shimmering beige stripes), whether all bottled water was collected from natural springs (!), and Derek's future career plans (none specific at present).

Roxy made a special effort to smile a lot at Sylvia and engage with everything she said like she was her special friend. A raised eyebrow from Nat let her know she was overdoing it a little, so she toned it down.

Roxy was *desperate* to tell Nat what she'd found out about Sylvia, but they hadn't been alone all evening. She had to be patient. The guests would shortly be retiring for the night, and Roxy would be able to launch straight into all that she'd learned as soon as she and Nat were alone in the kitchen.

"Let me help you load the dishwasher," she heard Kathy say, as the others left for their rooms. Roxy inwardly groaned.

"But you're a guest!" Roxy protested. "I can't let you do that. Please, please, sit down in the lounge and help yourself to a drink."

"But I *insist,*" said Kathy. "I'm doing an online course in personal development, and for a challenge, we have to go out of our way to do one good deed a day." She held her head up proudly and said, "It's always good to learn and grow."

"Yes, but..." Nat looked a little bewildered. "Are you sure?"

"Yes," Kathy said emphatically.

Nat shook her head. "Well, okay...if that's really what you want."

Kathy sang Country and Western songs as she loaded the dishwasher and Nat and Roxy cleared the dining room. They waited to see if Kathy had an ulterior motive for offering to help, but when she was done, she simply gave them a huge smile and said, "Deed done for the day."

Roxy smiled back. "Thank you, Kathy. Now *please,* go ahead, and sit yourself down with a nice drink."

"Raise a glass to Dash for us," Nat added.

"I sure will," Kathy replied.

Nat closed the kitchen door behind Dash's mother as she left and waited a few moments. She whispered, "I'm not sure about her."

"She is a bit strange. Anyway, forget that. Listen to this." Roxy explained all about Sylvia being Helen and everything she'd learned.

"No way!" Nat whisper-shouted. "I *thought* there was something fishy about her."

Roxy laughed. "You think everyone's fishy, Nat."

"But even if she does appear a bit dodgy, why would she kill Dash or hurt Michael? And wasn't she asleep by the time Michael was attacked? He stayed for a good while to chat with Sage and Dr. Jack, even after the others had gone to bed. They were talking about subatomic reality and how that related to spiritual enlightenment, or something like that. Sage told me. Of course, it's all rubbish, but that doesn't change the fact that Sylvia couldn't have attacked Michael when she was here, in bed."

"I guess you're right," Roxy said. "But, she could have snuck out. I didn't lock the door until past midnight, because Ada, Lily, and Derek stayed out late."

"Well, it's *them* we need to look at, I reckon," said Nat. "Lily wanted the Hilton contract so she could have bumped off Dash to give her a better chance of landing it, Ada could have done it in revenge for Dash humiliating her, and Derek...well, maybe he was jealous of his brother, so much so that he killed him."

"Come on!" said Roxy. "Derek wasn't even in the city when Dash was killed."

"Good point," Nat said. "But he could have attacked Michael. Maybe Michael's attacker wasn't the same person who killed Dash. Maybe Derek believes Michael was the murderer and was doling out his own form of justice."

"Oh, I don't know what to think," Roxy admitted. "It's just too complicated, but I can't stop thinking about it. I need to do *something*. Oh, and I found all this out because of a note someone posted under my door this afternoon. Don't you think that's strange?"

Nat stared at her. "That is weird. Who would do that? Do you recognize the handwriting?"

"Nope," said Roxy. "They wrote it all in capitals. The writing's very shaky like someone wrote it with their opposite hand."

Nat sighed. "A poison pen letter! Look, I sound so, so, *so* incredibly boring and square, I know, but you should really hand that over to Detective Johnson."

Roxy wrinkled her nose. "Yes, you're right. But, oh, you know he's going to grill me like a cheese sandwich. I'll have to psych myself up for another interview. Which reminds me, Sam still thinks I should speak to the reporters, give them a simple statement to get them off my back. One of them accosted me in the street earlier."

Nat shrugged and said casually, "Sounds like a good idea to me. Can't hurt, can it?"

"Oh, easy for you to say!" Roxy said, feeling a wave of anxiety immediately rise up and wash over her. "I'm the one who has to stand in front of all these cameras that are beaming my face across the world and say stuff that makes some kind of sense. It's terrifying."

Nat flashed her a wicked grin. "You're the boss. That means you get all the headaches, responsibility, and horrible jobs. Congratulations!" She threw her hands up in the air and laughed. "Sorry, girl. Look, I believe in you.

Go ahead and do it. In fact, do it right now. Go out there and find a reporter. The more you wait around, the more afraid you'll become."

Roxy could hear her heart thumping, even in her temples! But she knew Nat was right. It was crunch time.

ROXY DID EXACTLY what Nat suggested, and trying not to think any more about what she was doing, she marched outside. She stood in the middle of the narrow cobblestoned street on which the *Funky Cat Inn* was located and looked up and down, straining to catch a glimpse of the woman with a mass of wavy dark hair, a flash of red lipstick, and a massive, menacing microphone. It was late in the evening. Roxy half-hoped that Mariah Morales had gone home.

"Roxy," a voice said behind her, so close that it made her flinch. She spun around and there—as if Roxy had, by thinking about her, manifested her out of thin air—was Mariah Morales, her bright red mouth stretched into a broad smile.

"Hello," Roxy said. Her voice sounded shaky and weak. Her shoulders drooped. Roxy hated that she sounded so pathetic. She instantly threw her shoulders back, lifted her chin and cleared her throat. "Hello, Ms. Morales. I want to make a statement."

"Wonderful!" Mariah said, throwing one hand up in the air and snapping her fingers. "Sheldon, we're ready. We'll record it and send it right over to the station." She looked around the street warily. "Wouldn't want to wait for a live slot and let anyone else get their claws on *this* story." Her voice became more intense. "Sheldon, come *on!* Are you ready yet?"

"Ready," grunted Sheldon from behind her. He held the camera at chest height and the recording light came on.

Instantly Mariah slapped on her trademark smile. "And with me now is Roxy Reinhardt, manager of the *Funky Cat Inn* where just a few days ago famous Instagram influencer, Dashiell Davies was brutally murdered."

Mariah continued to set up the segment as Roxy heard blood thunder through her ears. She barely registered what Mariah was saying until...

"What would you like to say to the world about this tragedy, Ms. Reinhardt?"

Roxy's mind went blank. She couldn't get her thoughts straight. In fact, she couldn't think at all. The only thing she could do was open her mouth, let the words come, and hope she sounded somewhat lucid. She couldn't even process what she was saying, not really. All she remembered afterward was "terrible tragedy" and "Detective Johnson," "justice," and "no evidence that our hotel food was responsible." "Thank you," Roxy said at the end of her statement. She walked away, leaving Mariah to close the segment in front of Sheldon.

As she made her way back inside the *Funky Cat*, Roxy felt something she had never experienced in her entire life. An incredible rush of relief and pride pulsated through her like she'd been "plugged in" for the first time ever. The mint green of Elijah's Bakery in front of her, the pink façade of the *Funky Cat* across from it, the dark blue of the sky above, and the bright orange of the streetlights were all so intense that she felt like someone had turned up the saturation on her vision. She wanted to skip, to run, to shout, she was so pleased with herself.

She had too much energy to go back to the hotel. Instead, she decided to track down Sage. It was late, but Roxy wanted a card reading even if she still wasn't *quite* convinced she believed in them. She thought back to the reading Sage had given Sylvia. Her memory was fuzzy, but hadn't Sage said that Sylvia's story had not yet been fully released, that something about it was still unresolved?

Roxy climbed the steps to the street where Sage had her apartment, but there was no answer when she rang the bell. Roxy put her ear to the door, but she couldn't hear a gong, drumming, voices, meditation music, or any familiar noise that would indicate Sage was home. Similarly, Roxy couldn't smell the aroma of incense unfurling under the front door. She concluded that Sage wasn't in. Roxy decided to try Dr. Jack's botanica, instead. Despite the lateness of the hour, it would be open, you know, for the witches.

Roxy hurried to the magical supplies store, and stepped inside, savoring the wonderful familiar smell. She could never quite put her finger on what it was, but it was musky and sweet with notes of wood and herbs. It was like walking into a hug that you weren't quite sure you wanted.

There was no one at the cashier desk, so Roxy weaved her way through the aisles of candles, cauldrons, handcrafts, statues, soaps, and skulls. Finally, she found Dr. Jack counting essential oils on a shelf, his back to her. Before she spoke out or identified herself, he said, "Hello, Roxy. How nice to see you."

Roxy felt shivers go up her spine. "How did you know it was me?"

"You have a very distinctive aura," he said. "Especially tonight. A very particular kind of energy, expansive. Did you achieve a goal of some kind?"

Roxy was dumbstruck. "Well, I did finally talk to a reporter outside the *Funky Cat,* something I was very nervous about."

"Aha!" he said. "Well done. Now, what can I help you with?"

"I'm looking for Sage," she said.

"She was due here earlier," he replied, "but had to cancel. She's staying the night at a hotel near her client's offices. She has a very early presentation there tomorrow morning."

"Oh," Roxy said, disappointed. "I was looking for a reading."

He held his arms out. "Hello?" he said.

Roxy laughed. "Oh, I know, but..."

"No charge," he said. "Come on, I *insist.* You look like you need a good reading. Let's do a fast one. One card. Pick it." He whipped out a tarot deck from his pocket and pointed it in her direction. "Go! No thinking, now. Thinking will overwhelm your intuition."

Roxy shut her eyes and picked a card at random. It was a card with a young man holding a medallion. The medallion had a star on it. "*The Page of Pentacles,*" she read.

"A wonderful card," Dr. Jack said. He peered at her.

"It means you're ready to manifest your dreams. This is a good time to start new projects. Look to the possibilities and potential of what you're doing and make concrete plans. Don't just *react* to how events unfold. Be proactive. Make things happen, Roxy. Push ahead."

CHAPTER THIRTY-TWO

R
OXY WAS TRYING desperately hard to heed Detective Johnson's advice. She bustled around her room going through her early morning wakeup routine, ruminating as she did so. She was *not* going to go investigating and poking her nose in where it was not wanted. Instead, she was going to focus on making sure that her guests had the best time with her that they possibly could, given the grisly events that had occurred and the possibility that one of them was the murderer.

She decided to organize another trip for them, and an idea popped into her head while she was in the shower. This time, why not go to Marie Laveau's grave? Since the steamer captain had told her about it, it had piqued Roxy's curiosity. She'd see for herself what it was all about, and she would take her guests with her.

Roxy was undecided about what she thought of New Orleans Voodoo, but she *did* want to know about the heritage of the city. It was undoubtedly a special place. There was something in the air, a certain type of magic, and she wanted to understand what it was. It wasn't just the Cajun and Creole spices, it wasn't just the allure of Mardi Gras or the soft warmth of soulful jazz. There was a *je ne sais quoi* of the place, a sense of mystery about which Roxy didn't tire of learning.

The cemetery would undoubtedly generate interesting content for the Instagrammers, and she put her idea to the influencers over breakfast. Everyone was keen to go along. Even Ada said she would join them if only for the historical aspect of the outing. "I do not believe in such witchcraft, though," she said. "I want that noted by everyone."

"And you think I do?" Nat said pausing as she topped up the coffee pots. "It's just something you have to know about, being in New Orleans. It's not like you're going to become a Voodoo priestess tomorrow!"

Ada opened her eyes wide. There was silence at the table.

"How dare you be so impertinent!" Ada said.

"Sorry," said Nat quickly. "I didn't mean anything by it, Ada. I was joking around, that's all."

Ada continued to look outraged before looking at Lily, Sylvia, Kathy, and Derek. They were staring at her, their utensils paused in midair as they waited for this latest drama to unfold. Ada caught sight of Kathy, whose eyes were wide, her mouth forming a small "O".

It was at just that moment that Elijah arrived. Without knocking, he breezed through the front door, sashaying his way through the lounge and dining area, one hand aloft supporting three boxes of pastries piled on top of one another. "Morning, everyone!" he cried without stopping. He turned to push the kitchen door with his behind. He gave Derek a little wave and a grin before disappearing into the kitchen.

Elijah's appearance had pierced the heavy atmosphere and Ada relaxed. She gave Nat a small smile. "That's okay, I forgive you. But don't do it again," she finished softly. Roxy breathed a sigh of relief, and Nat hurried into the kitchen, glad to have a bolthole.

"Let's go to Marie Laveau's this morning and get a light lunch afterward," Roxy said brightly, keen to dispel any lingering remnants of tension. "Because I don't know about you, but I'm not keen on going at night."

Everyone felt the same. So she, Nat, Lily, Sylvia, Ada, Kathy, and Derek set off toward the old cemetery soon after breakfast. Roxy also called Evangeline to see if she wanted to join them, but she said, "I've been one hundred times before, cher, since I was a little girl. My mama had plenty a wish granted by the Voodoo Queen. Say hello to her for me, won't you?"

Michael didn't want to come either. "It's just a tourist trap, Roxy. I want to experience the *real* spiritual heritage of New Orleans. Plus, my head still aches."

Roxy thought his response was a little rude but didn't say anything. She kept what he'd been through at the forefront of her mind. She brushed off his dismissal and prepared herself to act as tour guide.

Roxy had thought that visiting the spot in the morning would take away the eeriness of the place, but she was wrong. The Saint Louis cemetery was incredibly quiet, the silence spooky. They could hear every footstep as they walked deeper and deeper into the cemetery. It was like walking through a miniature, abandoned city. Eventually, they came upon Marie Laveau's grave. It was a huge gray box of a mausoleum nestled in among those of others. X signs were scrawled all over the tomb, some with rings around them.

"This feels too weird," whispered Lily, shivering even though the sun was out.

Roxy felt the same. It seemed as though even the birds had stopped singing. She told herself not to be so ridiculous, that Marie Laveau was long dead (1881!), and any stories of her spirit lingering around were just superstition.

"Marie Laveau was a hairdresser by day," Roxy told the assembled group, "but at night she was known as the Voodoo Queen, sought after for her potions and charms. She was immensely powerful and many people were enthralled by her. It is said that even politicians, lawyers, businessmen, and the wealthy were influenced by her."

Ada hovered at the back of the group with a guidebook. "This is very interesting from a *historical* perspective," she said. Her voice shook a little.

Just then, they heard a voice coming out from behind the mausoleum. "You come to see me?" the voice bellowed, in thick, foreboding tones. Everyone jumped. Ada screamed. Lily launched herself across the group and grabbed Roxy's arm.

Derek jumped out from behind the grave. "Haha!" he cried, showing more energy in this one moment than he had in the entire time he'd been in their company. "I scared you all, didn't I? The looks on your faces! I should have recorded it on my phone! Now *that's* an Instagram story!"

"Derek!" Kathy scolded him. "You nearly gave us all a heart attack!"

"Who was the one who screamed?" Derek asked, a sneer playing on his lips.

Ada stared at him in stony silence.

"It was Ada," Lily said, seriously. "But I don't blame her. That was really scary. Perhaps you should do tours around here. You would be great at scaring the tourists half to death. Some people like that kind of thing."

"That's an idea," Derek said. He dug Lily in the ribs with his elbow. She frowned and moved away from him.

Roxy was absolutely furious. He was sabotaging her outing, turning it into a highly unpleasant experience. How could he be so mean? "Does anyone want to make a wish?" she asked to distract them from Derek's prank. "When you make your wish you have to turn around, shout it out, and mark your "X" on the tomb. When it comes true the custom is to return here, circle your "X," and leave a gift. That's why there's all these flowers and beads. Is anyone going to make a wish?"

"I don't know if I dare," said Sylvia.

"Oh, I will!" said Kathy. "I will ask for justice for my son."

Kathy walked up to the tomb, turned around and shouted out, "Justice for my son's murder! Dashiell Davies!" She took a pen from her bag and marked an X on the grave. "The Voodoo Queen better help me," she muttered. "I hope she and Jesus work together!"

"I wouldn't say that if I were you," said Ada.

KATHY TURNED TO Ada, her eyes devoid of any life. She didn't even smile, not even a forced one. "Don't tell me what I should and shouldn't do," she said. "When your child has been murdered, then and only then will you be qualified to give *me* advice."

Ada had the decency to mutter, "Sorry."

Roxy took that as a cue to leave the cemetery and took them to an Italian restaurant for lunch. Pasta and pizza was always a comforting choice, and it felt like they all needed some solace. The restaurant she took them to—Mandinelli's—was famous for suffusing traditional Italian food with Creole and Cajun spice to make a truly unique New Orleans foodie experience.

As they settled down to eat, Roxy checked her phone. There was a message for her on the *Funky Cat* Instagram profile. A private message. She clicked on it. She guessed it was to discuss a booking. But it wasn't. *Check this out,* the message read. Attached was a video. Looking furtively around to see if any of the group was watching, Roxy pressed "Play."

All she saw was a jerky video of a pair of men's booted feet. But then she heard the audio.

Do you see how you're talking to me?

Roxy thought it might have been Dash's voice, but she wasn't sure.

I'm recording you!

The voices were quiet, so Roxy brought the phone up to her ear. She kept switching between listening and looking at the screen.

Stop that!

This time it was a different voice. The camera jerked upward, and there was Michael, glaring into it. She was sure the other voice was Dash's now. Michael called Dash a name and slapped the camera out of his hand so that the view from the device jerked and twisted. It ended up facing a ceiling.

"No way," Roxy whispered to herself. Maybe Kathy had been right about Michael after all. Maybe he wasn't so nice.

Why are you so against the Hilton idea?

It was Dash's voice again. He sounded perplexed and angry.

Michael replied. *Because the Hilton idea is ridiculous! You and I agreed we wouldn't go down the commercial route because...*

No, you decided, and I have to go along with it like I always do! But I'm not doing it anymore, Michael. I'm not! I swear to you!

Dash was really angry now. Roxy heard Michael let out a growl of anger, and the video cut off.

Roxy sat still, her heart thumping.

"Are you okay, Roxy?" Kathy said, leaning over toward her.

Roxy moved the phone out of her view. "Oh yes, I'm fine," she said quickly, smiling at her.

Kathy frowned. "You don't *look* okay."

"I was...well, someone messaged me about a booking and asked for a discount for a certain number of nights. I was just trying to do the math in my head." She forced a laugh. "Math isn't my strong point." Neither was lying.

"Oh, let me take a look," said Kathy, holding her hand out for the phone. "I used to be a middle school math teacher."

"It's okay, don't worry about it," said Roxy with a smile. "I've forwarded it to my work email already. It'll be fine. Now I just need to head to the bathroom real quick. Please excuse me."

Roxy dashed to the restroom at the back of the restaurant. She wanted a minute alone with the phone to reply to the direct message. But she couldn't. There was no bar for her to type her reply into. She looked at the profile of the account that had sent her the video. It was clearly a fake one. There was no profile picture and only the name 'XgXgXg' which, of course, meant nothing.

Roxy slipped the phone into her pocket and sighed deeply. She cast a glance at herself in the mirror. She looked the same as she always did—slim, slight, and small, with a blond pixie haircut and a face that others told her was beautiful, but which looked just ordinary to her. There was a strength, a steeliness, to Roxy's eyes though. Just then the door to the bathroom burst open. She flinched. Kathy barreled through the door.

"I have to use the little girl's room too," Kathy said. "And I thought I could help you with that math."

Roxy smiled. She was starting to feel a little irritated. "Seriously, it's all right," she said. "Have you decided what you're ordering?"

"No, it all looks too delicious to choose!" said Kathy. "I do have a favor to ask you, though."

"Sure, what is it?"

"You know we've been talking about holding a celebration of Dash's life?"

"Uh-huh?"

"Well, we've decided to hold a large outdoor event on the weekend. I spoke to the city about it this morning. Since Dashiell admittedly *did* love a good time, we thought a street party would be the right thing to do. That way, we can invite his fans as well as his friends."

"I think he'd have loved that."

"So my question is, can you be one of the caterers? I know you can't do *everything*—I'll get other people to cook food too—but I've so enjoyed the cuisine at your place that I'd love for you to get involved."

Roxy hugged her. "Of course, Kathy. We'd be honored."

They went back to the table, and Roxy played the role of carefree host with apparent ease. But inside, her mind was *tick tick tick* with ideas. Who had sent the video? It had shown her a very dark side of Michael. Maybe Dash and he weren't such great friends, after all. Maybe, just maybe, Michael had *faked* his own attack. Maybe it hadn't happened like he said at all.

CHAPTER THIRTY-FOUR

"**E**XCUSE ME!" JOHNSON said. "Attention!" He looked annoyed. "And turn off that darned radio."

"Yes?" Evangeline said, twisting toward him, her hands on her hips. "What is it?"

Unannounced, Detective Johnson had arrived at the *Funky Cat* on the morning of the street party to celebrate Dash's life.

He turned up at the worst possible time—when everyone was hard at work in the kitchen. Lily looked stylish and impractical in slacks, heels, and a silk blouse, but she had brought her own apron and rubber gloves. Sylvia was there in dungarees and a work shirt. Derek showed up cloaked in a hoodie. The guests had generously offered to help with the food preparations. They'd eaten breakfast at 6 AM so they could be in the kitchen by 7, and no one had made a murmur of complaint. Even the glamorous Ada, who wore a Versace tracksuit, hadn't pitched a fit when she was splashed by the crab boil.

Evangeline, of course, was the kitchen manager and

behaved in a way that was rather Gordon Ramsay-esque, although without the incessant cursing. She certainly wasn't going to pamper Sylvia, Lily, and Ada just because they were Instagram stars. Roxy bit her lip at times when she heard Evangeline barking orders at them, but the truth was no one seemed to mind.

It was an all-hands situation so they rolled up their sleeves, literally in Sylvia's case, and got on with their tasks. Evangeline's old radio blasted out happy jazz tunes that had them dancing around the kitchen, and there were back slaps and shouts of laughter as they happily went about making cornbread patties, stirring gumbo, and assembling po' boys. Everyone seemed enthused by the prospect of a party. Derek almost raised a smile at one point. His mother, Kathy, was with Sam. They were setting up at the site of the party—hanging flags, arranging the stage, and organizing where all the caterers' tables would go while back in the *Funky Cat* kitchen Roxy teamed with Lily to make what seemed like a million *oysters en brochette*.

Sharing the tasks, Roxy and Lily skewered the oysters, bacon, and onion before rolling each skewer in cornflour. Later at the event, they would deep-fry them. They would also cut toast into triangles and brush them with a Meunière sauce made from parsley, lemon, brown butter, and red wine vinegar. After they had been fried, the cooked oysters, onion, and bacon would be served on top of the toast, and a twist of salt and pepper would complete the dish. Roxy had only made it once and that time under Evangeline's watchful eye, but today Evangeline had some ten other dishes going. They were on their own, but there was an easy, warm atmosphere of camaraderie in the kitchen and they were all focused on their tasks. Roxy's mind was as far away from Dash's murder or any other disaster as it could get.

That was until Detective Johnson showed up. Immediately the happy bubble around them burst with a pop. It was almost like Johnson carried a big pin with him.

"Look, I don't know what it is with this place, but any time something happens around here it seems to involve y'all. So I'm here to tell you no messing around today, y'hear? No funny business. This event is for Dashiell Davies. The police department has been liaising with his mother, and if *anything* untoward happens, the attention of your local law enforcement will snap onto the *Funky Cat* faster than you can say 'Instagram'. Is that clear?"

Roxy peered around to see the influencers looking taken aback. Ada glared at Johnson, Lily looked as though there was a nasty smell under her nose while Sylvia, like Evangeline, stood with her hands on her hips. Derek seemed to attempt to merge with the pots and pans as he tried to make himself invisible. They clearly weren't used to being spoken to like that. Roxy, on the other hand, had a little more experience. She walked up to the detective and kept her voice low. "Of course, Detective," she said quietly. She hoped he would match her tone. She was mistaken.

"Good!" he bellowed even louder than before. "And don't think that because y'all are some kind of famous in the strange world you live in that I won't zero in on you. Behave, alright? The law has no respect for celebrity or anything else. Law's the law."

"Thank you, Detective Johnson," said Roxy calmly. "We'll make sure to remain law-abiding. You have my word on that."

"Don't you rush me!" he said. "It is very likely the

murderer will be in the crowd today so we'll be keeping a close but discreet eye on the proceedings. Watch yourselves, okay?"

Roxy heard the word "murderer" with a jolt.

Johnson continued, "The toxicology reports are back. Mr. Davies was incapacitated with a form of poison, then suffocated." Johnson proceeded to stride around the room, thumbs tucked into his belt loops that sat under his large belly. He looked at each person carefully, and the food they were preparing, before moving on. He reminded Roxy of a Wild West sheriff inspecting his usual suspects.

It got so quiet in the kitchen as he did this that every single bubble popping at the top of a boil could be heard. Roxy could hear *tap-tap-tap* as Derek gently banged his model airplane against the chrome counter. Despite the news of the manner of his brother's death, he seemed unfazed.

Eventually, Johnson said, "Alright," but very warily as he watched Roxy out of the corner of his eye as if she were some criminal mastermind and the three influencers and Derek were her henchmen. "Well, I'll be seeing y'all later."

Roxy shook her head as soon as he was out the door.

"What was *that* about?" Nat burst out when he'd gone. She shook herself like a dog. "I can't *stand* that guy!"

"Neither can I," Ada said.

Their view of Johnson was something both Nat and Ada could agree on. They looked at each other a little more warmly.

"Let's try and forget about him," Roxy said, switching the music back on. The radio station was playing a compilation of popular Nat King Cole tunes. The lively melody of *Route 66* rippled from the radio. Evangeline and Sylvia starting singing softly along, shaking their hips as they continued to prepare the food. Soon they were all moving at least one body part in time to the music. Well, not Derek, but even he didn't leave the room.

"Sing us something, Nat, cher," Evangeline said.

"Nah, I have to save my voice for later. They like the big tunes do this crowd. Besides I can't do better than ole Nat, now can I?"

"You're singing at the event?" Roxy asked.

"Yep, with Sam and Elijah. Kathy asked us."

"Ah, that's nice."

Roxy would have been perfectly happy to while away the rest of the morning making oyster skewers with Lily, listening to some mellow jazz, and forgetting about everything else. The repetitive rhythm of the cooking was cathartic, and the smells of Creole spices were so soothing. But it wasn't to be. A short while later, Kathy bustled into the kitchen looking for her. She flashed a huge smile, hooked her arm into Roxy's, and pulled her out of the kitchen. "Come with me, girl."

They walked out of the front door and into the cobbled street.

"Wow!" Roxy said.

CHAPTER THIRTY-FIVE

R OWS AND ROWS and rows of flags had been hung, strung from one side of the alleyway to the other, in every color Roxy could imagine. When they came out onto the main street, Roxy could see that the flags continued, tied to streetlights and storefronts and electricity poles, anything that was high enough. They continued as far as Roxy could see.

"Look," Kathy said, "they run all the way from your door to the party.

"Kathy!" Roxy said. "Dash would have *loved* this!"

Immediately, Kathy's cheerful smile turned into heartrending sobs. She collapsed onto Roxy. Being that Kathy was the bigger woman and Roxy was tiny, Roxy staggered backward under the heavier woman's weight. With some effort, she managed to right herself, but Kathy crumpled down onto the sidewalk. She stayed there and curled up in a ball, her head on her knees. She began to cry and cry and cry. She just didn't stop.

At first, Roxy patted her on the shoulder, and said, "Kathy, Kathy," but her voice was drowned out by Kathy's cries. Eventually, Roxy sat next to her, her arm around her shoulder and her heart hurting as she listened to Kathy's sobs, unable to do anything or say anything to help.

They stayed sitting on the curb for what seemed like an age. Vehicles passed by, their drivers and passengers staring at them, and Roxy was *so* glad not to see Mariah Morales and her ilk prowling around with their cameras, ready to capture the scene and splash it all across the state news. There was no sign of any reporters at all.

As Roxy continued to comfort Kathy, she spotted the priest who had performed Dash's memorial service as he came around the corner. He walked toward them.

"Father John!" Roxy called out.

Kathy looked up.

The priest picked up his pace when he recognized them and with gentle hands brought Kathy to her feet. He wiped her tears away with his soft, fat fingers. "May the Lord bring you peace, my child."

Kathy blubbed, "I...don't...think...that's...possible, Father!"

"It will be, with time," he said. "Put your trust in the Lord. *Choose* to put your trust in the Lord."

"Okay," Kathy said like an obedient little girl. "I can do that...I think. Thank you."

"You will be blessed for your faith," he said. "There, there..."

Kathy visibly calmed at his words and began to breathe normally.

Father John turned to Roxy. "I came here to see you."

Roxy was a little taken aback. "Yes, Father?"

"I was wondering if you would speak at the event today. Of course, Kathy is speaking. Derek is not, due to his shy nature. Michael is paying a tribute to Dashiell, their work and fans. We, Kathy and I, that is, talked earlier, and wondered if you would like to say something. As a sort of representative of the city of New Orleans."

Roxy bit her lip. "Me? But I'm not even *from* here."

"Yes," he said. "I can tell that by your accent. But you're a businesswoman here now, and that means you are part of our community. I have talked to Michael too. He explained that you were a kind person. Perhaps you saw some qualities in Dash that you admired and that you can speak to?"

"Oh, yes," Roxy said. "Of course. He was adventurous and wild and brave, for sure. He was very encouraging too, and certainly knew how to have a good time!"

The priest nodded triumphantly. "That's that, then. You'll give a small speech?"

Roxy's stomach lurched. Speaking in front of a huge crowd of people wasn't her idea of fun. They were expecting thousands—not only local residents but many, many fans. Many more than turned out at the funeral. This time Dash's followers had had plenty of notice, and people were traveling from all over the country. Some were even coming from Europe! Roxy looked at Kathy, hoping that she would say it was inappropriate.

But she didn't. She looked tearfully in Roxy's direction. "Please do," she said. "It would mean a lot to me."

Roxy gulped. "Okay," she said quietly. Her eyes were wary. The priest looked at her quizzically. She cleared her throat and straightened up. "Sure," said Roxy, more confidently now. "I'd love to."

"Excellent!" Kathy gave a little jump and clapped her hands. "Now, I want to show you the rest of the preparations," she said. "And to show you where you guys need to bring the food later."

The trio started to walk. Kathy went a little way ahead and Roxy strolled alongside Father John.

"Thank you for helping Kathy and Derek like this, Father. I know you've been a huge support to them," Roxy said.

"Ah, no worries, young lady. It's my job. They've been dealt a terrible hand," the priest replied.

"Do you think Kathy will be alright?"

"With the love of God and her faith, I believe in time she will be."

"And Derek?"

"That, I don't know. I don't know the young man well. I only met him at the funeral service. I don't think he shares his mother's faith. You take care of them in your way and I will do so in mine. Together we'll do the very best for them."

"That we will, Father."

"WOW, IT'S NEARLY 10 AM already! We're starting in an hour," Kathy cried as she showed Roxy around the site of the party. "Here's where you'll speak." The stage was flanked with beautiful pillars graced with streamers and crisscrossed with more flags in bright colors. "Here's where you'll serve your food."

Roxy saw a few partygoers come down the street and glanced at her watch. "Look! People are trickling in already! I'd better get everyone to load their food into the van and bring it down. Where are all the other caterers, Kathy?"

Kathy bit her lip and looked down at her phone. "I told everyone to come at 10:30. Hopefully, that won't be too late!"

Roxy smiled encouragingly. "I'm sure it will be absolutely fine. Come on, why don't we go back to the hotel and get ready?"

Kathy smiled. "Sure! I think we'd better go at a jog, or we'll be late for our own party!"

"Okay, let's hurry!" said Roxy.

They headed back to the hotel quickly, and Roxy went into her room. Before changing, she grabbed a pen and pad and dashed into the kitchen where only Evangeline remained. Everyone else was upstairs getting changed into their party clothes.

"Aren't you getting your glad rags on, Evangeline?" Roxy asked.

"Oh, no, cher," the older lady replied. "I'll be headin' home. Can't be doin' with all these street parties anymore. I've been jumpin' up in carnival since I could jump...naw, since *before* I could jump. Too many parties will take the party spirit right out of you. I can't get excited anymore. Too old."

"Yeah, I get it," said Roxy. "I'm not one for parties myself. I always *thought* I wanted to go, but when I'd get there I'd wish I was at home curled up with a good book." She was jabbering away, rushing through the kitchen drawers like a hurricane.

"You just take this food and feed it to all those young people, y'hear? What you lookin' for, cher?" Evangeline asked.

"I'm looking for some bags."

Evangeline walked to her left and pulled open a drawer. She dragged out a small pile of brown paper bags and held them out. The elderly woman looked at Roxy quizzically. "What do you want 'em for?"

"I'm just giving everyone a little goodie bag," Roxy said. "You know, seeing as it's nearly their time to leave us."

"Great idea," said Evangeline. "What are you puttin' in 'em?"

Roxy paused, her eyes resting on bottles of spices lined up on the window ledge. "Cooking spices!" she said, hurrying over. "I-I-I'm gonna give each one of them a jar of your special Cajun spice blend, so they can make their own New Orleans-style meals when they get home."

Evangeline sniffed. "It's not a matter of having the right spices. N'awlins cookin' is much deeper than that. There's soul involved."

"Oh, I know, you're right," said Roxy. "But at least they can try. And it's a nice gesture."

Evangeline nodded. "Hmph, awright, but I hope you're not expectin' me to help you bag it all up, cher. I'm still stuffin' these tartlets."

"Oh, but I need your help. I don't know the recipe."

"I don't make it up each time I use it, you know."

"You don't?"

"Nah, I make up a batch every so often." She pointed to the walk-in pantry in the corner. "Top shelf, back left corner.

Roxy dashed over to the pantry and seeing a huge Mason jar full of a spice blend on the highest shelf, climbed onto a step stool to retrieve it.

Evangeline peered over her tartlets as Roxy staggered out of the pantry carrying the glass jar that was nearly as big as she was and just as heavy. "Do you need a hand with that?"

"No, it's fine!" said Roxy, breathlessly. "I got this."

She strained to place the jar carefully down on the counter and took a breath before saying "Oh! I need containers."

"Don't you worry, cher, I got some lovely glass jars, just the right size. I was savin' them for my tomato basil jelly, but you can use 'em and I'll get some more." Evangeline pointed to the pantry again. "Box on the floor on the left, just as you go in the door."

"You're a lifesaver, Evangeline."

Evangeline smiled fondly as she watched Roxy dash back into the pantry and come out again carrying a cardboard box full of unused canning jars. Roxy spooned the spice mix into six jars.

"I've got some labels somewhere here." Evangeline rooted around in a drawer and brought out some brown tags. "Now, you have lovely handwritin', write *Evangeline's Cajun Spice Mix* on 'em and tie them around the rim before you put the lid on."

Roxy did as she was told. As she wrote, she asked, "Tell me, what's in your mix, Evangeline? What makes it so fantastic?"

"Well, there's the usual paprika, garlic powder, cayenne pepper, oregano, onion powder, thyme, salt, and pepper."

"And?" Roxy pressed. "Isn't there something special you put in it? Something your grandmomma passed down to you?

"Ah, they would be my special ingredients."

"And what are they?"

"Well, that would be tellin', wouldn't it?"

Roxy looked at her. "But won't you ever tell me? What will I do when this batch runs out?" She waved over to the huge Mason jar that she estimated contained enough spices to last at least five years. "I won't be able to replicate your meals if you don't tell. Our guests will be disappointed if I don't use it in the cooking."

Evangeline looked at Roxy's sweet, innocent, slightly bewildered face.

"Guess you're right. I did invite you to run this place after all."

"So what are they?"

CHAPTER THIRTY-SEVEN

E VANGELINE LEANED OVER to whisper in Roxy's ear. "Lemongrass and a touch of saffron."
Roxy frowned. "But, but...Aren't they mostly used in Indian and Asian cuisines?"

Evangeline tapped her nose. "Exactly, cher."

Roxy paused, then smiled, nodding. "Okay, okay. Unconventional, I'll give you that, but okay."

After she'd attached the labels, Roxy wrapped ribbon around the necks of the jars, finishing them with a bow. She tightened the lids on the jars and they were ready.

She counted out the brown bags and labeled them, one each for Lily, Ada, Kathy, Derek, Sylvia, and Michael. Writing Michael's name made her think of the speech she was due to give later but even that couldn't distract Roxy at that moment. She slipped a jar of spices into each bag and a note she had written into one of them.

She heard footsteps come down the grand stairway outside. She folded over the tops of the bags, popped them all onto a tray and rushed into the hallway. She stood in front of the door determined that not a single one of her guests would leave before she'd handed them their bags. She'd track Michael down at the event.

Nat, Kathy, Derek, Ada, Lily, and Sylvia gathered in the hallway. They looked great in their bright colors. Well, in all honesty, Derek didn't look *that* great but then he never did. His eyes were dull and sunken, and he looked moody. As ever, he was fidgeting with his model airplane. Roxy felt herself feeling a little sorry for him.

"Come on, let's go," Nat said. She made for the front door.

Roxy dashed forward and put herself between Nat and the assembled group.

"Hi, everyone," she said brightly.

Nat, who was in black as usual but wore her turquoise sparkly Doc Martens and a matching neckerchief, said, "Is Sam here yet?" She peered out of the door. "He's going to have to drive all the way inside the alleyway. There's no *way* we can lug all the food up to the street."

"Nope, he's not here yet," said Roxy, still facing the group.

"I'll call him," Nat said, pulling out her phone. Then she nodded at the brown bags. "What are those?"

"Oh yes," Roxy said as if she'd forgotten them. The tray they lay on might as well have been burning hot for all she was able to ignore it. She addressed the group. "They're just a little thank-you from those of us at the *Funky Cat*. For staying with us. Something to remind you of New Orleans when you get home. Make sure to open them in private, though. I've included something pers—Oh!" The front door to the *Funky Cat* opened suddenly, pitching Roxy forward and sending the brown bags on her tray flying to the floor.

"I'm so sorry, Roxy!" Sage said as she walked in. "Are you alright?"

Roxy was fine, but at that moment she wasn't concerned about herself. Lily had reached down and was picking up the bags. She was handing them out indiscriminately!

"No, wait..." Roxy looked on in horror. But it was too late.

"Thank you so much, Roxy," Sylvia was saying.

"Yes, thank you, Roxy. You're too kind," Kathy said.

"I think I'd better put this in my room. It'll get lost at the street party," Ada added.

As everyone headed to their respective rooms to deposit their gifts, Roxy was left in the hallway holding one bag—Michael's. Nat looked at her perplexed. "What was all that about?"

Roxy shook her head. "Nothing, absolutely nothing."

Nat shrugged. "Oh, come on! Don't be a spoilsport. We still have to load all the food into Sam's van, and he's not even here yet."

Roxy fixed Nat with a glare. "Nothing is going on, all right?" she said. "Come on, let's sort out the food."

They went into the kitchen and began stacking the dishes on a rolling cart. "By the way," Nat said, avoiding eye contact with Roxy. "I just want to say that if ever I come across as a bit of a jerk, I'm very sorry. I know I get a bit edgy and a little inappropriate at times, and I also know that's no excuse. I get anxious, you see. It makes me a bit mad. Sorry, Rox."

"It's alright," said Roxy, finding a smile from somewhere. "I understand. Just be careful, take deep breaths, that's what I do. And if you see me blink rapidly five times in a row, you'll know what it means, okay?"

"Yes! It can be our secret code!" Nat said with a smile.

"That'll do!" Roxy said, laughing. She gave Nat a quick side hug. "You know I love you, Nat."

"I love you too, Rox. Thank you for keeping me on here." Nat's eyes shone.

"Come on, none of that. We've got work to do. Let's hurry up with this lot."

"I'll go and enlist some help," Nat said. She left the kitchen, soon returning accompanied by Lily and Ada. Sam came in behind them.

"Hi, Roxy," Sam said, his deep, gravelly voice as seductive as ever.

"Hi, Sam," she said, briskly. She had no time for flirting. Not today. "Thanks for coming to help."

They transported dish after dish after dish of food out to Sam's van while making sure to save some space for Elijah, who carried over piles of boxes of pastries from the bakery. When Roxy picked up the last set of plates, she turned to Evangeline, who was now loading the dishwasher. "Thank you, Evangeline, for helping us! What would we do without you?"

Evangeline came over, drying her hands on a towel. She put her arm around Roxy's shoulder. "I know what you're up to," she said quietly.

Roxy's eyes widened. "You do?"

Evangeline grimaced but pulled Roxy to her. "I recognize a fellow warrior when I see one. You do your best and seek justice. I know you need to do that for that young man. It's just in your nature like it is in mine. But be careful. Promise me that, okay? You're out in a big crowd. Small things have the tendency to get dangerous in crowds. Even carnival can get crazy. Just promise old Evangeline that you'll be careful."

"I promise," said Roxy, relaxing. For once, she didn't feel nervous or anxious, even with such an abundance of warnings. "I'll be fine. Don't worry about me. Like you said, I just want to see justice done."

Evangeline gave her an affectionate smile. "You know, cher, you're more like me than I thought. The first day you came in here you was like a timid little mouse. Like your cat coulda eaten you whole." She laughed. "Sorry, cher. But now, you're somethin' pretty different. The moxie's strong in you. Moxie Roxy." She laughed and patted her on the shoulder. "Run along, sugar. I know you'll do great."

"Thanks, Evangeline!"

Roxy rushed out and packed the last of the food into the van. Sage, Nat, and Elijah had already led the influencers, Kathy, and Derek out of the alleyway—they were walking to the party. They couldn't get lost because the street decorations signaled the way. Roxy planned to walk with them, but since they had already left, she swung herself into the van's passenger seat beside Sam.

"Hey, pretty lady," he said, giving her the half-smile that made her kneecaps feel like they were melting.

"Hey," Roxy replied softly.

CHAPTER THIRTY-EIGHT

"**I**T LOOKS AMAZING," Roxy said.

The block over by the river where the party was being held was normally a rundown industrial area. Now it was alive with color.

"Kathy sure doesn't play around, does she?" Sam said, sliding into a parking space.

Roxy spoke sadly. "I guess for your murdered son, you'd do anything. Money, effort, time, no object."

"Indeed," said Sam. "She must also be very determined. She would have needed a permit. How did she get around Detective Johnson to pull this off? Did he find a compassionate side?"

Roxy looked at him. "Compassionate? Him? He came to speak to us all this morning. He stared us down, each and every one of us, like we had murdered Dash in cold blood." The truth was, one of them *had* murdered Dash in cold blood.

Once Sam had parked, Roxy slid out of her seat and got to unloading. Lots of people were arriving now, all wearing bright colors and laughing and joking and drinking. One vendor had started up a bar at the side of the street. A crew was setting up a modern sound system on the stage while a wall of enormous speakers stood to one side. It looked like the event was going to be *loud*.

Roxy smiled at the scene, her feelings bittersweet. Dash had so wanted to experience the joy of New Orleans for himself, but he hadn't had the chance. Roxy hadn't known him well or for long, but she knew that he loved to grab life by the horns, to explore, to learn, to grow, and above all to *experience*. Roxy doubted he'd *ever* have settled down in one place like his mother wanted him to. He was an adventurer, right down to his bones. Excitement coursed through his veins. Wind was in his sails. There was always something to be enthusiastic about, some new territory to conquer.

Now that was all over.

But Roxy looked over the growing crowd and felt something move deep within her. People were here celebrating. They clearly loved his message. It touched the hearts of strangers, of people everywhere. And they had been so affected that they had made long journeys to be at the party today, to celebrate Dash one last time.

Roxy hoped that she would be able to absorb his message into her life too. In fact, it felt like she had done so a little already. Where she had allowed her anxieties and fears to clip her wings, she now felt herself growing more expansive. Where she had seen problems, she now saw possibilities. Where she had seen danger, she now saw adventure. She also recognized that she had the potential to be a leader.

She knew it wasn't just Dash who had helped her. It was a sprinkle of Sage who gave Roxy the confidence that everything would be all right. It was a touch of Evangeline, who was so no-nonsense that Roxy now saw many of her anxieties as simply plain silly. It was a dusting of Elijah, who just like the sugar he scattered over his pastries, showed her how to have fun. It was a smidgeon of Sam, who always encouraged her to "go for it". And it was a nip of Nat, whose "Nat-itude" and big heart pulled no punches.

Roxy realized how far she had come since she'd climbed onto the bus headed for New Orleans a few months before. She smiled to herself as she methodically unloaded Sam's van and placed all the food on their table. There were a *lot* of dishes, and it took a good while, especially as Nat, Kathy, Derek, and the influencers were nowhere to be seen.

Roxy saw that Michael was there, sitting behind the podium on the stage. He was staring into space. She walked over to him. She handed him his bag with the jar of spices, gave him a sympathetic nod, but otherwise left him alone. She saw him briefly look inside the bag before looking up again to resume staring at the horizon.

Before long, old school reggae began to play. It *totally* lifted the vibe, and both Roxy and Sam couldn't help briefly doing a little dance. Roxy imagined herself being so bold as to rock right up to him and dance *together* but she tamped her thought down. She couldn't afford to be distracted.

"I wonder where Nat and the others are. I haven't seen them, have you?" she said to him.

"No," said Sam. "But if I know Nat, she'll be at one of the cookout grills."

"*That's* true," said Roxy. Nat loved her grilled chicken, but Roxy was starting to get worried. Where were the others?

The crowd had really grown now. It was getting more and more difficult to pick anyone out of it. Roxy made her way up onto the podium, and peered around, looking for Nat. Thank goodness she loved to wear black, at least. For once she would stand out among this sea of color!

Finally, Roxy *did* see her and the rest of the group. And, sure enough, they were standing by a barbecue. It was on the other side of the crowd. "We've got all the food in the world here!" Roxy said to Nat when she sauntered over. "Yet you run off to the first man with a pair of tongs!"

"I worked in that kitchen this morning until I was sweating like a crawfish," said Nat. "Heck, probably *smelling* like a crawfish. I needed something different for my palate." She ripped some meat off the chicken leg she held. She looked around at the party, the colors of the crowd, the music, the food, and the way people were dancing. It was starting to look like a music festival. She saw Sage and Elijah dancing, Sage's slow and lazy moves contrasting with Elijah's peppier, upbeat ones that picked up the staccato off-beats of the reggae rhythm. "This is pretty amazing."

"Are you ready for your speech?" Sam called over.

"My what?" Roxy asked.

"Your speech, aren't you saying something? Kathy said she was going to ask you."

"Yeah, she did." The truth was that Roxy had forgotten all about making a speech. Now that things were really rocking, though, she was starting to feel edgy.

Kathy didn't look too great, either. She had on her trademark smile and a full face of makeup, but her skin underneath was pale, and her blush stood out too brightly on her cheeks. Her blue eye shadow looked wrong too, like she had made herself up as a clown. Her hands shook.

As the influencers helped themselves to food, Roxy sidled up to Dash's mom. She linked her hand in hers. "It's going to be okay, I promise." Kathy looked like she was about to vomit.

Before long, Father John stood up on the podium and addressed the crowd. "Hello, New Orleans!" he boomed.

CHAPTER THIRTY-NINE

"**G**REETINGS TO YOU all," Father John said into the microphone, more quietly this time. "We are gathered here to celebrate the life of Dashiell Davies in the vivid style that he was known for. His associate, Michael O'Sullivan, has put together a video montage of Dash's life. Please enjoy this tribute."

The priest stepped aside, and the whole crowd stopped and quieted to watch the huge screen. Roxy turned and craned her neck to see.

What followed was a beautiful montage of pictures and videos: of Dash on top of a mountain, of Dash skydiving, of Dash fooling around at some Hawaiian resort doing the hula on the beach under the twinkling stars, of Dash hanging out of a train in India, of Dash waving underwater while scuba diving. *Man,* this guy had done so much.

And how he laughed as he did it all! How he smiled! He had so much light in him, and it beamed across the crowd. People began to cry, and Roxy found a tear slipping down her own cheek.

Then Michael's voice thundered out from the speakers, a recording over the video.

"Dash, you were a hero—my hero—one of the world's brave people, one who refused to compromise, one who refused to play the game, and one who refused to stop dreaming. You lived life to the full in every moment, in every sense. You never said no. You always said yes. You never said, 'It's not possible.' You always said, 'How can we make this happen?' My life is forever changed because of you, and so too are the lives of millions of others. I know you wanted the world to relax because you told me that so many times.

"You know what, buddy? I regret a lot of things. I regret the way I spoke to you sometimes. I regret that I ever told you to be serious, or to be realistic, or to take your time. Especially that last one, because there *was* no time to waste. And you knew it. You just went at life, full speed. You DASHED! Your name suited you down to the ground.

"You wanted to build schools, dig wells, build solar power and clean water systems, give people jobs, the tools to support themselves and their families. When we had money, you gave it all away." Over the sound of the tribute, a yell rose from the middle of the crowd. The crowd shushed and Michael's voice carried on speaking without interruption. "I swear, buddy, you didn't get the chance to do everything you dreamed of, but I'll do it, and I'll do it for you. I've been close to the edge, but I have a reason to live now—your memory, your mission, and your spirit live on in me. I'll do it, buddy. And I know you'll be watching me do it from the other side."

Now people were crying in earnest. Even though it was daylight, they had turned on their phone's flashlights and were waving them above their heads. Father John called Kathy up to the stage.

She'd rubbed her eyes so much that she had black rings around them where her eye makeup had smudged. All her vitality and her brave, cheerful smile had gone. She was a broken woman.

She went up to the mic and began to speak. Her voice was choked with tears. "I was going to come up here and say so many good things about Dashiell. But I can't." She dropped her chin onto her chest, and it stayed there.

Roxy could feel the hearts of the people in the crowd going out to her.

"I'm so sorry," Kathy said suddenly. "I killed him."

What? Roxy's heart started beating too fast. It felt like everyone in the whole crowd took a sharp intake of breath.

"I did." She put her hands up in the air. "I thought it was the right thing to do at the time, but it wasn't. I did it because I have a huge amount of debt, and I wanted his money. I knew he had left all his money to me. I was blinded, totally blinded, by worry about my future. But now I see...I can't bring him back. I was crazy! I must have lost my mind! But I did it. I did. And I am so, so sorry." She broke down, sobbing hysterically.

Roxy was pushed from behind. As he passed her, she saw Detective Johnson barging his way to the front. The shove shook Roxy and propelled her into action.

"No!" she shouted. She pushed past the detective, her slight stature allowing her to weave more quickly through the crush of people in front of the stage. She rushed up the steps and onto the platform, wrenching the microphone from Kathy's hand.

Kathy launched herself at her. "Give that back!"

But Roxy wouldn't. She was standing in front of hundreds and hundreds of people, but she gripped the mic all the tighter and jerked it away from Kathy long enough to say, "She's lying! Kathy didn't kill Dash! Derek did! Dash's brother! Kathy's other son! She's only confessing to protect him!" She pointed to Detective Johnson. "Arrest him!"

Johnson had stopped amid the crowd. He didn't move. The throng fell into a silence so deep that Roxy felt she might drown in it. The heat of embarrassment rose to her cheeks.

"Detective!" Roxy hollered almost pleading now. There was a sudden movement in the crowd, and she spotted Derek. Roxy pointed, her forefinger straight and stiff. "That's him! Somebody! Anybody!"

"It's not true!" Kathy cried. "It was me! Not Derek!"

Chaos ensued. Derek, who had been watching the stage, attempted to bolt from the crowd.

"Get him!" Roxy shouted.

The crowd started roaring. Some people were stunned and let Derek through while others tried to grab him. Far from his usual lethargic self, Derek proved to be as quick as a fox and wriggled out of their grasp.

"No! No!" shouted Kathy above the crowd. "He hasn't done anything wrong!"

Derek feinted and dodged his way around the throng, but eventually, several burly men linked arms and together they acted like a trap, encircling Derek, and preventing his escape. A cop pushed his way through the crowd to place Derek in handcuffs.

Roxy turned to Kathy. "I'm so sorry," she said, "but the truth had to..."

Kathy had gone purple. She lunged at Roxy and

grabbed her by the neck. Her warm hands closed around Roxy's airway and squeezed. Roxy felt herself begin to lose consciousness, and she stumbled. She saw Kathy's face—three versions of it—swim in front of her eyes.

Just as the world started to go black, Kathy's grip on Roxy's neck loosened. Sam had grabbed Kathy's arms, and he pinned them behind her back while she screamed, "Derek! Derek!" She kicked out at Roxy, who fell to the floor.

"Give it up, Kathy," Sam said. He was holding her tightly and, unable to even thrash against him, she slumped, defeated. Detective Johnson arrived at his shoulder and led Kathy away.

Sam bent over Roxy, who was still lying on the floor, his dark eyes clouded with concern. He put a hand to her head, "Are you all right?"

"I think so." Roxy felt her neck gingerly. "Yes, yes, I'm good. Thank you."

She braced to push herself up, and he helped her to her feet.

"You really didn't want to give that speech, did you?" he said.

"I did give a speech. It just wasn't the one anyone was expecting."

CHAPTER FORTY

L ATER, ROXY, SAM, Nat, Elijah, Sage, Lily, Sylvia, Ada, and Michael were gathered in the lounge of the *Funky Cat*, nursing hot milky drinks even though it was still only afternoon. Evangeline, after hearing about the commotion on her radio, had come back to the hotel to take care of them. They were drinking sweet hot chocolate laced with brandy and topped with whipped cream and a dusting of chocolate powder. It was going down a treat.

They watched Detective Johnson on the TV. He looked very pleased with himself. "Derek Davies has admitted to the murder of his brother, Dashiell Davies. He has confessed fully. Fratricide is a heinous crime, and our thoughts are with the rest of the family."

Sage shook her head. "I accompanied Kathy to the police station. Her soul is very damaged, poor love. She was hysterical at times, and at others, her spirit left this plane to inhabit another. She told me Derek had committed the crime to help *her,* and out of guilt and a misplaced sense of maternal feeling, she confessed to it falsely. Kathy has been having financial problems and Dash had helped her a lot over the years. In the past few months, Dash had stopped giving her money because he felt she was wasting it, and that Derek was enabling her in her bad habits. Derek was furious about this, and he killed Dash so that they'd inherit all of his money. Thing was, until Michael announced it in his tribute to Dash, Derek didn't know that Dash had given all his money away.

"Kathy had no idea that Derek had killed his brother, but when she looked in Derek's brown bag, she found your note, Roxy. Once she heard Derek yell out from the crowd once he learned that Dash had donated all his money, she figured it out."

Roxy sighed deeply. "I'd written that I would expose him unless he confessed. I had hoped the note would encourage him to be honest, that I would flush him out, but Kathy must have got his bag by mistake after they fell on the floor." Roxy pursed her lips in frustration before continuing. "So Derek killed his brother, just for money? That's terrible."

"Yes," said Sage, looking pained. "Just awful. And poor Kathy, it will take a long time for her spirit to shed such a weight. Maybe not even in this lifetime."

"What a mess," said Roxy. "But how did Derek manage to kill Dash? They live in another state. How did he make it here and back home without Kathy noticing he was missing and how did we not know he was in the hotel? Surely we would have heard something? *I* would have heard something?"

Sage shook her head. "Kathy admitted to me that they'd come to the city to see Dash around the time he arrived here in New Orleans. They planned to ask him for more money. When he was killed they were actually staying in a rundown B&B nearby and tracking his movements because they wanted to catch him when he was away from Michael. They knew Michael wouldn't approve of what they were doing. After Dash's death, they waited a few days to show up here so it looked like they'd come from home. But Kathy genuinely didn't know what Derek had done. I'm sure of it. Who would suspect one son of killing her other son? Kathy's bewilderment was real."

Roxy sighed again. "My goodness. I suppose Derek must have sneaked into the hotel that night, perhaps during the drama over Ada's dress. He must have hidden somewhere to wait for Dash to fall asleep before going to his room to kill him."

"So," said Nat. "Are you going to tell us, Roxy? How did you know it was Derek?"

Roxy cradled her hot chocolate. "You remember the night you were attacked, Michael? The 'Evening of Love and Light'? Kathy had said Derek was going to talk to the priest. Well, when I mentioned that to Father John he looked confused and said he'd only met Derek at the memorial. I think Derek told Kathy he was going to see Father John that night, but instead, he lay in wait for Michael and attacked him on his way back to the Hilton."

"But why did he attack me?" Michael asked.

"That boy was full of jealousy. His soul is very dark," Sage said. "Extremely dark. As dark as dark gets." She looked very grave. "We may never know what was truly in his heart."

"Wow," said Sam. "It was lucky you ended up speaking to that priest, Roxy."

"Yes," she agreed. "It proved to me that Derek was a liar. I also remembered that when he and Kathy arrived here, Sage said that Derek *knew* where Dash's room was —even though he'd supposedly never been here before."

"That's right, he did," Sage said, nodding slowly. "I got chills when I met him for the very first time. I knew something wasn't right. My intuition was talking to me, but I just wasn't sure *what* it was trying to tell me."

"He must have watched the Instagram video Michael made when they first arrived. That's how he worked out how to get to Dash's room the night he killed him," Roxy said.

"But what about the poison? We never did find out exactly what killed Dash," said Ada.

"Our food was never in the frame. Detective Johnson knew Dash had been murdered from the outset and how but deliberately didn't tell us, leaving us to wonder if the food he'd eaten here was involved in some way. Johnson thought that if suspicion fell on the hotel and if the killer was one of us, they would relax if they thought the investigation was headed in the wrong direction. He thought they would make a mistake and reveal themselves. I can't tell you how much I didn't appreciate that tactic when he told me this afternoon. He threw the reputation of this hotel on the fire to help his case!"

"So what did Derek kill him with?" Elijah asked.

"They couldn't work it out to start with, but when he came into the kitchen this morning, Johnson saw the model airplane Derek always carried with him. Apparently, the poison consisted of noxious fumes from some kind of glue. The police think that Derek held model airplane glue to Dash's nose while he was asleep to render him unconscious and then suffocated him with his pillow."

"Ugh," Nat said grimacing.

"What a complete ass," Michael spat.

"Goodness, you're quite the detective, though," Sylvia said to Roxy.

"Oh, it's nothing. You know, I was convinced it was you at one point. Someone put a note under my door trying to implicate you. Now I think it must have been Derek."

The color drained from Sylvia's face. She shook her head. "Oh no. Really? I'm so glad you saw through that."

Roxy considered talking to her about her ex-husband and the murder case, but she was too tired to even think. "I hope you don't mind," she said to everyone, slipping off her shoes and tucking her feet under her. "I need to relax. Let's chat about other things."

"Yes," said Nat, clearing her throat. "And I'll start. Ada, I just wanted to say that I'm really sorry for speaking to you badly at times." She was blushing red, but to her credit, she looked up and kept eye contact. "I was really out of order, and I'm so sorry."

Ada actually smiled at her. "That's very gracious of you, Nat. Thank you. Let's talk no more about it. It's all forgotten." Ada reached out and clasped Nat's hand. Nat responded with a squeeze and a smile.

"I will ask Archangel Michael to bring healing to us all," Sage said. "He will not let us down."

"And while Archangel Michael is doing his thing, I'll do everyone's laundry for free," Sam said, standing.

"And I'll provide the beignets!" Elijah piped up. He literally bounced out of his chair.

"Well, I'm goin' home," Evangeline said. "I've had enough excitement for one day. 'Bye, y'all."

Roxy sank back into the couch, allowing the cushions to envelop her. She beamed despite her exhaustion.

Harmony, peace, and the bonds of friendship had been restored, and her world was just as she liked it. Even Nefertiti jumped into her lap and stayed for a while.

Ada, Sylvia, Lily, and Michael, despite coming to the end of their stay at the *Funky Cat Inn*, seemed reluctant to leave. They continued to chat with Sage, Nat, Roxy, Sam, and Elijah all through the evening and well into the night, talking about their lives, their hopes, their dreams, their careers, their families, what they would do next, and how much they had enjoyed their stay at the *Funky Cat Inn*, murder notwithstanding. It was a long, meaningful, and expansive discussion; social media wasn't mentioned even once.

CHAPTER FORTY-ONE

ROXY, SAGE, AND Nat sat together in Roxy's tiny office. Sage sat on a stool beside Roxy in the office chair. They were staring intently at Sage's laptop screen. Nat lounged on the floor, sprawled out on a beanbag, which suited her just fine.

"Well, it's not *all* terrible," said Roxy, checking their Instagram page. "We've gone from 5,000 fans to 105,000!"

"That will translate into plenty more bookings," said Sage, crisply. She even *sounded* different when she was talking about business. "Visibility is key here. We need to appear *everywhere*. The more followers we have, the better."

There was a knock on the door, and Sam poked his head in.

"Hello, ladies."

Sage briefly raised her eyes from the screen. Nat waved. Only Roxy looked directly at Sam. "Hi Sam."

"Roxy, can I have a word?"

"Sure." Roxy waited patiently for Sam to continue.

"Outside," he said.

"Oh, okay." Roxy pushed herself out from behind the desk and went out into the hallway where Sam stood.

"Look, I wondered, um, well, if..." Sam trailed off.

"Yes?" Roxy prompted. There was tension in the air, definitely tension.

"If, well, if you were alright." Sam's voice gained strength. "You know, after the other day. I mean, Kathy strangled you. That can't have been fun."

"Well, no. No, it wasn't. But you stopped her, and thank you for that. Things would have been a lot worse if not for you, but I'm fine now."

"Oh, right, well." Sam looked down at his feet before raising his head and trying again. "But you're not injured, or scared, losing sleep? I'd understand if you were. You nearly blacked out."

"No, no, I'm fine, thanks." Roxy was trembling now. Why did she do that around Sam? She remembered the vow she had made to herself. She would not get involved. Not with Sam, not with anyone. It would be unprofessional of her, and she still didn't know if she trusted him completely. And besides, she didn't have the time. "Anyhow, was there anything else?"

Sam looked directly at her. He was resolute now, having seemingly made a decision. "Just the laundry. I came for the laundry."

Roxy went back to her office where Sage and Nat were chatting about the relative merits of the different social media platforms.

"But, Sage, Instagram is where the kids go. Facebook is for old folks."

"Sylvia's followers aren't kids, and they're on Instagram, sweet petal. And look how many Facebook fans we have—65,000!"

Roxy laughed. "I hope everyone's doing okay. Shall we check up on them?"

"Oh, yes, great idea!" said Nat. She got up off her beanbag and stood behind them.

"Let's try Lily first," Roxy said.

Sage navigated to Lily Vashchenko's Instagram page. "Aha!" Roxy said. "She *did* get the Hilton Hotel deal!" There was picture after picture after picture of Lily posing in front of the Hilton, wearing Hilton-branded slippers, in front of the Hilton-branded pool. If it had Hilton on it, Lily was posing with it, on it, or next to it.

"Good for her," said Nat. "She really wanted that deal. It's all she could talk about when we were walking to Dash's party."

"Dash really wanted it too," Roxy said sadly.

"What about Sylvia?" said Nat.

Sage typed in *Sylvia Walters,* and nothing came up. "That's strange," said Roxy. "She's not on there."

"Do you think she deactivated?" said Nat. "She *can't* have!"

Sage closed her eyes. "Search for her *real* name," she said.

Roxy gasped. "What was it again?...Oh...erm...Oh, yes! Helen Matheson." Sage typed the name in. Roxy's heart was beating hard. "Oh my goodness, Sage, you're right!"

Sage clicked through to the profile. Before, Sylvia's Instagram feed had been full of well-curated pictures of lifestyle and travel. It was beautiful, for sure, but there was nothing particularly adrenaline pumping about it.

And now? Her profile picture was one of her standing alongside Oprah!

"No way!" Nat said.

"Uh-huh!" Roxy responded, finding it hard to believe herself. *"The truth will set you free!"* Roxy read from the page. *"Tell your story—the good, the bad, and the ugly. Learn from your mistakes, and speak your truth. Fight for justice!"*

Sage broke out into a beautiful smile. "This has been a learning experience for us all. Truly transformative. I vividly remember the reading I gave her. I could *feel* some inner tragedy had not been expressed. Often, I can tell exactly what a person has been through in life. I can look at them, and I *feel* their story. I see images, hear voices.

"But in her case, I didn't get anything in particular. She'd hidden her story well, somewhere no one could see or sense it; somewhere where even *she* would not see or sense it. It was buried so, so deeply. But unfortunately, when we bury our story, we bury our soul with it. She was walking around a shell of a person, always worried, always looking over her shoulder. And her throat chakra was completely blocked. It was surrounded by dark, damp energy. Having a cover story will do that to you."

Sage paused for a moment and tipped her head to one side. "You know when you try to relax, but you have a test the next day, and you haven't studied for it, and you feel disaster looming? She was living her whole *life* like that, never able to relax. Her poor soul must have been *so* tired." Sage peered at the screen and smiled. "Not anymore, though. Look at those eyes. I see joy, relief, and freedom. And a picture with Oprah? You have to be putting out some special energy into the Universe to achieve that!"

Roxy laughed. "That's fantastic. I want to find out more about what Sylvia...sorry, *Helen's* doing right now." Sage hit up Google and typed in "Helen Matheson." There was a Wikipedia page stating that she *had* been to jail for the death of her husband and was now using her platform to campaign for justice and help domestic violence victims.

"She has found her purpose," Sage said. She paused. "What about Ada Okafor? Let's see what she is doing." Sage searched for Ada and quickly found her profile.

"Oh, her last post is from a while ago!" Roxy pointed at the picture on her account. Ada was wearing a white coat. "Look, she's gone back to medicine!" Roxy clicked on the photo and up came the caption. "*I'm back in medical school, training to become a surgeon. Thank you, Instagram, for the fun times! See you in seven years!*"

Sage smiled at that too. "She's realized there are more important things than Versace limited editions."

"Thank goodness for that," Nat said. "I hope Michael's holding up okay," she added.

"He sure is." Sage grinned. "I don't need to check Instagram for that. He's always talking to Dr. Jack, and he's even thinking of apprenticing with him in spiritual matters. It would all be done online of course. Michael is traveling all over the world as he honors Dash's memory. Check out his pictures. You'll see!"

Roxy typed *Michael & Dash* into the bar and found their Instagram page. It was full of pictures of Michael here, there, and everywhere. In each picture, Michael held a large photograph of Dash. There were pictures of him with street children, on boats in the Caribbean, in soup kitchens, and at the top of skyscrapers.

Roxy clicked on one of the pictures. Michael was standing on a platform, an amazing view over London stretched out behind him.

Dash always said the sky was the limit. Now I'm in the sky, in one of the tallest buildings in Europe. I'm toasting you with a glass of champagne, Dash. I'm living it up, just for you!

Roxy read it out, and then they settled into a comfortable, bittersweet silence until the laptop suddenly went *ding!*

"Ooh, look! We've got a message!" Roxy said.

She clicked on her inbox.

"It's from *The Magnificent Luxury Travel Show!*" said Nat peering over Roxy's shoulder.

Roxy shook her head. "It's probably just a scam."

"No, it's not!" said Nat. "It's a great TV show! It's total vacation porn."

"Nat!" Roxy said, swatting her. She opened the message and read.

Dear Roxy Reinhardt,

We have watched how you handled recent events at your hotel with grace and poise.

We love the look of the cuisine you serve, and the spiritual, historical, and cultural events you organize for your guests.

We would like to feature you in one of our shows. Please contact our scheduling producer at your earliest convenience at the email address below.

Yours sincerely,

Tiffany Schuster

Executive Producer

"Yes! I told you we would be on TV soon," said Nat, punching the air. "Oh my goodness, this is like a dream! Roxy, this is worth thousands in publicity. You've made it!"

Roxy couldn't believe her eyes. She looked out of her office door through to the lobby. In the room beyond, she could see the table that Nat had brought back from the flea market they had visited with Lily in Sam's Rolls. When Nat had got ahold of the table, it had been scratched and faded, one leg was wobbly and the side detail was caked with grime. Now, the deep mahogany finish was smooth and shiny, the fine filigree detail exposed, the wobbly leg fixed. Set on top of the table was her other flea market find—a dramatic two-foot-high gold statue of a woman. She was a dramatic figure; her hair flowed behind her, her long dress twisted around her body. In her hands were a bow and arrow, her elbow pulled back as she took aim, her intense gaze focused on her prey. Every time Roxy looked at the statue, she felt a thrill course through her body. It inspired her. The woman was powerful, determined, a servant to no one. That was just how Roxy wanted to be.

"Is this for real?" Roxy said, finally.

Sage flashed her a grin and gave her a hug. "You bet, honey."

"I can't believe it."

"Well, you better believe it, mate," Nat said. "'Cuz, it's happening. You better hold on, Rox. You're going to be famous!"

A ROXY REINHARDT MYSTERY

LOUISIANA LIES

USA TODAY BESTSELLING AUTHOR
ALISON GOLDEN WITH
HONEY BROUSSARD

LOUISIANA LIES

BOOK THREE

Published by Mesa Verde Publishing
P.O. Box 1002
San Carlos, CA 94070

Edited by
Marjorie Kramer

CHAPTER ONE

ROXY SLID HER body over the smooth silky, supple leather. It responded to her like a glove, molding itself to fit her form. In front, a length of polished walnut gleamed so brightly that Roxy's face reflected back at her while under her feet was carpet so thick and soft, she felt as though her feet were suspended in midair. It was always a treat for Roxy to ride in Sam's Rolls Royce. She wasn't a very materialistic person, but even so, she couldn't help but enjoy the experience of luxury.

Sam was apologetic every time they got in it. "Just my little extravagance," he'd say, going a little red.

"Well, we certainly make a scene," said Roxy. As they cruised along, people turned to look at them as they drove by. She looked out the windows at the mash-up of sleek modern buildings created from chrome and glass, and the traditional, colorful, ornate Louisiana architecture that comprised New Orleans.

Sam grinned. "That's NOLA for you. Scenes galore."

"Yep," said Roxy. "I don't think I'll ever get used to it.

And the people! I can't believe one of my best friends is an *actual* spiritualist, and we're on our way to meet one of our guests who's conducting a séance! How surreal is that?"

Sam laughed. "I wouldn't have it any other way. Makes for unpredictable, exciting times. So, tell me more about your guest. The big cheese."

"Her name is Meredith Romanoff," said Roxy. "A spiritual medium and psychic. She's very well respected and famous in her circles. At least that's what Dr. Jack said."

"So what is she doing here?"

"She's holding a series of events. Tonight's just a small one for private clients, but tomorrow she's got a huge public workshop. Over a thousand people are going. It's being held at one of the hotel conference centers, but she prefers to stay in smaller, more personable surroundings, which is why she's made a reservation with us. They booked out the *Funky Cat* even though there's only three of them. She's visiting with her husband and her assistant."

"But why are we meeting them at the botanica?"

"They were going to check in first, but traffic was bad coming into the city, and they ran out of time. So I said we'd pick up their luggage and take it back to their rooms so that it's all ready for them when they arrive."

"Always going the extra mile, hey Roxy?"

She smiled. "That's me, Nothing's-Too-Much-Trouble Roxy."

Sam smoothly pulled his maroon classic car right in front of the botanica. The magical supplies store was housed in an old, converted, shotgun-style building right in the middle of a commercial district. It wasn't grand,

and it looked out of place among the sleek, modern structures that surrounded it, but it was even more eye-catching thanks to its color. The wooden boards were deep indigo, and the intricate metal fretwork that decorated the frontage was painted gold. The storefront was separated from the sidewalk by a small porch and was dominated by a huge picture window that displayed a selection of the wares stocked inside.

Crystals, oracle card sets, skulls, candles and all kinds of herbs and powders in jars filled the window to bursting. Roxy often thought that Dr. Jack could hold a scavenger hunt based on the window display alone. Roxy and Sam went inside and found a cluster of people browsing the store. A pile of bags and cases was stacked by the door.

"Hi, there!" Roxy said brightly. "We've come to..."

"*No,*" Dr. Jack said firmly to the woman standing in front of him, his purple face matching his velour three-piece suit. Dr. Jack loved to dress flamboyantly, and sometimes even threaded beads into his graying beard, but now he was exhibiting something much more conventional—fury. "That is absolutely unethical, and I condemn it 100%!" he cried.

"How dare you?" the woman in front of him shouted back. She pointed a thin, bony finger at Dr. Jack. It reminded Roxy of a bird's claw. Roxy knew immediately that the woman was Meredith Romanoff.

"You presume to tell me—*ME*—that you condemn such a huge aspect of my work? Well, *that's* a fine welcome!" Meredith Romanov's soft blonde hair shook as did the ruffles that decorated the front of her blouse. The blouse stretched over her ample chest while the tassels that hung from the hem of her long skirt and which spread over her stout hips trembled. Roxy was

462   ALISON GOLDEN & HONEY BROUSSARD

struck by how Meredith's hands seemed at odds with her body.

In the photograph Roxy had seen, Meredith had looked as though butter wouldn't melt in her mouth, but the Meredith now in front of her offered a very different impression. Her face was red; her mouth twisted in an ugly, tortured line. She was spitting fire. Butter would be reduced to a runny puddle inside a second in the face of such an onslaught.

"Please, Meredith," a man next to her said in a placating, soothing voice. It was like he was speaking to a young child. "Now, now." The man's bald head shone under the store lights, and his cheeks were bright pink. A pair of gold spectacles hung on a slim gold chain around his neck. He dabbed his brow with a folded, pristine white handkerchief. His pressed khaki slacks were perfect. The elegantly crumpled linen shirt he wore, the sleeves rolled up neatly, indicated that sometime earlier today he had anticipated some kind of heat, but perhaps not this kind.

"Please refrain from doing this now," Roxy heard him say. "You must put yourself in the right frame of mind for your session." The man enunciated all his words with glass-cut precision. His appearance and upper-crust demeanor made him the type of person that Roxy usually felt deeply intimidated by, but he was talking to Meredith so gently that Roxy found it impossible to be scared of him.

"I can get in the right frame of mind instantly," Meredith spat. Her voice was hard. She took a deep breath, and her next words were far more measured. She delivered them with a silky veneer to her tone. "But I suppose you're right, darling. Sometimes you do talk absolute trash, but on occasion you make sense. This is one of them."

The man rolled his eyes and smiled. He chuckled. "Thank you for the high praise, darling."

Meredith caught sight of Roxy staring at her, Sam behind her. She did a double-take and immediately assumed a warm, friendly expression. "Oh, hello," she said with a smile. Roxy wasn't sure it was genuine. "You must be...aren't you from the cute little hotel? Oh, I can't remember your name, I'm ever so sorry."

"It's Roxy," Roxy said brightly. "Roxy Reinhardt. This is..." She reached out to introduce Sam.

"I'm Sam," the tall man interjected simply, nodding at the gathered group. His shirt stretched around his broad shoulders as he folded his arms. "We know you're about to begin your meeting, so we won't disturb you. We came to pick up your bags and take them back to the hotel."

Meredith looked Sam up and down admiringly. She winked at Roxy. "What an attractive couple you make."

"Oh, we're not a couple," Roxy said quickly, feeling heat rush to her cheeks.

Meredith laughed. "Not *yet*. But I guarantee you the universe is aligning and then, well, you'll see. Now, yes, please take the bags. That would be wonderful. Thank you."

"I'll help," a young man said as he walked over to the pile of bags by the door. He had a very soft young face, red hair, and freckles. Roxy hadn't even noticed him until he spoke. He was very slight and short, and his presence was so unassuming that he was almost invisible. Roxy wondered if he was Meredith's son. He looked about the right age. "Is that okay, Meredith?" the young man asked, immediately disabusing Roxy of her theory. Her son would have called her "Mom."

"No, no, it isn't, George," Meredith snapped. "You need to be focusing on your responsibilities and getting things ready."

"Actually, I have already…"

"Well, then, get your mind right and meditate," said Meredith. She was terse and abrupt again. "I've told you before, you have a tendency to allow yourself to be overwhelmed by vast amounts of other people's energies, and then you don't come through as a clear channel. Anyone who needs something, you want to help. Stop being so soft and focus on what *you* have to do. You're not here to save the world or to be a 'nice guy,' you're here for a very specific purpose. And that is to help *me*." Meredith caught sight of Roxy staring at her again, "And all those lovely people we are trying to help."

Watching Meredith, Roxy felt humiliated on George's behalf, but the pleasant young man smiled. "Yes, you're right, Meredith," he said. "I'll go in the back room right away and cleanse the energies." He disappeared.

"That's more like it," Meredith said, tight-lipped. "Sorry about that, Roxy. That was George, my assistant. And this is Charles, my husband. And *this* is Terah, my old school friend." Meredith walked over to a woman browsing the racks of scented candles. She put her arm around the woman's shoulders. "We are catching up for the first time in forty years! Can you believe that?" Terah stiffened at Meredith's embrace. She wore a black eye patch over her left eye, the strap reaching over her ears and disappearing beneath her shoulder-length straight mousey hair. Terah nodded at Roxy. "We're still waiting for one more person to arrive, a private client of mine.

This is Dr. Jack, of course, but I believe you are already acquainted," Meredith finished.

Jack was still hovering, his arms folded across his chest, two creases between his eyes indicating his mood. Roxy was very aware of him. He was not radiating his usual calm, accepting aura, and she felt a little anxious. Meredith's husband Charles, the man with the glasses on the gold chain, gave Roxy a friendly nod and a small smile.

"Hello, Charles, Dr. Jack, Terah. I hope you're looking forward to a good evening," said Roxy nodding at them all. "We'll take the bags now and see you later back at the *Funky Cat Inn*." She turned to Sam, who, his face expressionless, picked up two heavy cases and took them outside to the car.

CHAPTER TWO

"**T**HANK YOU SO much," said Meredith. "Oh, and before I forget!" She went over to the counter and rummaged in her purse. "You *must* have a copy of my new book, Roxy. You look like the type of person who would be very..." Meredith put on a pair of bright white plastic-framed glasses and looked at Roxy over the top of them, "*receptive* to its message."

From her bag, Meredith pulled out a dust-jacketed hardcover and brought it over. The older woman carried it in both hands reverently as if it were a treasured holy text. She held it out, looking at Roxy intensely with her dark blue, almost violet eyes. "Do *you* have any spiritual gifts, dear?"

"Oh no. I...I don't know. I don't *think* so," said Roxy. "I just...well, I don't know much about it."

"She's quite intuitive, our Roxy," said Dr. Jack, suddenly piping up. "She's very intelligent, too. She's solved two murders."

Meredith looked Roxy up and down, appraising her.

"Well, isn't that interesting? Do read the book, Roxy, and let me know what you think. You have a certain...presence that attracts me."

"Well, thank you, um, Ms. Romanoff. I will. Thank you for the book." Roxy took it and tucked it into her purse. "I'll make sure to begin it tonight."

Meredith patted her on the shoulder. "There's a whole new world waiting for you, young woman."

Roxy, rather dumbfounded, simply smiled. "Thanks again. I'd better be off."

"Yes, me too. I have to prepare to converse with the spirits of New Orleans. I'm sure they have *a lot* to say," said Meredith. "Goodbye, now. See you later, Roxy."

"And oh," Roxy said turning back to her. "We'll have a *wonderful* dinner ready for you on your arrival. Evangeline is preparing it for you as we speak. She cooks the best, most authentic New Orleans cuisine you could hope to find."

"Sounds delicious!" said Charles. His features had relaxed now, and his cheek's pink hue was fading.

"You're so greedy, Charles," Meredith said with a not altogether pleasant laugh. She flicked his chest with her hand. "It's all he thinks about. Well, thanks, Roxy. We look forward to your hospitality. Perhaps we can talk about my book over dinner?"

"Yes," said Roxy. "Let's do that." She smiled but was already experiencing a feeling of dread. There was something unnerving about Meredith. "Bye, then." Meredith raised her hand in a small wave. "Bye."

Roxy headed out to the Rolls where Sam was loading up the final bags. "Sorry," she said. "I didn't help you with any of them!"

Sam laughed. "No worries. You were charming the

clientele as per your job description of hotel owner. And you seemed to be doing a great job."

Roxy smiled wryly as they got in the car. "Yes, but you got pegged as a lackey when you're hardly that."

Sam shrugged. He was unconcerned. "It's okay by me."

They climbed into the car and Roxy, once again, slipped down into her seat. "Seriously, though," Sam said, "look at you. You've really grown into your role—so in command, in control, so impressive!"

"Really? That Meredith was giving me the heebie-jeebies. She made me feel very uncomfortable."

"She was quite a character, wasn't she? But you've had plenty of experience in managing characters now, haven't you? Those Instagram influencers you had were hardly a piece of cake, and that novelist who stayed last month, she was a piece of *work*. All that method acting she insisted upon doing to 'get inside her characters' heads.'"

"Aw, she was alright. It was her Great Dane that was the problem. Nefertiti simply didn't like him.' Nefertiti was Roxy's white Persian cat. "Once I'd shut Nef in my room and the dog had stopped howling, she was able to get on with her book."

"I don't know how you put up with all the guest's demands. You have the patience of a saint. Don't you have *The Magnificent Luxury Travel Show* team coming to film you soon?" said Sam. He reached forward to turn the ignition on. The engine purred into life, but it was so quiet that Roxy could only tell it was running by the swinging needles on the dials in the dashboard.

"Yeah, next month," Roxy shivered. "The show won't air for about six months, though. Oh, look!" She glanced in the wing mirror and saw a large black executive car with tinted windows pull up behind them. "I'll bet that's Meredith's private client." Sure enough, a very tall, black-suited man with a thin, straight, black tie and shades got out of the back seat. He buttoned his jacket as he hurried inside the botanica. Under his arm was a small light-brown dog. "Wonder who that is, then?"

"Who knows?" said Sam. "It's quite common for business people in these parts to have spiritual advisers. They come from all over the state to meet them. Many of the entrepreneurs do huge deals and work with a lot of money while some are more...well, *dangerous* than others. There's some dodgy dealers and gangster types here and there. They seek out spiritual guidance to help them make decisions, that kind of thing. It helps them feel in control, that things will work out, that they are protected, and for some who are working near or over the line, it probably legitimizes what they do in their own minds."

"I suppose," said Roxy doubtfully, "I wonder if it works, though. If all this spirituality, voodoo, magic, if it's really real?"

"I don't know if it works," Sam said eventually, long after Roxy had asked her question. "And I certainly don't know if it's real. But there are a lot of people who believe in it, heart and soul. Sage and Dr. Jack for a start, of course. Who am I to tell them it's all hocus pocus?"

"Yeah, that's how I feel, too," said Roxy. "I mean, before I came here I didn't know anything about it. I wouldn't have even known what a medium was," She laughed. "Actually, I'm still not clear. Is it...do they...talk to spirits?"

"You got it," said Sam. "Usually they talk to people's loved ones who have passed away. But it can mean talking to other spirits, too." He grinned. "I've never felt so New Orleanian, explaining this to you. And I'm no expert."

"It's all a bit weird to me. Talking to spirits? The dead? Spooky. I'm a simple by-the-book sort of gal." Roxy chuckled. "If you can see it, touch it, I'm in. The simpler, the more straight-forward, the better."

"Nothing too crazy, huh?"

"No, siree. Have you ever been tempted to take up crystals or cards or whatnot?"

"No," he said. "The magic in my life is music, I'd say."

"The sax is your wand," Roxy said, then worried she sounded like she was mocking him. "Well, you're certainly very good with it," she added, making things worse.

What Roxy really wanted to know was how Sam knew so much about spiritualism and *gangsters*. There was something about him that didn't add up, and everyone knew it. He ran a modest laundry company with just three or four vans and spent a lot of his time doing renovations on the hotel. He had a limited edition Rolls Royce Phantom, and had *bought* the guesthouse, seemingly with a snap of his fingers, so that it wouldn't be purchased by developers. Sometimes he was spotted around town associating with shady-looking characters. So where *did* he get all his money? It was an unanswered question. When anyone mentioned money, Sam got all cagey.

If it had been anyone else, she'd have distanced herself. But this was *Sam*. He was so kind, so chivalrous, so brave, and there was an unspoken agreement that she and her friends would just drop the subject. Nevertheless, this unresolved issue, and others primarily their mutual attraction, hung in the air and at times energetically swirled around them, disturbing the atmosphere.

Sam turned on the radio. His car was permanently switched to a jazz station, and the voice of Ella Fitzgerald singing *Mack The Knife* immediately bounced through the posh car, distracting Roxy from her thoughts and setting her foot a-tappin'.

In the middle of it, Roxy's phone buzzed. She didn't recognize the number. "Hello?"

"Hello, Roxy, it's Meredith Romanoff. We are about to start the séance. The spirits say they want you here. No, they *insist* that you come."

Roxy's head whirled. "What? The spirits? But I have to work on dinner and...the spirits, you say?"

"Yes," said Meredith. "I absolutely insist you come back immediately."

"Oh...right, well," Roxy said. "Are you sure?" Attending a séance wasn't exactly how she had planned to spend her evening, but she didn't want to antagonize Meredith, especially now she knew about her temper.

"I'm sure. The spirits were very clear. They want you here. Now."

Roxy was suddenly struck by a burst of adventure. "Hmm, well, all right, why not? Just give me a few moments. I'll be there shortly." Roxy hung up her phone.

"What was that about?" Sam said, raising his eyebrows. "We need to turn around?"

"'Fraid so," said Roxy. "Meredith wants me at the séance. She says the spirits are calling me, and she wants me there." Roxy turned to look at Sam, her eyebrows raised as high as they would go. "Guess I'm about to find out if it's all hocus-pocus, huh?"

CHAPTER THREE

"COME ON, ROXY, hurry up," said Meredith.
"My private client is here. And I've allowed Dr.
Jack in, despite our argument, just to show that
I'm the bigger person." Meredith didn't elaborate on the
reason for the dispute as she ushered Roxy into the back
room of the botanica where it was dark, the only illumina-
tion being a reproduction oil lamp that sat in the middle
of a small circular table.

Deep purple velvet fabric lined the room entirely and
draped on the floor while ribbons that held the curtains
aside during daylight hung limp and forlorn in the
corners. Against one wall stood what looked to Roxy like
an altar of sorts—a side table covered in the same velvet
fabric as the walls. Candles, large and small, some used
and misshapen, some pristine and new, covered the table.
In the center stood a statue of a woman and in front of
that was set a skull. The floor was covered in dingy char-
coal carpet tile.

Around the small, circular table sat George—Meredith's assistant, Charles—Meredith's husband, the rangy

businessman Roxy had seen getting out of his car though he no longer held his dog. There was also Meredith's school friend—Terah and Dr. Jack. Meredith stood by the altar, the flickering candles casting shadows across her face that made her look quite terrifying.

"Look," said Meredith, pointing to an empty chair, "it was fate, Roxy. You were destined to be here, to fill the last chair."

"Thank you for inviting me," said Roxy, taking her seat gracefully. Her elbows rubbed against Terah and Dr. Jack who were on either side of her.

Meredith sat herself down and closed her eyes. She breathed in slowly. After a few seconds, she opened her eyes again. "The room is cluttered energetically with curiosity and confusion so let me disseminate this heavy energy. It appears like a gray cloud, and it will only interfere with our process," Meredith said. She huffed. "So it always goes with humans."

"Would you like me to clear it for you?" George offered.

"No," Meredith snapped. She flicked her hand at George, much like she had at her husband earlier, and tutted. "Now, let me introduce everyone again. That will integrate our energies well enough. This," Meredith continued, gesturing at the tall suited man who was still wearing his sunglasses despite the gloom, "is Royston Lamontagne. He is a private client and the main reason we are here today. He is a very important person who does extraordinary and wide-ranging work in the music business and he—very wisely—connects to the spirit world to help him succeed."

Royston Lamontagne nodded slowly, his full mouth in a straight line, apparently somber, but his true expression mostly indiscernible thanks to his shades. He reminded Roxy of Nefertiti who had regarded the novelist guests' Great Dane similarly except in her feline case, an ice-cold blue-eyed stare sat in place of sunglasses. Roxy wondered what had happened to Lamontagne's little dog.

Meredith turned to her. "Royston, this is Roxy Reinhardt, the owner of the *Funky Cat Inn*, the hotel I am staying at while I am in New Orleans."

At her words, Lamontagne sprang to life and spoke for the first time. "What is she doing here?" the businessman said in a deep, gruff voice. "Hoteliers are notorious for spreading gossip. I don't want my business shared with half of New Orleans and their grandmothers."

Meredith smiled and spoke carefully, her voice all syrupy. "I know it's unorthodox, Royston," she said. "But the spirits requested it. She will be useful in some way, you'll see. Who knows how? The spirit world will tell us. Roxy, you are bound by an oath of silence. You will not repeat any information the spirits divulge in this room. Is that clear? In fact, that goes for all of us. What is said in this room, stays in this room."

"That's fine by me," Roxy said, wondering what on earth she'd let herself in for.

Meredith gestured at Charles and George. "Everyone, this is my husband Charles and my assistant George." Then she nodded at the woman. "And this is Terah Jones, an old school friend of mine." Lamontagne shifted in his seat and opened his mouth to speak. Meredith moved swiftly to head him off. "She'll be fine, Royston. I have checked in with all the spirits, and they promise me this grouping is the most auspicious combination of energies.

Terah happens to live in New Orleans and recently reconnected with me.

"You contacted me, Meredith, but hi, everyone," said Terah to the room. Meredith shot her a stern look, but Terah met it head-on, and Meredith moved along.

"And this is Dr. Jack, of course," said Meredith. "The proprietor of this rather humble botanica." Jack caught Roxy's eye and minutely lifted his eyebrows and widened his eyes. "Are we all clear? Does everyone know who everyone is? Has your curiosity about each other been placated and your trust built?"

Roxy nodded her assent, unsure if Meredith wanted them to speak out loud.

"Well?" Meredith demanded. Obviously, she did. There were murmurings of agreement.

"Yes, darling," Charles said soothingly. "We are all in equilibrium now."

"Let me check you are telling the truth," Meredith said. "I will breathe in the room again." She closed her eyes and took a deep breath. As she exhaled, a smile spread across her lips and she sighed. "Yes, the cloud is gone. What remains is intrigue about me and my gifts, and the wonders the spirits are about to share."

Roxy wondered what her friend Sage would have made of all of this. Sage—a spiritualist, and a computer programming genius—was devoid of ego, something Meredith Romanoff seemed to have in spades. Roxy couldn't believe that Sage would have viewed the medium, famous though she apparently was, very favorably.

"Okay, George, turn out the lights," Meredith said, briskly.

George got up and blew out the candles.

"And *don't* trip up on the way back to your seat," Meredith's stern voice rang out. "We don't want the spirits startled."

But there was an almighty crash as George *did* trip. He'd stumbled into a chair. Roxy heard Meredith's exasperated sigh and imagined her rolling her eyes.

"Sorry," George mumbled.

He quickly sat down and switched off the lamp that sat in the middle of the table. The room went completely black except for a tiny crack of light that seeped in around the frame of the door that led into the store area of the botanica. Meredith tutted again. "That's no good, no good. What kind of place is this?"

There was a scraping of chair legs. Someone got up and pulled a heavy velvet curtain across the door. With that, even the tiniest shaft of light was extinguished. The room was now pitch black. Roxy didn't particularly like the dark, and this experience, among these strangers, was new and peculiar and a little discomforting. A small well of panic formed in her chest and threatened to rise out of control, but she breathed in deeply to calm herself.

When she'd first arrived in New Orleans, Roxy would have sprinted as fast as she could away from a situation such as this. Now though, she was much, much braver. Life had so much to offer, she'd learned, if you stuck around for it, if you opened your mind and took it all in.

"Okay, now everyone, silence," Meredith ordered. "I must raise the spirits and see if they are willing to speak to us. This might take some time. It can be tricky if they are not in the mood." Meredith began to talk in a booming, commanding voice. "Spirits of New Orleans, all those who are favorable, come unto us in this moment. Spirits of the earth, of the air, of the fire, of the river, come unto us."

Roxy heard Meredith inhale through her nose and puff out a long breath through her lips. "We are here now, to learn of your wisdom from the other side. We revere your grace, your beauty, and your wisdom. We understand your ownership of higher forms of life, of knowledge, that which is gained through your experiences both here on earth and in other realms, and we humbly ask that we may gain your insights so that we may make progress and prosper."

Roxy felt this talk was very strange indeed. She opened her eyes wide in the darkness, hoping that might enable her to see something, anything.

"Royston Lamontagne!" Meredith shouted so loudly and suddenly that Roxy flinched. She imagined everyone else did too, although she couldn't see the slightest thing in the darkness. The source of Meredith's voice changed a little, and Roxy could tell that she was standing. "We are here to attend first to Royston Lamontagne!" Meredith said in such a deep voice that Roxy almost doubted it was her speaking. "Royston, your humble question for the spirits please..."

"I want to know how I should proceed in my business. There are signs that a very difficult deal may turn nasty, and I wish to know the best steps to take to protect my safety and the safety of my business, but most of all, that of my dog Fenton."

"Spirits, we bring this question to you!" lamented Meredith. "Please, give us the answers we need."

There was a long silence. Meredith began to hum in a high, light, singsong voice, like a child's. No answers from the spirits seemed to be forthcoming and as she waited, Meredith's humming got louder and louder. Roxy could hear the older woman's clothing rustling and concluded that Meredith was swaying from side to side.

BANG!

The single sound reverberated around the room. The humming stopped. There was a clatter as something landed on the table, followed by a thud as something large and heavy fell to the floor.

CHAPTER FOUR

F OR A SECOND, Roxy ran all kinds of visions in her mind as the well of panic threatened to take her over again. Was this part of the séance? Had an evil spirit just made its presence felt? Everyone else seemed to be wondering the same thing. A silence stretched out into the blackness.

It was Dr. Jack who broke it. "Meredith?" he said.

There was no answer.

Someone got out of their chair and suddenly, with a tiny *click,* the room was far too bright. Roxy, as if in slow motion and shielding her eyes from the brightness, turned to see Dr. Jack, his hand reaching behind the curtain as he turned on the light switch. Still squinting, she looked wildly back to the table and her eyes landed on George, his eyes growing wide as he stared at the floor.

Roxy looked down. Meredith lay there, her hands by her ears, her mouth open in surprise, and her eyes staring. A rapidly growing dark stain in the middle of her chest marred her white blouse, the ruffles of which no longer shook. This was no performance. This was *real.* The image was horrifying but as much as she wanted to look away, Roxy kept staring at the woman lying on the floor. Then she noticed the gun on the table and time seemed to slow down even further.

Slowly the occupants of the room became aware of one another and what had just happened. They all stared at each other wordlessly, in complete and utter shock.

"What?" Terah breathed after some seconds. "What?"

"Who...who did that?" said Dr. Jack, looking at each of them in turn.

Royston Lamontagne shook his head, his hand at his mouth, his sunglasses still obscuring his eyes. He stood and half fell, half stumbled around the room, muttering something about "Fenton." Meredith's husband Charles had turned completely white and looked like he may fall down himself from the shock. George let out a wail that pierced Roxy's body like a dagger.

"I'm getting out of here, *now*," said Terah, gripping her purse and rushing to the door.

But Dr. Jack was faster. He dashed from his chair to intercept her. "Oh no, you don't," he said. "We must stay here. We have to call the police." He turned to everyone in the room, shaking. "One of you here did this. I don't know who, but I know that you have committed a murderous act. Not only will the police punish you, but the spirits will, too, mark my words. Now, come outside into the botanica, but you must *stay* in the building. I'm calling Detective Johnson, New Orleans PD."

Everyone filed out of the room, all of them deathly silent except for George, who was sobbing his eyes out, his face red and moist. Roxy turned to see Charles hang back just a little. He kneeled and clutched Meredith's hand.

He kissed it. "Goodbye, my sweet darling," he said. He stayed there for some time until Roxy went over to him and gently encouraged him up.

Outside in the botanica, Dr. Jack locked the front door. Then he locked the door to the backroom. "We must protect the crime scene." He turned to the small group—Roxy, Terah, Lamontagne (who had now been reunited with his little dog Fenton), Charles and George. Jack's eyes were full of sorrow. "I don't know what on earth is going on. Neither will Detective Johnson. But the spirits do, and you can bet it will all come out. Whoever did this, you have violated a sacred space, taken an innocent life. You are playing with life and death as if they are mere children's games. The killer, whichever one of you it is, has made a grave error. A very grave error indeed."

"What's all this then?" Detective Johnson said as he stepped into the botanica after Dr. Jack had unlocked the door to allow him to enter. He looked in all directions and Roxy tracked his eyes as he took it all in—the incense burners, the skulls, the crystals, the essential oils. Undisguised hostility emanated from him as normal, but Roxy thought she discerned a little vulnerability behind his eyes.

"Someone's been killed," said Dr. Jack.

Johnson's gaze swiveled as he took in not just the strange objects in the botanica, but the strange people. Charles, George, Lamontagne, and Terah stood or sat around the botanica desultorily looking about them. "You told me that already," Johnson snapped. His shiny head reflected the different colors rotating through the botanica as the low, early evening sun shone through the windows onto the crystals which dispersed the light into tiny rainbows. "Who's the vic?"

"Meredith Romanoff, the renowned psychic and spirit communicator," said Dr. Jack grimly, wincing at Johnson's overfamiliar and disrespectful manner.

"Renowned what?" Johnson said waving his hand dismissively. "Never mind." He rounded on George, who was sobbing in a corner by the oracle decks. "And who's this then? The son, I presume?"

"No," George said, gasping through tears. "I am, was, her assistant spirit communicator."

Johnson threw his eyes to the ceiling. "Right. Okay." He turned and caught Roxy's eye. He started in surprise. "You! Why do I always find *you* at some crime scene or other?" He curled his lip and growled.

"I don't know," Roxy said truthfully. "I can assure you, Detective, that I'm no happier about this than you are."

Johnson fixed his unwavering glare on her. "I'm watching you. Just know that, Ms. Reinhardt." He turned to Dr. Jack. "Well, where's the body?"

"She's not a body. She's a person," George wailed. "Oh..." He threw his head forward over his lap and embarked on another jag of prolonged sobbing.

Roxy looked at Charles, who was still ashen. He sat on a seat in front of the counter, looking almost dead himself. He had barely moved as much as his eyes since Johnson arrived. They were fixed on a point on the floor.

"In the backroom," replied Dr. Jack to Johnson.

"Look, I have to get to an important meeting," said Royston Lamontagne. He spoke around his little dog who was licking his face hungrily. The businessman marched up to Johnson, looking him directly in the eye. He removed his sunglasses to reveal piercing, angry black eyes. His shoulders were squared and his fist, the one that wasn't under Fenton's chest, was clenched. "I must get away as soon as possible. I have business to attend to."

Johnson snorted. "You could be having coffee with the President for all I care, but you'll not get away any earlier. You'll leave when I say you can."

Royston's lips pursed with obvious fury, and he glared at Johnson. But wisely, he said nothing and threw himself down on a chair next to Charles.

Johnson nodded at Dr. Jack. "In there?"

"Yes. Let me unlock the door." Johnson put plastic covers over his shoes and briefly disappeared inside the room. Everyone else in the store was silent and still except for George, whose sobs had petered out to be replaced by tiny sniffs punctuated by the occasional heaving sigh.

Johnson reappeared and spoke into his radio, "Back up for forensics and questioning at... What's this place called again?" he asked the room.

"*Dr. Jack's Botanica,*" Dr. Jack replied.

"Erm, *Dr. Jack's Botanica,* 22 52nd Street. Be quick about it, y'hear. Homicide."

The door to the botanica opened and in strutted a young officer. He thrust his chin into the air. "Officer Newman Trudeau," he said to Roxy who was standing just inside the doorway. "Where is Detective Johnson?"

Before Roxy could answer, she heard Johnson groan. "They sent the country boy, did they?" he said.

"My name is Officer Trudeau, sir," the policeman said. His eye contact was solid for a few long seconds until it stuttered under the unblinking gaze of the senior detective. Trudeau looked away.

"Question everyone here about everything," Johnson ordered, "Dr. Jack... you're not a real doctor, are you?"

"Well, that depends what you view as certification," Dr. Jack explained. "I was trained in the herbal medicine of the Andes mountain people, and..."

"That'll be a 'no' then," Johnson said. "Jack, where can Newbie... sorry Officer *Newman* Trudeau conduct his interviews? Is there another back room? Or will we have to transport y'all back to the station?"

"There's only a restroom," Dr. Jack said.

"Will a chair fit in there?"

"Yes," said Dr. Jack.

Johnson grinned nastily, showing imperfect teeth as he looked at Trudeau. "Just the thing."

"But sir, wouldn't it be more professional to take them to..."

"No," said Johnson abruptly, "it would not. Question them one by one in the restroom and try to do it properly, boy. I don't want any rookie mistakes. I'm going out to get a sandwich. I expect the interviews to be done and recorded effectively by the time I get back. I want you to present to me all the evidence in a coherent fashion on my return. Understood?"

Roxy saw Officer Trudeau's hands shaking. "Right, sir. Yes, sir."

Johnson swaggered out and wedged his large form behind the steering wheel of his unmarked police car. With a powerful surge of acceleration that, Roxy suspected, was for his onlookers benefit, Detective Johnson drove off.

Officer Trudeau, on the other hand, clearly felt humiliated and now, with his superior gone, his humiliation morphed into self-importance. He assembled his features into an expression that he clearly hoped telegraphed authority and opened his mouth to speak.

"Now, look," his words came out croaky. He cleared his throat and tried again. "Now look, I don't want no talk of ghosties and ghoulies in your interviews, y'hear? None of that nonsense. You'll stick to the facts and only the facts. Okay?"

"Yes, sir," Terah said. "Absolutely, sir. I'm with you. I'm not sure I believe all that either. Seems as though being on good terms with the spirits didn't exactly help Meredith any, did it?"

"Hmph, let's keep our opinions to ourselves too, shall we? Now, Jack or whatever your name is, put those chairs in the restroom."

"You'll only need one. There's no room for a second. One of you will have to sit on the toilet."

"You," Officer Trudeau said, pointing at Roxy. "Let's have you first. Get in there. And fast. I don't have no time to waste."

Roxy sighed. Why was it always she who got interviewed first? She felt a little bit sick. Johnson made her feel uncomfortable, but this Officer Trudeau seemed almost worse. While Johnson was officious and arrogant, Trudeau had something to prove, and it seemed unlikely he would give up until he'd proved it.

Roxy followed the police officer into the rest room and shut the door behind her. With them both in there, there was no room to turn around.

"I think you'll have to sit on the toilet, Officer. That way your witnesses can get in and out easily," Roxy ventured carefully. It wasn't a very luxurious restroom, just a simple small room with white tiles on the walls and floor, a toilet, a sink, and a small window.

"Absolutely not," Trudeau said again. They engaged in an awkward dance as they tried unsuccessfully to change places by squeezing sideways and sidling past one another. It was impossible.

Grudgingly, Trudeau finally accepted Roxy's argument, and she was treated to the sight of an officer of the law sitting atop a toilet seat interviewing her as she sat on a chair next to the sink. They were uncomfortably close together, their knees almost touching. Trudeau's humiliation was now total.

CHAPTER FIVE

"RIDICULOUS," ROXY HEARD Trudeau mutter under his breath. He balanced his phone on the edge of the basin and set up the recording. He looked at her, his gray eyes so penetrating that she had to look away for a moment. "State your name and date of birth."

"Roxanne Melissa Reinhardt, 2, 27, 1995."

"Occupation?"

"Manager of the *Funky Cat Inn*."

Trudeau then spoke the date, time, and location of the interview. He omitted the fact that they were in a bathroom. On his knees, he set a paper notebook.

"Right," he said. "Tell me what happened."

Roxy explained the evening's events as Trudeau feverishly wrote everything down.

"Do you have any previous connection with Meredith Romanoff?"

"None," said Roxy. "She was recommended my hotel by Dr. Jack. She wanted to stay somewhere more intimate than the big impersonal chain hotel where her main event is taking place. Oh! That'll have to be canceled now. Oh dear." Roxy looked at the floor for a moment. "Well, anyway, I came here to pick up her baggage as a courtesy, but she called me back and invited me to attend the séance. That's the only reason I am here, her request. She said the spirits were demanding my presence." Roxy could hear how silly her words sounded, a view reflected in Officer Trudeau's expression. He raised his eyebrows just a fraction and pursed his lips.

"Do you know anything about the relationship between the owner of this store and the victim?"

"Dr. Jack? Nothing."

"Was there any tension between Meredith Romanoff and anyone else this evening?"

Roxy swallowed and thought back to the argument between Dr. Jack and Meredith that she had chanced upon when she had arrived at the botanica. "Well, yes. I mean, I'm sure it doesn't mean anything..."

Trudeau slapped his pencil down onto his notebook. "I didn't ask you if it *meant* anything," he snapped. "I'm not searching for the meaning of life like you hippie-types. I want *information*. Stick to the cold hard facts, not what you think they mean." He sighed, exasperated, and picked up his pencil again. Clearly he'd been a student of Detective Johnson's interview methods.

"Are you new? To the New Orleans police force, I mean?" Roxy asked, before realizing that she wasn't being very tactful. "I... I'm just curious. I've not seen you around before."

"No, I am *not* new to the police force," he said. "I've been working in a rural part of the state. But that doesn't mean I'm not tough or cut out for detective work in the city."

"No, no, of course not. I—I see," Roxy stuttered, but Trudeau continued.

"I've shut down some real bad dog-fighting rings in my time, I can tell you, and I've also solved a lot of gun crime cases. It's not all sleepy farms in rural Louisiana, despite what you might have heard." Roxy had clearly hit a nerve. Trudeau was babbling. "In any case, I can tell you're not from this area by your accent. It's very obvious. Do you know about rural poverty, and the crimes it causes? Of course, you don't."

"Actually," Roxy said sharply. "I grew up in poverty myself, in Ohio. I am well-acquainted with the drug problems and other crimes that happen in these communities. I know how tough it is."

"Right," said Trudeau. He stared at her, then his expression softened and he quickly looked away. In that second, Roxy recognized a fellow traveler. She knew that Trudeau had had a similar upbringing to her, one where shoes ended up with holes in the soles yet didn't get replaced, where cockroaches scuttled across the kitchen, where sleep was merely a short respite from the constant strain that living in such tenuous circumstances brought about. Empathy was strong in Roxy, and she felt for him. Trudeau was trying to prove himself in the big city, to better his life, just as she was. All was forgiven for a moment as she caught on to the bond they shared.

"Continue with what you were saying," he said, more gently this time.

"Well, Meredith and Dr. Jack were arguing when I arrived," Roxy said. "I'm quite sure he didn't kill her, though. He would never do that."

"Stick to the facts, Miss Reinhardt. What were they arguing about?"

"Honestly? I can't tell you."

"You *have* to tell me," he said, all of a sudden so loud and intense that she flinched.

"I mean, I can't tell you because I don't know. It was some deep, spiritual, philosophical principle thing. I didn't really get it."

"Fine," he said. "What about the other people? What was she like with them?"

"Meredith seemed kind of sharp with her assistant George, the one who was crying a lot, and dismissive of her husband Charles. The other two, Terah, and the businessman guy... um, Royston... she was fine to them."

"And to you?"

Roxy thought about the book in her bag. "Actually, she was quite... erm, taken with me. She invited me along to this séance because she said the spirits wanted me there."

"The *spirits* wanted you there?" Trudeau smirked. "Okaaaay."

"Well, I don't know much about all that, spirits and stuff, but she took an interest in me, and considering she was my special guest, at the hotel I mean, I thought I had better honor her wishes...I mean, the spirits' wishes."

Trudeau was listening carefully to her now, genuinely interested. "Hmmm, you've got business sense, I will say. I could never work in hospitality. All that pandering."

"I prefer to see it as kindness."

Trudeau shrugged, "Kindness don't solve crimes."

"No, I suppose not."

"So tell me what happened in the room before the victim was shot?"

"It happened very quickly. There were six of us there. It was completely black. You couldn't see a thing, not a thing. Then just a couple of minutes in, there was a bang and silence. Dr. Jack turned on the light, and there was Meredith on the floor, dead. There was a gun on the table. That was it, really."

"And for those couple of minutes, what was happening?"

"We were seated around the table, and um, well, Meredith started talking."

"To who?"

"To, um...the spirits."

Trudeau looked up from his notes, one eyebrow raised. Roxy shrugged and pressed her lips together. She *did* sound crazy, she knew it, but it was the truth.

Trudeau asked Roxy a few more questions, but she had nothing to add, so he let her go. She left the restroom, the door swinging behind her, and joined the others who were waiting in the shop.

"Was it really bad?" Dr. Jack whispered to her. "Are you okay?"

"It was fine, really," said Roxy, placing a hand on his forearm. "I'm so sorry this happened here, Dr. Jack. You must feel awful."

He looked pained. "The Universe has a reason for everything. Even though sometimes it is difficult to fathom what that reason might be."

Roxy nodded, unsure what to think.

Trudeau called in Royston Lamontagne. "Not the dog, thanks."

Lamontagne handed his little dog to Terah, who immediately started stroking Fenton's head and talking baby talk to him.

While she waited to be dismissed, Roxy sat down behind the counter and called Nat to let her know what was going on and why she wasn't back. "You'll have to get all the dinner preparations finished up without me," she said. "It looks like I'm going to be here a while. I'm sure we'll be back soon, but it's..." She looked up at Charles and George and lowered her voice. "Well, the joyous, welcome party idea that we had in mind isn't going to be appropriate, obviously."

After Trudeau was finished with Lamontagne, the others traipsed into the bathroom in turn as Trudeau called their name—Terah, then George, Charles, and finally Dr. Jack. There was nothing at all to do while they waited. Roxy sat with her thoughts, but her mind kept going back to the image of Meredith lying dead on the floor. She tried to distract herself by reading Meredith's book, but she couldn't concentrate and was reduced to skimming the pages, taking in very little before she would find herself replaying the scene of Meredith's shooting in her mind.

"Roxy, do you know?" It was Terah. She pointed. "Are those *real* human skulls?"

"I don't think so," said Roxy with a shudder. "I sure hope not. I'm pretty sure Dr. Jack wouldn't have real ones in here. Would that even be allowed?"

"Some practitioners of dark magic do use real skulls," Charles interjected, his voice monotone as he stared into space. "Perhaps we've stumbled onto a dark wizard."

"Surely not," Roxy said quickly. The idea hadn't even occurred to her. "Not Dr. Jack. That's just something from storybooks, right? It can't be real."

"Unfortunately, it is," said Charles. "There are bad people in this world, Roxy. People with malevolent intentions." He nodded toward the back room. "Obviously."

CHAPTER SIX

OFFICER TRUDEAU FINISHED his questioning and stood guard at the doorway to the botanica, waiting for his superior's return.

Johnson arrived some ten minutes later, looking happier than Roxy had ever seen him. "Right," he said, addressing Trudeau, and ignoring everyone else. "Get yourself outside and tell me your findings."

"I don't think that it's very professional to..." Trudeau began until he saw the dark stormy expression that formed on Johnson's face.

"Listen, I am the lead detective here," Johnson said. "Whatever I do is, by default, professional, got it?"

Reluctantly Trudeau followed Johnson outside and the two men spoke for a while. Roxy watched them through the glass doors. They were gesticulating and mouthing noiselessly while tension mounted inside the store as the minutes ticked by. Who was the killer? Did the police know? Would they let everyone go? Would they arrest someone? Would they arrest *everyone*? Roxy bit her lip. Of course, she knew she was innocent, but

Johnson was always suspicious of her, and if she weren't the murderer, which one of her companions was? It had to be one of them.

She looked at them all. Dr. Jack was behind the counter closing out the register for the day. Terah sat sideways on a chair, her legs crossed, her foot jiggling. She scratched her face where the strap of her eye patch met her hairline. Lamontagne leaned against a wall, scrolling on his phone, occasionally kissing the fur between the ears of his little dog which he still held under his arm. Charles sat on a plastic chair next to Lamontagne. He leaned forward, his elbows on his knees, his hands clasped between them, staring into space, unseeing. George sat on the floor against the wall. He quietly sipped from a bottle of water, his face red, but blank, occasionally flicking his eyes to look at the two detectives standing outside.

Through the window, Trudeau and Johnson seemed to come to a decision. Trudeau pulled out his handcuffs. Roxy tensed and inhaled. When Johnson forcefully opened the door and strode through it, everyone looked up. Immediately they were all alert. Even Lamontagne looked up from his phone. Fenton yipped.

"Jack! Come here!" Johnson pointed at a spot on the floor in front of him.

Dr. Jack moved from behind the counter and walked easily to stand in front of the detective. Johnson quickly grabbed the botanica owner by the shoulders while Trudeau scurried behind him and slapped on handcuffs.

"What? Wait…"

"Jack Lavantille, you are arrested on suspicion of murder," Trudeau said.

"What?" Roxy said moving over to the trio. "On what basis?" She looked wildly between the two policemen. "It can't be Dr. Jack! He would never do such a thing." The men ignored her.

Trudeau continued, "You have the right to remain silent. Anything you say can and will be used against you in a court of law. You have the right to an attorney. If you cannot afford an attorney, one will be obtained for you before police questioning."

"What are you doing? I didn't kill Meredith," Dr. Jack said desperately, looking at George and Charles. "I didn't, I swear." His expression was open, his eyebrows high. He shrugged as he stood with his hands behind his back.

Johnson snorted as Trudeau grabbed Jack by the upper arms and pushed him toward the door.

"I am a man of the light!" Dr. Jack shouted behind him to the group who were now standing together in the middle of the store as Trudeau led him away. "I would never kill anyone!"

"Man of the *what?*" said Johnson. Then he waved. "The rest of you are free to go."

"Roxy, lock up my store!" Dr. Jack called behind him.

"Don't worry, Dr. Jack!" she called back.

"You'll do no such thing," said Johnson. "The forensics team is still in the backroom, they'll lock up when they're done, and I don't want to see or hear another peep out of you, Ms. Reinhardt. Is that clear?"

"Yes, sir." Roxy followed Johnson outside.

"I swear, Roxy, I didn't do it!" said Dr. Jack, as Trudeau pushed his head down, guiding him into the back of the squad car.

"I believe you!" Roxy said. "Don't worry, this will get sorted out!"

"Tell Sage!"

"Yes, of course." Roxy's words faded on her lips as the patrol car door slammed shut.

But as Roxy stood on the botanica steps and watched the squad car drive away, she questioned what she'd just said. How could she believe Dr. Jack so readily? She barely knew him, and she'd been around long enough to know people were not always what and who they seemed. As she thought, a black town car pulled up. She was roughly pushed aside as Royston Lamontagne passed her, obviously eager to get away. He jumped in the car, and with a squeal of tires, the car zoomed off, Fenton's tiny, beady brown eyes watching her steadily out of the window.

Roxy went back inside the botanica and saw Terah leaning over Charles, her arm on his shoulder. She was saying something to him quietly, and after Charles nodded briefly, she walked to the door, her arms now folded. "I'm off," she said. She lifted her hand and pointed her car keys in the direction of a sedan that was parked across the road.

"Bye, Terah," Roxy said gently and watched as the woman crossed the street, climbed in her car, and drove off. There was a noise beside her and she turned to see Charles, Meredith's husband, staring at the back of Terah's car.

"They're all gone," Charles said. His voice was feeble. He sounded broken.

Seeing the devastated man next to her, Roxy pinched herself. She needed to take action. She didn't have time to ruminate or hesitate, for that matter.

"Charles," she said. "I'm going to ring Sam. He owns the *Funky Cat* with me. He will collect us and take us back to the hotel. You can go to your rooms and regroup.

In a while, if you're up to it, we can have dinner. You can eat in your rooms, or downstairs, or whatever you like. Or, obviously, if you'd rather not eat at all, that's fine. We were going to play some live jazz music for you afterward, but, um, in the circumstances, it's entirely up to you. Whatever makes you feel comfortable. We're here to take care of you."

George joined them. The two men both looked terrible. George had awful bloodshot eyes from all his crying while Charles was so white his skin looked almost transparent.

"Okay," George said tearfully. He could barely stand. Charles, clearly beyond words, just nodded.

Roxy felt awful for both of them. "Just a moment or two," she said. "Sam will be here soon. The hotel isn't far away."

She made the call, and they stood waiting for Sam in silence. The two men looked like complete zombies, but Roxy was beginning to feel nervous. Her mind was racing. What if Johnson and Trudeau were wrong about Dr. Jack? What was going to happen next? Was she going back to the hotel with a killer? Two even? Questions whirled through her head, but she stuck out her chin and put a brave face on for her two guests.

Thankfully, Sam was as quick as she'd promised he'd be. As he got out of the Rolls Royce, his face was a picture of sorrow and concern. "I'm so, so sorry about what happened," he said to them. "I can't even begin to imagine what has happened here this evening."

"Thank you," Charles said in a monotone.

George began to cry again, then sniffed and shuddered as he repressed more tears.

Sam opened the back doors for the two of them. He mouthed over the top of the car to Roxy. "Are you okay?"

She nodded and got into the front passenger seat next to him. As usual, jazz was on the radio, but Sam quickly turned it off, and it was a smooth, mournful, silent ride back to the *Funky Cat Inn*.

When they got to the cobbled street where the hotel stood opposite *Elijah's Bakery*, Sam pulled right up to the entrance. Elijah looked out of the window as they drove past, and immediately came out and walked up to the car, his purple zebra-print shirt making Roxy squint. "Our new guests!" he said gleefully. "I'm Elijah, owner of this here bakery! So pleased to…" He stuck out his hand then noticed their glum faces. His hand sprung back. "What's happened? Somebody kill your cat?"

Roxy winced.

"Elijah," Sam said firmly as he got out of the car. He planted a strong hand on Elijah's shoulder and took him aside to discreetly explain what was going on.

"Sorry about that," Roxy said to George and Charles. "Everyone was excited to meet you. Obviously, the news hasn't spread yet. I do apologize."

"It's nobody's fault," said Charles.

"Please, come inside," said Roxy. "I can show you up to your rooms, your bags will be there. Charles, I can move you to a different room if you wish. So you don't have to have the room you would have shared…"

"It's okay, Roxy. Our original room will be fine. Staying there will help me to feel close to Meredith." It was the most Charles had spoken since Meredith's death.

"Yes, well, okay, you can decide whether you want to come down for dinner or have it upstairs, or not at all. Whatever you prefer."

"You're a very kind spirit," said George. "Thank you, Roxy."

"Not at all," Roxy said.

Roxy's cat, Nefertiti, met them at the door, meowing plaintively at Roxy, wondering why she had been so late.

"Sorry, Neffi," Roxy whispered, bending down to give her a quick tickle under the chin. "Plans changed. I'll come back and feed you in a moment or two. Just wait a sec."

Roxy showed George and Charles up to their rooms. Opening the door to Charles's bedroom, she felt a horrible tug on her heart. She looked at the bed where Meredith Romanoff should have been sleeping that night. It was all so very, very sad. She glanced at Charles. He'd hesitated at the doorway and was surveying the bed too. She saw him grimace before he gathered himself and stepped inside the room.

After she'd made sure the two men were settled in, Roxy gratefully went downstairs. She wanted to go to her room to rest and collect herself, but as she descended the stairs, she stopped mid-flight. Five pairs of wide eyes stared up at her.

CHAPTER SEVEN

"WHAT'S GOING ON?" Evangeline asked.

"Sam said Meredith Romanoff has been shot!" Sage exclaimed.

"Are the police coming?" a voice piped up. It came from Nat.

"Sorry if I put my foot in it." That was Elijah.

"Are you alright?" Sam asked.

They all crowded around her as she reached the last step. Nat, her assistant and Girl Friday, reached out to hug Roxy. Roxy gratefully allowed herself to be enveloped by her tattooed, pierced, grunge-clad, English friend. As Nat released her, it was Sage's turn. Sage was wearing her trademark robes, this time in summer-pink, a shade that matched the ribbons that were threaded through her dreadlocks. She was good friends with Dr. Jack.

Evangeline patted Roxy's arm. This gesture from the elderly woman who used to own the hotel when it was a guesthouse was an unusually warm expression of affection. Elijah kissed Roxy on both cheeks and whispered, "Sorry again," in her ear while Sam stood stoically to one side.

"Thank you, everyone. It's been an unpleasant evening. Will you let me have a few moments in private, and then I will be happy to answer all your questions." Roxy smiled weakly, and the crowd parted to let her pass. She walked over to the door that led to her private quarters, and in silence, went inside and closed the door. She sat down on the bed and put her head in her hands.

As she sat there, Roxy felt something small and moist nudge at her knuckles. She didn't look up. Momentarily, she felt another poke. It was sharper, more emphatic this time, and accompanied by a buzzing sound that sounded like a particularly insistent, and slightly asthmatic bee. Roxy's white puffball of a kitty, Nefertiti, was now wiping her cheeks against Roxy's hand. She wasn't going to give up. Finally, Roxy looked up and gave her cat a weak smile before scooping her into her lap.

"Oh, Nef-nef, life isn't straightforward is it? When we got up this morning, who'd have thought that a few hours later we'd be in the middle of another murder investigation?" Roxy gave a big sigh and lay her cheek down on Nefertiti's back. Her fur was as soft and as white as a cloud and was as comforting as always. Roxy closed her eyes for a moment.

She didn't allow herself to relax for long, though. Roxy fed Nefertiti quickly, and while her fluffy cat wolfed down her food, Roxy freshened herself up. She washed her face and scrubbed hard at her cheeks as though by doing so she could erase the evening's devastating events. She soaped and washed her hands three times before drying them and going back into the bedroom. She looked around and started to pace. She went back and forth quickly. It wasn't a very big room. Nefertiti trailed behind her, mewing. Roxy nearly tripped over her as she turned.

"Meeeooowwwww!" Nefertiti said impatiently.

"Sorry, sorry!"

Roxy bent down and scooped Nefertiti up again. "Oof, you're getting heavy. You need to get out more, Nef-nef. Less food, more action. Now come on, we need to face everyone. I'll feel better if I do." Roxy put her cat down and made sure to walk in front of her, confident that Nefertiti would follow her wherever she went. And indeed she did. One behind the other, the cat behind her owner, they left the room.

They found Sage in the lounge, laying out tarot cards and crystals in intricate patterns on the table. To Roxy, who had a birdlike, tense, nervous energy, Sage seemed like a strange, exotic creature. Normally her peaceful demeanor was communicated by her floating robes, smooth-as-honey voice, creative, colorful hair, and unhurried movements. Even her hair creations seemed like works of art, especially when compared with Roxy's "wash and go," short-cropped, naturally blonde style. Sage often wore flowers in her natural afro hair or opted for flowing mermaid-style wigs and weaves in a variety of colors. Tonight though, her gorgeous face was drawn with worry. And despite the ribbons in her hair, she was pinched and otherwise unadorned.

"Have you heard about what happened?" Roxy said gently. She pulled out a chair and sat down at the table next to Sage. "About Dr. Jack?"

"No, honey, I have not. I have been waiting for you to tell me. I know that it is terrible, though. I can feel it," she said, arranging and rearranging the crystals on the table as if once she got the right formation, everything would be okay again.

Roxy told Sage about the séance, about Meredith being shot dead, about Meredith's husband and assistant staying in the guestrooms upstairs. Sage turned, her big brown eyes connecting with Roxy's. "It is so sad that that poor woman was killed." Sage lay a hand on Roxy's arm and looked at her with her soulful eyes. "Now, what is it you really want to tell me, honey? About Dr. Jack."

Sage had increasingly been spending more and more time at the botanica, leaning on the counter and talking life, the universe, and everything in between with Dr. Jack. Secretly, Roxy wondered how long it would take for them to admit to each other they were head over heels in love. Everyone else could see it. They didn't need spirits to tell them that.

"He's...he's," Roxy cleared her throat. "He's been arrested." Roxy looked dubiously at Sage. "For Meredith's murder. They say he shot her."

Sage jerked her head away from Roxy, frowning. "What? That's ridiculous. Jack would never do something like that. I know him. I know his *soul,* and it's as pure as anything, trust me. That man is like an angel on earth." Sage sat back as she comprehended the news. "So *that's* why his phone was off. I wondered why I was feeling *so* disturbed." She half-rose from the table. "I must go to him. He will need comfort and spiritual sustenance."

"No, no, I don't think you should do that." Roxy rose too, her hand out, placating Sage. She could just imagine how Detective Johnson would react if they turned up at the police station now. "Nothing will happen until morning. They might have let him go by then. Besides, I don't think they would let us see him."

Sage hesitated, but she could see the truth in Roxy's words and slowly she sat down again. "Perhaps you're right. I don't need to be with him physically anyhow. I can send healing and freeing energy to him from here. He will still feel it and know that it's from me." Sage leaned over the table and resumed moving her crystals around, albeit more absentmindedly.

"It can't have been him," said Roxy, although she couldn't be sure, not really. She watched Sage as she moved the crystals from one position to another. It was mesmerizing to see how they changed color with each new position as they interacted differently with the light coming from lamps around the room. "Hopefully Detective Johnson and Officer Trudeau will see sense and let him go soon."

"What grounds did they have for arresting him?"

"I'm not sure," said Roxy. "Well...I guess it was because he and Meredith were having a big argument before the séance began." Roxy flushed. "I told Officer Trudeau about it. I have no idea what it was about. Dr. Jack said that something Meredith was proposing was unethical."

"Hmm, I wonder what the problem was. Dr. Jack certainly enjoys a debate on spiritual philosophy sometimes," said Sage, "and things do get heated at times, but he'd never *shoot* someone. He doesn't even own a gun!"

"I know, I know, none of it makes any sense at all," said Roxy. "We can only hope things will work out and the truth will prevail. Justice will be done, right? Isn't that what you tell me—the universe will see to it, and all that?"

Sage shook her head. She suddenly looked very tired. "Eventually. But not always in this world." She ran her fingers over the tarot cards. "I'll do a reading later. Now I just want to be a source of support." She shut her eyes and stayed still and silent for a long while. There was chattering coming from the kitchen, and Roxy was itching to see what was occurring in there, but she daren't leave the table and risk upsetting Sage. Disturbing the "healing energies" would not portend well, she was quite sure.

Sage breathed in carefully through her nose and slowly opened her eyes. "It may not be the time to go to Dr. Jack, but perhaps I can help Meredith's husband and her assistant. They've had a terrible shock."

"Yes, they have," said Roxy. "I'm waiting to see if they want dinner. I'm trying to be warm and welcoming without being intrusive and disrespectful, if you know what I mean?"

"I do," said Sage. "Let's just be kind. I think that's the most important thing. You can't go wrong with kindness."

"No, you can't," Roxy agreed. She headed toward the kitchen, Nefertiti still trailing in her wake. "Not in the kitchen, princess. It's unhygienic. Go play." Roxy pressed her hands against her cat's sides and spun Nefertiti around. Nefertiti stalked off, mildly annoyed. Roxy sighed after her with a little smile.

She pushed open the kitchen door with her hip and found Nat and Evangeline cooking up a storm. Elijah was leaning against the counter eating one of his own pastries, chatting to them. As soon as he saw Roxy, he stood up straight and shoved the remainder of his pastry into his mouth, wiping his hands together to brush off the confectioner's sugar that was stuck to his fingertips.

"Roxy! What is happening, girlfriend? I cannot *believe* you are embroiled yet *again* with that awful Johnson fella! That's some voodoo bad luck, that is." He wagged his finger from side to side, his lips pursed.

"Are you okay?" Nat asked, coming from around the counter. "You weren't hurt were you?" Nat, as usual, wore black jeans and black Doc Marten boots. A black band T-shirt exposed her arms that were covered in tattoos and currently cradling a huge mixing bowl full of cake batter.

"No, no, I'm fine. It wasn't a very big room, but whoever it was that shot Meredith seemed to be quite certain of what they were doing. One shot and that was it, she was dead. The police think Dr. Jack did it."

"What? Are you serious?" Nat rolled her eyes. "That Detective Johnson is *such* a fool. Of course, it wasn't Dr. Jack. He and Sage are *made* for each other. She would never go for a *murderer*!"

"But wasn't it obvious who shot the gun? You know, when the lights went up?" Elijah was incredulous. "I mean, in the dark, how could they tell who they were shooting? They could easily have missed or even shot the wrong person. Risky." Elijah popped another pastry into his mouth, frenetically munching as he thought about this.

Nat's eyes grew wide. "Hey, perhaps you're right. Perhaps the wrong person was killed. Perhaps the bullet wasn't meant for Meredith at all?" She looked at Roxy, her eyebrows nearly above her hairline.

"Oooh, very possibly, Nat," Elijah said. "Not sure we can trust Detective Johnson to work that out, either. He's not that bright. You need to get a-sleuthing, Roxy. You know, like you have the last two times?"

"No, I do not," Roxy said. The feverish speculation Elijah and Nat were indulging in was giving her a headache. She most certainly did *not* want to get involved.

CHAPTER EIGHT

"CHER," EVANGELINE SAID warmly, walking up to the three young people and cocking her head on one side as she looked at Roxy with her big brown eyes. She hugged her. Evangeline was a very no-nonsense old woman at the best of times, and after the shock of Meredith's murder and the arrest of Dr. Jack, her concern and affection caught Roxy off-guard.

Roxy gulped back a sudden lump in her throat. She didn't want to cry. The image of Meredith's body was accompanying Roxy everywhere she went and what had happened in the past few hours was starting to hit her hard. The room swam a little, but she told herself she couldn't break down. She *had* to be strong for Charles and George, for everyone at the *Funky Cat Inn*. That's what a leader did, how a leader was. That's what *she* was. Roxy cleared her throat. "The air's spicy," she said, by way of an excuse for her watery eyes.

The air *was* spicy. It was filled with Creole and Cajun aromas. The room was hot, too. Nat's and Evangeline's cheeks were flushed, and they had rolled-up their sleeves. Condensation formed on the windows.

"Well, at least our guests will eat well," Nat said. "Everyone feels better after six courses of Evangeline's finest."

"Eatin' at all's a task when your heart's been ripped out, cher," Evangeline said to her. "They may not feel like eating nuttin'. And mind yer mouth, y'hear? Don't you go sayin' anything harsh to them good people, will ya?"

"Of course, I won't!" Nat said. "Why would I do that?"

"It has been known, cher," said Evangeline. "You can't deny it."

Nat sighed and her shoulders sagged. "Look, I know I haven't always been the most sensitive of people. But I'm different now, I promise. And I'm doing better."

"Actions speak louder 'n words, cher," Evangeline said. "You keep workin' on holdin' your tongue. You show Roxy you can do it. You owe it her."

Nat's cheeks flushed even more, her eyes glassy in the spicy, steamy air.

Roxy changed the subject quickly. "So what was the spread planned for tonight? Maybe we can holdover some courses until tomorrow."

"First course is crudités. You know, carrots, celery, cucumber, asparagus, and some beets, with Cajun chicken dip." Nat pointed to some trays covered with brightly-colored vegetables aside a pale yellow sauce.

"That might work," Roxy said. "Light, fresh. They could take some to their room."

"Next was to be deep-fried crab cakes," said Evangeline. "We don't have to fry them until they say so. We can always save them for another night."

"We have a veggie option if they prefer, deep-fried okra," Nat pointed out.

"We'd planned a Cajun-spiced beef broth," said Evangeline.

"That might work, too, if they want to eat lightly," Roxy said.

"Then the fourth course is the main: oyster pie, roasted potatoes, greens, and beetroot salad. The cheese course, of course, after that."

"And what's for dessert?"

"Berries cooked in red wine, apple juice, and sugar," said Nat.

"Over homemade macadamia and white chocolate ice cream," Evangeline added.

Roxy let her mouth drop open. "Wow, that sounds fantastic as usual. How do we eat it all?" she said.

Nat laughed. "We always say that, but we always manage!"

"So true," said Roxy. "How long 'til it'll be ready? I want to offer them food as soon as possible so that Charles and George can get to bed early if they wish."

"It'll only be ten minutes or so," said Nat.

"You find out what they want to do, and come tell us, cher. We'll work around whatever they want," Evangeline added.

"Okay, great," Roxy said. She rang up to Charles and George's rooms and explained the situation. To her surprise, they both agreed to come down for dinner—all six courses.

"It's what Meredith would want," Charles said. "We'll dress for dinner in her honor."

After relaying the message to Nat and Evangeline

and the others—Elijah, Sage, and Sam—Roxy dashed to her room. Nefertiti was curled up on her bed.

"Hi, Princess," Roxy said, giving Nefertiti a scratch as the cat stretched out her full length, her soft belly fur spreading like a concertina, her claws retracting lazily. "Oh, to be a cat, huh? Just sleeping and eating all day long. How lovely that must be." Roxy let out a slightly envious sigh. "But there's no time for cuddles and relaxing now." Nefertiti sat up and shook her head, looking up at Roxy with her piercing blue eyes. "Oh, okay, just *one* cuddle," Roxy said. She bent down to give Nefertiti a squeeze and a kiss on the top of her head. Then she rushed off to shower.

As she let the jets of hot water pound against her, Roxy wondered what to wear. Earlier that day, she had planned on wearing her midnight blue dress, the one that had silver threads all over it, along with an abundance of silver and crystal jewelry, but now it clearly wasn't appropriate. A black dress felt a little too literal in the circumstances, but neither did she want to dress down in jeans. In the end, she settled on a dark green skater dress that didn't draw too much attention. She added single pearl earrings, but no necklace, and flat pumps.

A short while later, they were all in the dining room, tucking into their crudités and crab cakes. Elijah, still in his zebra shirt, sat at the end of the table, clearly not knowing what to say to Charles and George, especially after his faux pas in front of them earlier. Sedate and somber weren't natural states for him, but he sporadically attempted conversation with Sage who sat next to him. Both Elijah and Sage regularly dressed as though they were ready for a formal dinner anywhere, anytime, so they didn't look ill-suited to the occasion. Sage was in her pink robes from earlier. But now Roxy noticed that her facial expression flickered between serene and stressed, and she wasn't very talkative, answering Elijah's questions only briefly. Sam had dressed in a black suit and tie and was gamely making attempts at conversation with Charles. Roxy's heart warmed to him for the effort he was putting in.

George and Nat were talking earnestly in quiet, gentle tones, their heads close together. Nat looked different. She hadn't just "booted" it this time. When it came to dressing for dinner, Nat often simply changed her work boots for a pair of snazzier Doc Martens. Today though, she'd put on a fresh pair of jeans and a band t-shirt that was more than simply monochromatic. The band logo plastered across the front of her t-shirt had some color in it —green, blue, and yellow to be precise, although the band name was indecipherable to Roxy's eye. George wore a pair of navy slacks and a Black Watch tartan jacket while next to him, Charles was wearing a blue bow tie and a navy blazer with brass buttons and beige pants. Evangeline had decided to sit the meal out and was busy in the kitchen doing the last-minute food preparations.

As Nat cleared away the first course and they waited for Evangeline to bring out the broth, Roxy heard Sam ask Charles about his work.

"I am a pediatric surgeon at Mercy West Children's Hospital in Greensboro, North Carolina. I specialize in the surgical repair of birth defects. I've worked at Mercy West for forty years, although I travel a lot."

"He's a pioneer," George said breaking off briefly from his conversation with Nat. "Fetal surgery. It's an emerging field. Charles is a leader in it."

"Wow, that's impressive, important work you do,

Doctor. Where does your work take you?" Sam responded.

"I travel to different parts of the country to help out where I'm needed, but I also have a foundation that provides surgery to children around the world, especially in poverty-stricken areas." Charles' voice shook. He looked away and blinked. "I—I...," he said quietly. He stood suddenly and flung down his napkin. "I was wrong. I'm sorry, I just can't do this!" he burst out. He threw the dregs of his white wine down his throat. "I'm going to my room. Sorry, I'm sorry. I just can't..."

Sage stood up quickly. "May I come with you? As one spiritual person to another? Perhaps we can provide each other with some solace?"

"Oh, I'm not really spiritual. That was M—Meredith's thing. I'm all about science, me." Charles was speaking in a big rush. His words came out harshly.

The conversation in the room died, and everyone looked at Charles. Evangeline came through the kitchen door carrying the broth but stopped abruptly when she noticed the scene in front of her.

"B—But, thank you," Charles said more graciously now. "I would, however, prefer to be alone." He sniffed and walked awkwardly out of the room as the others watched him in silence.

"Would y'all like some broth? It's pipin' hot 'n' hearty. Just what y'all need on a night like tonight," Evangeline chirped brightly. The awkward silence broken, the remaining diners gratefully allowed her to ladle the steaming liquid into their bowls. Cutlery and crystal rattled as they turned their attention once more to their food.

The evening continued in a subdued mood. Later

when Nat softly crooned *I'll Be Seeing You*, accompanied by Sam on the saxophone and Elijah on the piano, it felt slightly eerie. It was a beautiful song, but it wasn't cheery. It had a bittersweet melody that went right into Roxy's bones and stayed there.

CHAPTER NINE

"HELLO?" ROXY SAID blearily, picking up her phone.

A peal of light bells had floated across the light of the early morning that streamed into Roxy's bedroom. She had stirred as the tinkle of musical notes woke her gently. Roxy had purposefully chosen the ringtone for its subdued, discreet quality. She had found over time that shocking her nervous system early in the morning with something as ordinary as a phone call was violent and unnecessary. Trouble was, the low volume and mellow nature of the sound meant it often took some time to rouse her. Nefertiti meowed indignantly as Roxy moved to sit up, waking her cat as she lay curled in a furry ball behind Roxy's knees.

"It's Sage, Roxy. Sorry to wake you up so early, honey. Dr. Jack has rung from the police station. He's still in custody. He wants you and me to go over there. Right now."

"Okay," Roxy said, sliding from between the sheets

and shaking herself awake. "Did he say what was happening? Like why they are still holding him?"

"No, nothing. Look, I think we should just get over there ASAP. I'm very anxious about him."

"I'll get dressed and meet you on Main Street."

"Perfect," said Sage. "I'll be there in two minutes. He sounds terrible, Roxy. Be quick, won't you?"

"As lightning," Roxy promised.

Roxy quickly fed the ever-hungry Nefertiti and slipped into jeans and a sweatshirt. She sat on the bed to lace up her tennis shoes, and within moments, she was stepping out of the hotel into the early morning light. The sidewalk glistened, a result of the overnight rain, but the sun was just beginning to peek over the tops of the buildings, promising a beautiful day. Glancing across the alleyway, there were lights on in Elijah's bakery, and she could see him filling his display cases with fresh pastries and loaves of bread. Despite their late dinner the evening before, he would have been up since the early hours, kneading, and proofing, frying, and assembling his baked goods. He looked remarkably fresh and alert, and on seeing her, gave her a wave.

As she promised, Sage stood at the corner of the alleyway where it met Main Street. She wore brilliant white flowing robes. A soft gray wig of long curls cascaded down her back, and she stood tall and proud. She looked like a Grecian goddess. After embracing Roxy in a quick hug, Sage announced, "Let's go. It's only a short walk."

They hurried down the street. It was so early that there was barely any traffic, and the only people they saw were dog walkers, runners out for their morning jog, and those on their way to an early shift.

Sage said, "He said he only had a second to talk. He'd had to *beg* Johnson to let him use the phone. He just told me things were really bad, and he needed to see us."

"Man," Roxy said, "I can't believe they're still holding him. I mean, why would Dr. Jack kill Meredith Romanoff? Unless..."

"Don't even think that, Roxy. He wouldn't do such a thing," Sage said her voice firm and resolute. "No 'unless' about it." When she turned to face Roxy, fire blazed in her eyes. "Seriously Roxy, I *know* his heart. It's not him. It's really not. Someone else murdered Meredith Romanoff."

"Okay," said Roxy softly. "I hear what you're saying."

Some doubt must have crept into her voice because Sage said, "Honey, please trust me on this one. Yes, people are complex. No one's perfect. But I have psychic powers, and I know Dr. Jack's complexity and his imperfections. I can promise you that the ability to kill another human being doesn't exist in him. Not even a little bit. He wouldn't harm anyone or any*thing.*"

"I believe you," said Roxy. "I trust you...your powers."

"Thank you." Sage reached out and squeezed Roxy's hand. It felt large and warm and soft as it wrapped around Roxy's cool, small, slight one. "Now, just give me a moment. I need to prepare my energy for walking into that police station. They are terrible places from an energetic perspective. All sorts of tortured spirits roam about, just like hospitals, but at least hospitals are healing places. There are strong, positive energies trying very hard to do good there. Police departments are just—ugh." Sage shuddered.

They walked the rest of the way in silence. As they got closer, Roxy felt her anxiety mount. Her palms began to sweat, and her pace picked up. She did not relish the prospect of coming across Johnson at any time, but first thing in the morning was especially tough. Perhaps Trudeau would be there. He wouldn't be so bad, but not by all that much. As it turned out, neither Johnson nor Trudeau were anywhere to be seen.

A young woman officer stood at the front desk. She looked startlingly young. In fact, Roxy suspected that the woman was younger than her, and that made Roxy feel old.

"Jack Lavantille requested our visit," Sage said to the police officer.

The young woman looked bored as she checked a list of names on a clipboard. She punched some numbers into a phone and spoke quietly into it. "You can meet him in the visitors' room," she said when she put the phone down. "I'll escort you. One second. Please sit." She gestured toward some scuffed utilitarian chairs in the waiting area.

Roxy and Sage both sat down. Now that she was paying attention, Roxy realized what Sage meant by the police station being filled with weird energies. Just sitting in the lobby made her feel uncomfortable and on edge. Stale air hung around the room, the noticeboard was filled with torn, faded, or out-of-date notices and the strip lights above were far too bright. They were threatening to give her a headache.

It seemed an age before the young woman police officer appeared from behind a heavy blue metal door at the side of the counter. She nodded at them in an unfriendly way. "You can come through now."

Roxy noticed the woman appraise Sage, taking in her

long mermaid hair and her white robes, clearly disapproving of them in all their floaty, exotic glory.

They followed the policewoman down a corridor and were led to a side room. "Go in," she said. "You have fifteen minutes."

Sage and Roxy walked over to a small booth. There was only one chair. On the other side of the glass partition sat Dr. Jack. He looked pale and defeated, his body slumped in his chair. As he caught sight of them though, he sat up, a nervous, desperate energy enlivening him. His eyes sparkled although there was no accompanying smile to soften his features. Another police officer stood against the wall behind him.

"Jack," Sage said. She ignored Roxy and slipped onto the chair in front of him.

"Sage," he said. He mustered a smile and looked behind her. "Hello, Roxy. Thank you so much for coming, both of you."

"Of *course* we would come," Sage said. She shifted over a little. "Roxy, do you want to take half the seat next to me?"

"No, I'm fine," said Roxy. "I'll stand here."

Sage gave her a grateful smile and repositioned herself in the middle of the chair. She put her hand on the glass, tilted her head to one side, and pursed her lips. Her big brown eyes were moist. Dr. Jack lifted his hand on the other side of the glass to match hers. Roxy looked down at the floor. She felt the moment too intimate for her to witness, but Sage and Dr. Jack didn't mind her.

"I can't believe they still have you here," Sage said. "What's happening?"

CHAPTER TEN

"**I** DON'T KNOW."

Dr. Jack shook his head. "They've questioned me three times so far, and they seem to be getting frustrated. They're not making progress, but that's because they're barking up the wrong tree. I heard Trudeau tell Johnson that there were no fingerprints on the gun. Johnson told him to check the scene for gloves. Of course, I have gloves at the botanica. I use them all the time to handle the crystals and other delicate objects, so I'm afraid they're going to say I used them while handling a firearm. Which, of course, is untrue. I've never even fired a gun, let alone killed anyone with one. It's unbelievable what is happening." The light in Jack's eyes dimmed a little and his chin dipped.

"Oh dear," said Roxy. The words slipped out before she could stop them. Jack and Sage looked at her as though only just remembering she was there.

"You both know I didn't do it, don't you?" Jack said.

"Of course!" Sage said quickly.

"Of course," said Roxy, not quite so quickly.

Dr. Jack studied her through the glass for a moment. "You're not 100% sure I'm innocent, but that's okay. In the material world, it is difficult for one to know who to trust if one solely uses logic for guidance. But, Roxy, if you go deep into your heart, and listen to your intuition, it will tell you the truth. I can only ask that you do that."

Roxy knew that she tended to overthink things, especially when she was anxious. She relied on facts and logic to help her make decisions most of the time. Using her intuition as Sage and Dr. Jack did practically all the time was extremely difficult for Roxy, and she wasn't at all sure it was a very sound practice. It sounded so foreign, baseless, and scary. The world didn't run on intuition and using it certainly went against all that she had learned growing up. Safety and security were Roxy's goals, and she mostly employed hard work, delayed gratification, and fact-based decision making to achieve them. Using one's intuition was the very opposite of that. It relied on making leaps of faith, trusting that things would work out for the best, and listening to one's gut, often in the face of evidence to the contrary. Roxy was quite sure her bank manager would not approve. "I really don't think you did it, Dr. Jack. Don't worry."

He smiled at her. "You're a very brave young woman, Roxy. Do you know that?"

"I'm not, not really. I'm not sure I would save someone else before myself if faced with a tiger."

"What about when that guest of yours murdered his brother. You went flying in to save the day." Sage was referring to the last time Roxy had gotten entangled with the police. A famous Instagram influencer had been murdered at the *Funky Cat.* Roxy had worked out that the influencer's sibling had killed him, and she'd confronted him in front of thousands of people.

"Yes, but that was because I wasn't thinking. I was overcome with...passion, emotion, righteousness."

"Exactly. You stopped thinking and went with your heart," Dr. Jack countered.

Roxy thought for a moment. "I see what you're saying."

Jack leaned forward on his elbows, his face up close to the glass. "Listen, we don't have long. Sage, I need your help."

"Do you want us to keep the botanica open, so you don't lose any business?" Roxy asked over the top of Sage's head, keen to put things on more solid, practical ground. "The witches will miss you." She gave Dr. Jack a silly smile. He had once told her he stayed open late "for the witches," but now he missed her little joke, and her smile died.

"I can serve customers, and do my programming work from behind the counter," Sage added.

Dr. Jack gave Sage a warm smile. "That would be most appreciated. Thank you for your offer, and you, Roxy, but what I want you to do is find out who the real murderer is. Roxy, you talk the language that the police understand, and you've shown your investigative prowess twice now. I would love it if you could turn it on again for me. Despite the anxiety you sometimes suffer, your perseverance and persistence are the catalysts for success. I'm sure you could succeed in proving my innocence. You're resilient. Nothing stops you, even if it tries to. I suspect you have a tougher history than many could guess at, and it's that which has given you a belief in justice and a back-bone when you've needed one."

Roxy nodded. She'd never known her father nor had any brothers to protect her. To survive, she'd kept herself to herself, and learned to navigate danger from when she was just a little girl. Seeing others suffering unjustly cut at her so.

Dr. Jack continued, "But this might be your biggest challenge yet. The furies will try to take you down. I understand the sacrifices you'll make, the risks you'll take, but I know justice burns brightly in you. Oh, you don't have to believe me right at this minute, Roxy, you can work with facts and logic until your heart takes over, but I need you. Will you help me?"

How could Roxy refuse such a plea? "Of course, I'll help," she said. "We'll find out who really did this."

"Sage, I need you to do some spiritual work to support exposing the real murderer. I know it's difficult work... very taxing, but I think it might be necessary, and it will lift the burden from Roxy, allowing her to move more freely."

"I'm working on it already," said Sage. "We have to get you out of here."

"Thank you," said Dr. Jack, tears welling up in his eyes. "You are more than I could ask for."

"I would fight a million soulless demons for you," Sage said, her eyes big and imploring. They smiled at each other and sighed in unison. Roxy looked away again.

"Don't discount Charles or George," Dr. Jack said. "They both look like wonderful men, but you must find out what lurks beneath. And who knows what history has passed between Meredith and Terah, and Royston Lamontagne, too. I'm sure there is a lot to uncover."

"I'll do everything I can," said Roxy.

Dr. Jack's eyes burned with gratitude. "When you work on behalf of truth and justice, you are blessed beyond your wildest dreams. Just hold out for an amazing reward. It'll come."

Roxy smiled. "Thank you. That the real murderer is put behind bars is reward enough."

"We'll get there," Dr. Jack said. "We just have to work as a team. Together we will be unbeatable."

"But Dr. Jack, before I take on this task, please tell me what you and Meredith were arguing about before the séance? You were both quite heated."

Dr. Jack sat back in his chair and folded his arms. "Meredith was involved in something I most definitely don't agree with. She wanted to invoke the practice during the séance, in my botanica. I said absolutely not."

"What...what did she want to do that you so disapproved of?" Roxy asked, almost afraid to find out.

"It's called spirit binding, Roxy. It means to bind a spirit to a vessel, a physical object, trapping them essentially. I believe it to be a cruel practice, like caging any being would be. It is for the benefit of the person who wishes to remain in contact with another's soul, but it requires the spirit's subordination. I don't support that, and I most definitely didn't want the practice carried out on my premises. It would be against everything I believe in. But of course, that doesn't mean I would kill anyone. I wouldn't, not for anything."

"I see." Spirit binding—that was something new!

The door opened and the young woman cop from earlier walked in, her thumbs hooked into her belt. She looked at the three of them. Sage sitting on the chair, her palm still placed up against the interview window, Roxy standing behind her, Jack on the other side of the glass. She jangled her keys and nodded her head at the door through which she'd just come. "Time's up," she said.

CHAPTER ELEVEN

W HEN ROXY RETURNED to the *Funky Cat,* she found Charles and George sitting at a small table in the dining room chatting in hushed tones. They both looked pale and tired.

"Hello, Charles, George," she said to them softly, not wishing to interrupt them unduly. They nodded in her direction.

"Hello Roxy," George said. His red hair, unbrushed, stuck up perpendicular to his head, and his freckles stood out against the pallor of his skin. His eyes were swollen. He wore sweatpants and a t-shirt, but even they were twisted around his body like it had been too much effort to put them on properly.

Charles was better groomed. He was freshly shaven and showered and wore a red plaid bow tie and a navy blazer over a white shirt and khakis. His glasses on their gold chain hung around his neck as usual.

Roxy headed through the kitchen to find Nat dashing about the kitchen as she stirred, sliced, sprinkled, and served. "Looks like Charles got his appetite back," Nat said. "He asked for our special."

The "special" comprised of such a big plate of food, Roxy had never been able to finish one, and she didn't have an especially small appetite. It consisted of a heaping plate of eggs, sausages, stuffed tomatoes, and beef cooked in tomato sauce over grits. Ginger-cranberry pancakes accompanied the dish along with coffee served just the way the guest liked it. Fresh beignets were available on the table too, just in case that pile of New Orleans goodness wasn't quite enough.

"As, it would appear, so did her majesty," Nat said, nodding toward the open door to the paved area out back where Nefertiti had her head in a silver bowl.

"Ah, she never lost hers," Roxy replied.

"Looks like she has a suitor, too. A big orange tom. She shared her food with him. The two of them had their heads in the bowl together. It was so sweet. When he left, I gave her some more." Nat grinned. "Maybe there'll be some fluffy orange and white kittens around here soon?"

Roxy grinned back. "No chance. She's been fixed."

"Oh, right." Nat turned down the corners of her mouth. "Well, that's a bit disappointing. I was quite looking forward to some little ginger puffballs running all over the place." She cracked some eggs into a bowl. "Where did you get off to so early this morning? Back on a health kick again? Out for an early morning run?"

"Unfortunately not," said Roxy. She explained about the trip with Sage to see Dr. Jack.

Nat shook her head. "I can't even process this right now. It's too much. Dr. Jack a murderer? Imagine!"

"I know, right? I don't know what to think. But I've

agreed to do a bit of digging. See what's what," Roxy replied. "And I need your help."

Nat looked up from her eggs in surprise. "You do?"

"Yes, I want you to focus on Charles and George. I want you to make them feel safe and comfortable and cared for. My mind's going to be everywhere, trying to get evidence and clues and whatnot, and I'm going to have to consider *them* suspects. So I'll really need you to step up, Nat. Do you think you can do that?"

"Sure," Nat said firmly. She was mixing the eggs in a bowl, but now she put them down and took a breather. "I know in the past I haven't always been the most...well, hospitable, shall we say, but you can count on me, Rox. I won't let you down."

Roxy gave her a side hug, and Nat responded with a grateful smile. "I know I can come out with some right old rubbish from time to time, and I know I can look a little, um, unapproachable, but I hope people don't think I'm venomous to the core!"

Roxy giggled. "Nope, you're a fluffy bunny under all of that...bravado."

Nat made bunny ears above her head with her hands and twitched her nose until she looked quite cute. Seeing Nat with her tattoos and combat boots looking so silly made Roxy laugh again.

"Anyway, Rox, enough with all the fun, what're you having for breakfast?"

"Oh, I was just going to have beignets and a café au lait. But since you're doing the cooked special, I would *love* some beef in tomato sauce over grits. I could eat that all day and all night!"

Nat gave her a cheeky grin. "Grillades and grits,

coming up! But you sure you want just that? You don't want the whole thing?"

"No fear!" Roxy said, her eyes popping. "I wouldn't be able to move for the rest of the day. And I need to be light on my feet if I'm going to help Dr. Jack."

"There's a coffee pot on the table already," said Nat. "You can help yourself to that and the beignets. Elijah already brought them over. Go and chat with our guests, and I'll be out with the food in a few. Sounds like you've had a challenging morning already. Let me look after you with a bit of food, *cher*," she said mimicking Evangeline.

Roxy gave Nat's shoulder another squeeze. "Thanks, girlfriend."

She went into the dining room and sat at the table just across from George and Charles. They were both reading now and looked a little more alive than the day before, but that wasn't saying much. At best, George didn't constantly have tears in his eyes, and Charles had regained some color in his cheeks.

Charles was working on a beignet. He had cut it into strips and ate absentmindedly as he sipped his coffee and read the local broadsheet newspaper. George was reading a book. Roxy looked carefully and saw that it was Meredith's book. She was unsure of what to say to them for fear of tipping this delicate calm into chaos and grief. Thankfully, George broke the silence. He looked directly at Roxy and pointed to an empty chair at their table. "Please come and sit with us. We would appreciate some company. We are not at our best this morning."

Roxy pulled the chair out and sat down. Charles looked up briefly and gave her a flicker of a smile but ducked out of any conversation by returning immediately to his newspaper. George made up for the older man's lack of conversation. "Roxy, I must say that your hotel is beautiful and so comfortable. My bed was just the right blend of softness and firmness, and the power of the shower was intense, so invigorating, and I needed that this morning although," he put his hand up to his head, "I think I forgot to comb my hair." He smiled sheepishly. "You have some fabulous energies here. Although we are staying under the most awful of circumstances, your hotel is easing our cares and woes. It's a wonderful place. Meredith would have loved it."

"Oh, thank you so much," Roxy said, touched by his words.

"Nat was telling me how it was before you took over, and how much you've transformed it. She said you chose the décor and such, and I must say, you've created an oasis for the spirit. Thank you so much for the hard work you've put in to make it such a soothing place. I have found it very restful and relaxing. It has truly relieved me —mind, body, and soul."

"You're very welcome, George. I'm so sorry that..."

"No, I'm sorry," George said, "that we have brought trouble to your door."

Charles started to speak without looking up from his paper. "The machinations of the spiritual world are some-times very strange. We did not expect Meredith to be killed by dark forces, but she was, make no mistake. A person picked up the gun and shot it, yes, but they were motivated by the forces of evil that constantly swirl through this world looking to wreak destruction. We regret very much that you were caught up in this." Charles turned over his page carefully so as not to knock from the table the small glass vase that contained a posy of pansies, viola, nemesia, columbine, twinspur, and alyssum. Roxy reflected on what a dichotomy Charles seemed. He sounded not at all like the man of science he had claimed to be the previous evening. He seemed steeped in the spiritual world.

"I'll send love and light throughout this hotel for as long as we're here. You certainly deserve it," George said. He looked around the large room. "The attention to detail you've put in tells me that you're a soul who cares very deeply, who understands people and their experiences. You want people to feel cared for."

"Yes, I do," said Roxy, smiling. That *was* her raison d'être. She wanted to take care of people.

George smiled. "And I do feel cared for. We both do. Very much."

"I'm so glad," said Roxy. "And seriously, if you, or you Charles, need anything, anything at all, please don't hesitate to ask. We're here for you."

"Thank you," George said. "And please ask us, too, for help. We have all the goodness of the spiritual world at our disposal, and we would be honored to share it with you," he said. "Our lights, and those of Meredith, will only burn brighter as a result of this tragedy. That is what those dark forces don't understand, that they only succeed in turning up the light as they attempt, injuriously, to snuff it out. It is self-defeating."

"You speak for yourself, young man," Charles said wearily, still flipping through the newspaper. Meredith's murder was featured on the front page at the bottom under "Local News." Roxy hoped Charles wouldn't see it. "This world is nothing but tragedy and pain. All goodness is an illusion."

"No, it could never be!" George said passionately. "Never! The dark forces are the only illusions! Life is beautiful! The world is full of love and light! We are not here merely to exist and then die. We are here to thrive! To help! The forces for good, the angels, and the archangels, and all the positive spiritual forces are here to support us."

Charles snorted. "You sound like a child."

Roxy's gaze flickered from one man to the other as she held her breath waiting to see how this conflict would evolve. George was trembling. He stood up, but before he could speak, the doorbell rang and Roxy heard the front door open.

"Yoo-hoo! It's only me!" Elijah, wearing chef's whites, appeared carrying a plate at shoulder height. It was covered with white starched linen napkins. Simultaneously, Nat came out of the kitchen carrying two plates—a full cooked breakfast for Charles, and Roxy's beef and grits. Both of them, on catching sight of the scene before them, halted in their tracks, their eyes bulging.

"I don't care one bit if I sound like a child. I choose innocence and goodness. I choose to *believe,*" George cried.

"Believe what you want!" Charles shot back. "If you want to be a fool, so be it!" He folded up his paper and threw it down smartly on the table next to his placemat.

"Hey, hey, hey," Nat said gently. "Let's not do this to ourselves, okay?" She eased up to the table and slid Charles's full plate carefully in front of him. "Please, eat. You will feel better." She turned to George. "George, are you sure you don't want anything cooked?"

"No, no, thank you, Nat," said George. "I am going to fast today, the better to connect my spirit with higher energies. I will only drink liquids."

"Okay then," Nat said soothingly. Her hand was up,

palm out, placating him. She knew she was talking to a highly emotional, stressed-out person. "Please sit down. The last thing we all need is an argument." Roxy observed her wide-eyed. This was a side of Nat she hadn't previously experienced. She was impressed by how calm and kind Nat was being.

"Yes, you're right," said George. Tears brimmed in his eyes, but he managed a weak smile. "Nat, you are very kind."

"I'm really not," Nat said. She sat down opposite Roxy and took a beignet for herself.

As she did so, Elijah slowly started to move again. Roxy looked over, and catching his eye, saw Elijah point at his plate and nod at the kitchen. She translated his meaning and dipped her chin in agreement. The baker quietly pushed the swing door open with his hip, dropping his shoulders, and widening his eyes in relief as he disappeared into the kitchen.

CHAPTER TWELVE

"I'M ONE OF the least kind people I've ever met," Nat was saying.

"No," George protested.

"No, really," said Nat. "I wish I was gentle and had a talent for making people feel all warm and fuzzy inside. But that's Roxy's specialty. I'm more like a razor. A rusty one." She shrugged. "Sharp and liable to hurt you. I think I was just made that way." She smiled.

"Other people may see the spiky outsides, all the thorns. But I see a gorgeous rose with stunning, fragile petals," said George.

Nat laughed, but not unkindly. "Are you sure?"

"Certainly," said George. "Maybe the thorns are necessary. Maybe they are there precisely to protect a beautiful, delicate flower from further damage in a rough, tough world. You're a wonderful person deep down, Nat, I can tell, but it seems you've lost sight of that and allowed negative energies to harm and change you. You've encased yourself in a form of armor, so to speak— thorns—to protect yourself. But you don't need to continue on that path. You can heal by surrounding your-self with more positive, supportive people, kind people like Roxy here. Has no one ever told you how fabulous you are?"

Roxy watched this interaction with big, shocked eyes. What made it so extraordinary was that Nat wasn't dismissing George. Roxy would have expected Nat to laugh off his words and throw her defenses back up, but she didn't. She had propped her chin on her hands and stared at him. She was listening to George intently. She hung on to his every word.

"You're right, George," she said. "How do you know that?"

George gave her a lovely, broad smile that displayed two rows of even, white teeth. "Let's just say, I can see it."

"But how?"

Charles sighed deeply. He sounded defeated, or perhaps cynical, Roxy couldn't decide which. He pulled off his gold-framed glasses and let them hang from their chain. He looked at Nat. "When you train to be a psychic, you develop a special kind of sight. George can see that about you as clearly as we can see you're wearing a black shirt."

"Really?" Nat said. Now Roxy was struggling to disguise her astonishment. She couldn't believe what she was seeing or hearing. The Nat she knew would have been melting with sarcasm at the turn this conversation was taking.

"Yes," said Charles. "Really."

"A certain sensitivity is inherent, but then the training expands that and brings so much more into awareness. That is partly what Meredith was teaching me," George added.

"Your food is good, by the way," Charles said. His voice was brusque.

After that, no one knew what to say for a while. It was Roxy who broke the silence in the end. "I hope you don't mind, but could I give you an update on the case?"

Both Charles and George looked at her expectantly. Charles put down his knife and fork.

Roxy sat up straight and pressed her hands between her thighs. She took a deep breath. "Dr. Jack is still in custody, but he hasn't been charged yet. There were no fingerprints found on the gun. I suspect they are struggling to find evidence to conclusively connect him to Meredith's murder."

Charles looked at her with such a penetrative stare that a shiver shot down Roxy's spine. "Do you believe he did it?" he asked her.

"Not really," Roxy said. "It would be so out of character as to not make any sense at all. But then, well, I don't know. I'm not an investigator. And life has taught me that anything is possible."

"If you..." Nat frowned at George. "If you can see all these things about people, can't you work out who killed Meredith?"

"It's not that simple," said George. "Unfortunately. And even if one can work it out spiritually, it's a devil of a job to get any law enforcement to believe you."

Charles shook his head. "Trust us, Meredith tried many times to convince the police of her suspicions as they related to certain crimes. They always regarded her as a crank. It makes sense. In their material world, law enforcement needs physical, scientific evidence to be able to take the case to a courtroom and get a conviction. The advice of psychics or mediums doesn't fall into the category of admissible evidence. Plus, they simply wouldn't believe her nor would they give any credence to what she had to say. They wouldn't even follow up on her information."

"They were wrong to do that," said George.

"No, they weren't," said Charles. "It makes sense given their paradigm. And let's face it, just as people cheat, hide, and lie in the material world, there are delusions and falsehoods in the spiritual realm, too. *We* may spend our time crossing between the two, but most people don't."

Roxy's head was starting to hurt from all this spiritual talk. "Well, Detective Johnson is a difficult man, but a dogged detective. I am sure between him and Officer Trudeau, they will find out who killed Meredith and the murderer will be brought to justice."

"Yes," said George. "It must happen. It must."

Roxy pushed her chair back from the table. "Now, if you'll excuse me, I need to go do some paperwork. I'll be in my office, just off the lobby. If you need anything, please do come and see me. My door is always open."

"Thank you, Roxy," said George. "I plan to stay here all day. I'm rereading Meredith's book. It makes me feel close to her. It...," he paused and gulped, "...helps."

"I plan on taking a walk." Charles looked out of the window. "Fresh air and sunshine will do me good."

"Okay, lunch can be whenever you like. Just call me," said Nat. "We usually have po' boys—they're special New Orleans sandwiches if you're unfamiliar with them—but I can whip you up whatever you feel like."

Charles smiled properly for the first time that morning, nodding down at his nearly empty plate. "I doubt I'll need any lunch after this."

Roxy grinned. "The Nat 'special' is fantastic, isn't it?"

"Absolutely," said Charles. "It wouldn't be hyperbole to say this is the best breakfast I've ever had the pleasure of eating, despite the circumstances. I feel much better, almost human again."

Nat blushed. "It can't be that good."

"It truly is, young lady."

For once, Roxy was glad to work on her accounts. It was a welcome break from all the otherworldly talk and thoughts of the murder. When she walked into her office she felt a little lightheaded, but she knew that by the time she was done, she'd feel much more grounded and stable.

As she worked, she heard Sam arrive. His toolbox rattled as he moved. He walked through the lobby and headed upstairs to work on the loft conversion, the next phase they'd agreed upon in their plan to update the building. She looked up briefly to wave at him through her open office door. He waved back and proceeded through the lobby to climb the stairs to the third floor.

Two hours later, when she was done, Roxy picked up the phone in the lobby and called him on his cell phone. "Hi, Sam. Sorry I didn't chat earlier. I was just working on the accounts. How's it going?"

"Pretty good," he said. "And don't apologize, Rox, it's fine. You're working hard on our business."

Roxy smiled. "What do you want for lunch? I'll bring it up to you."

"That would be awesome. What about a po' boy?"

"Coming right up! What filling would you like? You can have shrimp, tuna, ham, beef, pulled pork, cheese, or a combination of any of the above, lettuce, tomato, whatever you want. Oh, and I'll bring you a bag of chips."

"Ham, cheese and salad, please," he said.

"You got it," Roxy replied. She put on a posh, funny voice. "The most exquisite po' boy in town is on its way up to you, good sir."

He laughed. "Goofball."

"See you in a few."

"Look forward to it. Love ya."

Roxy put down the phone, her cheeks burning. *Love ya?* What did *that* mean?

She went into the kitchen and set about making Sam's sandwich. Soon after taking over the *Funky Cat*, Roxy had promised herself that despite their attraction to one another, she would not mix business with pleasure when it came to Sam. He was her work colleague, part-owner of the business, and supplier of laundry and handyman services. That was all he was, she reminded herself, and that was how things were going to stay. But keeping her rule wasn't easy, nor was it easy to stop thinking about how things might be different. Now, despite her promise, Roxy couldn't help but wonder what Sam had meant by his comment. She was so distracted that she kept looking through cupboards for the ingredients she needed until Nat came into the kitchen.

"What are you doing?"

"I'm just making Sam some lunch. A po' boy."

"What's he having in it?"

"Ham and cheese and salad. But I can't find them." Roxy kept opening and closing cupboard doors. She was on her second circuit of the kitchen.

"Well, you won't find them there, silly. They're in the fridge!"

"Oh! Goodness, you're right. Duh." Roxy slunk over to the walk-in refrigerator and immediately found what she needed.

"What's gotten into you?" Nat asked, grinning. She peered at Roxy. "You've gone all red."

"Have I?" Roxy said breezily.

"You sure have," Nat folded her arms and leaned back against the counter. She pressed her lips together in a triumphant smile.

"It's nothing, nothing," Roxy said quickly.

Nat raised her eyebrows.

"It was hot in the office, that's all."

CHAPTER THIRTEEN

ROXY FELT HEAT increasingly flush her cheeks as she took Sam's lunch up to the loft. *Don't be so ridiculous,* she told herself. *It's just Sam. Friendly, old Sam.*

She was so busy giving herself a good talking-to that when she climbed the final flight of stairs, she didn't notice Sam sitting on the top step. She nearly tripped over him.

"Oh!" she said. The po' boy and chips flew off the plate at breakneck speed, but Sam was fast. He caught the sandwich intact with one hand and the plate with the other. The chips scattered all over the stairs, though.

"Oh, man!" Roxy said.

"I got the most important bit," Sam said with a grin. He tore off a bite of the po' boy. "Chips are unhealthy, anyway."

"I'm such a fool," Roxy said, bending over to pick each chip off the steps one by one. At least now she had a plausible reason for blushing—and an activity to hide it.

"Hey, leave the chips for now," Sam said, placing a

hand gently over hers as she continued to scrabble around. His touch was like an electric shock coursing through her body, and she jumped. He let go. "Accidents happen. Do you want to see how the loft is coming along?"

"Yes, yes, of course!" Roxy pushed strands of her short hair behind her ear and brushed her face in confusion.

Sam put down his lunch, and they walked up the remaining stairs. At the top, there was a landing and a door that opened up to the loft space Sam was converting.

"Wow," Roxy said as soon as she stepped inside.

It was a long way from being finished, but the room looked a lot better than the last time she'd seen it. Before they had started on the project, she and Sam had sorted through boxes and boxes of items that could be credibly called junk, but out of respect for Evangeline—who had accumulated it all—they had tactfully marked it "miscellany." It had been an exhausting process.

"Oh, I haven't seen that in thirty years!" Evangeline would exclaim, as she took items out of their dusty old boxes and set them on the floor. This was usually followed by, "I must keep it!" Many frustrated looks had passed between Sam and Roxy until they became resigned to the fact that Evangeline wasn't to be parted from her memories. They needed to come up with a solution that respected her wishes but also allowed them to renovate the space.

Roxy had confided her frustration to Elijah during one of their regular "business and coffee" chats one day. Elijah offered Evangeline some unused storage space above the bakery and he and Roxy, along with Nat, Sage, Sam, a couple of Sam's laundrymen, and Elijah's two bakery assistants had spent an afternoon forming a human chain to move the boxes from the *Funky Cat* to *Elijah's Bakery*.

It had been an exercise in teamwork and cooperation that had warmed Roxy's heart. They had all kept their cool, respected each other's wishes, and had come up with a resolution that made everyone happy. Roxy couldn't have imagined concluding an issue so successfully before she had arrived in New Orleans. Until that point, her life had seemed a neverending round of power struggles. Struggles she had usually lost.

After they had cleared the space, Sam had cleaned the loft from top to bottom. It hadn't been touched in a very long time, and the dust lay so thick in places it was like carpet. Sam had filled multiple vacuum bags with nothing but gray dust, and then he had set about scrubbing the room down.

"Are you *sure* you want to be doing this?" Roxy had asked him.

"Yup, it'll give you a new room to play with. I'm mostly glad there are no rat hideouts or bird nests up here. If there were, we'd have been looking at a whole different operation."

As it was, the only major issue was some minor dry rot that was easily remedied. Handy as he was, Sam had simply cut out the old damaged wood piece by piece and replaced it with new lumber. Roxy could see his repairs had made things as good as new, if not better. After that, Sam had set about renovating the space.

Now, when Roxy stepped into the loft, her heart swelled with joy. The room was going to look *awesome!* Beams had been installed across the high, sloped ceiling and painted a rich mahogany color. The rickety window at one end had been replaced with a brand new frame, and it was *gorgeous*. It was circular with leaded glass that splayed out from the center to the edges like spokes. It looked like a giant wheel and let in plenty of light especially in the afternoon when the sun's rays showered the room with a golden glow and made it perfect for a nap or a relaxed drink while taking in the magnificent views across the city. Roxy knew that Nefertiti would be sure to find her way into the room unless they kept the door shut. Neffi was a sun worshipper and heat-seeking missile rolled into one.

At the other end of the room was a platform. A small, spiral staircase led up to it. It was encased in a delicate, filigree, wrought iron balustrade. Next to it, Sam planned to install another circular window that would offer the room even more light and even more of a view. Next to the room, on the landing, a luxury bathroom had been built and there was even access to the rooftop. It was the perfect, romantic hideaway, one that Roxy hoped would be popular with honeymooning couples and others wanting to get away from their regular, stress-filled lives.

"Sam!" Roxy said. "It looks incredible!"

"Yeah?" he said, shoving his hands in his pockets and looking modest. "It does look pretty good, doesn't it? It's coming along."

Roxy walked over to the window. "It's just...wow!" She looked out. There was a fabulous view over the rooftops of New Orleans. "This is just...well, I can't find the right word for it. 'Special' isn't enough." She turned to him. "Thank you, Sam."

"You're welcome." He hesitated before venturing, "Perhaps *you'd* like this room? We could switch things around so that guests stay in what are your personal rooms now."

Roxy walked up and down the large loft—it was the first time she'd been able to do that without worrying dry rot was going to bring down a beam on her. She turned and grinned at him, but shook her head. "Nuh-uh. We can charge a premium for this room." She looked around again. "It *would* be lovely to sleep here, though." She smiled at the thought. "So, tell me, how d'ya get so good at everything, huh?" Excitement over the room was overwhelming her shyness of earlier.

Sam shook his head. "I'm not good at everything," he said, "by any stretch."

"Aw, come on! You're courteous and kind, for a start. You can play the sax like a professional. You have a successful laundry business that you run standing on your head. You can do electrics and plumbing and just about every type of DIY trick known to man." She also wanted to add the fact that he clearly had tons of money, but she observed their rule of not speaking of it and held her tongue.

"You're too kind, Roxy," he said. "But look at you. You came here and started a new life knowing no one and nothing about New Orleans. You solved two *murders*, no less, and took control of managing this place without any experience at all. Took it from a rundown, if somewhat charming, guesthouse to a luxury boutique hotel that is constantly sold out...And you're still kind and as down-to-earth as ever. You've got a lot of things going for you, too."

"Thanks, it's sweet of you to say so," said Roxy. They smiled at each other for a long moment before Roxy started, her expression switching to deadly serious as a memory hit her. "That reminds me...murder. Dr. Jack called Sage and me down to the police station this morning. He asked us to investigate the case of Meredith's shooting. He says the police think it's him, but that they've got the wrong man. He maintains he's innocent. Sage is working on her side of things, asking angels and spirits for help and whatnot. I agreed to look into it, too, but for information the police will accept as evidence."

"Now *that's* a dream team," Sam said.

Roxy began pacing. It helped her thought process. "The people in the room with Meredith Romanoff when she died were George, Charles, Dr. Jack, a businessman called Royston Lamontagne, and an old childhood friend of Meredith's." Roxy looked at the plain wooden floorboards beneath her feet and counted the names of the people on her fingers. "Terah...Terah...I forget her last name. Jonas? Oh, I know, Jones! Terah Jones. And me. We were all in the room. Any of us could have done it."

"You're going to need to talk to them all."

"Yeah," said Roxy. "It's a fine line to walk, you know? With Charles and George. They are devastated, understandably, and I absolutely can't upset them further. If they're innocent, that would be terrible. At the same time, they could easily be involved. One or *both*. I'm not quite sure how to handle it. Now, concerning the other two, Royston Lamontagne and Terah Jones, I have no such qualms, but getting them to talk to me will be the issue. The thing is...well, Lamontagne seems to be the kind of person who's 'too important' to talk to likes of me. He'll be easy to find, though, with a name like that. I'll just Google him. Meredith said he was in the music business. I'll Google Terah Jones, too, I guess.

"Give it a go now," said Sam. "But wait here. I've got something to show you. One sec."

Sam walked over to his toolbox at the other end of the loft. He began to rummage. Roxy, in the meantime, hit up

Google on her phone. As she expected, searching on *Royston Lamontagne* brought up hundreds of hits that all pointed to the same person. He appeared to run a company called *Lamontagne Promotions. Terah Jones* was more of a mixed bag, with results popping up from all over the country. She tried again. *Terah Jones New Orleans* was much more fruitful.

"Ooh!" said Roxy out loud. "She's a dog walker! *Terah Jones Dog Walking Services!* And there's a number right here. I can call her now. Great."

Sam came back. "Now you can start getting somewhere. I've gotta get back to work myself, but I wanted to ask which floor stain do you like the best?" He held out some tiny samples. "I want to keep the original floorboards for the most part. I switched out the couple that had dry rot and aged them so that they fit in. But now you need to decide on a color. *Cream White, Rich Pine,* or *Mahogany?* Which do you think will be best?"

Roxy took a look around the room. She imagined the cathedral ceiling and all the walls painted in white, and the room flooded with daylight. "Okay, I know this sounds crazy, but a navy blue or forest green, even an aquamarine stain would give it *so* much more character, and provide an amazing start for the color scheme."

Sam dropped his hands holding the rejected stain samples. "Genius! I'd never have thought of that. You're a little wilder than you know, Rox."

Roxy grinned. "Hardly, but thanks...I'll take that as a compliment...I think?"

"It is *definitely* a compliment."

"Well, on that note, I'm going to walk on the wild side and call Terah Jones right now. I'll see if she can talk."

"Great plan," said Sam. "I'll install the other window this afternoon."

"Amazing, I can't wait to see it." Roxy hurried out. "See you later. Don't forget what's left of your po' boy on the stairs. Watch out for chips underfoot. I'll send Nat to vacuum them up!"

CHAPTER FOURTEEN

HALF AN HOUR later, Roxy was at the waterfront waiting for Terah. The waters of the Mississippi sparkled in the early afternoon sun, creating a glare that made Roxy squint. When she had called Terah on the phone earlier, Meredith's friend had confirmed that she *was* a dog walker, and she was about to take two dogs out for some exercise. Would Roxy like to join her? They'd arranged to meet by the river in Audubon Park, next to where the boat tours started.

The park was a little way from the *Funky Cat Inn*, so Roxy took a cab as far as she could. It was a lovely change of scenery, a truly serene setting. As she strolled across the park to the meeting place, Roxy was surrounded by towering trees and abundant stretches of green lawn. Flowers and shrubs bloomed everywhere. "I should come here more often," she said to herself as she walked down to the waterfront.

"Hello, Roxy," someone said behind her.

Roxy turned to find herself a few feet away from Terah. With her were two ferocious-looking German

Shepherds who strained on their leashes, their teeth bared. Roxy jumped back in shock.

"Rex! Tyson! Down!" Terah commanded, but the dogs took no notice. "I'm sorry," she said, backing away. "These boys are a little over the top."

"You don't say," Roxy said, looking at the dogs warily. She was much more of a cat person.

"The look of relief on the owner's face when she hands them over to me says it all," Terah continued. "I'd stop walking them in a heartbeat, but she is by far my highest paying client, so I'm hanging on for as long as I can. They need some serious training." She pulled again on the dog's leashes as they strained against her. Despite the challenging and fearsome dogs, Terah seemed to Roxy to be more relaxed than she had been at the botanica the previous evening.

"Right," said Roxy. "Great." She blew out her cheeks. "Perhaps they can smell my cat."

"I'll put their muzzles on. Just give me a few moments and stand well back." Terah tied the dogs' leashes to a nearby bench and got to work. "I *hate* to see dogs muzzled," Terah said. "But if they bite someone, we'll all have bigger problems, so it's the lesser of two evils."

It was warm, and Terah was sweating. With a tissue, she wiped her forehead, then under her good eye. As she discreetly lifted her eye patch to wipe sweat from her cheekbone Roxy caught a glimpse of an eyelid that was closed, permanently, it looked like.

Terah saw her looking. "Car crash. Years ago now," she explained simply. She pointed to the path ahead, "We can walk along, but you'll need to keep some distance between you and the dogs. They obviously sense something. They were being quite good until they saw you."

"I don't know much about dogs, honestly," said Roxy. "I've never had one. I have a cat, Nefertiti. She's as soft as a snowflake." They started to walk.

Terah smiled, although in the circumstances it looked more like a grimace. "I shouldn't complain. As jobs go, dog walking is pretty cushy."

"How did you get into it? Dog walking, I mean." Roxy asked. The dogs were calming down a little now they were moving, but Terah was having to lean back to counteract the strong forward motion of the dogs. Her arms were outstretched and taut.

"I fell into it, really—and only recently. I used to work in human resources for a corporate in Dallas, but I started getting a lot of pain in my hands and back. Eventually, I was diagnosed with arthritis, probably a much-delayed consequence of my car wreck. The drugs didn't work, and I don't like taking them anyway, so I came here to see a holistic doctor, and his treatment worked! I rarely have an attack anymore. I mean, I'm pretty skeptical when it comes to these things, but if it works, it works, right?"

"Absolutely."

"After a while, I felt much better, and I realized there was no way I wanted to go back to my old job," she laughed. "I started this dog-walking gig by walking my doctor's dog, would you believe? Word spread, and my books are full now."

"That's awesome," said Roxy. "It sounds like you've come a long way."

"Yes," said Terah. "But," her face darkened, "I just can't believe what's happened to Meredith."

Terah and Roxy continued to walk through picturesque Audubon Park, Roxy a little way off to Terah's left to avoid the attention of the German Shepherds. Terah shook her head. "I just find it so unbelievable that this Dr. Jack person would kill Meredith over a simple argument. There's *got* to be a bigger backstory. Maybe they crossed in the past, and he finally got his revenge."

"What makes you think that?" said Roxy.

"Well, no sane person would kill over a few angry words, would they? Maybe his sanity is the issue. Perhaps he's insane. That might explain it."

"Dr. Jack isn't insane," said Roxy. "I know him."

"For how long?"

"Oh...well, a few months."

"You see," Terah said, as if she'd solved the case already. "You can't really know someone in that short length of time. You only know the personality they've presented to you. The right person can easily put on an act. Some can keep it up for years."

"I would agree with you, but my friend Sage has known him much longer. Many years."

Terah shook her head. "Never trust a friend's view of their friend, Roxy. They can't see clearly, and they are biased. I've found that out to my peril more than once."

"Oh?"

"Back in the day, Meredith and I had a mutual friend who swore to me that Meredith was utterly trustworthy. But Meredith, when she was younger, had a dark side. I sensed it was there but ignored my instincts and believed my friend's judgment. The result was I let myself get close to Meredith, and she led me on a merry dance, that's for sure." Terah laughed.

Roxy frowned. "What happened exactly?"

"I knew Meredith forty years ago, and I knew her well, good and bad. I certainly didn't see her through rose-tinted spectacles like those hordes of credulous fans she has now. The fame, the public image of Meredith Romanoff doesn't affect or fool me. I believe it to be merely a façade. I doubt she has changed much since high school, and she made many enemies back then. Does that surprise you?"

Roxy thought for a moment, looking out over the trees. "Well, she does—did—have, well, an abrupt way about her. But...she could be charming, too."

"Exactly!" Terah exclaimed. "Charming *and* abrupt, some would say rude. She was such a contradiction. Knowing her as I did, it was shocking to see her become so rich and famous with a public brand that presented her as an all-knowing, kind, *beneficent* actor. Her fans treated her like a goddess, almost like she was the second coming.

"So what *was* she like in high school?" Roxy asked.

Terah was in full flow now. "Well, I first knew Meredith by reputation only. We went to school together, a small Texas town. She was kind of a big deal in high school, but I wasn't a friend of hers. She was a friend of my friend, Lizzie Jo. At the time, I had a boyfriend who was captain of the football team. He was the first guy at school with a motorbike, long, flicky brown hair, big shoulders, and dreamy eyes. You know the type. He was smart, too, the whole package. Very unusual."

"Yes," said Roxy. The type of boy she'd never gone anywhere near in high school. And who had never gone anywhere near her.

"I'm not sure why he liked me. I was into art, not cheerleading or anything like that. I was overweight, too, but back then, I did have this lovely long wavy blonde hair that all the girls envied, and he said he loved my eyes. Anyway, all the popular girls—including Meredith—were furious when he chose me over them. It made me something of an outcast but I didn't mind too much. I wasn't one to run with the cool girls.

"Meredith, however, she was known for her bragging and her big ideas as well as for taking over anything that she was involved in, no matter who was originally in charge or had the most expertise. She had a posse of mean girls around her. And even then, Meredith would say she could see ghosts and spirits and made out she had special powers."

Roxy stayed quiet. Terah was running her mouth, and she didn't want to stop her.

"Eventually, Meredith befriended me. I was into art and she would come to visit me during lunch and pretend she had this amazing newfound interest in urban art." Roxy frowned. "That's graffiti to most people. At the time, I didn't realize how dangerous Meredith was, and I welcomed her into our tightly-knit high school artist community. I admit I was a little blinded by the lure of her street cred. She seemed exciting, and I was a little intoxicated by her. I introduced her to our art space and helped her settle in.

"She wasn't very talented, but soon she started this huge project. She convinced the teachers to let us do a big mural on the side of the gymnasium. I was elated at first and came up with all kinds of designs. But pretty soon Meredith made it very, very clear that it was *her* project, and we had to do what she wanted. All my ideas were trounced in favor of hers, which were lame, in my opinion. Then she pursued my boyfriend, and he ended up dumping me to date her." Terah shook her head. "I think he was her goal all along. So that was that. Art was poisoned for me, and I'd lost my boyfriend as well. All thanks to Meredith."

"That must have been horrible," said Roxy.

"It was at the time, but it was long ago. The pain of her betrayal faded, we all grew up and moved on, but I never forgot her."

CHAPTER FIFTEEN

"SO IF YOU'D had no contact with Meredith in years, how did you reconnect?"

"Meredith contacted me a few weeks ago to say she was coming to the city. I suspect she looked me up on social media. I was surprised to hear from her, but she seemed nice enough and invited me to her reading. I was curious, to say the least. I mean, my memory of Meredith did not fit with the impression I had of a 'medium and psychic healer,' as she called herself. I thought those sorts of people were supposed to be earthy and kind. Meredith was not kind or earthy when I knew her. And I suppose I was skeptical of her reason for contacting me and felt I should be on my guard—a kind of 'keep your enemies closer' approach, if you will. I couldn't tell if she was seeking to make up for her high school sins or if her motives were less benign, and there was something more suspect beneath the surface. I wanted to find out. I did not want to be taken for a fool like last time. So I went along to see what was what."

Roxy nodded. "So what do you think now? Do you

think she was genuine? Like, did she have actual psychic powers? Or was she just a quack making a quick buck?"

"Well, if she were a fake, it wouldn't be for the money. At least I don't think so," said Terah. "Her husband Charles is rolling in cash. I think if she were cynically fooling people, it would be to bolster her ego, to exercise control. She loved having power over people. Back when we were teens, I would see her say this or that, or give someone a certain look, and then revel in how it made them behave. She was a master of manipulation. And, of course, she would love all the prestige and attention she got. Fame is a powerful drug."

"Hmm, there's also what one might think of mediums to consider," Roxy said. "Some people say it's all made up, and they're fakers. Others really believe in them. They think mediums can contact the dead and have all manner of special gifts. I don't know what to think about them, to be honest."

"Me neither. I have an open mind about that. Irrespective of whether contacting the spirits is truly a thing or not, I really couldn't say if Meredith was a good actress, or if she truly believed she could speak to the dead. I *can* say that, based on experience, either could be true."

"I see what you mean," said Roxy.

"Meredith was very convincing, but she was always a chameleon, you know? She could endear herself to anyone and be whatever someone wanted her to be so that she could wiggle her way under their skin. She certainly endeared herself to my high school boyfriend." Terah laughed. "It all seems very silly now. I haven't thought about it much over the years, only in passing, but it was painful at the time.

"What else made you distrust her?"

"Well, back in the day, she was always *starting* something or other, always with her at the center of it, always with her as the queen and the rest of us as her adoring pawns. The mural was one such project, another was a synchronized swimming team. Then there was the tribute band for some girl group that was famous at the time. There was always something. And she acted like she *loved* you but it was just to suck you in. Then, once you were caught in her trap, she'd control you within an inch of your life—what you did, said, who you could hang out with. If you resisted, she'd tarnish your name throughout the whole school with something private she'd wriggled out of you earlier or some derogatory information she'd found out. As you can imagine, at the time that was a *big* deal."

"Nasty," said Roxy. "So did she...did she try that with you? Use threats to control you?"

"She tried," said Terah. "She really did. But after she stole my boyfriend, I found out something about *her* that she didn't want *anyone* to know about. I told her what I knew, and I also told her that if she tried to blackmail me like I'd seen her do to others, I'd expose her. From then on, we were like a pair of bulls, keeping our wary eyes on one another from a distance."

"So what happened? What was this information she didn't want anyone to know about?"

"She didn't move to our high school until her junior year. I had an aunt who worked in the office at her old school, and she told me that Meredith was busted by the school for selling drugs. It was quite some scheme she was running, with passwords and secret drops, and a whole roster of clients only too willing to give her the money they made bussing tables or bagging groceries after school.

She was lucky that she didn't pick up a criminal record. The deal was that she had to switch high schools and she had to keep her nose clean. In exchange, no further action was taken regarding her drug dealing and her past actions were kept under wraps. I'm not proud of it, but I used this information as leverage. Once Meredith knew what I knew, we had an uneasy truce and went through the last year or so of high school at a brooding, respectful distance."

"You two really have a history," said Roxy. *And Meredith was a lot more complicated than I have given her credit for.*

"Yeah, but it was a long time ago..." Terah jerked her head. "Wait a minute...You don't think *I* killed Meredith do you?" Her face transformed as anger and disbelief took hold of her. The lid of her good eye lowered and her skin went pink except for that around her eye patch which remained resolutely white. "You've not met me to *question* me, have you? I thought you just wanted to talk about Meredith because you were, well, *upset.*"

All of a sudden Roxy became keenly aware of the German Shepherds who were still pulling away from Terah and growling at other dogs as they walked by. Terah snapped the dogs' leashes to bring them under control. Roxy took a big step backward. "I'm just trying to find out all I can about Meredith. You know, as a way to process what happened. I haven't experienced too many murders," she lied.

Terah turned her head to one side and squinted. She was a short, sturdy woman, and her appearance along with the struggling German Shepherds made the trio an unwelcoming proposition. People who passed gave them a wide berth.

Roxy felt an icy cold grip of fear clutch at her heart. She began to wonder if Terah's story of the rivalry between two young women was as one-sided as Terah had made out.

"You're playing amateur detective," Terah spat through gritted teeth.

A confrontation like this would have sent Roxy scurrying away just a few months ago, but now she lifted her chin. "Look, I don't know you from Adam. You don't know *me* from Adam. Dr. Jack is a good friend of mine, and he's asked me to find out who really murdered Meredith because it wasn't him."

"How do you know? That's just what he's telling you. He's hardly going to blurt out that he did it and ask the cops to cart him off to federal prison, is he?"

"Well, no," said Roxy. "But I believe him. I do."

"And do you believe *me?*" Terah pressed, "When I say I didn't kill Meredith?"

"Yes," said Roxy. "But in the same vein, if you did it, you're not going to just admit it either." Roxy thought after she'd said it, that that might have not been the smartest thing to say.

"This is ridiculous. I don't even know how to shoot a gun," Terah said. "Why are you getting yourself involved in all this, anyway? The cops are handling it, surely. They are the professionals. What are you?"

"Dr. Jack asked me to look into the case to prevent a miscarriage of justice."

Terah turned to look at her. She pursed her lips and tipped her head on one side. Her anger seemed to evaporate as she regarded the much younger woman next to her. Her outstretched arms that each held a leash bobbed up and down as they continued to walk along. "You don't owe him that," said Terah. "You have a job, and it's not investigating crime. Why not just let the police do their thing while you do yours?"

Roxy didn't reply directly. She didn't want to say that in her experience the New Orleans Police Department wasn't always as thorough and impartial as one would hope. "It's not ideal, but that's how it is."

"I don't know, Roxy. You're a young woman with a bright future. I was very impressed when you turned up at the botanica. Meredith mentioned that you were the owner of a very swanky boutique hotel. Charles even showed me some pictures. I was expecting someone much older. You're doing very well. My advice would be to stay out of all of this and focus on your own success. Don't get caught up in other people's troubles."

"But—"

"You were in the wrong place at the wrong time at that spirit reading. We both were. We had to look at Meredith's dead body, at her dead eyes..." Terah shivered. "That's enough for either of us to deal with. There's a reason for cops, you know. They're trained for that sort of thing."

"I know, but..."

"Trust me on this, Roxy. You can't save the world. You can't save anyone. And if you do, you won't get thanked for it. My advice is to put blinders on and stare straight ahead. Focus on your own life and success."

"And what about helping friends?" Roxy said. "Are we just supposed to sit by and watch them suffer?"

"Friends are overrated," said Terah. "You put all the effort you can into helping them. Then when you're down? They turn their backs."

"I think you're being overly cynical," Roxy said,

thinking about Sam and Nat and Sage and Evangeline and Elijah. Many times when she'd been down, they had helped her back up. None of them were perfect, but they were kind, good, and decent people. She trusted them. "Why are you so bitter?"

"Experience," Terah said. "You're still young. You'll learn as you get older."

"I'll learn no such thing." One of the dogs snarled at Roxy, and, despite herself, she flinched.

Terah laughed. "You're so sweet. You think life is all rainbows and fluffy bunnies. You've probably never come across anyone who's betrayed you yet."

"You know nothing about me," said Roxy. "I've had my share of troubles. I just *choose* to believe that there are good people out there. And guess what? When I made that choice, I began to *find* good people."

Terah sighed. "Ah, the innocence of youth."

"No," said Roxy. "It's not that."

"I don't mean to be condescending," said Terah. "You just don't know yet. You can't know yet. You haven't experienced enough of life."

This conversation was making Roxy angrier by the second. "Sorry, but I just don't agree," she said. "Look, if you want to talk more, call me at the *Funky Cat Inn.*" Roxy held out her business card. It had on it a line drawing of a cat that looked rather like Nefertiti wearing a trilby hat at a jaunty angle and holding a saxophone.

"I'm staying as far away from it all as possible," said Terah. "And you should, too."

"Goodbye, Terah," said Roxy. She was so furious at the older woman's condescension that she marched at speed to the botanica, over two miles away, and didn't get the least bit tired.

CHAPTER SIXTEEN

"**M**ADE ANY PROGRESS, Roxy?" Sage
asked, bluntly.

She hadn't looked up when the bell
above the door announced Roxy's arrival, choosing to
glare instead at her laptop while fumes of incense swam
around her. Eastern chime music played through the
botanica's sound system lending the place an even more
mystical air than usual. How Sage knew who was
standing next to her when she hadn't even looked up was
a mystery that Roxy had faced many times. It was one she
had given up trying to solve, instead rating it as one of
Sage's many unfathomable spiritual gifts.

Her directness told Roxy that Sage was in "all business" mode. It was such a transformation from her more
common mystical, mellow persona that it still had the
power to take Roxy aback. When Roxy had first met Sage,
she was genuinely intimidated by this no-nonsense behavior, and it wasn't until Elijah had explained that when
Sage was in the "real world," this was how she was, that
Roxy learned to be cool with it.

"Not much," Roxy replied. She flopped down in a chair next to a shelf full of huge crystalline rocks of deep purple and shimmering green hues. "I went to see Terah Jones, one of the people who was at the reading. She was an old school friend of Meredith's. She told me all kinds of stories about Meredith's antics back then, and how they'd had a feud. Then she got mad when she realized I was digging for clues. I didn't get any sense about whether she was involved in Meredith's death one way or the other. What about you?"

"I've been doing the spiritual divination as Dr. Jack asked," Sage said. "I've used all sorts of tools: Oracle cards, tarot cards, cowrie shells, tea leaves. I haven't gotten *very* far, but I think I have one piece of information. I could be interpreting things wrongly, but it might just be accurate."

"And what's that?" Roxy asked.

"I think—remember, I *think*—the killer is a man. The energy I'm intuiting is male."

"Okay..." Roxy said, processing, "well, that only eliminates Terah. Apart from Dr. Jack and me, that would leave Charles, George, and that businessman Royston..." Roxy struggled to remember his last name, "Lamontagne."

"Remember, though," said Sage, "it is just an idea at this stage. We all have both male and female energies. Our male energy causes us to be active, it leads us out into the world to achieve things. Our female energies are more nurturing, caring, more introverted. It could simply be that all I'm sensing is the male energy it requires to kill someone. I need to do more work."

"What will you be trying next?"

"I think I'll try smoke scrying," said Sage. "It's kinda

difficult though. I might go see a friend of mine who is an expert. She's been doing it for years, and her family for generations."

"What did you call it?"

"Smoke scrying. You stare at the smoke so intently that you go into a trance," Sage said, nodding at the incense stick and the smoke that curled upward from the tip in a chaotic dance. "Then you receive messages. Or you see pictures in the smoke."

Roxy frowned. "How does it give you messages?"

"It's hard to explain," said Sage. "You might hear them. Not directly, like you would if someone in the room was speaking to you, but you can hear them all the same. That's called clairaudience. Other times, you might just know something. That's called claircognizance."

"Gee, I have a lot to learn. I've never heard of either of those."

Sage gave a big smile. It was like the sun coming out on a cloudy day. "It's a big deal in my world, honey. There's a huge body of study and literature behind it." She nodded at the bookshelf on the other side of the store. "It's all there waiting for you, whenever you want it."

Roxy's head was already starting to hurt a little. She liked to think she was open-minded, but sometimes mysticism stretched her in ways she wasn't quite flexible enough for. "Thanks, maybe some other time. I think I should go see Royston Lamontagne now. And I still have to talk to George and Charles. I'm dreading that. What if they accuse me of suspecting them too as Terah did?"

"They'll be fine," Sage looked at her from under her eyelashes. "*If* they're innocent."

Roxy nodded in acknowledgment of her point, but she bit her lip.

"Don't be afraid," said Sage, kindly. "You'll do great. I know it."

Roxy smiled. "Thanks. I'm certainly going to try. I used to be much more afraid of talking to someone 'big and important,'" Roxy made air quotes, "like this businessman. Now I push through. He's human, just like everyone else."

Sage smiled. "Imagine him with just his underpants on if you have trouble. I find that usually helps." She laughed, her white teeth standing out against her dark skin, strong and straight. "Shall I give you a quick blessing? Help you on your way?"

"Sure!" said Roxy. She appreciated Sage's offer, even if she doubted it would help.

Sage came out from behind the counter, and wafted her hands back and forth in the air around Roxy's body. She hummed a beautiful and haunting tune, and then sang, "Golden light surrounds you still...Can you do it? Yes, you will!" She stood in front of Roxy and made as if she were sprinkling invisible fairy dust all over her.

Roxy laughed happily. "That's so weird. I feel warm and calm all of a sudden!" Perhaps her lack of belief didn't matter all that much. Perhaps it was the love and kind thoughts of her friend that counted and that she responded to.

Sage winked as she went back behind the counter. "At your service any time, pretty girl."

"Thanks, Sage." Roxy almost skipped outside and, as she walked the short path to the street, quickly typed *Lamontagne Promotions* into her phone. She put the address straight into her maps app and found it was only a 15-minute walk. She wouldn't call first, she'd only get brushed off. On her way, she stopped to pick up a free daily paper from a stand on the sidewalk and stuffed it in her bag. She'd read it later.

When she arrived at the address, she craned her neck to peer upwards. *Lamontagne Promotions* was located in a very tall, art-deco-style building. Turquoise windows and gold chevron detailing on the shining stone façade distinguished it from the chrome and mirrored glass buildings around it. Roxy pushed her way through the gold and green rotating door into the gleaming lobby, suddenly feeling nervous in her sweater, jeans, and tennis shoes. She looked very out of place among the people walking purposefully through the reception area. All the women wore skirts or pantsuits, sleek up-dos or bouncing waves, a full face of makeup and high heels. The men were just as sharp in their tailored suits and shiny brogues. It seemed no one edgy or unconventional worked for this company, and certainly no one scruffy.

But Roxy wasn't about to fall prey to feeling awkward or bad about herself as she'd done so many times before. This was a *new* season. She held her chin a little higher, pulled her shoulders back, and put on a big smile as she walked toward the reception desk. She arranged her face into an expression that she hoped was nonchalant as she leaned against the high table and said casually, "I'm here to see Royston."

The receptionist who was groomed to within an inch of her life looked at her closely. Roxy was glad there was a desk between them. The woman couldn't see how beat up her tennis shoes were. "Yes, madam. And you are...?"

"Roxy Reinhardt. I'm the owner of the *Funky Cat Inn*. Royston and I are involved in some business." Technically, this was true. Murder was a business alright.

CHAPTER SEVENTEEN

"**O**KAY, LET ME call his office." The receptionist carefully pressed the numbers on her phone with the pads of her manicured fingers. Despite her efforts to protect them, her long nails made clicking sounds against the phone's glass surface. She listened in to the receiver. Her perfectly symmetrical, tattooed eyebrows drew closer together just a smidgeon, and her long false eyelashes batted like exotic fans as she blinked before speaking to Roxy once more. "He's in a meeting at the moment." She eyed Roxy, considering. Roxy held her gaze almost, but not quite. The woman's oversized eyelashes were extremely distracting. "Go upstairs. You can wait in the lobby there. He might finish up and agree to see you when he's done," the receptionist finished. Roxy took off before the woman could change her mind.

"The elevators are over there," the receptionist called after her, pointing in the opposite direction. "He's on the top floor."

578   ALISON GOLDEN & HONEY BROUSSARD

"Oh, yes, of course." Roxy, feeling silly, caught sight of the golden pair of elevators a little way down from the reception desk. She walked over with as much dignity as she could muster and waited for the elevator to arrive. There was a ping, and the doors opened. Roxy got in and scanned the buttons. There were 10 floors. She hit the button on the elevator panel and began her ascent.

As soon as the elevator doors opened, Roxy was startled to find that she was in full view of *another* receptionist who sat behind a big desk, facing her. The woman, who had a bottle-blonde, topknot hairdo, stared at her with shrewd and unfriendly blue eyes. Roxy strode toward her appearing much more confident than she felt.

"I'm here to see Royston. We are involved in a business."

"I am Mr. Lamontagne's assistant, and you don't have an appointment," the woman snapped. "Who are you?"

"I am Roxy Reinhardt," Roxy said holding this woman's gaze much more easily. Her eyelashes were her own. "Owner of the *Funky Cat Inn*."

"I've never heard of it," the woman said snootily. "And if I haven't, Mr. Lamontagne won't have, either."

The woman radiated aggression. Roxy clenched her fists, summoning her courage, and tried again. "I'm a friend of a friend."

"Mr. Lamontagne doesn't much believe in *friends*. In fact, he doesn't have any. Business associates, only." The woman folded her arms. "Listen, I need you to be very clear. Explain to me why you are here. Am I meant to disturb Mr. Lamontagne because you're here to sell him Girl Scout cookies or something? If you have a demo, you can just leave it in that box, and I'll give it to him." She pointed to a box on the desk. Roxy looked at it. Royston Lamontagne either received a lot of music demos or his secretary didn't empty the box very often. It was full of thumb drives.

Roxy *itched to* give this rude, officious woman a piece of her mind, but she managed to hold her tongue. "I'm here about the murder of Meredith Romanoff."

"What murder? Oh, that...." The assistant frowned and peered at Roxy. "You're not the police?" Roxy stared back at her, neither confirming nor denying her question. "I think I'd better call the legal department," the woman said picking up her phone.

"No," said Roxy quickly. "I just want two minutes of Mr. Lamontagne's time."

"He doesn't have two minutes. Every minute of his day is accounted for and scheduled." The receptionist leaned on her desk, her arms still crossed. She looked incredibly pleased with herself as if she'd got Roxy in a "gotcha" like the cat who got all the cream.

"Okay, one minute then. Please. It's important."

"You're rather persistent, aren't you? You show up here uninvited, without an appointment, you lie about being a friend of Mr. Lamontagne, and you are connected to the murder of a medium. You sound like the last person to whom I should offer Mr. Lamontagne's invaluable time."

Roxy opened her eyes a little wider. "Please?"

The woman sighed. "Fine. I can't promise anything, but if you're desperate, you can wait over there. I'll see if he'll give you a couple of seconds between items on his schedule."

"Thank you," Roxy said. She looked to her left where

there were several leather armchairs and a coffee table with glossy brochures arranged carefully across the top. She walked over and sat down. For a few minutes, Roxy did nothing, and as she waited, she began to feel nervous. Her foot jiggled as she traced her finger in patterns on the arm of the chair.

From the coffee table, she picked up a brochure entitled *Lamontagne Promotions News*, a large, glossy, trifold brochure. Roxy skimmed through it. Across the front was emblazoned a picture of a group of young men standing on a street corner looking dangerously louche. They wore big chains, rings, and belts. On their heads were knitted beanies or baseball caps on backward. The subheading under the picture announced that they were rappers nominated for an industry award. Next to this, in parentheses, it said *Management: Lamontagne Promotions*. Inside the brochure, there was another image, this time of a jazz quintet playing in a club. It was labeled with the group name, *Dirk West Five* and also had the *Lamontagne Promotions* notation in the corner.

Roxy looked up the company on her phone again. This time she navigated to a website. There she learned that Royston Lamontagne was a music promoter specializing in rap, jazz, and soul. He managed nascent but talented groups and solo artists and seemed to have fingers in many music-related pies. His company listed club ownership, tour management, a record label, and music festival organization as just a few of its activities. In fact, anything related to music in the South seemed to involve Lamontagne somehow.

As she read the website, Roxy remembered something she'd seen on the front page of the newspaper she'd picked up earlier. She pulled it out of her bag. The front-page headline read *Label Languishes After Voodoo Vexation*. The paper reported that a deal to sign a rapper to the *Lamontagne* music label had fallen through after magic was reportedly used by a competitor to scupper the deal. According to the reporting, losing the signing had cost the label hundreds of thousands of dollars, and now it was even rumored to be struggling to stay afloat.

Roxy read the article twice over before the sound of voices disturbed her. She looked up to see the assistant talking to her boss, Royston Lamontagne. He still had his little dog under his arm! Lamontagne and his assistant muttered, their heads together before they looked over and the assistant pointed at Roxy. The big man quickly shook his head and disappeared into the room behind his assistant's desk.

Roxy stood as the woman wiggled over in her tight pencil skirt, a barely concealed smirk on her face. "Sorry," she said insincerely. "He said he's far too busy to see you, and you'll have to make an appointment. The next we have available is in six weeks."

"*Six weeks!*"

"Mr. Lamontagne is a very busy man."

"So I gather," said Roxy. Six weeks was far too long, though. By then the murder investigation would be long wrapped, and if things didn't change, Dr. Jack would be in prison. "Is there not any way I can get squeezed in sooner? I'm willing to meet him somewhere else, wherever's convenient."

"I'm afraid not." The woman's voice was as smooth and syrupy as molasses. "The elevator is over there," she pointed.

It was rare that anyone could make Roxy feel small anymore, but this receptionist was certainly trying her very best. "Okay," Roxy said, getting up. She stuffed the newspaper and glossy brochure into her bag. "Thank you for your help."

"You're so welcome. Anytime. Well, *six weeks' time*." The assistant giggled and wiggled off.

CHAPTER EIGHTEEN

"WHAT WOULD YOU like to do tonight, Charles?" Roxy asked.

George and Charles were slumped in armchairs in the lounge. George was flicking through a New Orleans guide on Voodoo, vampires, graveyards, and ghosts, but Charles leaned on his elbow, chin on his hand, staring into space.

"Oh, I don't know," he said. "Anything that you want to do, George?"

"I think we need to get out. Why don't we have dinner in a restaurant, and then head to the *Palace of Spirits*? Let's all of us go. The two of us are sad sacks. A few friends will take us out of ourselves."

"I think Meredith mentioned that place," said Charles. "She..." he sighed heavily, "...said it was probably just a tourist trap."

"But still, I'd like to visit. It's a museum located in the former home of Marie Laveau's aunt," George countered.

"Who?"

"Marie Laveau. She was the famous *Voodoo Queen*."

"Perhaps she can exert some spiritual influence from beyond the grave and ensure justice for Meredith." Charles jiggled his hands in front of him. He was joking, but George's eyes lit up.

"Yeah, she might!"

"Evangeline, the old owner of this place, believes in all that," said Nat, walking in the room and overhearing the tail end of their conversation. "She said her mother used to visit Marie Laveau's grave and had plenty a wish granted by the old girl's spirit. Perhaps she'll go with you. Or Sage. They could act as tour guides."

George smiled warmly. "I knew you'd understand."

Nat would normally have been the *last* person to understand, but around George, she seemed somewhat different. Softer.

They decided to go to *Bramwell's* on St. Charles Avenue, an upscale Creole restaurant that was one of the most expensive in town.

"In Meredith's honor," said Charles, "Our treat."

Sage joined them. She took some persuading.

"I'm busy working with the angels on Dr. Jack's behalf, honey," she told Roxy. "I don't think they'd appreciate me taking the night off."

"Nonsense. Ask them for guidance, they'll tell you what to do. Isn't that what you tell me?"

Sage sighed. "Yes, you're right." She paused and appeared to stare blankly at the wall although Roxy knew her mind was with the angels. "Okay, they're saying yes. I'll come."

Evangeline couldn't make it. "I've just got myself a new puppy, cher," she said down the phone. "I've been wantin' one for ages, and now I don't have guests to look after, I have the chance. I've called 'im Pinkie after his ridiculous pink ears. He's a French pug, don't 'cha know!" Roxy heard some snuffling. "Shush, shush, now Pinkie-winkie. Mommy on the phone," she heard Evangeline coo. Roxy's eyes widened. "I can't leave him," Evangeline added.

"Of course. He sounds adorable." Roxy wondered if Evangeline had taken leave of her senses. Training a new puppy was a lot of work and a French pug? They were a handful. But she could still hear Evangeline talking to her pup with a voice full of love. Roxy left her to it.

"Of course I'll come!" Elijah said when she asked him. "I know the *maître d*."

"Is there a *maître d* or restaurant owner you *don't* know in New Orleans, Elijah?"

"Hmmm, let me think." Elijah tapped his finger against his cheek and looked up to the ceiling as he thought for a moment. "Nope," he said pointing his forefinger at Roxy. "I know them all. Now, what time are we going? Do you want me to get us a table? They're often booked up, but I'll sweet talk Mateo."

Sam agreed to join them, and so it was Roxy, Sage, Nat, Elijah, Sam, George, and Charles for the evening. They dressed in all their finery. Roxy finally got to wear the royal blue one-shoulder dress she'd found in a vintage clothing store on Magazine Street a few weeks back. Sage wore her trademark robes, this time in bright mango, a matching scarf wrapped around her head. The men wore sharp suits, Elijah toning down his appearance this time with a forest green ensemble. But the surprise of the evening was Nat. She wore a black t-shirt, nothing new there, but this one was flecked with diamante and—she was wearing a skirt!

It was true that the skirt reached her ankles from

beneath which poked some patent, night-blue Doc Martens, but still—a skirt! Also, she was curiously wearing some long, elaborate—but delicate and feminine —silver earrings in addition to the cuffs, bars, and studs that curled around her outer ears. Roxy quickly recovered from her astonishment and linked her arm in Nat's. "Ready, girlfriend?"

"Ready, boss. I've fixed Nefertiti her own feast, cooked chicken and kibble, and left it for her in the court-yard. Maybe that ginger tom will come by and make it a romantic meal."

"Maybe," Roxy said wondering what had come over her friend.

They piled into a luxurious black minivan and soon arrived at *Bramwell's*. It was housed in a magnifi-cent, traditional New Orleans mansion. It was painted white. On all sides of the building were huge floor-to-ceiling leaded windows and black shutters across two stories. Pairs of pillars supported an elaborate wrought-iron balcony on the second floor that wrapped its way around the mansion and provided outdoor dining for the restaurant's clientele. Down-stairs, noise from the busy, chattering diners poured out of the open windows and onto the green lawns outside. On the third floor, more windows jutted from the roof.

Inside, a fireplace with a huge, dark, oak surround reached to the ceiling, dominating the entryway. Lights cast by the colored, leaded glass in the windows gave the reception a warm, muted, early-evening glow. In the dining room, the interior walls and ceiling were painted a muted sage green with white paneling detail, white majestic columns, and white tablecloths. An elegantly tiled floor was marked in a black and white checkered pattern.

As Elijah had predicted, the restaurant was full, the air humming with the sounds of diners.

"Mateo, we are here!" Elijah swept up to the welcome station. An older, distinguished man in a tuxedo gave him a small bow, the glow of the lights bouncing off his oiled salt and pepper hair.

"Good evening and welcome to *Bramwell's*. Sir, I have a special table ready for you, as you requested. Please," he said, looking at the group, "come with me."

Led by the *maître d*, they wound themselves around the restaurant tables to a small private back room. The other diners paid them no heed as they passed, but Roxy looked around as she walked. *Bramwell's* dress code was certainly formal. No one in the restaurant was casually dressed. The women wore floor-skimming, shiny dresses with big, expensive jewelry while most of the men wore tuxedos. Through the air came the warm, delicate sounds of mellow jazz. A man in a white tux sat at a white grand piano, his fingers dancing across the keys effortlessly.

"Wow," said Nat, whispering in Roxy's ear. "You sure they'll let us eat here? It's super schmancy."

Roxy laughed. "We just came from the *Funky Cat*," she whispered back. "We're schmancy too, remember!"

Roxy was looking forward to the evening. She glided into the seat that the *maître d'* pulled out for her. He picked up her napkin, shook it out with a flourish, and laid it on her lap. Sam, catching her eye from across the table, gave her a small smile.

"Here is your waiter, *Mesdames et Messieurs*. "Let him know if you need anything. Enjoy your meal."

"Thank you, we will," said Roxy.

"Thank you, Mateo," Elijah said, winking at him.

Despite the heavy circumstances, the evening turned out to be a glorious form of escapism. The food was extraordinary. The menu comprised haute cuisine with a Creole twist. For her appetizer, Roxy ordered Louisiana lump crab with avocado and a hard-boiled egg topped with gribiche dressing on top of homemade seeded bread. She followed that with an entrée of slow-roasted duck soaked in an orange-sherry sauce. As they ate, they talked about everything except the murder, everything except Meredith. Mostly, Sam, Sage, and Elijah, the three native New Orleanians told the four non-natives tales of the city.

CHAPTER NINETEEN

"**S**O," SAID GEORGE, sipping on his turtle soup. "What do you know about Marie Laveau? Or any type of Voodoo?"

"My family's Catholic," Sam said, "but a lot of the Voodoo and Catholic traditions are...I guess, more inter-connected than you might think. The Saints feature in both, for example."

"Sam is correct," Sage chimed in. "Did you know that the Africans, when they were shipped here and forced into slavery, weren't allowed to practice their religion so they allied each of their gods with a saint and practiced covertly.

"Oh, interesting," said Charles.

"Marie Laveau was a kind woman, a lifelong Catholic as well as being known as the *Voodoo Queen*. She held Voodoo ceremonies in New Orleans that thousands came to, but she also attended church regularly. She worked all sorts of magic. It's all woven into the fabric of everyday life here, I guess. You'll see signs of her everywhere. Or nowhere. It depends on how you look at things." She trailed off and pursed her lips, seeming far away.

Elijah piped up. "You've heard of Voodoo dolls, of course?"

"Yes," said George.

"Don't you stick pins in them to hurt people?" Nat asked.

"I don't think it's quite that simple," Elijah said frowning.

"No, it isn't," Sage said, coming back to the present with a chuckle. "It's a popular misconception and something of an old wives' tale. Most commonly they're used to help people, or to communicate with loved ones who have passed on."

Elijah grinned. "My grandmother told me a story once about how she was courted by someone who wasn't so good for her. She kept trying to leave the guy, but he'd do something nice, and she'd just fall in love with him all over again. Her friends were very worried about her, so they took her to a Voodoo priestess for help. This Voodoo priestess told my grandmother to make a doll of herself and tack it to a tree upside down. It was supposed to make her stop caring about her sweetheart. So that's what she did. And it must have worked because later she met my grandfather and was married to him for over sixty years."

"And you are here with us!" Nat chimed in.

Elijah smiled. "Damn straight. My grandmomma never really believed in it, though. She said it must have been the placebo effect, but you never know. Either way, she looks back on that moment as a turning point in her life."

For dessert, Roxy ordered a bruléed parsnip tart with wine-poached pears and bourbon ice cream. By the time they picked up the bill, the food, wine, and music had alleviated any heavy feelings they had felt at the beginning of the evening.

"So shall we go to the *Palace of Spirits* then?" Sam asked, pulling on his jacket. "I heard that's where you were interested in going, George."

"Now?" Nat said doubtfully.

Roxy nudged her in the ribs and giggled. "Thought you didn't believe in any of that old *rubbish*."

"Really, Nat?" George said. He sounded disappointed.

"I didn't before, I'll admit," said Nat. "But hearing all these stories, I'm beginning to change my mind...Are you sure it's safe, Sage? We're not going to awaken some crazy spirit, are we?"

"No, honey," said Sage. "They can be fearsome, yes, but only to protect innocent people from others who want to cause them harm."

"This may be a dumb question," Nat said as they walked out of the restaurant, "but am I innocent?"

George took her hand in his. "Yes, you are. You have a good heart."

Nat blushed and pulled her hand away, but not so quick that Roxy didn't notice. Roxy felt her jaw drop a fraction and quickly clenched her teeth.

"And if you're in doubt," George said, "I've cleansed my soul so I can be like an angel on earth. I'll protect you from anything evil."

"Really?" Nat replied.

"Really."

They caught another cab to the *Palace of Spirits* on Bourbon Street, which turned out to be buzzing with nightlife and lit up with color. People, many of them tourists judging by the fact that they stopped every few yards to take photos with their phones, were roaming around, laughing and talking, walking in the middle of the street as they made their way down it. When the cab stopped on the corner, Sam told the driver to wait until they were done.

"I don't know," the cab driver said, looking nervous. He glanced down the street. "How long are you gonna be?"

"Not long," said Charles. "Ten minutes at most."

They walked until they arrived outside a tiny shop, a small sign that dangled from the overhanging roof announcing that they had arrived at their destination. They stood in silence looking at it.

"Not the kind of palace I'm used to, that's for sure," Nat said in her London accent. "Not very palace-y, is it?"

The *Palace of Spirits* was incongruously named. In reality, it was a tiny store in a building that needed some attention. The exterior paintwork was scuffed and peeling. The windows needed washing. A drainpipe outside was stuck with torn and peeling posters that seemed to act as Band-Aids, propping it up and holding it together. The small windows were stuffed full of...stuff. Figurines, beads, cards, masks, feathers filled the brightly-lit space. The doors to the store were open and Roxy could see the inside outdid even the window. She could see bottles, fans, crucifixes, books, jewelry, skeletons, candles, all manner of knick-knacks. It was like Dr. Jack's botanica on steroids. There was a black t-shirt hanging from the doorway. It had a skull on it.

"Look, Nat, there's something for everyone here." Roxy tapped Nat on the arm and pointed upward. Nat looked up and scowled. She looked decidedly uncomfortable despite George's assurances.

"I'm not sure about this. I wish Meredith were here," Charles said. "This doesn't seem like a good place. She'd know how to deal with difficult spirits better than any of us."

"Don't worry," Sage said. "We're here for a good reason. It can't hurt, and it might just help. You never know. Let's go in and see if we can connect with a senior spirit, maybe even Marie Laveau herself!" Despite the liveliness all around them, Roxy began to feel a little nervous.

Sage led them inside. There was no one in the outer part of the shop so they continued to the back room, this one dimly lit. Skeletons, skulls, even a wrought iron gate were laid out there, along with beads, an altar, and wreaths long since dead and dried out. Beyond that, there was a doorway covered with a black lace veil. Sam took the lead through it into a dark room illuminated only by flickering candles.

"STOP!" someone yelled. They all jumped out of their skin. Roxy screamed.

A woman appeared from another back door—a very tall, skinny, terrifying-looking woman with alabaster, almost transparent skin, and straggly, jet-black hair that fell around her shoulders. She had an angular face with a diamond-shaped chin and thin, dry lips that were peeling. The woman was dressed entirely in black and glared at them with small, dark eyes, clearly unafraid of the group in front of her despite there being seven of them.

"Let's get out of here!" Nat whispered frantically.

"Wait!" George said to her. He turned back to the woman. George wasn't very tall, but he drew himself up to his full height and spoke. His voice sounded strong and confident, but Roxy heard a shaky undertone. "We would like to connect with your most senior spirit," he said. "To ask a favor."

The woman replied through gritted teeth as though she were suppressing some kind of rage that had presumably and inexplicably been caused by the strangers in front of her. Her hard low tone sent shivers down Roxy's spine. "They are not here right now. The *Palace of Spirits* is out of bounds. I *suggest* you come back tomorrow," she added although it clearly wasn't a suggestion at all.

"Okay," Elijah said quickly. "Let's go. I don't think we're going to get anywhere tonight."

"Are you sure?" Sage tried to cajole the woman. "We come with pure intentions and good hearts."

The woman in black inhaled deeply, her eyes blazing. Like George, she drew herself up to her full height that, to Roxy, seemed rather tall, almost as tall as Sam.

"Okay, okay, we hear you. Let's go, people," Sam said before the woman could say anything to frighten them further. They started filing out of the room into the street except for George who stood his ground until Nat caught his sleeve and started to pull him away from the woman.

"We're not afraid of you and your darkness!" George shouted at her. "I'm sending out positive healing energy at this very moment. There's a sinister ritual being performed in that room, I can feel it." He pointed to the door through which the woman had emerged.

"Clever boy," the woman growled.

"You won't get away with it," George said firmly. "You won't!"

The woman said nothing, her pointed chin lifted, triumphant.

Nat laughed, though it sounded like she was almost crying. "No problem. We'll just be going now."

The group scurried back the way they had come, dodging and weaving through the tourists back to the cab. As soon as the car doors closed, they breathed a collective sigh of relief.

"To the *Funky Cat Inn*," Roxy said to the driver. "As quickly as you can."

"What was *that* all about?" Nat asked George. She was squeezed in the corner of the back seat next to Elijah and Sage and had to look around them at George. "What did you mean by a 'sinister ritual'? How did you know?"

George was frowning. "There was dark energy, the blackest. I'm still feeling it. It's so heavy." He leaned his head back. "I'll need time to understand what it means."

They were all silent as they drove back to the *Funky Cat*, even Elijah. Roxy looked out of the window, her elbow on the window ledge, her palm propping up her chin, her lips pursed. She had that leaden feeling one gets after something has gone badly wrong.

CHAPTER TWENTY

"ANYONE WANT A nightcap?" Roxy asked brightly when they arrived back at the hotel. She was trying to rescue the evening.

"I have to head off, Roxy girl," Elijah said. "I have an early start."

"Me too, honey," said Sage. "I have a marathon meditation session set for tomorrow morning."

"I'm going straight to bed." Charles let out a deep sigh.

"I'll be contacting the spirits for some time yet. I need to go to my room right away." George was emphatic.

Roxy nodded. She didn't have any enthusiasm either. "You're right. It's best that we all go to bed and wake up bright and early in the morning, hopefully in better moods."

Outside the hotel, they said their farewells and dispersed. "Night, Roxy," Sam had said simply before he left. Roxy disconsolately watched the cab drive him and Elijah away. She hung her head and went inside.

"How you doing, girlfriend?" Nat asked her. She wound a loose arm around her friend's neck.

"Oh, I don't know. Things just don't feel...*right*, you know? I feel out of sorts."

"Yeah, that was weird what happened back there."

"I think I'm going to bed. There's nothing to be gained from staying up given the mood I'm in." Roxy moved to lock the front door.

"Yeah, me too." Nat left her and walked through the lounge toward the kitchen. She lived in a unit behind the hotel.

"Night, Nat," Roxy called out.

"N—, hey, look!" Nat whispered. She held her fingers to her lips and beckoned Roxy over. Roxy padded lightly to where Nat was standing. "Looks like Neffi has had a better night than we have," Nat said, pointing.

Roxy looked over to the sofa and there entwined together fast asleep, their tails twitching, was Nefertiti and her ginger tom.

At some point during the night, Nefertiti must have abandoned her stripy orange friend, or he'd abandoned her because when Roxy woke the next morning, Nefertiti was curled up beside her. Roxy stroked her gently, staring up at the ceiling, her thoughts turning to the investigation immediately.

Roxy knew she needed to question both Charles and George. Of course, she didn't want to amplify their grief, but the clock was ticking. She knew that today she'd have to engineer some kind of opportunity to talk to them about Meredith's life and death.

She didn't relish the prospect, but the thought of Dr. Jack languishing in a cell under the firm hand of Detective Johnson was enough to spur her into action. Even more important was her commitment to him. Roxy was utterly reliable. When she gave her word, she gave her heart and soul along with it.

"I'm going to talk to one of them over breakfast, Neffi. Charles *or* George—it doesn't matter which one. That's my goal." Roxy got up, had a quick shower and dressed for the day. She nipped over to Elijah's bakery to pick up fresh beignets.

"Morning darling!" Elijah called out. He was wearing chef's whites and a hair net. It always surprised Roxy to see him kitted out so bland and dorky. It was such a change from his "off-duty" attire, but then perhaps that was the point.

"Thought I'd save you the walk across the cobblestones. Have you got my order ready?" she said.

"Of course I have. Just like always." Elijah sauntered over to a side counter. "And I gave you a bonus, something new I'm trying—top box. Don't open it now. Come back and tell me what you think." He handed her two big white boxes that when piled on top of one another were so tall she could barely see over them. "Are you okay?"

"I'll manage," Roxy replied. "Just an ongoing hazard of being small." Elijah went around her to open the door and then had to dash across the alleyway to open the front door to her hotel when he saw that she couldn't manage by herself.

Once in the kitchen, Roxy opened the boxes, excited to see what Elijah had made for her. He often tried out new recipes on her guests. They were always fabulous. Elijah was such a perfectionist that he would never let anything leave his bakery unless he was certain of a positive reception.

The first box contained beignets, as usual. She turned to the second and took off the lid. There, on a paper plate covered with a paper doily, were five piles of sweet, chocolate-y deliciousness. Each pastry comprised of two choux buns that were sandwiched together, topped with chocolate ganache, and further topped with whipped cream. Roxy sliced one open and more ganache oozed out from inside the buns. "They're called Religieuse," Elijah would tell her later.

"I can see why," Roxy had replied.

Roxy didn't have to taste one to know they would be divine. She debated whether to save them but decided they would make an impressive sight first thing in the morning and quickly slid the doily with the pastries onto a china plate and along with the beignets, put them on the serving table in the dining room.

"Good morning, Roxy," George said when he strode in. "Those beignets smell like heaven."

Roxy grinned. "Freshly made this morning. I picked them up myself. They are still warm. But look at what else I have for you." She showed him the plate of choux pastries with a flourish. "New and fresh from *Elijah's Bakery* just minutes ago. Try one."

George didn't need to be asked twice. He took a bite and closed his eyes. "Hmmm, these are *gorgeous*. Melt in the mouth."

"Sorry, sorry, sorry I'm late!" Nat said, running in and throwing her apron over her head. Her dark hair was spiky and unbrushed. She'd obviously just rolled out of bed.

"Hey! Don't worry about it!" George said to her smiling. This morning, he was her exact opposite. He was bright-eyed and smiley, his face scrubbed pink, his hair freshly jelled, and his clothes casual but neat. "We all had a late night last night. Looks like Charles has slept in, too."

"Yep. I'm tired." There were dark rings under Nat's eyes. "What would you like for breakfast, George? I am *not* too tired to make whatever you want." She cast a nervous glance over in Roxy's direction as she checked her manager's reaction.

"I don't normally go for a hot breakfast, but I'd love some oatmeal if it's not too much trouble."

"Of course not!" Nat said. "I'll get to it right away. Oh, and I'll bring some juices and coffee and tea in. Roxy, I'm really sorry."

"It's fine, Nat, honestly," said Roxy kindly.

"Do you want anything?"

"I think after that dinner last night, I'll stick with a beignet and some tea," said Roxy. "I still feel full."

George sat down at the table and began to munch on another choux pastry.

Roxy took a deep breath. She had him alone. Now was her chance to question him.

CHAPTER TWENTY-ONE

"YOU'RE CONCERNED," GEORGE said.

Roxy looked at him over the table. He put his hands under his chin and looked back at her steadily, a warm smile on his face. Roxy had never met an adult who was so comfortable with eye contact. He had the credulous, artless gaze of a six-year-old.

Roxy nodded. "You're a good reader of people, George. I'm worried about Dr. Jack. Honestly, I think it's very unlikely he killed Meredith, especially over such a minor argument, but I'm willing to keep an open mind. Do you know if there was any history between them?"

"I don't think so," said George. "At least Meredith never mentioned any. She simply asked me to book a small private room in New Orleans for her reading. It was me that found Dr. Jack's botanica. She had never met him before."

"Did Meredith ask you to do a lot of things like that?"

"Of course. She was supposed to. I was her assistant. I did whatever she wanted." He gave her a broad grin. He had a slight gap between his front teeth. "And I did it with a smile."

Roxy shifted in her seat. "Look, George, I'm going to be direct now," she said, eyeing him carefully. "Meredith didn't seem very kind to you. I noticed her, well, um, snapping at you and ordering you around."

George's smile faded, and he looked down at the tablecloth before lifting his eyes to Roxy once again. "She didn't have to be kind to me, Roxy. She wasn't on this earth to be kind. She was here to be brilliant and sharp and a psychic genius, which she was. It was an honor to be her assistant, her apprentice. I was learning from the best. How she treated me was neither here nor there."

Personally, Roxy thought that Meredith could still have been kind. Kindness didn't cost anything, after all, and it made one feel a lot better. "Didn't you ever want to quit, though?"

"Yes, at times," said George, breaking eye contact and looking down again. "But I'm not a quitter, Roxy. I can bear anything including being treated roughly now and again."

"Yes, but why would you?"

"She was powerful, a great medium," said George, casting his direct gaze at Roxy once more. "I wanted to learn from her. Being snapped at was a small price to pay for the experience of being in close association with the great Meredith Romanoff. It's something I'll have on my resume and in my soul forever."

"But, still..."

"Look, I am as devastated as anyone by Meredith's death. I have no idea who in that room could have killed her. I can barely believe it happened, but it did, right in front of me, and I can promise you that I am not the murderer. I don't have it in me to kill an insect, let alone a person."

He pressed his lips together and flashed his eyes wide at her. He raised his hands, his palms upward, and shrugged his shoulders. Roxy nodded. She couldn't see him as the killer either. "Beautiful day today," she said, gesturing out of the window at the blue sky, the sun streaming through. "Do you have any plans?"

"Not yet. Perhaps I'll go outside. I do that a lot. I like to commune with nature, and I haven't been able to do so much of that in the last day or so. I get messages from the birds and the trees. They have their own language."

"Huh. How does that work?"

"Well, what I mean is that when you're spiritually 'in tune,' you can *sense* them communicating. We are all connected to each other and everything."

"I highly recommend Audubon Park," Roxy said. "I went there yesterday. It's peaceful. Huge, too. You could wander for hours without seeing it all."

George smiled again. "I might just do that. Thanks, Roxy. Perhaps Charles will come with me. I want to keep him busy. Stop him brooding."

At that moment, Nat came out of the kitchen with George's oatmeal. Their eyes locked, and she sat down at the table nursing a coffee. From that moment on, Roxy didn't seem to exist. Intrigued, she sat back in her chair and folded her arms to observe this unexpected interaction. She smiled a little. What an unlikely combination! Who would have ever guessed that skeptic Nat with a tongue so razor-sharp you could practically cut yourself on it and gentle spiritualist George would have gotten on so well?

For the next thirty minutes, there wasn't a single lull

in the conversation between the pair. They talked about anything and everything, from their childhoods to the current political situation. Nat even asked George his opinion on re-birthing and hypnosis. When Roxy stood up after finishing her beignet and coffee, they were so engrossed in their conversation that they didn't even notice. Roxy cleared her throat.

"I'm going to see if Charles is all right. It's nearly nine o'clock and I'm getting a little concerned."

Nat and George looked at her as though they'd suddenly remembered she was there.

"Okay," George said. "But I'm sure he's fine. Sleeping in isn't unusual for him. He's more of a night owl."

"I'm probably being silly, but after, well, everything, I'd like to make sure. I'll call up from the lobby phone to see if he wants his breakfast brought up to him."

Roxy excused herself and walked into the lobby where she picked up the phone on the reception desk. She wasn't surprised to find Nefertiti sitting there, looking very regal indeed, her blue eyes matching the décor and her paw draped over the phone, as if to stop her owner from making the call, from doing anything other than pay attention to her.

"Sorry, Nefertiti, love," said Roxy, delicately removing her paw to one side. "I need to make a call." Roxy dialed Charles' room number and looked down at Nefertiti as she waited for him to pick up. Neffi gazed back at her with what Roxy imagined was contempt. *How dare you carry on with your life regardless of me, human!* Roxy scratched her cat under her chin and Nefertiti stood and raised her tail high in the air while the phone buzzed and buzzed. Charles didn't answer. Thwarted, Roxy returned to the dining room, her heart beating a little faster. Nat was laughing at some story George was telling her and Roxy felt a ripple of irritation course through her at their obvious lack of concern and even more their delight in each other's company. Roxy considered pulling rank and asking Nat to clear up break-fast, but relented when Nat looked over and gave her a huge smile.

"No reply," Roxy said. "I'll take something up to him."

She grabbed a plate of beignets and a cup of coffee and walked out of the room, pausing at the bottom of the stairway as she wrestled with her thoughts. Maybe he was asleep? Perhaps he'd taken a sleeping pill or two and was out for the count?

Roxy shook her head, frustrated by her overthinking, a bad habit of hers, she knew. "I'd better go check," she said to Nefertiti, who was now winding her way around Roxy's ankles, still plying for attention. Roxy hurried up the stairs to the first floor where Charles's room was located. She knocked on the door. There was no answer. "Charles?" she said. Then a little louder, "Charles?" After another three knocks, there was still no answer, so Roxy tentatively opened the door. "I'm coming in," she called. Inside, light flooded the room. The bed was neatly made. The drapes were open. Charles was nowhere to be seen. "Charles?" Roxy went into the bathroom. Nothing had been touched. Fluffy white towels hung neatly on their rail. The bar of soap by the basin still had its wrapper on—the custom *Funky Cat Inn* paper seal that featured the face of a cat who looked very much like Nefertiti was unbroken.

Roxy looked around again. Charles' toilet bag sat beside the basin, and there was a book on the heavy wood-paneled nightstand. In the closet, Charles had neatly arranged his clothes, and they hung from hangers completely undisturbed. She counted two button-down shirts, two jackets, and a pair of pants along with ties and a belt. The clothes he had worn to *Bramwell's* were folded neatly on the back of a chair.

It was all very strange.

Roxy hurried back downstairs. "George," she said. "Did Charles mention he was leaving? Or going out?"

"No, why?"

"Well, he's not here. His bed hasn't been slept in. All his things are there, but his room is untouched."

"Oh," George said, frowning. He got out his phone from his pocket. "I'll give him a call." He held the phone to his ear for far too long. Roxy tapped her foot, her heart beginning to pound. George's frown deepened. "I don't understand."

"He didn't slip out while we were in here having breakfast, did he?" said Nat.

"I'm sure he didn't," Roxy said. "We'd have heard the front door. And like I said, his room hasn't been touched. Like he hadn't been in it since it was refreshed yesterday."

"Well, he must have been in it at some point because he came out with us last night," Nat said. "Perhaps he's just persnickety. He is a surgeon after all."

"Yes! That's exactly what his room is like—like an operating theatre. Sterile. Perfect. Everything laid out just so."

"Are you *sure* he's not upstairs?" George said.

"Not even in the closet," Roxy replied. "I checked. Why don't you go and look?"

They all went upstairs to Charles's room.

"Well, he's obviously not here," Nat said immediately. She looked in the closet.

"I'm going to call him again," said George, his voice high, his words tumbling out in a rush. "Something's not right here, I can feel it." As soon as George hit the call button, they heard the sound of a phone ringing.

Roxy rushed over to the side table and pulled open the drawer. "Oh dear, his phone's here."

George's cheeks turned several shades paler.

"I'm getting a terrible feeling about this," said Nat.

"Me too." Roxy was beginning to feel sick.

"Me three," said George.

CHAPTER TWENTY-TWO

"I HAVE TO go look for him," said George. "Maybe he went back to the *Palace of Spirits* since they wouldn't let us in last night?"

"Ah, yes. That's probably it." Roxy's heart lifted a little.

Nat grimaced. "Do we have to? I think we should call Johnson and let him know. It's not like Charles got up early to go out. He hasn't been here all night."

Roxy's heart sank again. "You're right. We probably should."

"No," said George. "Not yet. I don't want that detective's bad energy infecting everything. Let's at least look around by ourselves for a bit. I'm sure this can all be resolved very quickly. Charles can't have gone far."

"I sure hope so. I'll call a cab right now. Sam's due here to continue working on the loft. Maybe he should join us in looking for Charles?"

"Oh, I don't think that's necessary," said George. "I'll connect with Charles' energy and that will lead me to him. Let's just keep quiet for now."

"I want to come to support you," said Nat.

"Me too," Roxy said.

George smiled. He drew them both into a hug. "I feel overwhelmed by the kindness of you two. When this is all over, I think I would like to live here forever!"

Nat's eyes lit up. "Yes, you could! You could stay here in New Orleans, and work in Dr. Jack's botanica. You could do readings for people!"

Roxy decided to stop being surprised. Obviously, this was a situation beyond her understanding. Was this really the Nat she knew?

"Let me ring the cab people. Sam can call us if Charles reappears. While I'm doing that, will you feed Nefertiti, Nat? And clear away the breakfast things?"

Twenty minutes later, the trio was standing in front of the *Palace of Spirits*. The place didn't seem nearly so scary in daylight.

"Here goes nothing," Roxy said, stepping inside.

The room that had been brightly-lit the night before was now illuminated only by the morning sun. They all looked around at the items on display—the flowers, both real and plastic, candles, jewelry, feathers, bibles, rattles, scissors, packets of candy, and strings of beads.

"People put their faith in this stuff, don't they?" Nat said, not sounding like her old cynical self. Roxy could practically hear the cogs of Nat's brain turning over as she processed all this information with the new perspective offered to her by George.

"Offerings," George explained, looking down at the assortment of items on the tables. "Hello?" he called out, walking toward the door at the back of the room that led to the decaying objects they'd seen housed in the room behind the main store the night before.

Roxy held her breath, waiting for the terrifying woman they'd met last night to jump out. But instead, a young woman appeared. She had a round face with no discernible cheekbones, round eyes and a petite mouth with Cupid's bow lips. Her skin was luminous and unlined. "Hello," she said with a soft voice. "Did you want to buy something?" She gave them a shy smile.

"Oh," George said, taken aback. "No, thank you," he said. "We're looking for Charles Romanoff—tall, bald guy, fifties, heavy-set. Has he been here?"

"I don't know," the young woman said, biting her lip and frowning. "We've had plenty of customers this morning already. We're always busy."

"What do you do here, exactly?" Nat said.

"We're a botanica," the woman explained. "And we have some historic artifacts in the back, so a little museum of sorts."

"*That's* what Charles would have been here to see," George said.

The woman shook her head. "No one's been back there today."

Nat stepped forward. She narrowed her eyes. "I don't think that's the only thing you do here. We visited last night, and there was this evil-looking woman, and..."

"Last night? What time?"

Nat looked at Roxy. "About ten-thirty?"

"I'd say so," Roxy agreed.

"You must be mistaken," the young woman said, sweetly. "I closed up at 7 PM myself. It's been locked up tight since then. Opened up this morning too, I did. No one's been here in-between those times."

"That's not true. Really," said Nat. "We were here. We saw her."

The young woman looked at her mildly, blinking slowly, a small smile forming on her cherubic lips. She didn't react to Nat's comment. "Would you like to come in? I can show you around," She smiled and stepped to the side, gesturing the way.

"No," said Nat. "No, thank you. Bye." She turned abruptly on her flat Doc Martened heel and marched outside, closely followed by Roxy and George, who nodded silently at the woman as he backed away.

Even though it was sunny, both Nat and Roxy were shivering. They stood in the middle of Bourbon Street, raising their faces to the sky and soaking in the sun's rays.

"Well, I don't know what to make of that, but Charles certainly isn't there," said George. "I have the sense he might have been, though, you know, since we were here last night. But who can say?"

Roxy shivered again, thinking about their encounter with the strange woman the night before. Her gut filling with dread, she said, "You don't think...You know that woman, and the ritual that was going on in the backroom that you said wasn't good, a sinister ritual, I think you called it? You don't think Charles' disappearance has anything to do with that, do you? You know, at a spiritual level?"

George's eyes widened with horror. "I hadn't put the two events together...but...you might be right. He may have picked up something when he came here."

"What? You mean, like, like...a virus?" Nat exclaimed.

George began to pace. He thrust his fingers through his hair. "This could be serious. Very serious indeed."

"The two of you are being ridiculous," Nat shouted, her arms flailing in the air. She was becoming more and more agitated. She started to pace. "Why are you connecting the thing from last night with Charles disappearing? There is absolutely no evidence to link the two," Nat said. "You're pulling stuff out of thin air!" She put her hands out in front of her as though to protect herself, or keep George and Roxy away from her. She looked panicked. "You're making all this up as you go along!"

George put his hands on Nat's shoulders and looked her in the eyes. She was breathless, but she stopped pacing and dropped her arms to her sides. "I don't know exactly what's going on," said George. "But last night I had dreams, terrible dreams, of darkness and blood and murder. I had to fight off all kinds of demons in the astral plane—that's the place in your mind where you go when you have dreams. I woke up exhausted. Maybe the same spirits came for Charles, and he couldn't handle it. I don't know!"

Nat slapped her palm to her forehead and growled. "George..."

Roxy, like Nat, didn't enjoy all this talk of dark, supernatural events, spirits, and demons. She didn't want to get caught up in it. And, privately, she was with Nat, she didn't believe in it. "I think we need to call Detective Johnson."

"That's what I said earlier!" Nat cried. "But you didn't listen to me. And now there's all this talk of evil spirits and viruses and things. Johnson may not be the nicest guy, but I prefer him to *this*!" Nat pointed back at the *Palace of Spirits*.

"Okay, go ahead," said George. "Call him."

Roxy pulled out her phone and called Johnson, a number that was now programmed into both her contacts list and her mind. They were still standing in the street.

"Reinhardt," Johnson barked, as if she were part of the police force, too.

"One of my guests is missing," she said. "Meredith Romanoff's husband. He's staying with me. We went out last night with him, but this morning he's gone. His bed hasn't been slept in."

Johnson spoke to her as if she were a very dim child. "And did you call his cell phone?"

"Yes. He'd left it in his bedside drawer."

Now it was Johnson's turn to growl. He said a few words Roxy couldn't quite make out. "I'll put out an APB for him immediately. Let's hope he hasn't gotten too far."

Roxy moved away from Nat and George who were now deep in conversation again and spoke quietly into her phone. "Do you think...could this be an indication that he's guilty? I mean, spouses are often..."

"Jack Lavantille is in custody for the murder. Have you forgotten?" Johnson barked. "This doesn't change anything in that regard."

"But have you charged him?"

"Not yet, but I will."

"You don't have the evidence," Roxy spat, surprised by the strength of her own emotion. "And you won't get any because..."

"Because you're covering for him?"

"No! Because he didn't do it!"

Johnson laughed. "Okay, then who did?"

"I don't know!" she said. "But it's worth investigating. There were other people in the room that night. Terah

Jones, who had a huge falling out with Meredith Romanoff in high school, for a start. Did you know about that?"

"I don't appreciate your impertinence..."

"And what about Royston Lamontagne, that businessman?"

"He's a very well-respected..."

"What? Are you saying that well-respected people don't commit crimes?"

"Listen to me, I have this investigation under control, Ms. Reinhardt. You would do well to leave things alone," Johnson said curtly. "As I said, I'll put an APB out for Romanoff. That is all." He hung up the phone.

"Ugh!" Roxy burst out. Frustrated, she squeezed her eyes and her fists tight. She looked at the screen of her phone as if by staring at it, Johnson would ring back.

"What?" Nat said as she and George looked over.

"Nothing," said Roxy. "Just Johnson being his annoying self. Let's go look someplace else for Charles. What about Dr. Jack's botanica?"

"Good idea," said George.

CHAPTER TWENTY-THREE

W HEN THEY ARRIVED at Dr. Jack's
botanica, they found Sage at the counter.
She was wearing long aquamarine linen
robes and having an involved conversation about essential
oils with a young couple. While smiley and attentive to
her customers, there were dark circles under her eyes.
Nat, George, and Roxy looked around the botanica as
they waited for her to be done.

When Roxy had first arrived in New Orleans, this
store had both charmed and intrigued her. It was so alien
and beyond her experience. And now? Now she browsed
the "love potion" perfume bottles, and "grounding"
healing crystals, and powder that promised to "banish evil
spirits" without blinking an eye. She took in the sights and
smells of the small shop and looked carefully up and
down the aisles. There was no sign of Charles.

Eventually Sage finished serving the couple, and they
left, happily clutching a brown bag. She rushed out from
behind the counter and greeted her visitors with a hug.
"Good morning, good souls. I had a wonderful meditation

this morning. How are things?" She looked at them, a hint of desperation in her eyes.

"Hi Sage," said Roxy. "Has Charles come by?"

"No, why?"

"We can't find him anywhere," said Nat. "He's left his phone in the hotel and disappeared."

Sage frowned.

"We've just been to the *Palace of Spirits*," George explained, "but he's not there, either. I'm getting a bad feeling. This isn't like him." George's forehead crinkled as he spoke. "We came here to see if you've seen him."

"He's not been here. I opened an hour ago. Perhaps he went for a long walk when he found he couldn't sleep. Maybe he's returned to the hotel since you left," Sage suggested.

Roxy shook her head. "Sam's there; he's working on the loft conversion. The front door is locked, so Charles would need to ring the bell to get in. I told Sam to call us if that happened, and he hasn't. Besides, if he went for a walk, he wouldn't leave his phone behind, would he?"

"Oh. No. Probably not." Sage went back behind the counter and sat down, looking thoughtful. Then she jumped back up, her eyes bright. "Do a reading, George! You're the closest to him, you would be the best person to do it. Take whatever you want from the shelves. I have cowrie shells, or you can use cards, or..."

"I can't," George said firmly. "I'm not authorized."

"Huh?" Sage said. "Authorized? What do you mean?"

"Meredith said I wasn't ready," said George. "She said the world and their grandmother's cat thought they were qualified to read these days when it's an art reserved for a select few. She said my spirit wasn't perceptive enough yet."

"Nonsense!" said Sage, shaking a pointed finger at him before taking a deep breath and biting her lip. "I'm sorry, honey. I didn't mean to burst out like that. She's right in a way. Many people without intuitive abilities proclaim that they can read, and they shouldn't. But anyone can tell that you're qualified. It's obvious!"

"Yes," said Nat. "I agree. Go ahead."

"No!" George said. "No, I won't!"

"George?" Nat said softly.

"I'm not good enough!" He looked wildly about him and on the verge of tears.

Sage looked at him with concern. "Honey," she said softly, clasping his shoulders and looking deep into his eyes. "I don't mean to offend you, but this woman, Meredith—I don't know much about her, but she sounds like she was trying to hold you down instead of lifting you up."

"No, she wasn't!" George said, tears falling freely now. "She loved me!"

Sage sighed. "Can I give you a hug, sugar?"

George nodded and fell onto her shoulder gratefully. After a few moments, Sage released him. "There, better?" George nodded mournfully.

"If everyone could get a hug from Sage, the world would be a much better place in my opinion!" Roxy smiled broadly at Sage who smiled back before turning to George again. He was still standing limply next to her, looking down at the ground.

"You don't have to read if you don't want to, George," said Sage, her voice warm and soft. "But I think it would be a good thing. Tell you what, why don't I get an oracle deck, and you pick the card? I'll interpret. We'll do it together. Sound like a plan?"

"Yes," George said, sniffing and wiping his eyes. He looked up, but not at anyone in particular.

"Let me get this deck set up." Sage reached into one of the long pockets in her robes and drew out three decks of cards. One set had a picture of an angel surrounded by golden light on the backs, the second deck had a woman looking into a crystal ball, and the third had birds, crocodiles, and monkeys decorating a picturesque jungle river scene. "Which one calls out to you the most?"

"The angels."

"I had a feeling." Sage winked at him. She went over to the counter and spread the cards across it in a long line. "Now, what are we asking about? Charles, or Meredith, or...?"

"Everything," said George. His face crumpled for a second before he lifted his chin and stood a little straighter. "I want to know what's going on."

"Okay, good. Hold that question in your mind, and pick whichever card feels right," Sage said. "Go ahead."

George's hand hovered over the cards, the light brown freckles that covered the back of it standing out against his pale skin. He pointed at a card. Sage slid it out from the pack and turned it over.

"*Illusions,*" she read. "Let's read the interpretation, then I'll offer my own." She reached into the pockets of her robes again and pulled out a book with a navy blue, silver, and violet cover. The corners of the book were worn and creased. Sage flipped to the right page and took a deep breath. "*You are a true master of illusion, especially when behind masks that you wear for others. This is a gift received through the hardships of your childhood. Your ability to adapt, to pretend, was essential for you to get the love you needed.*"

George gasped.

"These masks can be helpful," Sage continued. *"You can bend to every situation and get along well with anyone. But they may hold you back from attracting situations and circumstances you desire. You sometimes fool even yourself with the personas you adopt. This card is telling you that you don't need to rely on these false guises anymore."*

Roxy watched George carefully. Did this have anything to do with the murder? Was *he* the murderer, and his "good spiritual man" persona just that—a persona?

"Now is the time to let the real you flourish. You are free to be yourself," Sage was saying.

"I'm not sure any of this is true," said George. "Maybe this reading is for someone else."

"Maybe, honey," Sage said. "But let me continue to the end." She glanced back at the book. *"Often, you pretend that you do not know the truth. You play dumb, and let others enjoy feeling superior to you."*

"Oh, my gosh!" said Nat. "That sounds just like how you were with Meredith!"

"No, I wasn't," said George. "Was I?"

"George, a truth punch is coming," Sage warned. *"Inwardly, you can be smug, secretly indulging in the idea that it is you who are superior to others."*

"I didn't think I was superior to Meredith."

"But once you step into yourself and acknowledge your truth, you won't have to play this game anymore. You will emerge as a true equal to others, both in the outer world and in your inner world. Accept the truth of who you are, and allow yourself to bloom."

George sank into a chair. "I've got a headache."

"I'm not surprised," said Sage. "That was a heavy reading."

"It was." George covered his face. "I'm embarrassed."

"Do you want to hear my interpretation, honey?" Sage asked him.

"Only if it's more positive than that."

Sage closed her eyes and took on a calm, meditative expression. "All right." She opened her eyes again. "Did you find any truth in the reading?"

"Maybe a little," George said into his hands. "I did let Meredith act superior toward me. She could be overbearing. By keeping quiet, I thought I was doing the right thing."

"Maybe you were, at the time," Sage said comfortingly. "But it seems like—I could be wrong—but it seems like maybe she was intimidated by your talent, and she threw you shade so that she could shine herself. She was afraid you'd eclipse her."

George broke down in tears. "I worshipped her."

"I know, I know," said Sage, rubbing his back. "It's not a good idea to worship humans though, honey. No one is perfect. They can't always have your best interests at heart, even if they want to. Do you get down on yourself a lot?"

"Yes," he said.

"And she put you down, too?"

"Uh-huh."

"You know what you need? You need some good friends to say positive, true things to you, to build you up. Encourage you."

"I'll go!" said Nat. "I think you're great, George." Nat took his hand and beamed.

George looked at her with a tear-stained smile. "Thanks, Nat," he said wearily.

"You're a genuine, kind, big-hearted person," said Roxy. "Anyone can see that."

"Thanks, Roxy."

"And I can tell that you have enormous spiritual potential. You could be a great healer; of hearts, minds, souls, and even bodies. See?" said Sage. "Doesn't that make you feel better? You don't need the stress of someone putting you down all the time, especially in the name of 'spiritualism' or whatever Meredith chose to call it. That's false prophet speak and not what this is about, at all."

"So...you don't think she was doing it for my benefit?" George said. "That's what I always believed. That she had my best interests at heart. You think she was putting me down in a way that would make her look better?"

"Well, none of us were in her head, so we can't know," said Sage. "But her behavior toward you had the *result* of keeping you down. Of you thinking bad things about yourself. Of you thinking that you're not even qualified to read an oracle deck!" She laughed, but not unkindly. "You're one of the *most* qualified people to read one! You care *so* much about people. And that's the most important thing."

George wiped his eyes again. "You think so?"

Sage gave him an indulgent smile. "I know so."

CHAPTER TWENTY-FOUR

GEORGE SMILED, THIS time with more energy. He spread his arms out wide in a stretch. "Well, we'd better go look for Charles, then. I'm worried about him."

"I'll come with you," Nat said.

"I'll go back to the *Funky Cat*," said Roxy. "Maybe he's there somewhere and we missed him. Maybe he collapsed in a corner or something. Who knows? I just have the urge to go back there. It's nearly lunchtime, too. Do you want to come back and eat quickly before you go out?"

"Thank you, Roxy," said George, "but right now, I have no appetite whatsoever."

"We'll grab lunch from a street vendor if we get hungry," said Nat. "It'll be quicker that way, and we can spend more time looking for Charles. George, we should check the hospitals while we're about it."

George blew out his cheeks at the thought. "Yes, I guess you're right."

"Okay," said Roxy. "Good plan."

"Sage, please let us know if he comes by here," said George.

"Sure honey, I'll call Nat's phone."

"And thank you so very much for that reading. I feel like a weight has been lifted. I hadn't realized how much of Meredith's energy I'd absorbed into my own."

Sage smiled. "You're welcome, honey. And I expect payment for it! In the form of you doing a reading for *me* one of these days." She winked at him. "May all the spirits guide you as you look for Charles. I'm sure he'll be fine. I can feel it."

"I sure hope so, and you can count on that reading!" said George.

"See you guys later," Roxy called out. She set off for the *Funky Cat* and Nat and George went in the opposite direction. Sage's talk had done George good. Roxy noticed a spring in his step, a light in his eyes, and a can-do attitude that hadn't been there before. Feeling lighter herself, she jogged all the way back to the hotel.

When she arrived, there was a squad car parked at the end of the cobbled street on which the *Funky Cat* was located. Her heart quickening, she picked up her pace as she ran over the cobbles to the hotel. The door was open, and she rushed in to see Detective Johnson pacing the lobby.

"You!" he said as soon as she appeared in the doorway. He spoke with such force it was as if he'd tossed a dagger in her direction.

"Um...hello," Roxy said. "How can I help you? Where's Sam?"

"The guy with that stupid car?" Johnson said. "He let me in. He's upstairs."

"Right..." Roxy said. She waited for the detective to announce why he was standing in her lobby.

"You've kept me waiting for 10 minutes," he barked.

"I didn't know you were coming."

"You were the one who called me! To alert me that Charles Romanoff was missing."

"Yes, we were at the *Palace of Spirits*."

Immediately Johnson looked suspicious. "What were you doing there?"

"Looking for Charles Romanoff."

"Well, that's what I'm here to do. Look for Charles Romanoff."

"I thought you were going to put an APB out for him." This was a very odd argument. Why was Johnson being so obtuse?

"Done that. But you may have overlooked something here. I've searched the common and service areas. Now I need to go through the bedrooms and the basement."

The idea of Johnson poking around all the bedrooms —hers included—made Roxy feel very uncomfortable. "He won't be in the basement. How could he get in? It's locked."

"If he was killed or apprehended, *someone* with a *key...*" Johnson squinted at her, "could have opened the basement and dumped him in there."

Roxy took a step back. His idea was ludicrous but Johnson's implication that she might have abducted Charles was chilling.

Five minutes later, Johnson came up from the basement. He hadn't let Roxy accompany him. She'd waited at the top of the stairs, feeling jittery even though she knew Charles couldn't possibly be down there. She had the only key. As Johnson took the last step he tripped over Nefertiti who he hadn't seen waiting under Roxy's feet.

"Darn it!" He nearly fell flat on his face and had to grab the wall to steady himself.

Nefertiti squealed and fled.

"Oh!" Roxy exclaimed. "Sorry!" She would have found it amusing if the situation hadn't been so serious.

"That darned cat is a health and safety hazard!"

"I'm sorry," Roxy said again. She gestured at the basement. "So...?"

"Oh yeah, he's down there," said Johnson, looking more annoyed than ever. He brushed out his suit creases. "Doing crochet with an alligator. They're both coming upstairs now to have a cup of tea. Put the kettle on to boil why don't 'cha?"

"What?"

"He's not down there," Johnson snapped. "Obviously."

"Johnson?" A voice floated from Johnson's radio on his chest.

He pressed the button. "It's *Detective* Johnson!" he hollered into it.

"Trudeau here, *Detective*."

"What do you want?"

"Time's up on Jack Lavantille."

"Who?"

"Dr. Jack. We have to let him go. We don't have enough evidence to charge him. Gun was clean, untraceable, and forensics said there was no way of identifying who shot it. The witnesses were bunched around a small table so close together it was impossible to work out the trajectory, apparently."

Johnson turned away from Roxy and walked into the

dining room so she couldn't hear the the rest of the exchange, but she could see him muttering furious words into his radio. A couple of moments later, the detective came back looking like he wanted to break the whole world in two. "I'll be in touch," he growled to Roxy, brushing past her so fast that for a second, a gust of wind made her short hair stand up on end.

She hurried out to watch him stride up the alleyway and get into this squad car. "Are you releasing Dr. Jack?" she called out after him.

"You'll find out soon enough," he shouted back.

"But what about Charles Romanoff? Don't you want to look in the bedrooms?"

Johnson glared at her and shrugged his shoulders before slamming the patrol car door. The engine roared into life and the car lurched forward as he drove it away at speed.

"Jeez!" Roxy said, as soon as he was gone. She felt the warm, tickle-y softness of Nefertiti press against her ankle. She bent down and picked her up, laying her cheek on the silky soft fur as she often did when she needed comfort. "The amount of frustration that guy generates could power the entire city, Neffi." She let out a big sigh just as her cat gave a big yawn. "I'll go and see Sam and update him on Charles. He'll calm me down."

When she reached the loft, Roxy saw the second round wheel-like window had been installed. The loft was flooded with golden midday light. "Wow!" she said.

Sam, who had his back to her and hadn't heard her arrive, jumped. He turned around, laughing. "Man, you startled me."

"I don't blame you, what with all this craziness going on," said Roxy. "That window makes all the difference,

Sam. It lights up the whole place. This space looks wonderful."

He beamed. "I'm glad you like it. I got that navy blue stain for the floorboards like you said. I'm going to tackle that next."

"I can't wait to see it all done!"

"So...did Johnson give you a hard time?"

"No more than usual," said Roxy. "He wanted to check out the basement. Charles wasn't there, of course. He wasn't at the *Palace of Spirits*. He wasn't at Dr. Jack's. It's like he's disappeared into thin air. George is so worried. He and Nat are out combing the streets for him."

Sam nodded. "I'm concerned myself. It's nearly 1 PM now. I've got a bad feeling."

"I have a bad feeling one minute, an optimistic one the next," said Roxy. "I'm up and down like a yo-yo."

"Shall we go out and look? I can put all my laundry van guys on it, too. I'll send them his picture if you can get one from George. Then you and I can go out in the car and search ourselves."

"Yes, let's do that," said Roxy. "I won't be able to relax if I try to do anything else. I hope he's okay."

"What's happening with Jack?

"They might be releasing him today. They don't have enough evidence to charge him, and they can't legally hold him anymore. I overheard Trudeau tell Johnson, time's up."

"That's excellent news," said Sam. "Maybe they'll start considering other suspects now."

"Yes," said Roxy. "We can only hope."

Her mind flew as she considered the logistics of leaving the hotel to search for Charles. "No one's going to be here at the hotel. Normally I'd get Nat to come back, but she's a big comfort to George right now. Sage is covering the botanica. Maybe I should call Evangeline? She might step in. And she could make dinner? Oh, but I don't expect dinner matters much. It's just for George, and I doubt he'll want to sit down to eat when Charles is missing." Roxy was rambling.

"Just lock up, Roxy. Put a note on a door."

"Yes, yes, that's a good idea. I'll leave a note with my phone number on it, just in case Charles comes back or anyone else stops by. I'll go into the bakery and let Elijah know what's going on, too."

As she crossed the street, a frown creased Roxy's forehead. There was so much coming and going, she could barely keep it all straight.

When she explained to Elijah that Charles Romanoff had gone missing, and she was locking up the hotel to search for him, Elijah looked very concerned. He insisted on handing her a big bag of white chocolate and macadamia nut cookies. "For energy," he said. "Are you sure you don't want me on the streets, too?"

"It's better if you're here," said Roxy. "That way you'll see him if he arrives. Plus, you have your bakery to run."

"Okay, girlfriend. I'll keep my eyes open. Good luck."

CHAPTER TWENTY-FIVE

OR THE NEXT two hours, Roxy and Sam cruised the streets in his Rolls Royce Phantom. Every now and then, Roxy caught sight of a man of Charles's height and stature. Her heart would stop, and she'd point. Sam would slow his speed as he drove past while she peered closely out of the window but each time, a closer inspection revealed the stranger wasn't him.

"My mind's starting to run away with me," said Roxy. "I keep thinking, maybe the murderer got to him, too. Or maybe he is the murderer, and he's taken advantage of the police's fixation on Dr. Jack to flee."

"Wasn't there any evidence to point to one of you in the room as being the shooter? Fingerprints? Ballistics?

"I heard Trudeau say there were no fingerprints found on the gun, that it wasn't registered, and that because everyone was sitting in such a tight circle, it wasn't possible to say from where exactly the gun was shot."

The Rolls was crawling along so slowly that cars

behind them were honking their horns. Sam ignored them. They needed to go slow—they didn't want to risk even the slightest chance of missing Charles.

"Move that big hunk of metal outta the road," someone yelled from behind.

Roxy turned back to see a man in a pickup truck waving his fist.

"Take no notice," said Sam. He was silent for a while, but he did pull over to let the cars pass before cruising off again. "I've just had a horrible thought," he said eventually.

"What?"

"What if..." He sighed. "What if Charles killed Meredith, and now he's gone and killed himself. A murder-suicide of sorts."

"But..." Roxy's head was pounding. "But when I've seen that before, on the news or whatever, it's usually done in one massive moment of anger. Like the husband goes into a rage and kills his wife, and then commits suicide immediately. Like it all happens at once. And there's lots of emotion, a crime of passion."

"That makes it sound almost romantic."

"It most certainly is not, but this feels different from that. Meredith's murder was planned, premeditated. There was no emotion at all. Whoever did it was as cool as a cucumber."

"You have a point," said Sam. "Yeah, you're probably right. I hope you are."

"I'm hoping he went out, forgot his phone, and then couldn't find his way back."

"Could be," said Sam, though he sounded doubtful. Roxy wasn't surprised. The idea seemed far-fetched even to her.

Just then, Roxy caught sight of a sign for *Modal Appliances,* the company she'd previously worked for as a customer service agent. She'd mostly dealt with irate customers who couldn't work out how to use their new or malfunctioning washing machines. Her memories hit her like a wave.

"Man," she said, slumping back in her seat.

"What is it?" said Sam, looking concerned, his eyes flicking from the road to Roxy.

"I don't know...it's weird how different my life is now, how fast it's changed. It's surreal. Just a few months ago, I was working in a call center. The job was so uninspiring, but it felt safe. All I had to do was go to work, do my time, go home again, and get paid."

Sam laughed. "You make it sound like jail."

"It wasn't much different. But in some ways I loved it."

"Okay, now you sound crazy," Sam said. "What do you mean by that?"

"Well...my whole life, I just felt kind of...unsafe, like there was nothing to cushion me if I fell, and that I was very likely to fall, like it was almost inevitable. Where I grew up, there was always someone hurting someone else. Robbing them, or attacking them, whatever. Life around me was always eventful but in the worst ways. Sirens went off constantly, cops came to arrest people at all hours, kids stole cars, fought, dealt drugs. There was always stuff happening, illegal, frightening stuff, always something for my mom to gossip about. She took delight in all the drama, was energized by it while I just *hated* it all."

"I can imagine," Sam said softly. "You feel things deeply. You're sensitive. I know some people say that as an insult, but I don't mean it that way. I mean it as a compliment. I think it's a good thing."

Roxy smiled at him. "Thanks. Not many people see it that way. Even me, at times. Sometimes I'd love a thicker skin."

"So after all that, you craved security and safety," Sam said, "so you got the most boring, most stable job possible. It makes sense."

"Yes," said Roxy. "Except I traded *everything* for safety. That place was dull, my boss was a bully, I had coworkers who couldn't stand me, and deep down, I knew I wasn't fulfilling my potential. I was restless but stuck and lacking in courage."

Sam nodded. "I know what you mean. I hate that feeling. That's what keeps me chopping and changing what I'm doing all the time. My father calls me a flake, a dabbler." He laughed. "Maybe I am, although I like to think I'm a polymath."

"A what?"

"It's a person who loves learning different things and who has skills in multiple areas. Others call it being multi-passionate. Perhaps that's a better word."

"I couldn't imagine any father *not* being proud of you. Maybe he is underneath?"

"I doubt it," Sam said. "But thank you, though. That's a kind thing to say."

"What makes you so sure he's not proud?"

"He hates entrepreneurs and business owners. Thinks they're lower class, unethical money-grubbers. And some of them are."

"What does he do?" Roxy asked.

"He's a plastic surgeon, a very accomplished one. He

works on all sorts of complex cases, disaster victims, burns, unique cases. He doesn't simply do cosmetic work, although he does that too. He's something of a hero in his field, a pioneer in new techniques. When he realized I wasn't going to medical school, he encouraged me into investment banking, but it just didn't suit me. I'm not that kind of detail-oriented, super-intense person. I like ideas and grand schemes and making new things happen! I want to have a big impact too, but in a different way from my father."

Roxy smiled. "Did you ever decide to implement the idea you had about training homeless people and giving them jobs?"

"Yeah, I did. I've got a couple of guys visiting the West Coast right now. They're visiting with an organization out there that does a similar thing with ex-offenders. They'll come back and give me a viability report on what they think, and I'll go from there. I've always wanted to help people. I just want to make sure it's the right thing—responsible, respectful, not patronizing, you know?"

"You *do* help people," said Roxy. "You're kind to everyone, and you already employ tons of people at the laundry. Your business helps them support their families and lead happier lives."

"But I want to do something on a grander scale," Sam said. "I want to make a *difference*. A big one."

"Wait! Is that Charles?" Roxy pointed out a man walking with a dog. "Why's he got a dog with him?" Sam slowed the car again and as they drove past, Roxy turned to see the man's face. It wasn't Charles. "I'm starting to get really worried now." She bit her nails, something she hadn't done for a long time. "Maybe that's why Charles disappeared. Maybe his memories were too painful, and he's gone and...Oh, I don't know! I just wish he'd come back!"

CHAPTER TWENTY-SIX

"I THINK WE'D better head back," said Roxy.

"Yes," said Sam with a sigh. "It looks that way."

Sam and Roxy had driven around New Orleans for hours, but there was no sign of Charles anywhere. It had gotten dark, and the rain was pouring so heavily they could barely see out of the car windows. The windshield wipers were pounding back and forth on the highest setting, but the rain still obliterated their view for all but a second. Seeing out of the side windows was impossible.

"I have no idea how we're going to sleep tonight," Roxy said. "We'll all be beside ourselves with worry."

"You need your rest," said Sam. "Do you want me to come in and take care of everything for the night, so you can sleep? I can lock up, take out the trash and get set up for tomorrow?"

"No, it's fine," said Roxy, smiling at him. He was so kind.

"Nat and George will need a lot of rest, too, they have been walking all day," Sam said.

"They're probably soaked."

Roxy was right. They drove back to the *Funky Cat* and found Nat and George trudging up the alleyway. They looked like drowned rats.

"Oh no!" Roxy said. She rushed from the car in the pouring rain and unlocked the front door. "Come in, come in! Come out of the rain." She waved goodbye to Sam, and he reversed back out onto the street. There wasn't enough room for him to turn the big car around.

Nat and George were so wet that their hair was plastered to their heads. Nat's mascara was running down her face in black watery streaks. George was shivering. They made squelching noises as they walked and left wet footprints behind them.

"No luck," George said. "We couldn't find him anywhere."

"Neither could we," said Roxy. "I'm so sorry, George. We can start again tomorrow."

George shook his head. "No. I'll eat dinner, shower, and go back out when it stops raining. I'll look all night if I have to." He was so exhausted he had to steady himself against the wall.

"You need to rest," Roxy said gently. "And there are places that are not safe in New Orleans at night. You don't know where they are and might stumble into them unawares."

"I don't care," he said, his voice strong despite his obvious exhaustion. "I don't care about rest *or* danger. I *have* to find Charles."

"Okay," Roxy said soothingly, calming him. She didn't object further, but the last thing she wanted was George out at night, lost or getting hurt, too. "Let's call Johnson, see if he's made any progress. Or done anything at all."

"Okay, could you do that? My head is spinning," said

George. "I can't see straight, and I can't think at all."

"Come and sit down in the lounge for a moment," Roxy said kindly. "I'll make you a hot drink and put together something hearty for you to eat." She secretly hoped he'd fall asleep and give up on his idea of going out again.

"I'll soak the chair," he said shaking his head. "Thank you but I'll go upstairs, shower and change."

"Are you sure you can manage?" Roxy said. "If you're dizzy it might not be safe to shower."

"I'll be fine," he said.

"Okay. What drink would you like?"

"A sweet milky coffee would keep me awake so I can head out again soon," he said.

"And you, Nat?"

"I could use a warm brandy punch."

"Coming up. I'll see you guys in a minute."

All of a sudden, the hotel seemed so empty with just the three of them. Evangeline rarely came over now, having tutored Nat in cooking skills so well that sometimes it was impossible to tell her crawfish pie from her mentor's. Now, Evangeline only cooked for them when they needed an extra pair of hands or help with a specialty dish. Roxy wished she'd asked Sam to stay but she didn't want to call him back—he'd been driving around all afternoon and was probably just as exhausted as they all were. Elijah would be early to bed in preparation for his oh-dark-thirty shift the next morning, and Sage would still be at the botanica. *Put your big girl panties on, Roxy.*

She went about fixing the drinks and an extensive exploration of the fridge uncovered some Andouille sausage gumbo. Roxy warmed it up and served it in bowls alongside some of that day's New Orleans French bread from *Elijah's Bakery*, its fluffy center and crispy crust the perfect counterpoint to the soft and spicy gumbo.

She walked back into the lounge with a tray containing George's sweet milky coffee and a warm brandy punch for Nat, two bowls of gumbo and bread, and a plate of the white chocolate and macadamia nut cookies Elijah had given her earlier.

"Charles!" she screamed in shock, then, "Charles!" again, this time overjoyed, nearly dropping the food all over the lounge's expensive antique rug.

Roxy put the tray down on the table and threw her arms around Charles' neck, even though he was soaking wet. Charles was wearing a light windbreaker, beige slacks the fabric of which was dark and wet down his thighs, and a pair of scruffy tennis shoes. He peered through his glasses that were spotted with raindrops and partially misted. His face and head were shiny with moisture while the little hair that he had hung down over his ears. He looked tired and cold.

Charles' attempt at reciprocating Roxy's hug was half-hearted. "Hello, Roxy," he said wearily. "How long have I been gone?"

Roxy struggled to answer. It felt like a week. "A day...I think? We went to *Bramwell's* and the *Palace of Spirits* last night. We haven't seen you since you went upstairs to bed when we got back."

Charles sank into a chair. "Thank goodness for that. I thought it had been three or four days. I completely lost track of time. You weren't too worried, were you?"

"Actually, we've been out looking for you all day, since we discovered your bed hadn't been slept in. Are you all right? Where were you? Where did you go?"

Just then, Nefertiti cantered into the room from the lobby. It was as though she'd heard Roxy's exclamations and wanted to see for herself what was going on. As soon as she saw Roxy, she stopped and then proceeded to stalk across the room before effortlessly launching herself up to her favorite spot, the chaise longue, where she watched Charles and Roxy with her piercing blue eyes.

"I'm sorry I worried you." Charles shook his head in disbelief. "It was all so strange." He clasped his hands in front of him as if in prayer and brought them to his lips.

Roxy was very curious, but Charles looked so disturbed that she didn't want to press further. "I'm just relieved you're safe and well. Do you want a drink?" She gestured to the tray she had brought for George and Nat. "Warm brandy punch? Coffee? Tea?"

"The punch sounds like a good idea."

Roxy passed him Nat's drink. "You just sit here and drink that." She reached over and handed him a deep orange throw that lay across the back of the sofa. "I'll bring you some towels. Nat and George are upstairs showering. They'll be delighted to see you. You won't disappear while I'm gone, will you?"

Charles gave her a weak smile and shook his head. "I'll take my drink upstairs. I'm going to change my clothes. I won't be long. I'll come back down, I promise. You all deserve an explanation."

Roxy rushed into the kitchen to make another punch for Nat, and because she felt she needed one too now, she fixed one for herself. She came back into the lounge with two warm brandy punches at the same time as Nat and George.

"He's back!"

CHAPTER TWENTY-SEVEN

"WHO? CHARLES?" GEORGE said, his face lighting up.

At that moment, there was a sound of footsteps on the stairs, and they turned to see Charles walking slowly down toward them.

George launched himself at Charles with some force. "Charles!" he said, a grin lighting his face. He hugged the older man tightly.

When George released him from his grasp, Charles looked at him with a grin. "Hi, George. I heard I worried you all. I'm very sorry about that."

"You did, you did," said George, his voice wobbling as though he were about to cry again. "I...I thought you were dead. That whoever had gotten Meredith had gotten you, too. I couldn't bear to lose both of you so close together. What a relief to see you."

"I didn't mean to make you worry," said Charles. "I don't quite know what happened. Shortly after we came back from the *Palace of Spirits*, something came over me. I had some kind of break with reality. I walked out of the hotel in the middle of the night and walked to Audubon Park. It was almost dawn when I got there, and it was just what I needed. I walked around it by myself, sheltering from the rain under the trees, watching the people and the wildlife. Do you know there are so very many species of birds there?" Charles wearily sat down next to Nefertiti who jumped away and re-settled herself in an armchair nearby. "I don't even know why, it was like I wasn't choosing to do these things, I just did them. I have no memory of how I got to the park and when I tried to find my way back, I got lost. I've been wandering the streets for hours."

"Why didn't you ask for directions?"

"I—I couldn't bring myself to speak to anyone."

"Like a spirit was controlling you?" George said. His eyes were wide and color was returning to his cheeks. "A dark, negative one?"

Charles shook his head. "I'm not certain. Going to the *Palace of Spirits* last night disturbed me, for sure. I was hearing voices. They made no sense, just words. There were other noises, screams, and the wind. I couldn't tell what was in my head and what was real. It was terrifying. Meredith had spoken of such things in the past, but I'd never experienced them myself until now. I felt like I was in a different world."

"You were," George said knowingly. "In some hellish realm, it sounds like."

"Sure was," said Charles. "I still feel a little strange now. Is there something I can do, George? To make me feel better, more stable? I don't want to take drugs, but I truly feel like I have been going mad."

"Sage has remedies," said Roxy. "All kinds and for all

kinds of things. I'm sure she'll be able to help get you into a better state of mind."

"Speaking to her might be very useful."

"Do you want me to call her?" Roxy offered.

"Yes, please. I've got a terrible headache and would love to lie down, but I'm frightened to close my eyes. Will she come to talk to me?"

"I'm sure she'd be glad to," said Roxy. "She'll be relieved you're okay. In fact, I'd better call everyone. They won't bother you, but we've been worried about you, and they'll be so glad to know you're safe."

Charles drained his glass of punch. "Aaahhhh! That was just what I needed. I'm going to take a soak in the tub, then change into my nightclothes. You'll send Sage up when she comes?"

"Yes," said Roxy. "I'll make sure she's the only one who disturbs you. She has such a warm, loving, motherly way about her, doesn't she? She'll put the world to rights for you. Everything seems okay when she's around."

Charles gave her a small smile. "Yes. Very much so. Well, goodnight then. And," Charles hesitated, a small shudder rippling through his body, "I'm sorry again for what I put you through."

"Goodnight, Charles," George said. He gave Charles another hug, a more restrained one this time.

When Charles had disappeared upstairs, Nat, George, and Roxy all flopped on the sofa and sighed with relief.

"Thank goodness for that," said Nat.

"Yes," said George. "I'm so glad he's back, although his story is troubling. There are clearly many dark forces around at the moment."

"You're probably right," Roxy said softly, "but let's not think about that for now. Let's get cozy with our drinks, and have a relaxing evening. Maybe we could play cards, or checkers, or something. Anything to relax and unwind after the day we've had." She pulled her phone from her pocket and scrolled through her contacts. She needed to call people.

"Cards! Yes!" said Nat. "We never play cards. I'm always meaning to." She rushed to the bookcase to pull out a card deck. "What's your favorite game, George?"

"Can't say I know any very well, except *Snap*."

"Oh, come on!" said Nat, digging him in the ribs and laughing. "That's baby stuff! Let's play poker."

"Oh, no," said Roxy. "Too intense. What about *Cheat*?"

"*Cheat*!" said Nat. "Yes, that's a *great* game!"

"How do we play?" said George.

Nat set about explaining while Roxy called Sage.

"Hi, Roxy!" Sage sounded cheerful.

"Charles's here, safe and well!" Roxy said into her phone, equally cheerful.

"Thank goodness for that," said Sage.

"He's feeling well, but a little weird. He's gone to his room and said he'd like to see you."

There were some muffled sounds of talking as Sage spoke to someone in the background. "They've released Dr. Jack. He's here, but he too needs peace and quiet. I'll be right over, honey, once I've got him settled."

Roxy called Sam. "That's fantastic! Shall I come over?" he said immediately.

"That would be lovely, but aren't you exhausted after today?"

"Yeah, but I'm feeling a little lonesome and it sounds a lot more fun at your place."

Roxy called Elijah. "Would you like to come over? Or is it too late for you? We're playing *Cheat*. Sam's coming."

"Why not? The more, the merrier! I can sleep when I'm dead."

With no small feeling of anxiety, Roxy called Johnson to let him know about Charles' reappearance. The detective wasn't in the office and his phone rang through to reception. Roxy left a message with the officer on duty, a small blessing that Roxy appreciated. She made up another batch of warm brandy punch while Nat patiently played a practice hand of *Cheat* with George.

"I don't think this game is all that ethical," George was saying to Nat.

"Oh, lighten up!" Nat said with a laugh. "It's just a game."

"Yes, I suppose you're right," said George, "although even games can be microcosms of reality. If we get used to cheating in a game, maybe then we'd think it acceptable..."

"Stop!" Nat tapped him on the arm and then gave him a quick side hug. "Stop taking everything so seriously!"

"Nat," Roxy said, hearing her stomach growl, "what are we going to do for dinner? I made this gumbo for you and George but with the others coming over..."

"I'm beat," said Nat, "*please* don't ask me to make anything."

"I wouldn't dream of it," said Roxy. "I can't see myself on my feet cooking up a pot of anything, either. What about takeout? Pizza?"

"Pizza would be perfect," said Nat. "What do you think, George?"

"I think pizza sounds wonderful," he said. "And

totally against my diet principles that demand I eat healthy, natural, colorful food to feed my spirit. I'm playing *Cheat* and eating pizza. What a day!"

Nat nodded. "Pizza's colorful! And it has vegetables. Come on, you can't be too strict with yourself *all* the time. Gotta let loose and have some fun, too! Besides this won't be any old pizza. This will be *New Orleans* pizza. How about a thin crust topped with cured pork shoulder, caramelized onions, and marinated artichokes along with a NOLA craft beer?"

"You're right," George said with a grin. "To celebrate Charles coming back."

"Keep those brandy punches flowing, Roxy!" said Nat, raising hers in the air. "Tonight's going to be a good, good night!"

Sage, Sam, and Elijah arrived together. Sage went upstairs to speak to Charles. Roxy ordered four large pizzas, with garlic bread and a portion of chicken wings on the side. She picked some chicken off the bone for Nefertiti. They played endless rounds of *Cheat*, which George became surprisingly good at, and when they had eaten and drunk enough, Nat gave them a slightly tipsy rendition of Billie Holiday's *Strange Fruit*.

Gently, she sang them to sleep on the couches, feeling full and satisfied and warm. It was just what they all needed after a tough day, but as Roxy reflected as she leaned back, her head against Sam's shoulder, her eyes closed as she listened to the slow, mellow lyrics that floated from Nat like sleepy smoke, they were still no closer to finding out who had killed Meredith Romanoff.

CHAPTER TWENTY-EIGHT

NXIETY ABOUT MEREDITH'S murderer continuing to roam the streets niggled at Roxy when she woke the next morning. She lay in bed thinking, Nefertiti nestled in the crook of Roxy's body as she lay curled up on her side. Roxy buried her hand in Nefertiti's long white fur, feeling the scruff of her cat's neck between her fingers, her fur tickling the back of her hand.

"I have one job, Neffi, one important thing—I *have* to make good on my promise to Dr. Jack. Even though he's been released, I have a feeling that Detective Johnson will still be on his back. Our favorite policeman will be trying ever harder to gather evidence against him, I'm sure of it." Neffi looked up at Roxy and gave a big yawn, her small, pink tongue curling outward sensuously.

Roxy carried on kneading her fur and talking. "When I make a promise, I do my best to follow through, it's only right. So today, I must take things up a notch. I have to find out who *really* killed Meredith. And that means I *must* speak to that scary businessman, Royston Lamontagne." Roxy rolled on to her back and stared at her bedroom's white stuccoed ceiling. "But not via that assistant of his. Perhaps Charles has his number. Meredith must have liaised with him directly at some point."

Charles was already in the dining room when Roxy made her way down. He was at the window looking out over the cobbled street. He looked much better than he had the previous evening.

"Good morning, Charles," Roxy said softly, walking up to him and putting her hand gently on his arm. "How was your night?"

Charles turned to smile down at her. He was a tall man, and Roxy was short. "Good morning, Roxy. I slept like a baby, thank you for asking. Sage performed some reiki on me, I believe that's what she said it was, and I fell asleep partway through. When I woke up, she was gone, and it was morning. I feel like angels have been stitching me back together in my sleep."

Roxy smiled at the imagery. "That's good. I'm glad you're feeling better. Can I get you something to eat? Drink?"

"I've been across the courtyard and had some coffee and a piping hot beignet with your friend, Elijah, already." He patted his stomach. "It was just what I needed."

"Perfect." Roxy hesitated as she attempted to formulate her request. "Honestly, Charles, I want to talk to Royston Lamontagne about...well, I want to talk to him. I was wondering if you had his number. And if you'd be willing to give it to me?"

"Yes, I have it. Royston gave it to me after...well, you know. He told me to call if I needed anything." Charles reached into his pocket for his phone before pausing, his head cocked on one side. "Roxy, are you sure you want to do this? You don't have to. It's certainly not your job. And I'm not asking you to. If you want to help solve the case, you're most welcome. I'm just concerned for you. This is a police job. It's not for you."

"Oh!" Roxy wondered how he'd known why she wanted to talk to Lamontagne. "I'm fine with it, I am. Don't worry about me. I'm tougher than I look. And for those moments when I fall, I have the best friends around me to pick me right back up again."

Charles smiled. "You're a brave young woman, Roxy."

She smiled back. "No, not really. It's simply that I believe very much in justice."

"That's very admirable of you. Let me get Mr. Lamontagne's number." He scrolled through his contacts.

Roxy tapped the number into her phone. "Thank you so much, Charles."

Charles touched her gently on the arm and looked into her eyes. "Thank *you*, Roxy. Thank *you*."

Roxy didn't waste a moment. She hurried into the kitchen, fixed herself a coffee—she was too wired to eat—then headed into her office. Nefertiti was sitting in a box of printer paper grooming herself, but Roxy was so focused on what she was about to do, that she didn't even notice her. Sitting at her desk, Roxy stared at her phone for a moment before confidently pressing the call button.

Royston Lamontagne picked up within two rings. "Who's this?" he demanded.

"It's Roxy Reinhardt, manager of the *Funky Cat Inn*."

"Who?"

Roxy drew herself up and spoke a little louder. "Roxy Reinhardt, manager of..."

"The *Funky Cat Inn*. Got it," he said. "Yes. I'm not deaf. Have we met?"

Roxy heard a small yip in the background. Lamontagne must have his little dog with him.

"We have met, Mr. Lamontagne. I was in the room when Meredith Romanoff was shot dead."

"Oh! The small blonde? Or the one with the eye patch?"

Roxy looked up. Unlike in her bedroom, the ceiling was wood-paneled and painted white. She pressed her lips together.

"Are you the one who showed up to my office unannounced?" Royston said. There was another small yip. "Stop it, Fenton."

"Yes. Your assistant said to call to book an appointment, so I'm calling now. I want to talk to you..."

"About what?"

"I think it might be better to talk in person," said Roxy.

"Why would I do that?"

"I want to talk is all."

"I don't do *talking* for no good reason."

"I wanted to see if you knew anything, about Meredith's murder. If you had any information that might shed some light on who might have done it."

"If I did, I'd have given it to the police."

"Yes, but..."

"Look, I don't have time to entertain any amateurs. I have a large and demanding business to run. Goodbye." Lamontagne rang off.

Roxy banged the palm of her hand on her desktop so suddenly that Nefertiti mewled loudly. She jumped out of the printer paper box and ran from the room.

"Neffi! Sorry!" Roxy called after her, but the cat was gone. Roxy half-rose from her chair to go after her when her phone rang again. It was Royston Lamontagne. Roxy snatched her phone up and banged the "accept call" button with the pad of her finger. "Yes?"

"Meet me at the club tonight. *XOXO*. Frenchmen Street. Midnight. You've got five minutes." The phone went dead.

"Oh, oh, oh!" Roxy walked back and forth as she considered what had just happened and what it might mean before grabbing her phone and her bag and rushing over the street to *Elijah's Bakery*.

Elijah, dressed in a violet suit, met Roxy and Nat in the street between their two businesses. A black shirt, tie, and black, metal-tipped, winklepickers completed his outfit. Roxy hadn't known what to wear but had decided to glam it up. She wore a rainbow-sequined, bodycon dress with blue shoes and a matching clutch. Nat wore what comprised 98% of her wardrobe—a band t-shirt, black jeans, and boots. It was chilly, so she'd brought a man's oversized jacket to keep herself warm while Roxy wore a shawl. It was 11 PM and the stars were bright. All three of them were in constant motion as they anticipated their night out.

"Okay, sugars! Let's be on our way," Elijah cried, rubbing his hands together.

"Where is this place, exactly? *What* is this place, Elijah?" Roxy had never been to a club in the city before. She had created all kinds of fantasies about *XOXO* in the hours since Royston Lamontagne had told her to meet him there.

"It's an underground jazz club. My friend Alphonse runs it," Elijah said.

"You really do know everyone involved in New Orleans nightlife, don't you?" Nat said.

Elijah shrugged. "Pretty much."

THEY WALKED TO the end of the street and hailed a cab. Ten minutes later it pulled up at the corner of Frenchmen Street. The driver couldn't get any closer to their destination. The way was barred by a band and their audience. A large number of musicians, Roxy counted twelve, were playing a combination of trumpets, trombones, clarinets, saxophones, and a set of bass drums. The loud, rhythmic jazz sounds from the impromptu curbside concert caused tourists, who had spread out across the street watching them, to dance, nod, and jiggle in time with the beat. Beyond them, clubs and stores were lit up in neon blue and yellow.

After pausing to listen to the band for a while, Roxy, Elijah, and Nat made their way down toward the club, and as they did so, music poured out from the buildings on either side of the street every few yards.

"Man, I can hear all kinds of music—jazz, blues, reggae, rock," Nat said.

"They play some of the best live music in the world on Frenchmen Street," Elijah said. "I'm surprised you've never been down here before, Nat. This is your home, where your heart is." They had to stop speaking for the moment as the sound from another roadside performance meant they couldn't hear each other speak. A quartet of men in pork pie hats blasted out jazz music from a saxophone, clarinet, drum, and a piano—on wheels.

"Oh, I don't kn—whoa!" Nat swerved to avoid clashing with a troupe of hula-hoopers who were walking calmly down the street, flickering, lighted hula hoops spinning around their waists so fast they were a blur. To their right, a man stood reading poetry from a lectern. All around them, locals and sightseers milled, causing Roxy, Nat, and Elijah to slow their pace to that of the crowd even though they were anxious to go faster.

"Wow, this is quite the place!" Roxy exclaimed. "It's like Mardi Gras without the costumes."

"XOXO is just there," Elijah called pointing to his right.

Roxy looked over, but all she could see was a big sign draped across the railings of a balcony that announced a musical theatre production later in the month. "Really? Where do we go? It's all dark." Roxy looked up at the building Elijah had stopped in front of.

"Not there, *there*," Elijah was pointing to some steps to the left of the building. They led down to a door, outside of which a big, burly man stood, and from which bright lights, the sounds of people talking, or more accurately, shouting, and the lonely strains of a trumpet, could be heard. Elijah led them down the steps, spoke a few quiet words to the guy on the door, and then beckoned to his companions to follow him inside.

When they opened the door that led into the cavernous space of the underground club—it was literally underground—an explosion of noise burst forth as a huge swell of chatter. The club was packed and the crowd seemed to heave as one. All ages mingled together, drinks in hand, half of them leaning in close to their companions so that they could converse with one another. It was dark except for the lights around the bar, the odd wall light, and spotlights pointing out from a stage in the corner.

Elijah inched his way through the crowd to the bar, nodding occasionally, clasping the hand of one man in greeting, waving to several others. Behind him, trying to stay close, were Nat and Roxy. They clung onto each other as they used their combined body weight to force their way through the throng.

Elijah leaned in to speak to the barman as he placed two cocktails and a beer on the counter. The barman pointed and Elijah looked over, nodding his thanks before taking the drinks and turning around just as Roxy and Nat reached him.

"Here we go, ladies. Mojitos for you and me, Roxy, a beer for you, Nat."

"You know, I'm a little more sophisticated than I look," Nat said tartly, taking her beer and giving it a swig in a fashion that disputed her statement. "A cocktail would have been fine."

"Where's Royston Lamontagne? Does he have an office at the back?" Roxy shouted hopefully. The noise was deafening.

"Oh no, this isn't Royston's club. He's visiting tonight. Looking for new talent, I expect. It's Karaoke night. Music promoters and record industry execs travel from all over to come here on Monday nights. Anyone can pick up the mic but this place is known for trying out up-and-comers who are hoping to get noticed. There'll be some really good voices singing on that stage later." Elijah pointed at the raised platform that was empty except for a mic stand and some speakers. Next to the stage was a piano and a drum kit. A sweaty man was weaving his way, hunched over, around the equipment, cable in one hand, a transformer in the other.

"Elijah!"

"Alphonse!" A slight, dark-haired man with skin that shone like spotlights in the dim light of the club embraced Elijah, slapping him on the shoulders, before standing back as best he could given the crush of the crowd. "What are you doing here?"

"We're here for the music, man, a good time. We're also looking for Royston Lamontagne. We were told he'd be here tonight. My friend here has a meeting with him."

"Really?" Alfonse swiveled to regard Roxy, looking her up and down. "Sing, do you?"

"Oh, no," Roxy gushed breathlessly. "I'm here about... something else. He told me to meet him at midnight."

Alfonse looked at his watch. "Yeah, he should be here soon. He comes most Mondays although he's been telling me to get some better talent in or he might stop coming by. The ones we've had in lately haven't interested him. I'll keep my eye out and give you a wave when he arrives."

"Thanks, man," Elijah said. The two men clasped hands before Alfonse was swallowed up by the crowd around him.

Another voice cried out, "Elijah!" Elijah turned. There was a crash from the stage. Roxy and Nat looked over and when they looked back, Elijah had disappeared.

"Now what?" Nat said, taking another swig of her beer. "Our connector and protector has gone."

"I guess we just wait for Lamontagne to appear. It's just a few minutes to midnight. Not long now."

"Look over there, a table. Let's get it, quick!" Roxy and Nat once again joined forces to shove their way through the crowd and scrambled to reach the empty table like it was a deserted island in the middle of an ocean. They crashed down onto the banquette in relief.

"Oh, but now I can't see a thing!" Roxy cried. "I'm never going to be able to see Lamontagne when he arrives."

"Stand on the table!"

"What? I can't do that."

"Course you can. Come on, I'll help you," said Nat.

And so, in her tight bodycon dress and her high heels, Roxy, helped by Nat, clambered onto the table to get a full view of the crowd and the door to the club. As she stood up, pulling down the skirt of her dress so that it reached her knees once more, she immediately spied the tall figure of Royston Lamontagne. He was standing in a corner near the bar. He looked exactly as he had at the séance. His suit was impeccable, his tie was thin and straight, and he continued to wear sunglasses despite the fact he was indoors and it was night-time. Under his arm was his tiny dog, Fenton. Lamontagne was talking to another, much shorter man whose rumpled shirt and rolled-up sleeves denoted sartorial credentials that were far less distinguished than his companion's.

"He's here. I'm going in." Roxy got down onto her knees and from there climbed from the table.

"Well, I'm staying put. You'll find me here when you're done," Nat said. "I'll take care of your cocktail while you're away." She winked at Roxy who took a deep breath, put her hands up in front of her and moved into the crowd.

Several minutes later Roxy emerged a few feet away from where Royston Lamontagne stood. And thank goodness she did. Jostled and inadvertently pushed along by the crowd, she had taken a long and circuitous route to reach him. Brushing herself down, and finger combing her short hair, once again grateful for the style's practicality, she walked up to Lamontagne and stuck out her hand, panting gently, her nerves having evaporated during her journey across the floor of the club.

"Mr. Lamontagne? Roxy Reinhardt, from the *Funky Cat Inn*. And Meredith Romanoff's séance. You asked me to meet you here. To talk."

Lamontagne looked at her. Or at least she thought he did. It was hard to tell what he was doing behind those sunglasses. She heard a drumroll and the crash of a cymbal from the direction of the stage. A bass guitarist began to warm up.

Lamontagne lifted his head to the stage and beckoned to her. "Five minutes, I said." He led her away from the club down a corridor. When they were far enough away that they could speak without shouting, he stopped and leaned against the wall.

"You're looking into Meredith's death?"

"Yes, um, as a sort of...adjunct to the police department."

"What do you want to know? Be quick."

"Well, how did you know Meredith?"

"I've been seeing Meredith for years. She gives me, well, let's call it advice. I've had many private consultations with her. This was the first public one. She's not been to New Orleans before. I usually see her when I'm traveling. This was the first time I agreed to meet her with other people being present. Big mistake. One I won't be making again, obviously."

"What sort of advice?"

"Adv...? Look, that's private. It's nothing. I'd ask her questions, and she'd give me answers. Sometimes I'd take her advice, sometimes I wouldn't. It was just a bit of fun, you know." Royston looked around. "Look, you're not going to tell anyone, are you? That I was there?" Lamontagne's little dog gave a yip and snapped at Roxy as if to warn her off.

"That depends, Mr. Lamontagne, on whether you've got anything to do with her death." Roxy could hear the band clearly now. Their beat was untidy and they weren't very tight, unlike the high, whiny voice that was currently singing along with them. Whoever it was, she didn't think they'd be scouted for a record deal that night, or anytime soon.

"Me? Are you kidding? Of course I had nothing to do with Meredith's death! We were associates, that's all. She gave me advice that I used to help make my business decisions. I've made a lot of money over the years, in part thanks to Meredith. Why on earth would I want to kill her? It would make no sense." Fenton yipped three times in a row in agreement. Lamontagne leaned down so that his lips were close to Roxy's ears. He was so tall that it was quite an effort for him. "If you want to find out who killed Meredith, look into that husband of hers."

"Why do you say that?"

"My assistant went to a retreat run by Meredith in Arizona. I wouldn't go because it wasn't private so I sent her instead. I was expecting great things, it being in Sedona and all. Those vortexes are supposed to be pretty powerful, but according to my assistant, it was a total bust. Charles ruined it. My assistant said that Meredith was harsh and rude during the retreat, but that it wasn't her fault. She confided in my assistant that Charles—because he didn't support her and her work—was causing 'energetic disturbances' that stopped her connecting with the spirits properly. She said that she had a vision that Charles was trying to kill her. Like he was trying to stop her from doing important work. I never saw him sabotage her but...Wait!

They both listened. From the club, the noise had died down. The crowd was silent, attentive. Roxy could hear the piano playing chords, just chords, allowing someone their moment to sing and, Roxy could tell, sing mightily. It was a woman, her voice low, deep, rich, awash with longing and mood. The voice swelled to a crescendo and then peaked as she belted out the chorus to a ballad full of sorrow and lost love. A few in the crowd whistled and cheered before being quickly shushed by others wanting to hear more.

"Oh my...Who is that? Who is *that*?" Lamontagne, Meredith Romanoff's murder forgotten, pushed past Roxy. "I have to see her. I have to." He disappeared through the open door into the club and the crowd that filled the room to bursting. Roxy stood where she was. She didn't need to see who was singing. She already knew. It was Nat. She was singing in front of people. Unfamiliar people.

WHEN NAT CAME to the end of her song, the crowd who had remained silent to the end erupted in cheers and applause. They drummed their feet and their hands on whatever surface was available to them. Nat stood and looked out, apparently bemused, perhaps confused, certainly unmoving. She swayed a little. Roxy stood at the back of the hall and watched as the crowd began to chant, "Who are you? Who are you? Who are you?"

Louder and louder they chanted as they pressed forward toward the stage. Nat looked around, unsure of what to do, fear beginning to cross her face as she looked from side to side, her feet planted to the spot. Cocktail umbrellas, beads, even a scarf were tossed onto the stage making Nat blink and stare. Then to her right, there was movement. A group of men led by Elijah appeared and barreled Nat off the platform. They formed a circle around her as they propelled her through the noisy throng to the back door where Roxy was standing.

"Get her out of here!" Elijah cried. "Quickly!" The

crowd had followed them and were now pressing in again, like a formless, mushrooming, many-headed monster that threatened to subsume them, gobbling them up. Roxy, startled, immediately grabbed Nat's hand. "Come!" she commanded Nat. They ran.

Outside, the cold air stung their faces as they sprinted, but it only served to propel them faster up the steps and down Frenchmen Street, and into the neighborhood beyond. "Can you run all the way back to the *Funky Cat*, Nat?" Roxy asked breathlessly. She hopped as she pulled off her high-heeled shoes one after the other to run barefoot.

"Yes, I think so, let's try it," Nat said laughing, the cold air making her eyes bright. "Phew, that was something wasn't it? I thought they were going to eat me alive. What a night!"

What a night indeed, Roxy thought wryly, feeling the wind blow her hair and her feet slap the pavement as they ran back to the safety of the *Funky Cat Inn*.

Roxy sighed and slumped back against her headboard. She'd packed Nat off to bed and was now sitting cross-legged on top of her own. It was 2 AM. Her laptop sat in front of her, the glow from the screen illuminating her face while Nefertiti squeezed into the space between the keyboard and Roxy's belly button.

Roxy considered everything Lamontagne had told her earlier. Could Charles really be the kind of person he'd described? Was his feedback, second-hand as it was, meaningful? Was Meredith right? Was Charles trying to kill her?

"Okay, *fine*," she said. She was going to do a little online sleuthing and see if the Internet could help her out. Her fingertips hovered over her keyboard. "Right. *Charles Romanoff*," she said, typing his name into the search bar.

The first result was his business profile, stating that he was—as he had told her—a pediatric surgeon in North Carolina with over forty years' experience. There were articles about his foundation and the life-changing work it did in developing countries. Roxy read that Charles had been recognized with several awards, as one would expect of a ground-breaking surgeon of his experience and stature. She quickly clicked over to view the image results. As she scrolled down the page, she saw pictures of Charles in his white coat, his green operating scrubs, with Meredith at events, with his colleagues, and out in the field among the people who lived in the impoverished villages where he did his work. She scrolled back up the page.

She stopped at a picture of Charles and Meredith. He had his arm around her shoulder. Meredith was dressed to the nines in an off-the-shoulder black dress and sparkling jewelry. Roxy peered in close. Behind them stood a woman. She was glaring, her red mouth twisted into a growl. Roxy scrolled back down the page again and suddenly caught her breath. Yes, there she was again.

This time, the woman was standing next to Charles, and they were surrounded by young children dressed in brightly-colored loose clothing, their hair cropped close or braided in cornrows. The caption underneath said they were in a village called Lietbhar in Sudan. This time, though, the woman wasn't growling. She was looking up at Charles, smiling adoringly.

Roxy continued to scroll. Sure enough, she found another photograph taken at the same time. The same village, same children, Charles and the woman, but this photo was different again. Not only was the woman craning her head to look up at Charles as she smiled, but he was looking down into her eyes, reciprocating. Roxy shifted her position on the bed. The scene looked a little too cozy for Roxy's liking. She thought that the look Charles was giving the woman wasn't of a type that would leave Meredith calm and collected had she seen it. She leaned back against her pillows and thought for a moment.

How had Meredith and Charles really been with each other? He had appeared attentive enough, but he had also seemed ambivalent about her work, sometimes believing in it, at others not so much. Meredith was also tricky, and Charles had looked long-suffering the first time Roxy had met him. She wondered if Charles might have fallen out of love with his wife. Or perhaps he was jealous of the fame and recognition Meredith received? Or he felt overshadowed. Or that she was a liability. He might have faced ridicule and censure from his peers and found her an embarrassment. Spirits and healings and readings were hardly compatible with a worldview steeped in science.

Roxy sat up again and went back to her search results. She clicked over to the foundation's website. On the *About* page, she learned that the woman in the photos was Stacey Wilson, a nursing administrator at Charles' foundation. She had worked for it for 20 years. Roxy's mind raced. Could Charles be having an affair? Was that where he had gone when he went missing? To meet with his mistress?

Roxy took a deep breath. "Calm down, Roxy girl. You have no basis for this thinking except for a couple of photos found on the Internet. Keep an open mind." She let out a big yawn with a groan but forced herself to consider the motivations of all the suspects before she would allow herself to sleep.

She had to admit, the murderer *could* be Dr. Jack. Perhaps she had overestimated his kindly, calm nature. It was possible that he had become so incensed with Meredith over the argument they'd had, that he'd decided to shoot her.

The murderer *could* be Terah. She might have killed Meredith in revenge for the treatment Meredith had meted out to Terah during high school. It seemed unlikely 40 years later, but it was possible.

It *could* be Royston Lamontagne, though Roxy didn't have a motive for him yet. Still, she could find one, she was sure of it. He didn't seem a very agreeable sort of person, and his lifestyle was of the type that would contain plenty of potential for shady dealings. She just needed to dig further. She was sure she'd find something.

The murderer *could* be Charles, a man who may be having an affair with his co-worker or may have felt his wife's livelihood an embarrassment, one that impacted him negatively or overshadowed him. Or he might have been so jealous of his wife's success that he was driven into a murderous rage. Oh dear, Charles had a lot of motives.

It might even be George. Perhaps secretly he wanted to break free of Meredith's vice-like grip over his life and gifts, or he had simply had enough of her humiliating him.

Roxy's eyes scanned her room, searching for something, anything that might provide a flash of inspiration.

Her eyes alighted on her purse. Meredith's book—it was at the bottom of her bag. Of course! Why hadn't she looked at it before? Maybe there were some clues in there. Roxy pulled the book from the bag, got herself comfortable, and immersed herself in the pages. There was no index, and while it was a thin book, it was no pamphlet. She'd have to skim it.

For half an hour, Roxy scanned the pages and found much that was interesting but not pertinent to her mission. The exercise was becoming tedious. She was losing hope that the book would prove to be of any use and was considering turning out her light when she came across some passages that mentioned George.

Nothing looked meaningful initially. Meredith described how the pair met—at a retreat she was running—and how he was "immature" in his psychic gifts, but very eager. Roxy got a bad feeling as she read the words. It did look like Meredith was determined to paint George in the role of a bumbling but well-meaning apprentice.

George came to me with an idea of how the spirit and soul interact, and I laughed at his spiritually juvenile ideas. Later, I explained how it all worked...

A couple of pages further in, George was mentioned several times in one paragraph. Roxy slowed down to read it carefully.

One day, a wealthy client from New Orleans came to see George and me. He was a businessman who wanted to use my spiritual powers to influence a business deal.

Roxy read on.

George and I worked with many spirits to produce the outcome the client wanted. It was strenuous work, and George—with his delicate constitution—ended up bedbound for three days while he recovered. I, being much more spiritually experienced and resilient, of course, was fine to carry on my work and life as normal.

The businessman, a famous, wealthy music producer, wanted to prevent a rival company from acquiring a major new talent.

Something clicked in Roxy's mind as she read these words. She knew she'd been given a piece of the puzzle, but it was just a sensation. She paused—her mind hadn't caught up yet.

"A music producer," she whispered to herself. "A major new talent." A moment later, she banged her hand on her quilt. "Of course!" She thought back to what she had read when she'd been waiting in Royston Lamontagne's office: Lamontagne's company had "bounced back" after a rival company had used Voodoo to stop a deal. One by one, pieces of the puzzle fell into place. Royston, far from having *benefited* from Meredith's "help" had *suffered* from it—when she and George had acted on behalf of a client who was a rival of Lamontagne's. Meredith and George had scuppered the deal that had caused the near-ruin of *Lamontagne Promotions*. Did he know they were the agents of his company's problems? Had he killed Meredith for her betrayal?

Roxy powered off her laptop, pressing the OFF button so violently that she thought she'd broken it. She twisted to place the computer on her nightstand, causing Nefertiti to give a little protest mewl. Roxy blew out her cheeks. She felt no closer to solving the case than she had when Dr. Jack had asked her to look into it. The only person who had been in the room with Meredith that she could be sure *wasn't* the murderer, was herself.

She had to come up with an *idea*, a way forward to break the deadlock. "I know!" she said, after a few minutes. Nefertiti looked at her mildly, her expression indifferent in the face of her owner's excitement. Roxy had come up with a plan. It was risky, criminally risky, but she was desperate. Her idea might be unorthodox, yes, but she was sure Johnson would forgive her once the murderer was in handcuffs.

"**Y**OU'VE ALWAYS FELT like an outsider," George told Nat, his voice wobbling. "Is that right?"

"Yes, and unconventional," said Nat. "Weird."

"But now..." George looked up. "Oh, hello, Roxy." He blushed. "I was just trying my hand at palm reading."

"Trying your *hand*," Nat laughed. "Get it?"

With her stomach growling, Roxy had walked into the kitchen to find Nat and George sitting at the counter. They were holding hands. Roxy shook her head and grabbed a beignet from a plate on the kitchen counter. She took a big bite. She was tired. It had been a very late night. "Yes, yes, whatever. Look, guys, I have the craziest idea. I think it might be slightly illegal. But I think Johnson might forgive me if it works."

"Illegal?" Nat said, shocked. "You?"

Roxy gave an awkward grin. "Your chutzpah is rubbing off on me. Watch yourself."

Nat frowned. "You know, Rox, nothing is *slightly* illegal. It either is or it isn't."

"Hmm. I plan to hold a reenactment of the crime scene tonight. I want to gather everyone at Dr. Jack's. Have someone act as Meredith, Sage perhaps, and have all those who were in the room with her the other night there too. I want to re-enact the murder to see how it went down, and if we can find out anything more."

George shook his head. "Terah might do it, Charles too if I ask him, but I doubt Lamontagne will play along. I mean, it is kind of intrusive, and he's a busy guy."

"You're right," said Roxy before grinning sheepishly. "But what if... the police ordered him to do it?" She raised her eyebrows, inviting their comments.

Nat screwed up her nose. "Johnson wouldn't do that for you."

"Neither would Trudeau," George said.

"Nope, you're right, again, they wouldn't. But what if the police officer calling wasn't...well, *official*?"

Nat's eyes opened up as wide as the plates she normally carried to and from the kitchen. "You mean, you're going to call them and pretend to be a cop?"

"Yep."

"That's dangerous," said George. "Jail-time danger-ous. Impersonating a police officer? Do you know what you're saying?"

"I know. But we have to get this case solved. And that's the best idea I've got. We have to flush out the killer somehow." It felt weird saying these things to George. She still didn't have evidence to conclusively eliminate him, but nor could she bring herself to believe he was guilty of murder.

George and Nat looked at one another, then back at Roxy.

"I don't know if it's a smart idea or a crazy one, but I

tell you what," said George. "I'll put a protective light around you so that no one can harm you, and that you'll get the result you want. I think that's the best thing I can do."

"And I can amplify that by setting up a shrine in the corner here." They turned to see Sage glide in the room, her sapphire robes wafting around her as she walked, her laptop under her arm. "I'm here to get your approval for the new website updates, Roxy, but before I leave, I'll place a crystal healing grid in the center and surround it with candles, mirrors, running water, and incense. They will magnify the impact of the protection field you'll be surrounded by. Then, before you carry out the reenactment, I will work with you to call the angels and make sure they travel with you. They will make sure you won't come to any harm.

"Thank you," Roxy said gratefully. "You are both fantastic. I'll call Dr. Jack now and get the room organized."

Nat shook her head in wonderment as Roxy made the call. "Is it shy, timid, little Roxy Reinhardt planning this?"

Roxy grinned. "I guess so!" She spoke into her phone. "Dr. Jack, can I use the back room tonight?" Roxy cradled her cell to her ear while she made herself a café au lait. "Is it open for use yet?"

"Sure," he said. "What do you want to do?"

"Um... just a little experiment."

"Sounds interesting," he said with a chuckle.

"I'll tell you later. I'm so glad they released you," said Roxy. "I was really worried."

"The spirits are working hard to free me. I can feel it," said Dr. Jack. "It isn't over yet though, Roxy. When Johnson released me, he said he was working to nail me.

According to his thinking, it had to be one of us in the room, and I'm the only one who had a disagreement with her."

"Don't worry," said Roxy. "I'm still working on it. So is Sage. It's all going to be okay."

"Much appreciated, Roxy."

"You're more than welcome."

Roxy hung up the phone and stirred two teaspoons of sugar into her coffee. Getting Royston Lamontagne to attend the reenactment would be her biggest challenge. She considered calling him right away but decided to wait a little longer.

"Hello!" someone called out from beyond the kitchen.

Roxy hurried through. "Oh, hi Sam."

Sam was walking through the lobby with his toolbox. "Hi, Roxy. How are things?"

Roxy followed him as he mounted the three flights of stairs to the loft. "Good!" she said cheerfully.

Sam grinned. "And it's still only 9 AM. Elijah told me you had quite a night last night."

"Yeah, it was a bit wild."

"People all over town are going to be asking who Nat is, you know?"

"Are they?"

"Sure they are. XOXO is *the* place for new talent in the city. Judging by the reaction Nat got, the music scene is not going to let her disappear into thin air. They're going to be looking for her. I hope she's ready for what's coming."

"I'm not sure she's even given it a second thought. I think she was a bit tipsy, to be honest."

Sam laughed. "Well, be ready for her. I'm not sure

how long she's got before she's found, and her obscurity well and truly disappears."

"Oh, dear. That might not be so good for her. I mean, she needs to stay on the down-low. I'd better tell Elijah not to say anything. His friend, Alphonse, runs the club. He saw us with Elijah. Immigration won't care a thing about Nat's singing voice if they find out she doesn't have a visa."

"Yeah, that's true. Be prepared to hide her then. She won't get a second chance."

CHAPTER THIRTY-TWO

"WHAT HAVE YOU got planned for today?"

"Today is floor staining day! Hence my glamorous attire," he said, gesturing at his scruffy T-shirt and track pants. "I'm gonna be covered with navy blue splotches before the day is out."

"I can't wait to see what it looks like!"

"Me either," said Sam. "Navy was a great idea of yours, Roxy."

"Thanks," she said. "I'm picturing a white four-poster bed, with blue covers to match the floor, velvet in winter... linen in summer."

"Sounds nice," he said. "I'll leave that part up to you."

"I need to get Nat up here for some more ideas. She's got a better eye than me. Then she can hit the flea markets looking for New Orleans antiques to spruce up the room." They'd reached the top of the stairs, just in front of the entrance door to the loft room.

"Well, just make sure she's not singing while she's doing it. Someone will hear her, and she needs to be our little secret."

"It seems a shame to keep her for ourselves. She would benefit so much from being able to express herself completely."

"Yeah, but if she doesn't want to get shipped out on the next plane, that's how it'll have to be." Sam sat down on the step and began to tie plastic bags around his shoes. "Just for a little bit of added glamor." He winked at Roxy and she laughed.

He tied up the second bag with a flourish and stood up. "Right, I'd better get to work."

"And I'm going to go organize my devious plan for tonight. Wish me luck."

Sam gathered himself and stood up. "Devious plan?"

"I'll explain later," she said. "I just hope it doesn't backfire on me." She hesitated telling Sam of her plan, unsure of his reaction and not wanting his disapproval.

"You're being very mysterious," he said. "I hope you're not doing something you shouldn't."

"I'm actually not sure of the legalities." Roxy bit her lip, wondering if her plan was a little *too* crazy. "Anyway, just hope and pray and wish or whatever you have that Johnson sees sense and decides not to arrest me."

Sam looked concerned. "Roxy, what are you doing?"

"Nothing, nothing much. See you, Sam." Roxy quickly spun around to go down the stairs, eager to be away.

"See you...," Sam said hesitantly. "Look, do you need me to do anything?" he called out. Roxy turned to look back at him. "You know, help fix something for you? I don't want you to get into trouble."

"I'll be fine," Roxy said, more confidently than she felt. "I'm sure it will all be just fine. I know it." But as she hurried down the stairs, butterflies fluttered in her stomach, and she wasn't at all fine.

She got back into her office and shut the door, grateful for the opportunity to be alone. There was a knock at the door, and Sage popped her head in. "Have you got time to look at these website updates, sugar?"

They spent a few minutes perusing the changes Sage had made. "All looks good to me. Thank you, Sage."

"You know, you and I make a great team, Roxy." Sage smiled her broad smile as she closed up her laptop. "We complement each other perfectly. Salt and pepper. Sweet and sour. Bread and butter. I am so delighted to be your friend."

Roxy leaned her head on the much taller woman's shoulder. "Likewise, Sage. Likewise."

"See you tonight, honey-bun!" Sage wafted away like she'd wafted in, her robes flowing around her.

Roxy thought about calling Royston Lamontagne again. Instead, she gave her laptop keyboard a sharp tap and opened her social media accounts, replying to every comment on Instagram and checking out the progress of the competition she was hosting on Facebook. The prize was two free nights at the hotel, probably in the loft room Sam was renovating, a free dinner for two, and a bottle of champagne.

An hour later, she went back up to the loft to take some new pictures—one of the wheel-like window at the end, and one of Sam laying down the navy blue floor stain —but she didn't linger. She posted them to her social media accounts and teased her followers about the grand reveal she'd do at the end once the loft conversion was complete.

There was another knock on her door. It was Nat.

Behind her were George and Charles. "I'm going to take them down to the riverside, probably take in a cruise. Wanna come?"

"Sorry no, I can't. What time will you be back?"

"Early evening, I expect."

"Okay, don't forget..." Roxy mouthed "the reenactment" and looked pointedly at Charles and George behind them. Nat raised her eyebrows confirming she understood. "Have a lovely time!"

Once they'd left, Roxy scurried across the alleyway to *Elijah's Bakery*. Elijah was in the kitchen at the back. He was building an enormous pyramid out of profiteroles. "What's up, girl?" he said as Roxy scurried in. He didn't look up, concentrating as he was on finishing his confectionary creation.

"Elijah, I just wanted to remind you that if anyone comes asking about Nat, you don't know her. We need to protect her from the authorities."

Elijah didn't say anything. He piped chocolate ganache on top of the pastries that comprised his pyramid's penultimate row, then using just his thumb and forefinger, eased the final profiterole on top. He stood back and admired his handiwork, a two-foot-tall construction made entirely out of pastry, chocolate, and cream. "There she goes."

"How do you do that, Elijah?" Roxy asked distracted from the purpose of her visit for a moment as she admired his steady hand.

"Chemistry, engineering, and a lotta elbow grease, lovely girl. Now, what did you say? Nat? Of course, my lips are sealed. She will be a mystery, a sprite, a faerie with a beautiful voice. People will talk about her, but no one shall find her. I will quite enjoy playing along." He drew his fingers from right to left across his mouth.

"Er, good. Right." Roxy wondered what Elijah was planning, but decided she didn't have time to explore things further just at the moment. "Thanks. Must dash." Roxy scurried back the way she came and slipped back into the *Funky Cat*.

Now that she was alone in the hotel except for Sam who was busy on the loft space, she buzzed with half-excited, half-nervous energy as she continued to work, her mind partly on her business tasks, and partly on the murder scene reenactment she was going to stage later. In truth, she didn't know how much information it would give her, but it was worth a try. She also knew she was procrastinating. It was time for her to call around to get all the suspects there.

"MR. LAMONTAGNE?" ROXY said, in her most serious voice. She briefly closed her eyes as she tried to calm her nerves. Her stomach had been in knots as she'd set her phone number to private. She lowered her pitch and added a little Southern drawl to her tone, hoping the businessman wouldn't notice the tremulous shake that was threatening to expose her as a fraud.

"Who's this?" Royston Lamontagne barked as he picked up his phone.

"This is Officer Anna Brown of the New Orleans Police Department, sir." Roxy winced. She felt awful—she'd never been one to lie, and it was a very uncomfortable feeling indeed.

"Yes, what is it?"

"I'm assisting Detective Johnson with his investigation, sir, and he's instructed me to contact everyone who was at the scene of Meredith Romanoff's murder. I appreciate that this is short notice, but we're holding a reenactment of the crime scene this evening at the botanica where she was killed. You are obliged to attend."

"What time?"

"7 PM, the same time as the original, um, meeting."

"I'm not sure..."

"It is imperative, sir."

Roxy heard pages flipping. Some people did still use paper calendars, then. "Okay. I'll move things around to be there."

Roxy's eyebrows shot up. She had expected much more resistance and felt a surge of relief. She forced her eyebrows to return to their normal position as she composed herself again. "Thank you, Mr. Lamontagne. I must impress upon you that your attendance is mandatory. Failure to show up could result in your arrest."

"I'll be there, Officer."

"I'm glad to hear it. Goodbye, sir."

Roxy hit the "end call" button. Her hands were shaking, and she felt sick. It had sounded like such a good idea in her head. Only now was she realizing how much of a risk she was taking. Surely she would get arrested.

She wanted to call Lamontagne back immediately, tell him it was all a joke and that he didn't have to go anywhere, but it was too late. She'd already committed the crime. There was nothing she could do to take it back. Her only hope was that she could uncover evidence that would expose the murderer. Then, perhaps Johnson would go easy on her.

Now that she had lied to Lamontagne and there was nothing to be gained by abandoning her plan, Roxy pushed herself to call Terah Jones. This time she played herself.

"Hi, it's Roxy," she said.

"Hello," Terah said tightly. "Called to accuse me, have you?"

"No," said Roxy.

"Hmm. What can I do for you?"

"We're reconstructing the scene of the murder tonight," Roxy said. "You know, to work out if we can deduce any more information about who might have killed Meredith."

"Who's we?"

"Um... well, everybody, all of us who were there—Charles and George and me and Dr. Jack and Royston Lamontagne. And you."

"No, I mean, who's putting this together?"

Roxy knew she was about to get a lecture on meddling in an investigation so she ignored Terah's question. "It's happening at Dr. Jack's place."

"Oh, sure, *that's* a good idea," Terah said. "Let's closet ourselves in a dark room, the scene of a murder, with the killer. They'll probably murder another one of us, you know, just for fun."

"I'm sure it won't come to that."

"You are far too sure of yourself, Roxy Reinhardt."

Roxy sighed and switched her cell phone to the other ear. "Will you come?"

"I don't know. When is it?"

"7 PM, tonight."

"That's not convenient."

"But everyone will be there," said Roxy. "You'll be the only one missing. It would ruin it."

"I don't know what good it will do, me sitting there with nothing to say, and all of us reliving our trauma."

"I know, it might come to nothing," said Roxy. "But there's a chance we might uncover something new, something that might make all the difference. I think it's worth taking that chance. For Meredith's sake."

Terah sighed. "Oh, all right. I'll be there."

"Thank you *so* much," Roxy said. "We'll get to the bottom of this."

Terah began to ask, "Are the police involved in..."

But Roxy only heard the start of her question before she hung up her phone. By the time Terah's question had registered, it was too late. Roxy fired off a text to George telling him that the reenactment was on and a few minutes later, he wrote back to confirm that he and Charles would be there.

Roxy sat at her desk for a little while, watching a tiny spider climb her office wall. It was a mighty task for such a little guy, and it had to scramble several times when it lost its footing. Each time, though, the spider recovered and went on its way, eventually reaching the ceiling and disappearing into a tiny hole under the molding.

As she watched the spider climb its Mount Everest, Roxy wondered what on earth had happened to her life. She'd gone from successful hotel owner to law-breaker in one phone call. From timid, beaten down, naïve innocent to brazen liar in just a matter of months. She'd had plenty of moments of doubt as she'd made this transition, but like the little spider, she'd recovered and carried on. Now she wondered if she hadn't gone too far. Perhaps she had. She'd now crossed a line, for sure, but recognizing her progress made her feel powerful. It was freeing. She felt unburdened, a little reckless, and a little scared of what she might be capable. She reminded herself that her transformation was for a good cause—finding Meredith Romanoff's murderer was paramount.

Roxy heard a clock chime outside in the lobby and

roused herself. It was lunchtime. She headed to the kitchen to make her lunch and Sam's. Instead of the usual po' boys, she whipped up some fried crab cakes. As she mixed the crab meat with flour, eggs, some seasoning, and deep-fried the mixture in a skillet, she thought about what she might learn later. She hoped that someone might drop a clue, or have a reaction, or some insight or memory that hadn't been remembered prior. Guilt or grief might prompt a confession, but that might be too much to ask for. Nevertheless, she felt excitement, optimism, and hope that the mystery of Meredith's murder might soon be resolved.

"Wow, what a treat," said Sam, when Roxy appeared with his lunch. He was standing on the landing outside the loft. He closed the door as she ascended the last few steps and sat on the floor. Roxy sat on the top stair. Sam devoured three crab cakes in nine bites and wolfed down the salad just as quickly. He drained the glass of passion-fruit juice she'd brought up, too.

Roxy laughed. "Looks like staining wood is hungry work! How's progress?"

"Take a look for yourself," Sam said, reaching to open the door.

The smell of the stain was so strong and pungent that it cut through Roxy's nostrils. The navy blue floor gleamed, though. It was still wet, making the floor like a vast indoor lake.

"Wow!" she said, standing. "This looks incredible, Sam! Thank you!"

He winked. "Only the best for Roxy and the *Funky Cat Inn*."

Roxy paused on the stairs and watched him for a moment: Sam, with his Rolls Royce, his good heart, his funds from a questionable source, and his helpful and protective ways. "Sam... can I ask you a quick question?"

"You can ask it quickly or slowly, it's all good with me." He stood now too, towering above her.

"I was just wondering, why are you spending so long renovating this loft for me? I mean, you surely have a lot of other things to do, and I could just pay someone."

"Are you saying you don't want me to do it anymore?" he asked, anxiety springing into his eyes.

"No, no, not at all!" Roxy said as she quickly pressed a hand to his arm. "I'm happy, no, more than happy, no, *delighted* with the work you're doing on it. But...it's just...you're such a busy guy, you could be doing much more good with your time, and I don't see why..." All the words twisted up inside her head, and she was sure he was getting her all wrong. "Oh, don't worry. Forget I said anything."

"No," he said. He looked at her with his kind eyes. "I enjoy doing this. And besides, I like spending time here. There's nowhere else that feels so...comforting." He grinned. "I like being around."

Roxy smiled back. "I like you being around, too."

"And I want you to have the best if I do say so myself."

Roxy felt she might be blushing. "Oh, thanks," she said. "That's nice to know."

"I really do," he said steadily.

He came closer to the edge of the landing. Roxy took a step up, their eyes locked. The tension in the air was loaded.

"Ow!" Something stabbed Roxy in the ankle.

"Are you okay?" Sam said, hurriedly. He looked down, concerned.

"Yes, I'm fine," Roxy said grimacing and rubbing her ankle. She blushed but with pain now. "Oh, I'm such a klutz."

Sam looked down and bent to pick up a screwdriver that was poking out of his toolbox. "Nope, I'm the irresponsible tradesman. I'm sorry."

"It's okay! It's fine, really. It's just a scratch."

"Are you sure you're all right?"

Roxy smiled as she let go of her ankle despite the still-stinging pain. She attempted to stand upright. "Absolutely. Well, I'd better be going. I have some work to do. Thanks, again, it looks awesome. The guests are simply going to love this room."

"Are you sure about that? It would be perfect for you."

"I know, but it looks so fantastic I think we should make it pay. It's too much of a lovely room to simply be my quarters."

Sam looked around the room, a cloud crossing his face. His shoulders sagged minutely, and he gave a small sigh before picking up his tools and getting back to work.

ROXY TOWELED HER short hair dry. She'd dressed casually in jeans and a shirt. Soon it would be time to leave for the botanica. She wanted to be early, but as she came out of her room, she found Sage and Elijah waiting for her. They both looked very grave.

"I might need you to play the part of Meredith, Sage."

"Okay, just give me a call to let me know if you do, honey, and I'll come straight there. Now though, we are here to get you ready," Sage said. Roxy frowned. "As we promised. The angels sent me a message that you need to be prepared. We're going to surround you with their gentle, powerful, protective force."

"Ah yes. And George was going to..."

"He will work his own magic. All the positive forces will compound together to look after you. Come on through to the shrine I've built."

Roxy looked at Elijah. "I'm just her assistant," he replied, shrugging his shoulders.

Roxy went into the lounge, and in the corner, Sage

had set up a table with a crystal grid in the center. Amber, clear, and black stones were placed in circles, a large clear rock in the center. Candles flickered, a water fountain tinkled, the room was infused with the fragrance of lavender. A granite bowl filled with dried leaves and flowers sat to one side.

"I've impressed each of these crystals with protective energies. And here in this bowl, I've mixed aloe, pepper, musk, vervain, and saffron. This will call the angels to you. Please light them for me, Elijah," Sage said. "Sit, Roxy."

Elijah whipped out a chair from the middle of the room and placed it in front of the table. With a lighter, he lit the dried flowers in the bowl. Immediately an earthy, spicy fragrance rose into the air.

"Close your eyes," Sage said softly. Roxy could feel the heat from Sage's hands as they hovered over her head. "Elijah, hand her the orb." Roxy felt a glass ball being placed in her hands. It felt cold. "Imagine a purple light surrounding you, Roxy, all around you, from the top of your head to the tips of your toes. Feel it wrapping you in its warm, protective aura. Now imagine the crown of your head opening and a stream of healing white light flowing from the top of your head, into your heart, and out through your arms and hands. Imagine ropes from your feet traveling down, down, into the center of the earth, grounding you, holding you still. See the white light above you, keeping you safe."

Roxy was feeling hot now. Her cheeks were burning; she could feel tiny beads of sweat on her upper lip. The glass orb in her hands was now warm too. Roxy felt Sage gently touch her head, then her shoulders, and finally her hands. "Take a deep breath in through your nose and out through your mouth." A strong smell of lavender again assailed Roxy, and she stifled a cough. "You are now prepared to embark on your quest. When you are ready, open your eyes, and be on your way, knowing that the spirits will protect and guide you."

Roxy opened her eyes. Before her, Sage pressed her hands together in prayer and bowed her head. Elijah reached over to take the glass ball from Roxy's hands. He pressed his lips together, raised his eyebrows and winked. Roxy felt wonderfully calm. She rose from her seat and left the *Funky Cat* without saying another word.

When Roxy got to the botanica, she was still feeling relaxed and composed. The setting sun, the darkening chalk blue sky, and the singing birds had kept her nerves settled. The bell above the doorway to the botanica tinkled and inside, she found Dr. Jack polishing crystals behind the counter.

"Greetings!" he said.

Roxy slipped noiselessly through the store to him. "Dr. Jack, I think I've done something rather...out of character." A frisson of energy almost caused her to shudder. The slightly reckless feeling she'd had earlier was back.

"Oh?" he asked, concern in his soft blue eyes. "You seem pretty cool with it."

"Yes, you see," she said, "I've been doing some investigating and well, it seems like everyone has a motive for Meredith's murder. I thought the best thing would be to reconstruct the crime scene. I thought that it might force some more evidence into the open.

"That sounds like a good idea."

"But Royston Lamontagne was being difficult, and I didn't think he'd cooperate, so when I rang him to tell him about the reenactment I pretended I was Officer Anna Brown of the NOPD." She smiled sheepishly, still quite shocked that she, reticent Roxy Reinhardt, had gone quite that far. "I...I...well, I impersonated a police officer."

"Ah," said Jack.

"He was the only one I pretended that to. With the others, I was just myself." She bit her lip. She couldn't decide if she'd been brave or as George had suggested, crazy. Every time she felt proud of herself for her action, a small voice inside her argued that she was mad. "Do you think I'll be arrested?"

Dr. Jack looked out the storefront window. "Hmm. You never know with that Johnson guy. He's pretty unpredictable."

"What about Officer Trudeau? Do you think he would take my side? Wait...I know! Trudeau!" said Roxy. "That's it! He'll understand." He was the poor country kid trying to make good, a little bit like her. He'd be much more lenient. "I'll give him a call."

"That's a good idea," said Dr. Jack. "I would be more comfortable with the police knowing what you plan here tonight. What if something happened? Think about it. One of us must be the killer. I don't want anyone else to get hurt." Roxy looked at Jack, her hand poised over her phone, her eyes big. "You really should get their permission for your plan, Roxy. It would be much safer and more honest that way. And that means it would be more spiritually ethical and accompanied by better energies."

"I'll call Trudeau now," said Roxy. She looked at the time on her phone. "Everyone should be here in about 15 minutes." She went outside to call Trudeau.

"Ms. Reinhardt," Officer Trudeau's voice filtered through her phone's speaker almost immediately. "What can I do for you?"

Roxy took a deep breath. "I thought I should notify you. I've invited all the people who were in the room when Meredith Romanoff was shot to Dr. Jack's botanica for a reenactment of the crime scene."

"You've done what?"

"Invited all the..."

"What did you do that for?"

"I thought it might help. Perhaps elicit some evidence or information that might result in an arrest."

"Oh, man. You do know you're meddling in an investigation? Detective Johnson isn't going to like it. At all."

"Yes, I know, but you don't have to tell him, do you?"

"I'm in the squad car right next to him, Ms. Reinhardt." Trudeau sounded genuinely sorry about that. "He already knows. You're on speaker. He's driving."

Roxy heard Johnson bark in the background. Her stomach sank. She decided she couldn't possibly mention she'd impersonated a police officer, not with Johnson listening in.

Trudeau began to speak, but his voice was muffled. She couldn't hear what he was saying.

"Johnson says absolutely not," Trudeau said coming through clearly now.

"I *said* I'll arrest you!" Johnson hollered in the background.

Roxy kept her voice steady. "On what charges?" She could hear the two men talking loudly to each other.

Trudeau spoke into his phone. "He says whatever he can come up with. He'll think of something. Stay put. We're on our way."

"No, no!" Roxy said to Trudeau. "It's okay. I'll just tell everyone to go home, and I'll go back to the hotel." She heard Trudeau talking to Johnson on the other end again. She listened hard to make out their words.

"We have to go to this other crime scene anyway, Detective," Trudeau was saying.

"You don't think I know that?"

"She says she'll cancel everything and go back to her hotel," Trudeau said.

"Tell her she'd better," Johnson barked. "Because we'll be over there the second we're done, and if she's still at that botany store or whatever it is, I'll lock her in a cell. TONIGHT!"

"You heard that, I guess," Trudeau said to Roxy.

"Yes," said Roxy, sadly.

"Better cancel it and go back to the hotel, huh?" Trudeau said, in an unexpectedly kind voice. "That's the right thing to do."

"Okay," Roxy said meekly. "If you say so."

CHAPTER THIRTY-FIVE

ROXY FELT CRUSHED, like all the life had gone out of her. Why had she come up with this mad idea? Why had she compromised herself to get everyone there? How was she going to find out who killed Meredith now? She slumped against the sidewall of the botanica and kicked a rock with her foot.

Behind her, she heard a car. Roxy turned to see a blacked-out Mercedes pull up in front of the botanica. Royston Lamontagne stepped out. He whipped shades from his suit pocket and slipped them on, despite the fading early evening light. Under his arm, he carried his little dog, Fenton. Lamontagne didn't look in Roxy's direction, but Fenton did. He bared his teeth and growled.

A swell of anger roiled up inside Roxy. She bared her teeth and growled back, wrinkling her tiny nose, and narrowing her eyes. Lamontagne didn't notice, he walked straight across the sidewalk and into the botanica. Roxy, her anger at her impotence propelling her forward, hurried after him. She'd been frustrated at every turn of this investigation. She'd been stonewalled, abused, diverted, suspected, and patronized. She would hold this reenactment even if it got her thrown in jail, even if meant the entire kingdom of angels turned against her, even if Fenton was treated like Lamontagne's handbag for the rest of his life! She had had it!

"Mr. Lamontagne!" she said as she crossed the botanica's threshold.

He half-turned toward her. "Don't talk to me," he said, roughly.

"Why not?" Roxy said.

"I have important business matters to attend to. When's this *reenactment* going to start, do you know?"

"In just a *few* minutes!"

Lamontagne held up his smartphone and gave her a withering look. She could see earbuds plugged into his ears. He sat down, still holding Fenton under his arm. He began texting.

Roxy looked at Dr. Jack behind the counter.

"How did your call go, my dear?" Jack asked.

Roxy took a deep breath. "Fine," she lied. She was piling lies upon lies. It didn't feel good, but she was in so deep now, she couldn't see what else she could do. Roxy leaned on the counter. Johnson and Trudeau would be here soon. What was she going to do? "Man..."

The tinkling doorway bell sounded, and Roxy turned to see Nat and George enter the botanica, deep in conversation. Roxy's heart flipped into her stomach. She wasn't expecting to see Nat. If Lamontagne recognized her from the club, there would be a commotion. Charles trailed behind them, jangling car keys with a rental company key fob in his hand.

"Hello," George said to them all.

Roxy dashed forward and put herself between Nat and Lamontagne.

"What are you doing here, Nat? Shouldn't you be getting dinner ready or something?"

"I thought I'd come and give George some moral support," said Nat, then added quickly, "as a friend, of course." She frowned at Roxy and leaned in. "Are you all right?" she said quietly.

"Yes, of course. Why?"

"You're acting all weird."

"No, no, I'm not."

Behind Roxy, Royston Lamontagne took his head-phones out and looked up at George with interest. "Meredith Romanoff's assistant, correct?" He seemed to not notice Nat at all. Nevertheless, Roxy took a step closer to her and turned around slowly to face Lamon-tagne. She hoped to shield Nat from the music producer's view, even though her friend stood smack-dab in the middle of the store.

"Yes, sir." George looked more confident in himself than Roxy had ever seen him.

The big man turned to Dr. Jack. "Give us a room, man."

Quickly, Roxy leaned in to Nat and whispered. "Look, why don't you go back to the *Funky Cat* and prepare supper for us for when we get back? We'll all be starving and have lots to talk about."

"Yes, why don't you do that, Nat? It would be lovely to have some of your gorgeous food to come back to." George beamed at Nat. She beamed back at him and after a moment's hesitation said, "Okay, toodle-oo." She waggled her fingers and walked out of the shop. Roxy inhaled deeply and closed her eyes. Her shoulders relaxed and dropped two inches as she let out a huge sigh.

Lamontagne was still talking to Dr. Jack, oblivious to the exchange that had taken place behind him. "The police aren't here yet so we can't progress with the reen-actment. I need a reading immediately."

Dr. Jack said, "You can use the same room as...well, the same room as before. Please." He opened the door to the backroom and stood aside.

George and Lamontagne filed past Dr. Jack. Lamontagne reached for the door handle, but Jack put his hand out to stop him. The big man turned to look back. "We need the door closed. We are discussing sensitive business matters. They are strictly confidential."

A shot of fear traveled through Roxy's body. Lamon-tagne and George in the same room? Alone? With the door closed? When Lamontagne may have already shot Meredith who along with George had nearly ruined Lamontagne's business?

"I don't think..." Roxy said warily.

"Roxy's right," Dr. Jack said. "I think we should keep the door open."

"That won't work for me at all, and it's completely unnecessary," Lamontagne said. Fenton yipped in agreement.

"It's fine, Dr. Jack," George said. His voice was sharp. Roxy felt the hairs on her arms stand on end. This was a much more confident George than she was used to.

"Are you sure?"

George lifted his chin and with his gaze firm, said clearly, "Yes."

The two men walked into the back room where

Meredith had been shot. Dr. Jack closed the door after George, his eyebrows drawn together in a frown.

Roxy bounded up to the counter. "What if one of those two is the killer, and something happens in there?" she said in a loud whisper to Dr. Jack. Her cheeks were flushed pink with alarm.

"My thoughts exactly," Dr. Jack said. His expression was grim. His eyes were dark and his lips were pressed into a thin line.

Just then, Roxy's face brightened. Her mind worked quickly. "The bathroom!" Roxy darted over, slipping inside and locking the door quickly. She sat on top of the toilet lid as Trudeau had done before her and pressed her ear up against the wall. *Yes!* Just as she'd hoped, she could hear George and Royston's conversation through the wall.

"Before we start," Lamontagne was saying, "do you know who killed Meredith?"

"No," said George.

Lamontagne snorted. "Some spiritual gifts you've got. Shouldn't they reveal things like that?"

"Not necessarily!" George shot back. Roxy could imagine the tops of his freckled ears turning pink.

"Look, you were just Meredith's assistant. You're nothing special. The only reason I'm talking to you now is that I have some very important business going down, and I need guidance."

"I am very capable, sir. The only reason you aren't familiar with the strength of my gifts is that Meredith prevented me from showing them to you. She didn't want me to outshine her. But now that she's gone, my powers are unfettered, and the spirits are talking to me loud and clear."

There was a long silence, and Roxy's racing thoughts rushed to fill it up. Royston Lamontagne was not acting like a killer who had a vendetta against George, and Roxy imagined the younger, shorter man's cornflower blue eyes blazing as he talked back to him. Had someone got to George, boosted his confidence? Nat perhaps? Or had George *pretended* to be sweet and wholesome this whole time? Roxy shook her head, trying to shake some sense into herself. George couldn't be the murderer, surely? If that were true, Roxy would feel for Nat. George was the best friend she'd made in a long time. Oh, this was all so confusing.

"Whatever," said Royston through the wall. "Right now, you're my only option. Give me my reading. I want to see what comes up."

Roxy continued to listen, her heart thudding so loudly that she worried they'd be able to hear it on the other side of the wall. George began to give Royston a reading from the cards he now carried in his pocket. As he did so, she looked in the bathroom mirror at herself. She noted her small body and short blonde hair. Other people may have seen a sweet, pliant, kind young woman who looked younger than her age, but as Roxy stared into her own eyes, all she saw was grit and determination. "Whoever you are, I'll get you," she whispered. "I will."

KNOCK, KNOCK. THERE was a rap at the bathroom door. Roxy leaned over and opened it.

"Hello," Terah said, scanning Roxy like she was assessing enemy territory for threats. With her one good eye, she took in Roxy's unusual position on the toilet and then looked up into her face.

"Hi, Terah," Roxy replied, her eyes shining and her voice unnaturally bright. "Not long until we start now. All we have to do is wait for George and Royston to finish their reading, then we can begin the reenactment."

"I hope it's not too long," said Terah. "I've got the German Shepherds tied outside, and they don't like being restricted for long."

Roxy glanced through the open door and saw the large dogs lounging outside on a patch of grass out front, shaded from the early evening sun by a tree. They were muzzled. She seriously hoped that Terah was *not* the killer.

"Is there anything I can do to make you feel more comfortable while we wait?" Roxy asked.

"Yes, please," Terah said tightly and gave the least genuine smile Roxy had seen in a long time, probably since she last saw her co-workers at Modal Appliances. "You could leave. I'd like to use, um, the bathroom."

Roxy sat up. "Oh, right. What for exactly?"

Terah eyed Roxy strangely again, "For the purposes you usually associate with a bathroom."

"Oh! Yes, of course." Roxy jumped up and squeezed past Terah. "I'd completely forgotten where I was. Excuse me."

Outside in the botanica, the bathroom door shut behind her, Roxy folded her arms around her waist and drummed her fingertips against her arms, willing Terah to hurry up. She didn't like leaving George and Royston unobserved. Royston still had a very strong motive for wanting George dead. After a couple of minutes, Terah having not emerged, Roxy walked up to the counter.

"I'm worried, Dr. Jack. One of them in the back room could be the killer. I don't like them being alone in there together."

"They're not alone. Charles has just gone in," Dr. Jack said. As he said it, there was a yell from the back room, and a thump as something hit the wall.

"Oh, my gosh!" Roxy ran to the door and tried to push it open, but it wouldn't budge. Shouts and more thumps were coming from inside. She tried again, but still, the door wouldn't give way. "Dr. Jack! The door's stuck! We must get inside," she said. The sound of a scream rose from inside the room, followed by a crash and a heavy thud.

"What's going on?" said Terah Jones, rushing up.

"No time to explain!" said Roxy. She stepped to one side as Dr. Jack tried the door, but he couldn't open it either.

"Come on!" Roxy said.

Dr. Jack pressed his whole weight against it, and it budged a little way. "It looks like something's pressed up against the door. Stand back!" Terah and Roxy gave Jack room as he ran at the door with his shoulder.

"I'm not getting involved," Roxy heard Terah say before there was a big bang as Dr. Jack burst through the door in a charge that was very unspiritual-like in its execution.

As soon as he was through, Dr. Jack stopped dead in his tracks. Roxy rushed up behind him and peered around his body. "Look," he said. The window was wide open. The curtains flapped a little in the breeze. Jack edged toward the light, looking around the room. Roxy heard a moan. On the floor, lay the long, languid figure of Royston Lamontagne. He was holding his head in one hand, the other covered his eyes as he rolled from side to side. Fenton was scurrying around the edge of the room, yipping constantly as he looked for a means of escape.

"Where are Charles and George?" Roxy whispered.

"They must have gone out through the window." Dr. Jack turned to her, his eyes wide. "Roxy, what the heck is going on?"

"I don't know, Dr. Jack, I don't know! Could one of them have taken the other hostage? Or are *both* of them involved together?" They stared at each other as the ramifications of what Roxy had just said dawned on them.

The screaming sounds of police sirens filled the air.

Roxy and Dr. Jack looked out of the open window to see two squad cars coming to an abrupt halt at the curb. Johnson and Trudeau jumped out of the first as horns continued to blare and lights flashed. Under the tree, the German Shepherds jumped to their feet and pulled at their leashes, barking loudly. Their muzzles prevented them from being more threatening, but their bared teeth and rigid, tense musculature were intimidating none-theless. Johnson and Trudeau eyed them carefully and gave them a wide berth.

"Roxy Reinhardt!" Johnson barked, striding inside the botanica.

"Detective Johnson!" she said, rushing from the back room into the store. "I'm so glad you're here. I have to tell you..."

"You are under arrest for impersonating a police offi-cer," Johnson said, slapping the cuffs on her wrists. "You have the right to remain silent and refuse to answer ques-tions. Anything you say may be used against you in a court of law..."

"What?" said Dr. Jack. "No!"

"You have the right to consult an attorney before speaking to the police and to have an attorney present during questioning now or in the future." Trudeau took over from Johnson, speaking so fast Roxy would have barely been able to understand him even if a torrent of blood hadn't been rushing through her head so loudly that she could barely hear anything at all. "If you cannot afford an attorney, one will be appointed for you before any questioning if you wish."

"No! Look! Listen! I..."

"Yada, yada, yada," Johnson said.

"How did you know?" Roxy asked.

"How did I know what?"

"That I pretended to be a police officer?"

"We're detectives, Ms. Reinhardt. It's our job to ask questions and find out things. You know, *detect*. Come on, let's continue this down at the station. You're headed for a cell, Roxy Reinhardt. Finally."

He clasped her upper arm so tightly that the force of his grip almost lifted her from the ground. He practically carried her to the patrol car. As he passed Terah who had flattened herself against the wall of the botanica, he nodded briefly.

Dr. Jack rushed around them and blocked Johnson's path.

"Don't arrest her," he said, "please."

"She committed a crime."

"She means no harm. She was just trying to..."

"I don't care if she was trying to feed orphans in Bangladesh," said Johnson. "A crime is a crime."

"Please, Detective, listen..." said Roxy.

"*Trudeau!*" he hollered.

"Please, Detective Johnson," she continued. "I was just working on the mystery of Meredith's murder. Charles and George have disappeared. Charles is driving a rental car. I saw him carrying the car keys. One of them, or both of them, have beaten up Royston Lamontagne. Someone could be in danger, or two people could be getting away..."

"You think I care about your cute story?" Johnson said.

"Who's in danger, Roxy?" Trudeau asked.

"Get her in the car!" Johnson barked, pushing Roxy at him.

"Hey!" Dr. Jack said. "Don't manhandle her like that!"

"Excuse me?" Johnson said. "And don't think I haven't got my eye on you, *Doctor*. You're not out of the woods yet."

"George has been kidnapped!" Roxy shouted as Officer Trudeau led her toward the squad car. "I think!"

"A likely story," Johnson said. "Just another one of your lies. Impersonating a crack detective now, are you?"

"No!" Roxy said, struggling against Trudeau's firm grip. For such a tiny slip of a woman, her efforts were laudable but ultimately fruitless. "I *know* I made a mistake. A big mistake. I shouldn't have pretended to be a police officer. But I..."

"Don't bother," Officer Trudeau said quietly. "Get in the car, then we'll talk."

"But..."

"Just trust me," he said. "This'll work out. I believe you."

"You do?" She looked at him carefully, studying him.

He looked back, his eyes clear and free of mischief or malice. "I do. Get in the car."

Roxy got in the backseat, finding it hard to maneuver herself with cuffs on her wrists even though they were quite loose, her wrists being tiny. She watched out of the police car window at the scene unfolding in front of the botanica.

Terah had come out to see her drive off while Dr. Jack was remonstrating fiercely with Johnson, his arms flying around, gesturing toward Roxy in the car.

In the back seat, the only thing Roxy could hear was Johnson hollering, "If you don't shut the heck up right now, I'll throw *you* in jail! *Again.*" Johnson's anger was making the German Shepherds a few feet away from him even more agitated, and they continued to bark without letting up.

Having shouted Dr. Jack down, Johnson stormed back to the patrol car, yanked the door open, and climbed into the passenger seat. He turned around to give Roxy a gleeful glare. "You just think you can do anything, don't 'cha?"

"I'm sorry!" Roxy said desperately. "I don't know what I was thinking. But *seriously,* George and Charles are missing, and I think..."

"You don't need to concern yourself with any of that," said Johnson. "I'd advise you to sit back in your seat, be quiet, and think about the disastrous consequences your recent actions are going to have on your formerly pretty little life."

Trudeau got behind the wheel while Roxy, on the brink of crying with frustration, flung herself back in the seat and leaned her head against the headrest. Part of her still had the energy to protest, to repeatedly tell the two policemen that they were letting a murderer, maybe two, get away, but the futility of her situation weighed on her.

She slumped back against the worn leather and looked miserably out of the window as Trudeau started up the car and cruised back to the station. It began to rain heavily, seemingly out of nowhere, and the rhythmic drumming of the rain against the window began to settle her. She tipped her head forward and leaned it against the windowpane, feeling with relief the coolness of the glass against her skin.

Roxy had been arrested. The indignity made her feel small. She considered what Detective Johnson had said— how might her arrest affect the rest of her life?

Maybe there would be a big fine. Or a short period of jail time. She thought about her friends. Nat and Sam and Sage and Elijah would hold down the fort, maybe employ someone in the interim to keep things ticking over— wouldn't they?

But what if they didn't? What if they fired her and hired someone else? What if they banded together, called her a criminal, and let her languish in jail? What if they refused to return her letters, her calls? What if they adopted out Nefertiti, and Roxy lost her too?

Roxy's mind had turned as dark as the sky. Her thoughts made her feel sick and her palms sweat. Exhausted, she closed her eyes and focused on the thrum of the patrol car's engine as it cruised to its destination, bracing herself despite her cuffed hands against the bumps and jolts as they navigated the city streets. When they arrived out in front of the police station they had to park some way from the entrance. Johnson treated himself to the only umbrella leaving Trudeau to escort Roxy in the pouring rain. At least Trudeau had his police cap.

By the time she stepped into the police station, Roxy was shivering from cold and shock. She was drenched through, her clothes stuck to her. She looked and felt thoroughly miserable. In the dingy lobby, a scruffy man ahead of her emptied his pockets at the custody desk while an exhausted woman slept on one of the chairs, a free newspaper sliding off her lap onto the floor as she snored.

Roxy felt the weight of her lost hopes and dreams pull

down her shoulders. Was this now her *life?* Disgrace? Humiliation? Loneliness? She thought back to her childhood. She felt she'd come full circle and then some. And now there was the question of George. And Charles. She might be disgraced, but what had happened to them?

"I'M DONE FOR the night," Johnson said. "I haven't time to talk to you now. Trudeau is in charge until I get back. We're busy chasing down the other two. Don't even *think* of doing any funny business." Roxy was sitting behind bars, her head spinning. "There are cameras in these cells, and I'll have Trudeau reporting back to me with regular updates." Johnson strode away but turned back. "I always knew you were trouble. Maybe now you'll learn not to meddle."

Roxy could not believe where she was. She was too stunned to cry or even feel any emotion at all. She sat on the cold hard bench, wringing her hands. All she could hear was the ticking of the wall clock in the hallway. Time dragged painfully slowly.

She wondered where George and Charles were. Was one of them in terrible danger? And if so, which one? She imagined them in a cemetery, Charles coolly lining George up with one of the graves so that he fell into it once Charles had shot him. She found it a struggle to visualize the scene, so she tried to imagine George shooting Charles in a temper, his hand shaking, his eyes bright with fury. She couldn't visualize that scene at all.

"Officer Trudeau!" she called out. She shook the bars of her cell putting her entire body weight behind the action, but all they did was rattle. Nobody came. Her voice echoed around the empty corridor outside her cell and died without getting any response.

Roxy sat on the bench for what felt like an eternity until finally, she heard the click of a door opening down the hallway. She rushed to the bars.

"Roxy." It was Trudeau.

"Officer Trudeau!" she said her body flooding with relief. "You must help me. This case has gone very wrong. Seriously, we have to do something. People could be in danger!"

"Yeah, I hear you." He unlocked the door and came into her cell, locking the door again behind him.

Roxy told him everything—how Meredith had stolen Terah's boyfriend, how Lamontagne had lost a major business deal thanks to Voodoo performed by Meredith and George, what Lamontagne had told her about Charles being unsupportive of his wife, and her suspicions that he was trying to kill her, Roxy's concerns that Charles was being unfaithful, and finally how George had been abused and downtrodden by his boss.

"Wow, it seems she made a lot of enemies. They all have a motive," Trudeau said.

"When I set up the reenactment, I had no idea who the murderer was. I thought it was most likely Lamontagne. I thought it might jog memories or someone might say something incriminating. But now they've disappeared, I think it must be George or Charles, or perhaps they are in cahoots together!" Roxy started to wring her hands again.

"Okay, okay, calm down. I understand what you're saying."

"Oh, thank goodness! Thank you for believing me!"

"Now I didn't say that missy, but we are on the case."

Trudeau's radio crackled. He pressed the button on the side and lifted it slightly so he could hear what was being said. "Suspect sighting AEO123KO. Leonidas heading south toward Oak. 35 covering." It made no sense to Roxy, but Trudeau's eyes lit up. He spoke briefly into the radio, "35 stay back. 43 on its way."

"I gotta run," he said rattling his keys. "That was good news."

"Huh?" Her situation seemed so dire that Roxy could barely process what he was saying.

"Romanoff's car has been sighted. They're still in the city. We put an APB out for them before we left the botanica."

"Oh, that's fantastic!" Roxy said. Her eyes shone, and now she clasped her hands together.

"I'm gonna follow up now. Perhaps we can bring them in before Detective Johnson even knows they've been spotted." He turned and stepped out of Roxy's cell, grabbing the door.

Roxy quickly stuck out her hand to prevent him from closing it. "Can I... can I come with you? I might be able to help."

Trudeau grimaced. "Absolutely not, Roxy. You're under arrest. Johnson will have my head."

"Please," she said. "I did give you all that intel. And I know them well. I might be able to advise you on how to approach when you find them. Yes, that's it—you *need* me there. And besides, when you solve the case, Johnson won't be able to say anything bad. You might even get a promotion." Roxy's words came out in a rush. She looked so eager—her eyes open wide, her eyebrows up as far as they could go, her whole body tense as she awaited Trudeau's answer. Her eagerness made her look even younger than normal.

Trudeau regarded her. She could see him weighing the arguments. "Oh alright! You can come, but I'll have to cuff you, otherwise, *I'm* breaking the law, and we'll both end up in jail."

"That's fine," said Roxy quickly. "Hurry, I don't want them to get away. And I definitely don't want to be sitting in here, wondering what's going on."

"Don't do anything funny or stupid. Remember, you're still in police custody."

"Don't worry," said Roxy. "I won't do a thing."

Trudeau led her out of the cell and handcuffed her wrists in front of her. They hurried through the police station and got in the squad car, all the while Trudeau listening to his radio following the communication between Control and the car that was on Charles' tail.

"Right," Trudeau said. He buckled Roxy in the front passenger seat before looking down at his police-issue phone. Roxy watched as he navigated to a tracking app.

"Where is he?" she blurted out.

Trudeau looked at the screen and the flashing dot that was traveling across it. "He's heading west on South Claiborne toward Boutte."

"How quickly can we get there?"

Trudeau narrowed his eyes. "We'll put the sirens on."

The torrential rain had calmed to little more than a spit, but the roads were slick. Nevertheless, the police officer pressed his foot down hard on the gas and shot out of the precinct parking lot and into the street. Soon they were weaving through light traffic at high speed. Roxy had never ridden in a squad car with its sirens on before and found it *quite* exciting.

Trudeau had beamed his phone display onto the patrol car's interior screen, and Roxy watched the pulsating red dot as it tracked Charles' and George's movements. They were gaining ground, but not quickly enough.

"I just hope George isn't involved, and he's safe," said Roxy. "I hope this isn't a getaway drive."

After five minutes, the red dot slowed to a crawl.

"Fantastic!" said Trudeau. "We can catch up with him. Look at the screen. Where does it say he is? What's the location?"

Roxy peered at the display. "Louiswood Industrial Park."

Trudeau spoke into his radio. "35 stand down. 43 covering."

"Is it just us following him now?" Roxy asked.

"Yep. I don't want to spook them. It's just you and me, kid." Trudeau looked over at Roxy and winked. She felt a shiver of fear run down her spine for the first time.

They continued weaving their way through traffic, driving through stoplights, sirens blaring all the way along South Claiborne Avenue until they were within a half-mile of their prey. Trudeau turned off his siren and then his lights as they quietly turned into the industrial park. At a crawl, they edged their way around the buildings, each corner they navigated bringing them closer to the red dot on their screen. Both of them were on edge, but silent and alert. As they rounded the fourth building, Roxy gasped. "There!" A white Mercedes sat outside one of the buildings, the rental car company sign still hooked around the rearview mirror.

"I'm going in." Trudeau brought the car to a halt and unbuckled his seat belt. "Hmmm, what am I going to do with you?" he said, frowning. "I'm going to have to leave you in the car..."

"Let me come with you. Please?"

"Much too dangerous. You'd be a liability." Trudeau wouldn't consider it. He had parked the squad car a little way down so that they had a clear view of the rental vehicle and the building it was parked next to. He'd also avoided setting off the motion sensor floodlights. They were shrouded in darkness. "Looks like they're in a warehouse," Trudeau said, sizing up buildings around the lot.

"Please let me come."

"No. What if you got shot?" he said. "I can't let you out. I can't. I'd probably go to jail myself. You're going to have to get down in the back and make sure you're not seen."

Roxy frowned and pursed her lips like a truculent toddler.

"Or maybe I should take you back to the station and lock you up."

"No!" said Roxy.

"Either way, I should wait for backup. It would be safer."

"But we don't have time! George or Charles might be in danger!" Roxy desperately wanted to enter the warehouse with Trudeau, but she had to see sense. "Okay, look, I'll lie down in the back and keep quiet."

Trudeau fingered his radio. "I'm calling for stealth back up, no sirens or lights. When they get here, stay down, y'hear?" He unbuckled her seat belt. "Get in the back now, and quickly."

"All right, all right," Roxy grumbled. She had a thought. "Hey! I can track you while you're inside. Give me your personal phone. You keep your police issue one."

"How will that help?"

"I'm not sure, but it can't hurt. We can talk too."

Trudeau thought for a moment. "Fine. But don't you tell *anyone* about this. Got it?" He handed her his personal phone.

"Not a soul," said Roxy. "Promise. Can't you take my handcuffs off, you know, just in case I need to rescue you or something?"

Trudeau squinted at Roxy, assessing. "No chance, you might escape. Then I really would be in trouble."

Roxy huffed. "Call your phone then and keep the line open. Oh, and put it on silent."

"It's already on silent," Trudeau said icily. "I'm not stupid. Don't overstep the mark, okay? I'm the cop here."

"Sorry," Roxy said.

Trudeau helped her out of the car and into the backseat. "See you in a while." In his haste, as he shut the door the lock didn't quite catch.

Roxy crouched in the back of the car as Trudeau moved carefully toward the building. The phone in her lap lit up.

"It's an abandoned warehouse," she heard him whisper. "There's a whole bunch of rusting car parts, covered in dust. Cardboard boxes disintegrating."

"No sign of Charles or George?"

"No."

Trudeau was silent for a while. "I think they must be upstairs."

"Be careful."

"I'm doing fine, thank you very much," he whispered back sharply.

With her cuffed hands, Roxy tried to reach through the grille that separated the front from the back of the patrol car. She wanted to see if she could manipulate the dashboard display and get another view of the scene outside, but it was impossible.

She looked around. There were no interior handles to the back doors of the police vehicle. She sat impotently for a few moments before, with a sudden burst of energy she shoved the half-closed door with her shoulder so hard it burst open and she fell out onto the tarmac.

Roxy quickly righted herself and darted into the front seat. She slipped down low and closed the door oh-so quietly. She held her breath. There was no movement outside and no sound from Trudeau's phone. She turned to the dashboard display, reaching out for it, but manipu- lating the screen with her hands cuffed together caused her to overbalance. She ended up flat on her face, sprawled across the driver's seat, her behind in the air.

She wriggled herself upright and tried again. This time she ended up with her head in the driver's footwell. She stared at her handcuffs, then looked around. She gave a big sigh. "Sorry, Trudeau," she whispered. One at a time, she wriggled her wrists out of the cuffs. Her hands were so slight and fine-boned that it wasn't difficult, although she did need to lick the back of her right hand to ease the cuff past her knuckle. Her left hand came out more easily.

Roxy grinned. Now she could reach forward and play with the screen.

"Are you walking or still?" she whispered into the phone.

"Walking," Trudeau whispered back. "Now stop talking. Only reply when I tell you to. I'm going up the stairs, and they may well be close. Be quiet now. Don't announce yourself."

She could hear the sound of his police-issue boots on the steps. *Don't announce yourself.* She hardly dare breathe. Then, the most horrifying sound came through the phone's speaker. It was a muffled voice, begging, pleading.

George! Roxy recognized the high timbre of his voice.

"Police! Put down the gun!" Trudeau yelled. His voice came through the phone so loud that it hurt Roxy's ears. There was a bang, a gunshot. Roxy clenched her jaws to stop herself from crying out. She heard a groan.

"Officer down! Officer down!"

"H E'S RUNNING AWAY!" Trudeau ground out, his voice tight with pain. "He's going down the stairs. He's going for the car!"

"What do I do? Are you okay?" Roxy whisper shouted into the phone.

"I don't know," he said. "He's shot me in the leg. I can't get up." He let out a holler of pain. "I just hope... is backup there yet?"

Adrenaline flooded Roxy's body. She turned to look frantically around her, but there were no police cars that she could see.

"Nope," Roxy said desperately, willing them to come. "Just me."

"Stay down," said Trudeau. "Just in case... stay down... Don't let him see you."

"Okay," said Roxy. "Hang on in there. Shall I call an ambulance?"

"No. Just stay where you are and get down."

Roxy slid down the front seat, hiding herself in the footwell, keeping as still as a mummy. She heard a noise, like a can being kicked, then someone swearing. She sat up just a smidgeon so that she could see the entrance to the warehouse.

The sight took her breath away. Charles, dressed in his slacks and white shirt, was running or rather lumbering away from the scene. He was not a fit, lithe man. Instead of getting in his car, he passed it, and she saw him toss something into the bushes just beyond the warehouse. He disappeared down an alleyway between two other buildings. Roxy quickly looked at the map on the screen and saw that it led to a six-lane street that ran through the business district.

Before Roxy knew what she was doing, she was out of the patrol car, running after him as quickly as her legs would take her. He was a lot bigger than she was, he had a good head start, but he wasn't fast. And she was so light she could practically float through the air.

"Charles Romanoff!" she hollered as she turned the corner between the buildings. Shocked, he turned immediately and stepped into the motion field of a floodlight. Immediately he was illuminated in bright white light. He put his hands up like a cat preparing to fight. Roxy, benefitting from the shadows, darted around the edge of another building and found herself in a small cul-de-sac. *Darn!* She could hear Charles' footsteps, and momentarily he slunk around the corner to face her with his hands curled like claws in front of him!

Roxy was panting with fear. Half-crouched, she looked up at him. "You killed Meredith, didn't you?" Charles stared at her, motionless. "And you kidnapped George because...why?" Charles continued to stare. He made no movement or sound at all.

"Because we thought he was on to us. He was getting

way too cocky. You know, what with his *magical* powers and all." Roxy's eyes widened, her mouth dropped open, astonishment wiping away the fear that she felt as her mind went blank. For there, in front of Roxy, walking from around the back of a building, a gun aimed straight at her, was Terah Jones.

"*Terah!*"

"Yup, pretty girl. You had no idea did you?" Terah's lip curled in amusement, her black eye patch bisecting her face. The two German Shepherds strained against their leashes in front of her, their muzzles absent.

Roxy looked back and forth between Terah and Charles. Charles was still in his fighting stance, a silent tension causing every muscle in his body to tremble. In contrast, Terah stood calmly, confidently, next to him, a small smile on her face. "Sit!" she commanded the dogs. They deferred to her immediately, sitting at her feet.

"What's happening here? What have you to do with all this? Are you telling me that all that talk about you and Meredith in high school was *lies?*" Roxy was incredulous.

"Oh no, it was all *true*," Terah cackled. "I knew Meredith in high school, alright. She *was* a drug dealer who got caught. She *was* controlling and toxic and manipulative. But more than that, she ruined my life. That boyfriend Meredith stole from me? That was Charles. This eye patch? It covers the injury I sustained when I crashed my car minutes after Meredith told me she had stolen him from me."

Roxy swung wildly around to Charles. She was having a hard time believing that this pink, bald, portly man was formerly a high school football player with flicky brown hair and a motorbike. "It was *Terah* you were

730 ALISON GOLDEN & HONEY BROUSSARD

having an affair with, not your nursing administrator at the foundation?"

This seemed to shake Charles from his stupor. He came to life. "What? Stacey? Good lord, no. Stacey's a good friend, but our relationship is purely platonic."

Roxy wasn't sure Stacey saw things in quite the same way. "And what about when you went missing? We were all *terrified* for you."

Charles lowered his hands. He spoke quietly, deferentially, like he was explaining to a patient about a surgery he was about to perform. "I'm sorry about that. I was with Terah. She and I were high school sweethearts before I started a relationship with Meredith. We got back in touch five years ago. We've been together ever since. I should never have let Meredith come between us in the first place. I was a fool."

"But I don't understand. Why were you at the séance, Terah?"

Terah shrugged. "Meredith invited me. She had no idea that I was having an affair with her husband, and I think she genuinely wanted to reconnect. Little did she know I'd harbored murderous thoughts about her for *years*. I found her approach quite amusing, and the séance was the perfect opportunity to pop her off. We hit on a plan to eliminate Meredith so that we could move on. We'd already wasted too many years because of her, and she would never have left us alone. She was vengeful and hateful and would have followed us and haunted us for the rest of our lives. We had to be rid of her once and for all, no matter the cost. Charles agreed, didn't you, Charles?"

Charles started to pant. Beads of sweat poured down his face, and he dabbed at them with his perfect, white handkerchief. However, he said nothing. It was as though he was as much under Terah's spell as the two dogs now appeared to be.

"You two are sick."

"And you're dead." Terah's voice hardened as she edged up closer, nudging the dogs out of her way, the gun still pointed at Roxy. "You've been playing with fire, Roxy Reinhardt, talking, and questioning, and *investigating*. People who do that? Well, they get burned."

They were a few feet away from each other, but not so far apart that Terah would miss if she fired her gun. Roxy felt like a target at a shooting range. In the distance, she could hear the wail of sirens and imagined the spinning blue light atop the police cars.

"The police are coming for you," Roxy said evenly, her voice trembling only slightly. "You're not getting away with this. You're not going to kill me, you're going to rot in jail for the rest of your lives."

"Terah..." Charles looked panicked.

"Shut up, Charles," Terah said.

"No!" Charles took off, running as fast as he could back to the Mercedes. Roxy didn't take her eyes off Terah as Charles receded in her peripheral vision. The dogs, sensing the heightened tension of the situation, started up again, barking, bearing their teeth, strings of drool hanging from their gums.

Terah dropped their leashes. "Go!" She pointed at Roxy.

Backed into the corner of the cul-de-sac, Roxy's eyes grew wide. Her hands scrambled at the surface of the building behind her. Panic began to overwhelm her. Instinctively, she half-turned to shield herself from the onslaught that was about to be unleashed upon her. She closed her eyes tight, crouched over, and threw her arms around her head. Every muscle in her small body fired, they were as hard as concrete, as she waited...

"Down! Down! Sit! Sit!" It was Terah. She was pleading. *"Please."*

Roxy opened her eyes just slightly and peered out the corners of them. Instead of attacking her, the dogs had turned their menace on Terah. The two dogs circled her. Terah had dropped her gun and put up her arms to protect her face as the dogs jumped at her, growling. Strong and heavy, they succeeded in knocking her over. She curled into a fetal position as they stood over her, snapping their teeth, dominating, and intimidating just as a patrol car squealed and skidded to a stop across the end of the cul-de-sac. Roxy jumped up and down, waving her hands like a maniac. It was Johnson!

"I thought you were off duty!" Roxy cried.

"I thought you were in a jail cell!"

CHAPTER THIRTY-NINE

"**R**EADY?"

ROXY WAS standing at the entrance to the loft. Sam was behind her, his hands over her eyes. It was good to be so close to him, to take in his smell and his comforting, strong vibe even if she couldn't see him.

She heard a clattering behind her followed by voices —Dr. Jack, Elijah, George, Nat, Evangeline, and Sage.

"Oh, hi guys." Sam didn't sound quite as cheerful as he had a moment earlier.

"We've come to see the unveiling." Nat's voice.

Privately, Roxy didn't get what all the fuss was about. Sure, Sam had stained the floor and installed the light fittings and mirrors, but there was no furniture in the room, so it was hardly worth this unveiling and covering her eyes and all. Frankly, it was a little embarrassing, but she decided to be a good sport about it.

"Okay, ready. Let's do this," she said.

Sam lifted his hands away from her eyes. Roxy opened them. She gasped.

The loft was finished! Completely finished. The walls were a beautiful, crisp white. The floor was so deeply navy blue that it looked like an ocean beneath her feet. Even better, Sam had installed a crystal chandelier that cast down sparkling splinters of light that made the floor look as though the sun was glittering upon waves. There was a large four-poster bed, complete with white and blue linens, and a white antique armoire and a white closet. Light blue velvet curtains were draped at the windows while white nightstands with brass lamps and blue shades finished off the look.

On top of one of them was a beribboned basket of custom cookies that on close inspection had been decorated with the *Funky Cat* logo, a cat wearing a trilby hat at a jaunty angle and holding a saxophone. Even Nefertiti matched the decors as she curled up on the white fluffy rug, so well camouflaged that there was a real danger of stepping on her.

"What!" Roxy said. "Am I dreaming? How did you *do* all this, Sam?"

Sam looked at her innocently.

"Sam?" she warned.

Sam put his hands in the air. "Okay, okay, I admit it, Nat and I hatched a cunning plan behind your back."

Roxy spun around. "You!" she said to Nat.

Nat grinned. "Well, I had to do *something* while I wasn't cooking. It was easy-peasy. Sourced the furniture at the flea markets and painted it all white. Bought a few trimmings to pull the look together, Elijah made the cookies, George and Sage blessed the space, and voilà!"

"My goodness," said Roxy, walking all around the room. "This is really special." She turned to her friends. "You guys!" She felt a little tearful. "This is incredible!"

Nat wrapped her up in a hug. "We thought you deserved it. We wanted to take a load off your mind."

"It looks fantastic, cher," Evangeline said. "Even better than when it was full of ma ole junk."

"It has great energy, Roxy," George said.

Elijah nodded. "You work so hard, Roxy. You deserve it."

"You do," said Sage.

Dr. Jack stood next to Sage. They were holding hands. "I want to give you something, too, for all your help."

"You don't need to give me anything, Dr. Jack," said Roxy. "Honestly."

"Well, it's a little too late for that," he said. "I put in a call to the police department." He gave her his phone. "Someone wants to speak to you."

"Huh?" Roxy, dazed with surprise, took the phone. "Hello?"

"Hello, Roxy, Officer Trudeau here."

"Hello. Are you okay? Is your leg healing well?"

"Yes, thank you," he said. "I'll be back to work in a couple of weeks."

"That's good," said Roxy.

"You're probably wondering why we're on the phone."

Roxy laughed. "You could say I'm curious."

"Well, Detective Johnson and I have been talking, and the New Orleans Police Department would like to award you a medal for your bravery in the capture of Terah Jones and Charles Romanoff."

"What?" Roxy said. "No way!"

"Yep. You did an outstanding job helping us catch them, Roxy. You were right all along. It wasn't Dr. Jack."

Roxy looked over at George. "I'm just so glad Dr. Jack is off the hook and that you and George are okay. Solving the case is just the filling in the beignets."

"All thanks to you," came Trudeau's reply.

"You helped!" Roxy said.

"Well, yes, but that's my job. So will you accept the award? Johnson will be mightily annoyed if you don't."

Roxy laughed. "Suppose I better had, then."

"I should say so."

"Thank you, Officer Trudeau."

"Call me Newman," he said. "Here, Detective Johnson wants a word with you."

Roxy winced and bit her thumb. "Okay."

Johnson came on the line. "I just wanted to say, um, thanks. And glad you didn't get hurt. Yes." Johnson cleared his throat. "That is all."

"I'm sorry about impers..." Roxy began.

"Let's not talk anymore about that, lady. It all came right in the end." There was a pause.

"All right, Detective Johnson. Bye then."

"Goodbye, Roxy." She ended the call.

Roxy?

"Woo-hoo! I think we should have a drink to celebrate!" said Nat. "Everyone downstairs for some champagne!"

"I second that!" said George. The skin on his face was a little raw from where he'd been gagged with duct tape but aside from that, he had recovered well from his ordeal.

Soon they were all down in the lounge, sipping on champagne. Sam prepared to play his sax as Elijah passed out mini pastries and *Funky Cat* cookies. "They're made with real Louisiana strawberries and pistachios, people!" Nefertiti snuggled on Roxy's lap.

"You know, George, I thought it might be you when you disappeared with Charles. I thought you might be in cahoots," Roxy said.

George hung his head. "I think I deserved what I got, honestly. I started thinking all kinds of bad things about Meredith. I attracted the situation to myself. When Charles came in that back room, he punched Royston, imagine! Then he put a gun to my head and got me to climb out of the window. I should have run when he was climbing through the window after me, but I was so shocked. I couldn't believe what was happening!

"He took me to that warehouse and tied me up. Then Terah appeared and demanded I tell her what I knew. But I didn't know anything! She said she was going to shoot me and leave my body for the rats to feed off. No one ever went to that warehouse anymore, she said. Charles never said a word and then suddenly just ran away. I think he knew that killing me would spell a very bad future for him in the spiritual realm. The spirits would not appreciate him killing me. He did tell me once that he thought Meredith was a complete charlatan, but he wasn't so sure I was a fraud."

Roxy shuddered. "It sounds awful."

"I'll get over it."

Nat patted him on the shoulder. "You're stronger than you think, George."

Roxy looked at them for a moment—the deeply warm and affectionate way they looked at each other. She wondered what was in store for them. They said they were just friends, and she believed them, but Nat had been very cagey. Roxy had found her wiping her eyes in the kitchen that morning, and suspected George leaving for home later that day had something to do with it. Nat had blamed her sniffles on the onions she was cutting up.

"How do you feel about Meredith now? Are you mad at her?"

"No," said George. "Whether or not she made up some schtick, she was still exacting and perfectionistic and brilliant and talented. She had high standards. At some level, she had a gift. And I owe her for showing me mine. I will say, though, that I'm glad Royston doesn't hold the part I played in that deal against me. Had I known that I was being asked to bring harm to another spirit, I wouldn't have done it."

"Hey, why don't we toast Meredith?" Roxy suggested. "She was a person, a human being who didn't deserve what happened to her."

"Absolutely."

"To Meredith!" Roxy said, raising her glass in the air.

Nefertiti chimed in, "Miaow!" and made everyone laugh.

Later, Roxy climbed up to the loft. She wanted to look it over at her leisure without anyone else in the room.

"Oh!" she cried when she opened the door. Sam was there.

"Hey, Roxy. Just admiring my handiwork." Sam smiled.

"You did a fantastic job. Thank you so much."

"You are very welcome. Are you sure you don't want to make it your own room?"

"Well, hmm, what do you think? It is lovely, but I feel

a little guilty for taking it over, not making bank from it. You're my co-owner, what do you think?"

They stood side by side looking up at the wheel window at the end of the room. Sam put his arm around Roxy's shoulders. Sparkles shot through her body at his touch. "I think you absolutely should move up here. I would be honored if you would."

"You did this with me in mind?"

"Sure I did."

"And you got Nat to furnish it like this, for *me*?"

"Uh-huh."

Roxy thought about the things she knew about Sam—his kindness, his attractiveness, his compassion, his work ethic—and she weighed it up against what she didn't know—his money dealings. Math wasn't her strongest suit, but she understood probability and risk assessment. Although in the past, she had avoided uncertain situations at all costs, she was now much more willing to throw the dice. If things worked out there were big rewards to be gained.

Roxy had changed. She was bolder, more forthright, less complicated. She used her intuition. She'd thought that a girl should never make a move on a boy, but she also used to think she should not stare down murderers, or impersonate police officers, or get arrested. Now she had done all of those things.

Roxy looked up at Sam. He was over six inches taller. She couldn't reach him unless he bent down. Bolder than she had ever felt before, she tugged at his shirt and said, "Come here, big man." As soon as their lips touched, Sam lifted her up and passionately kissed her as she flung her arms around his neck, her feet a foot off the floor. She may have been a charlatan, but Meredith Romanoff had been right about something. The universe *had* aligned just so, and Sam and Roxy *did* make an attractive couple. The future was theirs to make. *Together*.

Thank you for reading this omnibus edition! I will have a new case for Roxy and her gang soon! To find out about new books, sign up for my newsletter: https://www.alisongolden.com

If you love the Roxy Reinhardt mysteries, you'll also love the sweet, funny, *USA Today* bestselling Reverend Annabelle Dixon series featuring a madcap, lovable lady vicar whose passion for cake is matched only by her desire for justice. This omnibus edition contains the first four books in the series and is available for purchase from Amazon here. Like all my books, the omnibus is FREE in Kindle Unlimited.

And don't miss the bestselling Inspector Graham and his gang, a detective series with twisty plots and characters that feel like friends. Binge read this *USA Today* bestselling series featuring a new and unusual detective with a phenomenal memory and a tragic past. Get your copy of

the omnibus edition comprising books 1-4 from Amazon now! This omnibus is FREE in Kindle Unlimited.

If you're looking for something edgy and dangerous, root for Diana Hunter as she seeks justice after a devastating crime destroys her family. Follow her journey in this non-stop story of suspense and action by purchasing the omnibus edition featuring the first four books in the series. This omnibus is FREE in Kindle Unlimited.

I hugely appreciate your help in spreading the word about this omnibus, including telling a friend. Reviews help readers find books! Please leave a review on your favorite book site.

Turn the page for an excerpt from the first book in the Reverend Annabelle Dixon series, *Death at the Cafe...*

A Reverend Annabelle Dixon Mystery

DEATH AT THE CAFÉ

Alison Golden

Jamie Vougeot

DEATH AT THE CAFE

CHAPTER ONE

NOTHING BROUGHT REVEREND Annabelle closer to blasphemy than using the London public transport system during rush hour. Since being ordained and sent to St. Clement's Church, an impressive, centuries-old building among the tower blocks and new builds of London's East End, Annabelle had been tested many times. She had come across virtually every sin known to man, counseled wayward youths, presided over family disputes, heard astonishingly sad tales from the homeless, and retained her solid, optimistic dependability through it all. None of these challenges made her blood boil and her round, soft face curl up into a mixture of disgust, frustration, and exasperation. Yet sitting on the number forty-three bus to Islington, as it moved along at a snail's pace, was almost enough to make her take her beloved Lord's name in vain.

On this occasion, she had managed to nab her favorite seat: top deck, front left. It gave her the perfect view of the unique kinds of streets London offered and the even more varied types of people. Today, however, her viewpoint afforded her only a teeth-clenchingly irritating perspective of a traffic jam that extended as far as the eye could see down Upper Street.

"I know I shouldn't," she muttered to herself on the relatively empty bus, "but if this doesn't deserve a cherry-topped cupcake, then I don't know what does."

The thought of rewarding her patience with what she loved almost as much as her vocation—cake—settled Annabelle's nerves for a full twenty minutes, during which the bus trundled in fits and spurts along another half-mile stretch.

Assigning Annabelle, fresh from her days fervently studying theology at Cambridge University, to the tough, inner-city borough of Hackney had been an almost literal baptism of fire. She had arrived in the summer, during a few weeks when the British sun combined with the squelching heat of a city constantly bustling and moving. It was a time of drinking and frivolity for some and heightened tension for others; a spell during which bored youths on their summer holidays found their idle hands easily occupied by the devil's work; an interval when the good relax and the bad run riot.

Annabelle had grown up in East London, but for her first appointment as a vicar, her preference had been for a peaceful, rural village somewhere. A place in which she could indulge her love of nature, and conduct her Holy business in the gentle, caring manner she preferred. "Gentle" and "caring," however, were two words rarely used to describe London. Annabelle had mildly protested the assignment, but after a long talk with the archbishop who explained the extreme shortage of candidates both capable and willing to take on the challenge of an inner-city church, she agreed to take up the position and set about her task with an enthusiasm for which she was noted.

Father John Wilkins of neighboring St. Leonard's Church had been charged with easing Annabelle into the complex role of a city-based diocese. He had been a priest for over thirty years, and for the vast majority of that time had worked in London's poorest, toughest neighborhoods. The Anglican Church was far less popular in London than it was in rural England, comprised as London was of a disparate mix of peoples and creeds, and Father John's congregation was largely made up of especially devout immigrants from Africa and South America, many of whom were not even Anglican but simply lived nearby. The only time St. Leonard's had ever been full was on a particularly mild Christmas Eve.

Despite its lack of influence, London's churches played pivotal roles in the local community. With plenty of people in need, churches in London were hubs of charity and community support. Fundraising events, providing food and shelter for London's large homeless population, caring for the elderly, and engaging troubled youths were their stock in trade, not to mention they provided both spiritual and emotional support throughout the many deaths and family tragedies which occurred.

The stress of it all had turned Father John's wiry beard a speckled gray, and though he knew his work was important and worthwhile, he had been pushed to his breaking point on more than one occasion. Upon her arrival, he had taken one look at Annabelle's breezy demeanor and her fresh-faced, open smile and assumed that her appointment was a case of negligence, desperation, or a sick prank.

"She's utterly delightful," Father John sighed on the

phone to the archbishop, "and extremely nice. But 'delightful' and 'nice' are not what's required in a London church. This is a part of the world where faith is stretched to its very limits, where strong leadership goes further than gentle guidance. We struggle to capture people's attention, Archbishop, let alone their hearts. Our drug rehabilitation programs have more members than our congregations."

"Give her a chance, Father," the archbishop replied softly. "Don't underestimate her. She grew up in East London, you know."

"Well, I grew up in Westminster, but that doesn't mean I've had tea with the Queen!"

Merely a week into Annabelle's placement, however, Father John's misgivings proved to be unfounded. Annabelle's bumbling, naïve manner was just that—a manner. Father John observed closely as Annabelle's strength, faith, and intelligence were consistently tested by the urban issues of her flock. He noted that she passed with flying colors.

Whether it was with a hardened criminal fresh out of prison and already succumbing to old temptations or a single mother of three struggling to find some sense of composure and faith in the face of her daily troubles, Annabelle was always there to help. With good humor and optimism, she never turned down a request for assistance, no matter how large or small it was.

When Father John visited Annabelle a month after the start of her placement to check upon a highly successful gardening project she had started for troubled youth, he shook his head in amazement.

"Is that Denton? By the rose bushes? I've been trying to get him to visit me for a year now, and all he does is grunt. You should hear what he says when his parole officer suggests it," he said.

"Oh, Denton is wonderful!" Annabelle effused. "Fantastic with his hands. He has a devilish sense of humor—when it's properly directed. Did you know that he plays drums?"

"No, I didn't know that. He never told me," Father John said, allowing Annabelle an appreciative smile. "I must say, Reverend, I seem to have misjudged you dreadfully. And I apologize."

"Oh, Father," Annabelle chuckled, "it's perfectly understandable. You have only the best interests of the community at heart. Let's leave judgment for Him and Him alone. The only thing we are meant to judge is cake contests, in my opinion. Mind those thorns, Denton! Roses tend to fight back if you treat them roughly!"

To get your copy of Death at the Cafe and three further books in the Reverend Annabelle Dixon series, Murder at the Mansion, Body in the Woods, and Grave in the Garage, visit the link below:
https://www.alisongolden.com/annabelle-boxset-paperback

For a limited time, you can get the first books in each of my series - *Chaos in Cambridge, The Case of the Screaming Beauty, Hunted, and Mardi Gras Madness* - plus updates about new releases, promotions, and other Insider exclusives, by signing up for my mailing list at:

https://www.alisongolden.com/roxy

BOOKS BY ALISON GOLDEN

FEATURING INSPECTOR DAVID GRAHAM

The Case of the Screaming Beauty

The Case of the Hidden Flame

The Case of the Fallen Hero

The Case of the Broken Doll

The Case of the Missing Letter

The Case of the Pretty Lady

The Case of the Forsaken Child

FEATURING REVEREND ANNABELLE DIXON

Death at the Café

Murder at the Mansion

Body in the Woods

Grave in the Garage

Horror in the Highlands

Killer at the Cult

Fireworks in France

As A. J. Golden

FEATURING DIANA HUNTER

ABOUT THE AUTHOR

Alison Golden is the *USA Today* bestselling author of the Inspector David Graham mysteries, a traditional British detective series, and two cozy mystery series featuring main characters Reverend Annabelle Dixon and Roxy Reinhardt. As A. J. Golden, she writes the Diana Hunter thriller series.

Alison was raised in Bedfordshire, England. Her aim is to write stories that are designed to entertain, amuse, and calm. Her approach is to combine creative ideas with excellent writing and edit, edit, edit. Alison's mission is simple: To write excellent books that have readers clamoring for more.

Alison is based in the San Francisco Bay Area with her husband and twin sons. She splits her time between London and San Francisco.

For up-to-date promotions and release dates of upcoming books, sign up for the latest news here: https://www.alisongolden.com/graham.

For more information:
www.alisongolden.com
alison@alisongolden.com

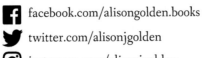

facebook.com/alisongolden.books

twitter.com/alisonjgolden

instagram.com/alisonjgolden

THANK YOU

Thank you for taking the time to read the first three books in the Roxy Reinhardt series. If you enjoyed them, please consider telling your friends or posting a short review. Word of mouth is an author's best friend and very much appreciated.
Thank you,

Made in the USA
Columbia, SC
08 September 2021